Sergei frowned. *Where were they?* He had chanced moving twice, and was now almost fifty meters away from the last Sauron he had killed. He had expected to be dead long since, but the hail of fire had not come. Sergei could not understand why the Saurons had not killed him already.

Suddenly, inexplicably, Sergei was seized with terror. That was why he could not hear them! They were not rushing to kill him, they were closing in on him to take him prisoner! Through him, the Saurons would find his village and obliterate his people. Again, acting almost before he was aware of it, Sergei bolted away from the river.

He had gone less than a hundred yards when a tripwire caught his ankles, and he pitched forward onto the gritty Haven soil. Before he could roll over, a soft-soled boot was put against the back of his neck, and next to it he felt the pressure of a rifle barrel.

Kamov closed his eyes, thought of his family, and prayed.

"Now where would you be going in such a quick hurry?" The voice from behind the gun barrel asked in clipped Imperial Anglic.

ALSO IN THIS SERIES
Created by Jerry Pournelle

CREATED BY
JERRY POURNELLE

VOL. IV:

WAR WORLD

INVASION

With the editorial assistance
of John F. Carr

WAR WORLD IV: INVASION

This is a work of fiction. All the characters and events portrayed in this book are fictional, and any resemblance to real people or incidents is purely coincidental.

Copyright © 1994 by Jerry Pournelle

All rights reserved, including the right to reproduce this book or portions thereof in any form.

A Baen Books Original

Baen Publishing Enterprises
P.O. Box 1403
Riverdale, N.Y. 10471

ISBN: 0-671-87616-3

Cover art by Gary Ruddell

First printing, August 1994

Distributed by
Paramount Publishing
1230 Avenue of the Americas
New York, N.Y. 10020

Printed in the United States of America

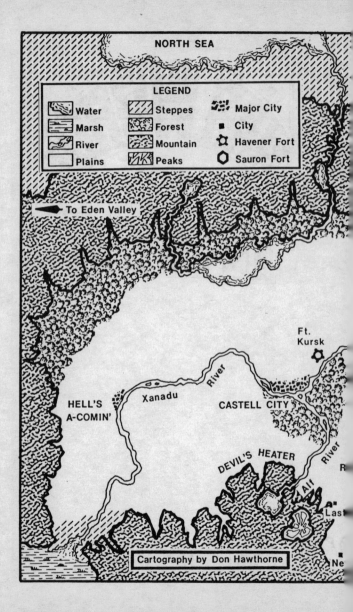

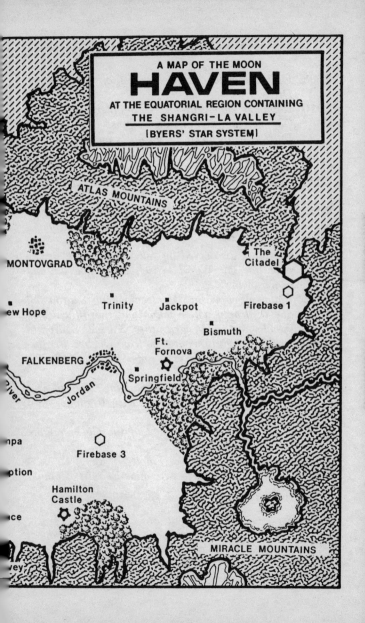

A MAP OF THE MOON
HAVEN
AT THE EQUATORIAL REGION CONTAINING
THE SHANGRI-LA VALLEY
[BYERS' STAR SYSTEM]

ATLAS MOUNTAINS

MONTOVGRAD

The Citadel

New Hope

Trinity

Jackpot

Firebase 1

Bismuth

FALKENBERG

Ft. Fornova

Springfield

Jordan

River

mpa

Firebase 3

ption

Hamilton Castle

ace

vey

MIRACLE MOUNTAINS

CHRONOLOGY

2008 *First successful interstellar test of the Alderson Drive.*

2010 *Habitable planets discovered in other star systems. Commercial exploitation begins. CoDominium Intelligence licenses all scientists and begins censorship of scientific publications. Most scientific research ceases.*

2031 *CoDominium Navy absorbs all other CD Armed Services.*

2032 *Captain Jed Byers of the CDSS Ranger discovers a planetary sized moon of a gas giant and names it Haven.*

2038 *Sauron is discovered by Avery Landyn, a survey pilot for 3M. World is rich in radioactive and heavy metals.*

2042 *Initial attempts by 3M at colonizing Sauron fail due to deadly native fauna and the difficulty of establishing viable agriculture. 3M sells Sauron to wealthy English Separatists from Quebec and former South African expatriates living in Canada and Australia.*

2098 *Saurons evict the CoDominium viceroy and declare their independence. They begin to build their own space navy.*

2103 *Great Patriotic Wars. End of the CoDominium. Exodus of the Fleet.*

2111 *Formation Wars of the Empire begin.*

2250 *Leonidas I of Sparta proclaims Empire of Man.*

**2250
2650** *Empire of Man enforces interstellar peace.*

2603 *Secession Wars begin. St. Ekaterina is nearly destroyed by Sauron attack. Sauron Coalition of Secession declares its independence.*

2618 *Third Imperial Fleet is nearly destroyed by Sauron armada off Tabletop.*

2622 Colonel Gary Cummings of the Imperial Marines arrives on Haven to coordinate the re-deployment of the 77th Imperial Marines ("Land Gators").

2623 The 77th Imperial Marines leave Haven for Friedland. Colonel Cummings retires from the Imperial Marines and is appointed General and commander-in-chief of the Haven militia, the "Haven Volunteers."

2624 A pirate ship, posing as a tramp freighter, attacks Castell City.

2626 The Black Hand, a small fleet of corsairs, attack Haven. The Militia destroys two of the ships by missile attacks from Fort Kursk. In retaliation, the survivors destroy most of Haven's near-earth satellites and relay stations. Only two space-worthy shuttles survive a determined attack on Castell's spaceport.

2628 David Steele crowns himself King of Haven. He controls Castell City and several satellite towns.

2636 King David Steele is deposed and new planetary government is formed. Last Imperial military ship passes through Byers' System.

2638 Piet van Reenan is exiled from Frystaat with a score of his retainers. They are sent to Haven on a chartered merchantman.

2640 Sauron First and Second Fleets destroyed at the Battle of Haven. The Home Fleet is destroyed at the Battle of Sauron. Only one Sauron ship, the Fomoria, escapes the destruction of the Home-world undetected. After a long series of Alderson Jumps, the Sauron Heavy Cruiser reaches Haven.

2644 Piet van Reenan mounts an attack on the Eden Valley. He forms an alliance with the Edenites and thus begins the HaBandari.

Table of Contents

Mpoh Aletti closed his eyes, leaned back in his chair, and thought *I'm bored bored bored*. Nothing ever happened on watch duty in the "Crow's Nest," a 270 degree ring of old-fashioned video monitors. The screens showed the typical approach trajectories to Ayesha, the insignificant little ball of rock and ice which Aletti called home—and which boasted the only refueling station in the Byers system. Besides occasional glimpses of Ayesha's sister moons—swinging in stately procession around the gas giant known as Cat's Eye—the screens offered only unchanging views of space. Even the moons were feature-less and dull—with the notable exception of Haven, which was the only other inhabited body in the Byers system. But Haven was nowhere near conjunction, mean-ing that duty in the Crow's Nest would be typical: four hours of mind-numbing drudgery. Aletti sighed, let the chair tilt back down to a level alignment—a gradual pro-cess in Ayesha's low gravity—and opened his eyes.

Screen four—which monitored the trailing approaches to the refueling station tethered some thirty kilometers over Ayesha's surface—contained a small, twinkling anomaly in its lower right quadrant. Before Aletti's jaw could fall fully open, the glistening speck burgeoned into a black, wedge-shaped atmospace vehicle: a fighter, stabilizers and wingtips glinting sharply as the shadowy arrowhead shape shot past the camera view to the right.

Aletti was just realizing that he should resume breathing when he noted a second speck, approaching along the same vector that the fighter had followed. This second speck also grew larger—but unlike the fighter, showed no signs of completing that growth. Aletti's jaw snapped shut, his Adam's apple pumped once; this craft was big—monstrously so—and jet black, which meant that it had to be a—

Aletti slammed his palm at the "alert" button to his right, missed it. Unable even to curse, Aletti drew back his hand, hit the button, and then hit it again. And again and again.

Long after the flashing crimson lights indicated that Ayesha's discretionary alarm circuits had been activated, Aletti was still hammering away at the console, mesmerized by the expanding mass of blackness on his screens.

For the third time, Survey Rating Markel rotated the trackball to the right, the 2-d image panning across the tethered refueling station: fuel bladders—arrayed side-by-side like two ranks of dull white sausages—hung motionless in the cold, star-speckled skillet of space.

From behind Markel, Survey Ranker Bender called for another update; "Proximity sensor report?"

Markel executed a swift, almost machine-like turn to face his superior. Among normal humans, the abruptness and precision of Markel's movement would have looked odd; amongst Saurons, it merely indicated a characteristically efficient use of time and physical effort. "Projected data now confirmed, Fourth Rank Bender. The refueling station is connected to water cracking facilities on Ayesha by a thirty kilometer tether. Liquid deuterium is pumped from Ayesha up to the station via tubes bundled about the tether itself. As expected, there is no sign of resistance; the spaceside elements of the fuel depot appear to be fully automated."

Bender's light blue eyes widened marginally. "By reason of exclusion, your statement suggests that the ground facilities might *not* be automated. Explain."

Markel indicated the image in the far left hand screen. "Current sensor data regarding the dirtside complex shows low heat signature, low power generation, no sign of auxiliary craft: all consistent with an automated facility. However, one feature suggests that it may be manned." Markel's index finger unfolded from his palm, indicated an irregular oval at the center of the screen; a partially disassembled radar array. "Typically, arrays as large as this one are situated near installations that handle a great deal of traffic—and which, therefore, tend to have resident populations."

One of Bender's eyebrows elevated slightly; he leaned forward to take a closer look.

Vance Trainor waited for the chirp of his pager to terminate, was annoyed when it did not. Another malfunction? wondered Trainor as he veered toward the wall of the corridor, letting the continuous stream of Ayeshan maintenance workers flow past him. He pushed aside the folds of his coveralls to get a clear view of the pager's LCD display, but never bothered to read the data it contained; the pager's red light was blinking steadily: a discretionary alert. Trainor felt the close-shaven hairs at the base of his neck struggle to rise, a sensation he had not felt since his last tour of duty with the Imperial Marines twenty-five years ago. Trainor tapped in his acknowledgment code—the one which identified him as the chief of depot security—and then turned the unit off. Remarkable to think that something as unused as Ayesha's discretionary alert system was still functional; almost every other subsystem in the fueling station seemed to be dead or dying. Trainor congratulated himself on the calm irony of that thought, silently reviewed the old OCS checklist of what not to do in a crisis; do not run, do not shout, do not allow yourself to exhibit any behaviors suggestive of concern or panic.

A wan smile on his face, Trainor reversed his facing, headed back toward the operations center, and unsuccessfully endeavored to forget the image of this pager's blinking red light—a light which meant that Ayesha had finally run out of borrowed time.

Bender tapped the passive sensor readouts. "The presence of the radar array cannot be taken as primary evidence of a manned facility. As you point out, Markel, the groundside power generation is quite low—too low to sustain life."

"They could have powered-down prior to our approach, Survey Rank Bender, hoping to trick us."

Bender shook his head. "In order to power-down before our arrival, any personnel on Ayesha would have needed advance warning of our approach. How would they receive that warning, Rating Markel? Their active sensors"— Bender once again tapped the video image of the half-disassembled radar array—"are non-functional, there is no evidence of a passive sensor array, and we have maintained absolute radio silence since our arrival." Bender rose. "In short, personnel on Ayesha would have had no way of knowing of our approach, and hence, no reason to reduce their power generation levels. The level we see, therefore, must be the actual level—which is insufficient to support life."

Markel nodded, but his words were not conciliatory. "If the ground facility is unmanned, then why was it equipped with a radar array?"

Bender frowned; Markel noted the change in his superior's expression, reflected that similar displays of extreme emotionalism had probably hindered the Survey officer's advancement through the ranks. "Even an automated facility may require a radar array, Markel, particularly if the facility handles a great deal of traffic."

"Logical—but if this facility *does* handle a great deal of traffic, then why is the array shut down—and partially disassembled?"

Bender's blue eyes brightened and his jaw grew rigid; memories of the Sauron homeworld—last seen wreathed in a bright, evanescent mottling that bespoke a devastating saturation bombardment from orbit—threatened to intrude upon his conscious thoughts. "The array is disassembled because there is no more traffic for it to handle; the war has shattered the Imperium, the Sauron Coalition, and the commerce that they fostered. As interstellar society continues this process of implosion, outback systems—such as this one—will tend to be the first to dismantle any machinery that facilitated contact with visiting ships." Bender nodded—signalling an end to the debate—and went back to his console.

Markel turned to face his own instruments. The Survey Ranker's explanations were logical, direct, sensible—but unsatisfying. Markel's eyes kept roving from screen to screen, first studying the tethered station, then the ground facility, and then the station again.

Trainor arrived in the operations center just as Ayesha's new Administrator, Henry Dorrit, was confirming the checklist of mishaps that had allowed the Saurons to catch the depot with its proverbial pants down. "Ladies and gentlemen, allow me to get this straight: because we're currently in the midst of a general overhaul, we're operating on batteries only; no fusion power. Secondly, since we need fusion power to open and close the protected berthing bay, flight operations were suspended, and all our shuttles are now undergoing maintenance."

"Actually, we still have two operational shuttles, Mr. Dorrit." No sooner had the Chief of Flight Operations offered this cheerless clarification than he seemed to shrivel, crisped by Dorrit's glare.

The Administrator continued his baleful litany. "And finally, since the interplanetary transmitter hasn't been repaired yet, we have no way of warning Haven that there are Saurons sitting on our—and their—doorstep." Dorrit—a recent emigre from Haven—seemed to put extra emphasis on this last item. He scanned the sheepish faces that ringed him. "Is that a fair description of our current situation?" Most of Dorrit's audience responded to his scrutiny by staring at the floor; there were a few nods and murmurs of assent.

Hands on hips, Dorrit scanned the room again, noted Trainor, nodded sharply. Trainor returned the acknowledgment with a slow, shallow nod of his own. Dorrit never saw Trainor's response; he was already stalking back and forth, hands behind his back. *Like a nervous j.g. on his first assignment*, thought Trainor; *Just what I need—a would-be Horatio Hornblower*.

Dorrit's attempt at a severe, authoritative tone was as artificial as his martial posturings. "Let's consider our military options, people. There's got to be some way to strike at the Saurons—or at least, some way to prevent them from docking with the station and taking on fuel. We could send a high voltage surge through the power lines leading to the station, a surge strong enough to burn out the fuel tanks' cryogenic elements. That would cause the L-hyd to heat up, sublimate into a gas, and explode. Then, if we—"

Hazeltine, a 40-year veteran of remote operations, shook his head once. "Sorry, sir, but that won't work. The storage tanks have individual, automated safety systems; if the temperature or pressure in any tank becomes excessive, its contents are vented to space."

While Dorrit resumed his pacing, Vance stared at the multiple images of the Sauron heavy cruiser that were being relayed from the automated cameras on board the refueling station. "How'd you find her?" he asked.

Dorrit turned toward Trainor, an un-officerly hint of impatience in his voice. "What?"

"How did you detect the Sauron vessel?"

Dorrit, turning back to the rest of his staff, snapped, "Visuals."

"There were no radio transmissions? No active sensors?"

"Mr. Trainor, as my chief of security, I wish you'd focus on the important business at hand. We are trying—"

"I appreciate the gravity of the situation, Mr. Dorrit, but I'll be able to offer better advice if I know *exactly* how the Sauron was detected."

Dorrit gestured at the youngest of the faces which ringed him: Mpoh Aletti. Aletti licked his lips nervously. "I detected the Saurons on visual scanning only, Mr. Trainor. They were dead quiet on their approach: no radio, no sensors; nothing."

Trainor nodded. "Describe their approach, Mpoh; how did they come in?"

"From trailing, sir, with a single fighter in the lead. The fighter made a straight run at the station; must have passed within 10 meters of the extreme starboard bladder doing better than 500 meters per second. Then the battle-wagon came in, right behind; same vector, but slower."

Trainor frowned, set his incisors over his lower lip and moved his jaw slowly from side to side, staring at the image in the main vidscreen.

Dorrit resumed his verbal brainstorming session. "What if we open the tankage valves now, before the Saurons complete their docking procedures? We could at least dump the fuel, instead of letting them get it."

Colette Kwan, in charge of fuel transfer engineering, coughed discreetly before disagreeing. "Mr. Dorrit, we don't have enough time left for that tactic. The Saurons would note the fuel discharge and manually reseal the tanks; they could even use controlled, low-power laser fire to weld the valves shut, if necessary."

Instead of responding with another gesture of annoyance, Dorrit leaned his lower lip against his index finger, a smile spreading across his face. He approached the console that controlled Ayesha's massive fuel pumping apparatus. "Correct me if I'm wrong, Mr. Hazeltine—or Ms. Kwan—but we have complete local control over the rate at which we pump fuel up to the station, do we not?"

Hazeltine and Kwan looked at each other, exchanged shrugs, nodded.

Dorrit reached down, toggled the automatic pumping

controls into the "off-line" position, and allowed his hand
to hover over the now-active manual controls. "Then, by
using manual overrides, we should be able to increase the
flow rate to a level that the station can't handle—like
overfilling a balloon with air. That would cause a fair
amount of damage, wouldn't it?"

Hazeltine   swallowed,   nodded.   "Yes—relatively
speaking."

"Then unless someone else has a tactical option that
we've overlooked—" Dorrit turned toward the pumping
controls.

For the fifth time, Markel traced the length of the
tether with the video image, studying the surface of the
main fuel line intently. Yes, there was no doubt about it;
the long vertical streak running along the center of the
main line was a radio receiver: a flexible, 30-kilometer-
long communications mast which was hidden—so to
speak—in plain sight. The receiver was not in itself proof
that Ayesha was inhabited, but on the other hand, if there
was no one at the base with whom to talk, then why had
such an investment been made in ensuring high quality
radio reception? Markel turned to look for Bender, discovered the Survey Rank to be absent from his station. He
paged his superior and then turned back to watch the
video image of the fuel lines; if there were dirtside inhabitants on Ayesha, they might decide to interfere with the
fuel flow—and if they did so, then Markel would be sure
to see it in the altered turgidity of the fuel lines.

"Mr. Dorrit, don't increase the fuel flow."

Dorrit turned, his hand still poised above the manual
pumping controls. "You have a better plan, Mr. Trainor?"

Vance shook his head. "No, but if you play around with
the flow rate, odds are that the Saurons will detect a
change in the appearance of the feeder lines. And if they
do, they'll come down here. Besides, you won't achieve
much by over-pumping. The tanks that are already filled

won't burst; each bladder seals as soon as it reaches maximum capacity."

"Yes, but the excess fuel pressure in the line itself will blow the station free of the tether."

Trainor shrugged. "That's not going to keep the Saurons from getting the fuel. After a day or two of EVA operations, they'll have chased the station down, corrected its tumble, and be ready to tap the tanks."

"So what's your alternative? To let these bastard Saurons dock and take on all the fuel they need?"

Vance shrugged again. "Sounds like a good idea to me."

"That," began Dorrit dramatically, "sounds like treason, Mr. Trainor." The operations center became silent except for the hum of the machinery. "In the day or two that those Sauron monsters will be busy trying to recapture and stabilize the station, pursuing Imperial ships could show up and make short work of them."

Vance shook his head. "These Saurons are not on the run from any 'pursuing ships;' if they were, they'd have grabbed the fuel tanks immediately—and they'd have done it with sensors hot, fighters out, and weapons ready. They certainly wouldn't be pussyfooting around the way they are now, with passive sensors and a single fighter. No, these Saurons know they've found a safe, sleepy byway, well off the main interstellar thoroughfares—and the fact that they haven't announced their presence suggests that a sleepy little byway is exactly what they were looking for."

Dorrit's posture became unnaturally erect. "Then it's our duty to make this byway a little less sleepy. And I mean to do just that."

"By destroying the refueling station? Even if you *could* deny them access to the fuel, that would only compel them to come down here and take possession of the processing plant."

"Good; that will give us a home court advantage. We can tear them up in zero gee."

Vance kept a scowl off his face. "What makes you think we can 'tear up' Saurons in zero gee?"

Dorrit's chin elevated slightly. "Perhaps you've forgotten your own local history, Mr. Trainor. Since the Imperium pulled the last of its troops out 17 years ago, there have been two occasions when pirates have troubled this system. Both times, the pirates avoided Ayesha and hit Haven instead—despite Haven's vastly greater defensive assets. Clearly, Ayesha is a daunting target."

Vance shook his head. "To pirates, maybe—but not to the Saurons. Take my word for it, Mr. Dorrit; you can't use the actions of a criminal to predict the actions of a professional soldier."

"And why not?"

"Because pirates fight for loot, not for duty or destiny. They know that zero gee operations against prepared locals can get messy, so—for them—that type of game isn't worth the candle. But Saurons don't fight for profit, nor do they conceive of soldiering as a noisome civic duty; combat and conflict are the very core of Sauron culture. Each Sauron aspires—and trains—to be ready for any challenge in any environment; hell, twenty of our best personnel wouldn't last 30 seconds against three Sauron EVA commandos. The way I see it, our best course of action is to take no overt action at all; most of us will survive if the Saurons continue to overlook us—and if we go deep underground."

"Underground?"

"If the Saurons mean to stay here in the Byers system— and all their actions indicate that they do—then they'll destroy those assets that they can't keep. Which means that they're going to blow the spaceside station, and when they do, this base is going to be at ground zero of the resulting deluge of debris." Trainor turned to leave.

"Mr. Trainor, you are not going 'underground.' You are going to set up a defensive perimeter around the pumping facilities, since, as you point out, the Saurons may attempt to take this facility if we give them problems with the station. And if they do attempt a landing, that's when the Saurons will discover that ordinary people can become extraordinary fighters when they're fighting to defend their homes." Dorrit's stirring rhetoric left the operations staff strangely uninspired.

Trainor sighed. "Dorrit, including myself, this station has four full-time security personnel—all armed with handguns." As though producing evidence, Vance drew his pistol and shook it meaningfully. "Do you really expect me to repel Sauron EVA commandos with *this?*"

Dorrit's face grew red and his voice was tight with suppressed anger. "I expect you to fight the Saurons with that and anything else available; I expect you to fight them the best way you know how."

"Is that an order—to fight them with any means available, the best way I know how?"

"Yes," Dorrit snarled, "and you will follow those orders to the letter, mister."

Trainor smiled. "To the letter, sir." The ex-Marine raised his handgun to a ready position and swept his thumb back; the safety disengaged with a sharp click. Tracking the muzzle along the length of the pumping control console, Trainor swung the weapon in a slow arc, squeezing the trigger at regular intervals.

Survey Rank Bender pointed to the close-up of the tether that dominated Markel's central video screen. "You are referring to the radio antenna that is coaxially mounted on the main fuel line?"

"Yes, Fourth Rank. If the entire facility were unmanned, there would be little need for—"

"Markel." The young Sauron sensor operator ceased speaking, discovered that Bender's eyes were no longer animated and bright, but as flat and blue as wind-scoured turquoise. "Markel, under normal operating conditions, how do we establish docking alignment at automated facilities?"

"By establishing tight-beam laser lock-on with the docking beacons."

"And what happens when the gimballing servos of those lasers are inoperative or damaged? How do we establish docking alignment then?"

Markel flushed. "We transmit coded binary instructions to the automated facility by radio."

Bender nodded slowly. "Which means that an automated facility must have a large radio receiver in order to accommodate ships which have suffered tight-beam laser failures—which, as you should know, is the most common form of battle damage. Consequently, such a receiver is not evidence of a manned presence."

Bender stared down at Markel—an impatient glare—then turned his back and left. Markel snapped off all but one of the video monitors, his finger thumping loudly against the smooth surface of the dynamically reconfigurable control panel; had Markel been anything other than Sauron, his motions would certainly have been suggestive of anger.

Mouth open, Dorrit stared at the even pattern of ten-millimeter holes that ran the length of the fuel pump control console. Then he emitted a decidedly non-military screech; "What have you *done?*"

Trainor snapped the handgun's safety back into place. "Following your orders to the letter, sir; I have fought the enemy in the best way I know how."

"By destroying our only offensive option?"

"An old maxim of warfare, Mr. Dorrit: if you know you can't win, then the definition of victory becomes cutting your losses." Reholstering his weapon, Trainor moved to the door, then stopped as though he'd forgotten something; he turned back to the operations staff. "I recommend you all head down to the lower levels."

Dorrit, sweat beading his brow, had recovered a semblance of dignity. "Mr. Trainor, you are relieved of your security duties—and if you make any further suggestions which encourage the personnel of this command to abandon their posts, I will have you shot." Dorrit turned his back on Trainor; already, technicians were swarming about the console, assessing the damage.

Trainor shrugged. "Have it your way," he muttered, and left for the lower levels.

Two minutes later—when Dorrit wasn't looking—Mpoh Aletti sidled out of the operations center to attend to the call of nature. However, this particular call of nature did not steer him toward the head. This call was more primal than the one associated with waste elimination; this was the primal call of survival. And, oddly enough, that call seemed to draw him toward the lowest levels of the Ayeshan complex.

Forty minutes later, Markel watched the image of the refueling station dwindle rapidly, becoming no more than a shiny mote at the center of his one active screen. The fueling had proceeded swiftly and the EVA teams had emplaced the scuttling charges without meeting a single person, although they had noted the presence of a few remote video sensors; probably there as a matter of record-keeping. Well, the record was about to end, and abruptly; though separated by a doorway, Markel heard First Rank Diettinger's voice clearly: "Charges status?"

Weapon's response was equally clear. "Telemetry indicates full functions, all, First Rank."

A long moment passed, one in which Markel had the opportunity to reflect on how the upcoming invasion of Haven might provide him with an opportunity to redeem himself in Bender's eyes.

Because the young sensor operator's thoughts were elsewhere, Markel only half heard Diettinger's command of "Activate." The scintillant speck at the center of Markel's video screen flared briefly and then was gone. The Sauron cruiser *Fomoria*—weapons charging and planetfall ordnance bays in readiness—continued to accelerate, making best speed for Haven.

From *The Book of Ages:*

It was long a characteristic of many cultures to build, to work at improving their know-how and their conditions of life. This was true of numerous cultures on Haven. Such efforts and their results, however, depended on more than intelligence, hard work, and self-discipline. Whether of citizens or tribesmen, such efforts depended on a degree of peace and hope, and on compatible government. On Haven, these crashed under the impact of the Saurons.

The short-term impact in particular varied with location. A few cultures in remote fringes of habitability—the Dinneh for example, and Maitreya's people—would not even hear of the Saurons for decades. But in the vast Shangri-La Valley, awareness was prompt and the impact immediate. That impact was heaviest on those who lived, and in many cases quickly died, in and near the valley's centers of government and technology.

Even in the Shangri-La Valley, however, there were those who, at the time of the invasion, dwelt or worked or traveled in back areas away from such centers. For them, the full meaning of the Sauron invasion took longer to sink in. . . .

THE RAILROAD
John Dalmas

Fedor Demidov sat with a book open in his lap, watching out the window as the railroad coach rocked and swayed its slow way up a grade. The terrain and forest outside could have been approximated in numerous places in his native Novy Rossiya: high hills that by some would be called mountains, and forest largely of the common Haven "pine." To his practiced eye, the area they were crossing had been clearcut about, oh, eighty years previously, and the replacement stand thinned at about age fifty, for fuel. In states like Novy Finlandia—*Uusi Suomi;* he'd have to watch himself on that. In states like Uusi Suomi, where forest was plentiful, forest thinnings, logging debris, and sawmill waste were the usual fuel in rural villages. In fact, they were much used in towns as well. Electricity was cheap enough, but electric cookstoves were very expensive.

There was a patter of quiet Finnish conversations in the car, which was mostly empty. Uusi Suomi's Foreign Ministry had reserved it for the two small groups of technical people: the one Demidov was with, and one made up of mining engineers, including a consultant from New Nevada. From the far end of the car, the consultant was holding forth loudly. Demidov allowed it to annoy him; the man was arrogant and offensive, as well as loud.

They were in the second of the two passenger cars. Demidov had the impression that the other was empty, except for the conductor who apparently had an office compartment in it. The rest of the train was of log cars; he could see them out the window, rounding a curve his own car had rounded moments earlier. They'd picked them up from different sidings along the line, and would leave them at the next sawmill they came to. On iron-poor Haven, where forest too was not abundant, lumber was valuable, and the management of forests quite technical and organized.

A voice began to speak from the loudspeaker at one end of the car, but he paid it little heed. It was in Finnish, a language in which he knew only a few polite phrases learned especially for this trip. Its rapid, tonal staccato and grammatical inflections hid even the scattered technical words it had in common with Russian and Americ.

Demidov glanced at Anna Vuorinen, the young interpreter in the seat facing his, and her stricken expression jerked his attention. She stared toward the loudspeaker behind him, and he turned as if looking might enlighten him. Virtually every other person in the coach was looking that way too, he realized now, and the conversations had died.

He turned back to the young woman as the speaker went silent. "What was it, Anna?" he asked in quiet Russian.

"Pirates," she said. "Extra-atmospheric fighter craft have been reported from several locations, and have engaged military aircraft near Fort Kursk."

Engaged! That meant destroyed; extra-atmospheric fighters would be infinitely superior to anything that any state of Haven could put in the air. For a moment, resentment flared in Demidov. Not at the pirates, but at the Imperium that had left the planet undefended.

Pirates were an aberration, but there had always been such aberrations, such predators, among humans. And the Imperium knew it. Yet some wretched bureaucrat in—what? The Ministry of State? Of War? Some faceless imperial bureaucrats had decided that the forty or so million citizens on Haven were not worth a squadron to protect them.

He overlooked that he was a bureaucrat himself. A bureaucrat was always the other person, usually someone you didn't know.

And Anna Vuorinen's husband was an officer in the Finnish air force. She'd mentioned that while they were getting acquainted at the Ministry of Forests the day before. So it was hardly suprising that the news had shaken her. But the border of Uusi Suomi was two thousand kilometers from Fort Kursk, and there were various places in the vast Shangri-La Valley that offered better looting.

He was thinking of pointing that out, when the conductor entered the car, a blocky man, gray of hair and mustache. He walked past the seated Demidov and his interpreter, stopping close ahead to talk to Veikko Ikola, Demidov's guide and principal host on this trip. Ikola lacked a doctorate, but as a silviculturist, an ecological engineer specializing in the management of forests, his reputation was international. He was said to look through the innumerable apparencies and recognize the key relevancies, then formulate working solutions more surely than anyone else in the profession. Which was why Demidov was there—to visit representative sites on the ground, ask questions and hopefully learn.

Ikola's conversation with the conductor was in Finnish of course, but he glanced at the Russian while they spoke. Then the conductor went on to talk to the man in charge of the group around the mining consultant from New Nevada.

Ikola stepped over and sat down next to Anna Vuorinen, across from Demidov. Although the Finn read technical papers in Americ well enough, in general conversation he used it clumsily, having particular difficulty following it when spoken. Thus the interpreter.

"Perhaps," Ikola said through her, "you would prefer to return to Hautaharju. Considering the pirate raid." On a world like Haven, with little or no high-tech military capacity, a mere raid by space pirates could be far more devastating than an earnest war between local states. "Our train will lay over at Tammipuro where we will eat while it recharges its storage batteries. There will be a southbound train there. We can go back on it."

"Do you consider that there is danger to your country?" Demidov asked. "Or to mine?"

Ikola shrugged and answered, this time in Americ. "Probably not. It is hard to know."

Demidov nodded. "I prefer to continue. I traveled 620 kilometers by rail, plus whatever we have come today. I would not care to return with nothing accomplished."

Ikola nodded, and returned to his seat across the aisle, where Demidov's two other hosts sat, the tall and massive Reino Dufva and the similarly tall but rangy Kaarlo Lytikäinen.

By now the conductor had finished what he'd had to say to the other group. The mining engineer, Migruder was his name, Carney Migruder, was laughing, a loud braying laugh that grated Demidov's nerves like fingernails on chalkboard.

The laugh ended with a long string of "huh huh huhs," releasing the Russian, and he glanced again at Anna Vuorinen. An attractive young woman, though not quite pretty. More interesting to him was her background. Her Finnish name had come with marriage.

Her background was as Russian as his own, though very different. Her spoken Russian was soft, the effect of having begun life among the peasant sectarians of "Pikku Venäjä." They were descendants of Russian religious deportees forcibly relocated on Haven more than five hundred years earlier. Entirely enclosed within the borders of Uusi Suomi, the sectarians remained calmly unabsorbed, culturally and linguistically. There was constant attrition, of course, of young people in reaction to the rigid rules of the sect. They went to the towns or to Russian-speaking states, and were assimilated. Anna's parents had broken away late, she'd said; they'd been nearly thirty, with three living children.

But the community remained closed, impenetrable from the outside, and the Finns had never tried to Finnicize them. The *Pikku Venäläiset* were hard working and productive, and used their land well. That was enough for the Finns.

Demidov had asked her to speak the dialect for him, and had understood only a little of it. It was quaint to an extreme. According to her it was not greatly changed from the mother tongue, at least in vocabulary and grammar. They still read the ancient bible—in cyrillic!— chanted prayers and hymns from ancient books, and recited a catechism centuries old. Apparently even pronunciations had not changed much; according to Anna, speech still largely fitted the ancient spellings.

Knowing it, though, had made it easy for her to learn the modern speech of Novy Rossiya, she'd told him. Certainly she spoke modern Russki fluently, despite her light accent.

Veikko Ikola watched the village of Tammipuro appear through the trees. Actually, the first he saw of it was the railroad siding with its loaded and unloaded strings of log cars. The village itself was almost like forest, its gravel streets lined with trees. Though not pines. Its trademark was its steelwood trees, the *tammi* in Tammipuro. He knew the place well enough, and a number of others more or less like it.

The morning was far enough along that they left their overcoats in the luggage rack when they got off the train. The local tavern doubled as the dining room for the railroad, and for whatever locals chose to eat out. At this

particular hour there were no other dining guests. As
was customary, the passengers would sit at a long trestle
table set up for them. Nor was there a charge; meals
were covered in their fare.

There was no menu. They simply needed to wait till
the food was ready. Some of the men went to the tap-
room, but Ikola sat down at the long trestle table and
waited. He preferred to do his drinking in more intimate
situations, with one or two friends in private conversation, or with Toini, his wife, at supper. Dufva and Lytikäinen too abstained, Lytikäinen because his temper,
never the best, was inversely correlated with his blood
alcohol. That was how Lytikäinen himself put it. Ikola
thought the problem was psychological; the forest super-
visor could get disagreeable just drawing the stopper.

Minutes later the mining experts returned with a large
pitcher of beer and a liter of whiskey, "bourbon"
imported from New Nevada. The loud consultant had
bought it. Migruder was his name, Ikola recalled, Carney
Migruder, a rather large burly man looking not quite
solid but not flabby either.

As usual the tavernkeeper had the radio on. The station played peasant music almost continually, energetic
music you could dance to. There was room to dance in
the dining room. Sawmill workers would dance there,
and the forest workers when they were in town, with
their wives and girlfriends, or with each other if they had
none there. But just now the railroad passengers had the
place to themselves. During trueday the forest workers
were away in the woods, working shift and shift, six hours
on and six off through four cycles, spending their off
time collapsed on their bunks. Busses brought them to
town for dim-day and true night, when woods work was
unsafe or impossible. Ikola knew their life first hand;
he'd lived it. Had grown up in a village much like Tammipuro, as had Dufva and Lytikäinen. You needed the
practical experience to be accepted into forestry curricula
at the university.

Migruder stood up, cleared his throat to draw their attention, then held his glass high. "Here's to Novy Finlandia!" he said loudly in Americ. "Long may she—do whatever it is she does!" He laughed then like a jackass, loudly and without humor.

Except for Migruder's laughter, the people there were silent as stone. Ikola had seen Lytikäinen stiffen, and had put a hand on his arm. The Nevadan was an official guest, invited by the Minerals Ministry to help evaluate some iron ore deposits in the upper foothills. Small concentrated deposits, typical of those developed volcanically, and potentially very valuable on iron-poor Haven.

The men from Minerals who accompanied the Nevadan raised their glasses stony faced. Migruder's mining expertise, Ikola told himself, must be very good indeed for them to put up with him. It was hard to believe that someone who found such pleasure in mindfuck, could do good work. He wondered if the man was married, and if so, what kind of husband he was, what kind of father.

Novy Finlandia! That was deliberate, thought Demidov. Migruder was either pathologically vicious or had a death wish. Or both.

Demidov knew more history than most Haveners. He was an avid reader, an accumulator of knowledge. Back on Terra, the Finns had had a long record of resistance, more or less successful resistance, to Russian dominance. Something that some Terran Russians—intellectuals and ruling circles—had found exasperating, and resented.

After the CoDominium was established, no Terran state was independent. So in Finland, the original Finland, a corporation was founded that sold shares in a new colony. In the worldwide depression of the time, however, even 7,000 shareholders were limited in what they could pay for. Thus the Finns settled for a place on Haven. Had chosen a place with much forest—hardly surprising, considering Finnish skills and traditions—and nearly six centuries ago had emigrated, moving families, livestock, and equipment.

They'd named their corporation *Uusi Suomi Yhtiö*— "New Finland, Limited." But some CoDominium bureaucrat, no doubt a Russian, had quietly entered it into the records as *Novy Finlandia*, the first word Russian, the second latinized Swedish. And once in the CoDominium computers that way, it was not only official. From there it got into all official and commercial computers and onto all map updates for Haven. Which was as close to being graven in stone on Mount Sinai as you could get. Of course, when the CoDominium collapsed, all that became null, and the Empire, when it arrived, accepted the name *Uusi Suomi* as official. But old habits die hard, and among other Haveners, "Novy Finlandia" was still common, if offensive usage.

The Finns, one of the most language-proud peoples, had resented it intensely at first, and still were sensitive about it. It would no doubt have been more acceptable had it been in Americ: "New Finland." But in Russian!

Another part of the original contract was that Uusi Suomi's territorial integrity was legally protected. But as with most of their contracts, the CoDominium ignored this one too. After BuReloc, the Bureau of Relocation, was established and forced deportations began, dissident Russians of various stripes were deported to Haven. Most went to mining districts, to work and die as forced laborers. Others were unloaded on the two established Russian colonies to accommodate as best they could; Demidov's ancestry included such deportees. But a shipload of religious dissidents had been unloaded in "Novy Finlandia."

It seemed doubtful that CoDo officialdom planned it that way. Aside from "trivial" matters—matters not coming before high-level officials—it seemed doubtful to Demidov that the CoDominium had gone out of its way to do vicious things, things not substantially profitable to one of its power factions. More probably some mid-level *apparatchik* had arranged it with the ship's captain out of spite. Tradition had it that shiploads of deportees had been put down nowhere near the site officially specified, for nothing more than a case of good whiskey, from someone who wanted slave labor and didn't have pull with BuReloc.

To make it worse, the newcomers had arrived in early winter with nothing to live on and little to make a living with. While the Finns themselves were still struggling to survive. At once there'd been a schism of sorts among the Finns, between those who wanted to leave the 2,800 newcomers to die, and those who refused to. The colony's council had voted to help them—indeed such help had already begun, unofficially—but the vote had been close. And the decision had held a proviso: aid to the Russians would come from a special fund of provisions; those who didn't wish to, need not give.

Fortunately the newcomers were mostly farmers, people with knowledge and skills, even with some tools. They could contribute effective muscle and work, though nothing of food, medicines, or initial shelter. At the end of the first years-long winter, nearly 1,200 still lived. But among those Finns who'd helped, the winter's death toll, not to mention other suffering, had been notably worse than among those who hadn't. The rift it had opened between the *halukkait,* "the willing," and the *sydämet-tömiä,* "the heartless," had taken several generations and the blurring of gradual intermarriage to close.

The fact that both the name Novy Finlandia and the burden of unwanted dependents were Russian, tied the two together in the psyche of the Finns. Migruder, Demidov told himself, was prodding a very sore spot.

The music was interrupted in mid-line by a voice in dry staccato Finnish, and it seemed to him it was something he should know about. He turned to Anna Vuorinen, questioningly. Her words, in Russian, were soft, almost murmured, her eyes unfocussed. "They say a Finnish squadron, the seventh Air Reconnaisance Squadron, has been attacked by the pirates, and most of it destroyed."

There'd been much more to the report than that. Apparently the information about the Finnish Squadron had preempted her attention. He didn't know if that was her husband's unit or not, but thought it must be. Judging from her face, her eyes. She excused herself then and left the table, which seemed to answer his unasked question.

He had another, and turned to Ikola with it. "Have the pirates visited Uusi Suomi, then?"

The Finn shook his head. "That squadron was on"— he groped for the Americ words—"it had our duty for the Council, at Sabbad."

Demidov nodded. Detached service in the south. The new Council of States had instituted an air patrol to discourage the corsairs that occasionally pillaged towns along the southern coast. The biplanes and triplanes they put in the air would mean little to space pirates though.

"And her husband was with the destroyed squadron?"

The Finn pursed his lips. "I think. From the way Anna react."

The food had been brought to their table more in the manner of a boarding house than a restaurant. It was plain but good, the sort of meal a solid working-class family might eat at home. Eating, Ikola told himself, served the additional function here of keeping Migruder's mouth occupied. Afterward the cook himself brought out individual bowls of a sweet but spicy dessert, and served each person himself.

When they'd finished, they reboarded the train. Both Demidov and Migruder had wanted to continue to their original destination, the town of Rajakuilu in the northeast corner of the country.

There were more than enough seats on the car. No one needed to sit beside anyone, or even across from anyone if they wanted to be alone. And indeed, most did sit alone. Why, Ikola asked himself, isn't everyone talking about the pirates? The place should be a-buzz. Yet he felt no urge himself to talk about it. Perhaps because so little was known—the skimpiest of information and no rumors at all.

One man was talking though. At the far end of the car, Migruder sat wearying his interpreter with his usual loud Americ. His monolog was rich in idiom and slang, well beyond Ikola's ability to follow, even had he been in the mood. It seemed to be something derogatory about someone.

One of the men from the Minerals Ministry passed on his way to the restroom. On his return, Ikola reached and touched his arm. "Sit," he invited, gesturing toward the seat opposite. The man hesitated, then sat.

"What do you know about Migruder?" Ikola asked.

The man shrugged, his face a grimace. "He is famous for his ability. As well as his character or lack of it. The Ministry studied the records of all the experts on Haven, and Migruder seems to be the best of them. We'll just have to put up with him for a few days."

"It's surprising someone hasn't killed him."

The man nodded. "His father is Baron Migruder of New Reno, very rich and influential. They fight like two land gators over a dead goat. The old man has disinherited him, or that's the report we have, but protects him nonetheless." The Ministry man shrugged and started to stand.

Just then Migruder hurried past him, headed for the restrooms at the end of the car.

Demidov still sat across from Anna Vuorinen, across the aisle from Ikola. And guessed it was Migruder that Ikola talked about with the Minerals official. What else? He looked at the young woman. "What did they say?" he asked.

She looked at him woodenly, and he realized she didn't know, hadn't listened. She must have been thinking about her husband, wondering if he was dead or alive. "Excuse me," he said. "I didn't mean to intrude on your thoughts. My question was idle curiosity."

She nodded slightly, then seemed to blank him out, her focus turning inward.

They rolled past a recent clearcutting, thick with seedlings knee high to a man, and lovely to Demidov's eyes. Haven pine produced two crops of tiny winged seeds in the long summer, the first remaining in the tough leathery pods. If a summer fire killed the stand, the pods, chemically changed by the heat, opened and released the seed onto the ash, where it germinated to produce a virtual carpet of seedlings. The later seed crop was born in pods much more fragile, which opened in winter storms. The spring thaw worked the seeds down into the needle litter. If fire then burned through before the early crop matured, the crowns might burn and the trees be killed, but of the needle litter, only the top centimeter or two were dry enough to burn. Last year's late crop, stimulated by the heat, germinated quickly then; at least what was left of it did.

In which case the new stand was often patchy and more or less thin and limby, but nature cared little about form factor or coarse knots, only presence and energy gradients. The trick in management was to use such general knowledge, along with the specifics of local conditions, to harvest the mature stand and obtain a new one without fire. The Finns, Ikola in particular, were masters at it, which was why he'd come here.

The loudspeaker sounded again. This time it wasn't the conductor's voice. He'd been sitting in his compartment listening to the radio, apparently, and switched on the speaker so the passengers could hear. It began in midsentence. Demidov watched as the woman listened. Her face paled almost to chalk, then the color returned to it as the report ended. Tears began to run down her face.

"Excuse me," she whispered, and getting up, hurried toward the restrooms. Ikola had been watching; he came over and sat where she had. "Radio gave names of dead flyers," he said. "One was *Luutnantti* Eino Vuorinen. I think her husband."

Demidov felt his own throat constrict, a burning in his own eyes, and thought for an embarrassed moment that he might weep. That would never do! He didn't know the woman well enough for that, and besides, what would Ikola think?

Through the long slow hours of early morning, most of the passengers dozed intermittently. The car rocked and swayed, the seemingly endless forest slid slowly past, and reading led easily to drowsiness. There were occasional short stops to pick up and drop off strings of log cars.

Migruder was the exception; he spent much of the next several hours in one or the other of the car's two restrooms, emerging more and more haggard. It seemed to Ikola that the tavernkeeper or cook in Tammipuro must have overheard the man's insulting toast and prepared a dessert portion especially for him. That would explain the personal service.

Toward midmorning, some of them adjusted their seats into beds, took their pillows from the overhead, and lay down to sleep. Even Migruder lay down between trips to the restroom.

The next news bulletin was switched into the speaker almost from the first word: The intruders had nuked Hell's-A-Comin' and Castell City! The mushroom cloud at Hell's-A-Comin' could be seen from Nothing Ventured, 215 kilometers away. Unofficial reports were that the intruders were not pirates! Supposedly, satellite transmissions had shown the ship to be a Sauron heavy cruiser!

Saurons! A chill rucked Ikola's skin. Talk of Saurons on Haven drove the report of nukings into the background. If Saurons had come ... If Saurons had come, the Empire had lost, and they faced a new empire, a

Sauron empire, that would make their old troubles seem trivial.

On the other hand— For unofficial report, read "rumor." Of course, rumors could be true; that was eighty percent of their fascination, but more often than not—

Drowsing was over with; no one was sleepy anymore. Nor likely to become so, Demidov thought. The conductor let the radio play continuously now. At least it wasn't dance music; under the circumstances it wouldn't have been appropriate. This was old music in the classical vein, played on an orchestral synthesizer. Dark music. He didn't recognize it; perhaps it was Finnish. Men adjusted their beds back into seats. Still nothing much was said for a few minutes. People began to draw together, talking sporadically in undertones. Lytikäinen and Dufva drifted over to sit again by Ikola.

Demidov looked openly at Anna Vuorinen. Her eyes occupied dark depressions in a pale face. He thought to start a conversation with her; it might draw her out of herself and her shock. But he could think of nothing. Partly it seemed too little was known, and the Saurons— The Saurons might be only a rumor. And partly— If it was true, it was too big and too new to confront all at once.

Even so, he found himself speaking. "Mrs. Vuorinen, do you know what music that is?" *Inane!* he told himself. *You're being inane!*

"It is 'Lemminkäinen in Tuonela.' "

"Thank you." He hesitated. "Was Lieutenant Eino Vuorinen . . . ?"

"My husband."

"I am terribly sorry."

"Thank you. Feel sorry for yourself." She said it almost bitterly, as if she held him somehow accountable. Then spoke further, contrite and clarifying: "It is kind of you to say so. But I feel—" She shrugged, a shrug that was half shudder. "I think our troubles are just beginning."

He turned inward, wondering if they were. There was no proof, only the rumors. He'd demoted the reports of nukings to rumors now, too, along with the Saurons.

But only for a moment, because the music was interrupted by another report from Hautaharju. The interpreter listened without changing expression. As if nothing more could affect her now. When it was done, she translated for Demidov without his asking. "Falkenberg has been destroyed by a nuclear explosion. Other places have been attacked by powerful weapons, believed to be orbital weapons. There has been a massive explosion at the power plant near Lermontovgrad, not nuclear, but a fire is said to be raging there, sending a smoke plume toward the east. It is thought to be radioactive." Her mouth twisted as if in cyncism. "People are warned to get out of its way."

As if they could, most of them, Demidov thought.

He tried to read then, but repeatedly found himself without a clue as to what his eyes had just passed over. He had to look again at the cover: *Physiological characteristics of the roots of pine seedlings in the Atlas foothills of. . . .* He set it aside. It seemed to belong to a time past. Not long past, but past and now irrelevant. It seemed to him that the days of managing forests for the export market were gone. They'd been there when the train had left Hautaharju, twelve hours earlier, but now they were finished. At any rate they were if the Saurons had come.

The conductor entered the car and walked along the aisle, speaking directly instead of through the speaker. He stopped by Demidov's seat and repeated in halting Americ: "We come to Sahakylä soon. We stop there. Eat and charge batteries."

Demidov wondered if Migruder was well enough to eat now. Or if he'd eat if he was well enough. It seemed doubtful he'd offer his foolish toast again. He looked

backward out the window. Rounding one of the innumerable curves was the long string of log cars they'd gathered. And would no doubt leave at the place they were
coming to.

"What is the town again?" he asked Anna Vuorinen.

"Sahakylä," she said. Then surprising him added,
"*Saha* means sawmill, and kylä is village. Sahakylä." As
if knowing, he might better remember. Or as if, with the
world coming apart, he'd never leave this country, and
had best start learning the language.

The thought triggered chills almost too intense to bear.
Was that it? he thought, and it seemed to him that the
answer was yes.

When they left the railway car at Sahakylä, Migruder
looked pale but generally recovered. In the dining hall,
however, though he bought another bottle, he drank quietly, moodily. To Ikola it felt that what the man had on
his mind was not the bombings nor the rumor of Saurons, but what had been done to him at Tammipuro. His
mood seemed not one of worry or shock, but of smolder-
ing resentment. Ikola was glad the man wasn't his
responsibility.

He sat down across from Demidov. The Russian had
impressed him at first as someone who perhaps thought
of himself as more refined than other people. His hands
were small for his size, and rather slender. But he'd com-
ported himself courteously and thoughtfully at all times.

"What you think of news today?" Ikola asked quietly
in Americ.

"I think—" Demidov began slowly, "I think it may be
the end of things as we've known them. The end of
civilized life for humans on Haven."

The Finn raised an eyebrow. "On Haven were terrible
times before. After wars destroyed CoDominium, and
Haven left by itself. Our ancestors fell to—" He groped.
"Primitive. We have come back long way. Come back
again if need."

The Russian shook his head. "If the Saurons have come, it will mean worse than primitivism. It will mean slavery!"

The Finn's eyes were calm but intent. "What will you do then, if Saurons are here?"

Demidov sighed and shook his head. "What can one do? Expend one's life as best one can."

"Expend?"

Demidov looked to Anna Vuorinen and spoke in Russian. "If the Saurons have indeed come, they will make slaves of people. And if they've come here, it means they've defeated the Empire. That is hard to believe, but perhaps they have done it. Then one can either be their slave, or one can expend his life with honor, and die fighting."

The interpreter didn't begin translating till after Demidov had finished, as if she was looking at the situation for the first time. When she'd repeated it in Finnish, Ikola peered at the Russian curiously.

"Only those two alternatives, you think?"

Anna passed his words on. "What else?" the Russian asked.

"Seventeen standard years ago when the Marines were pulled off Haven," Ikola replied, "the Empire was still very powerful. There were wars of secession, but the Navy was large—immense—and loyal."

His Finnish was flowing more slowly than it might have, and Anna kept pace not many words behind.

"Sauron was also powerful," he went on, "but not nearly so large. And if the Empire was beset by wars of secession, the Sauron slave worlds were less than loyal to their masters. They might, perhaps, fear to revolt, but surely they would do such sabotage as they could. Do you really believe the Saurons could have defeated the Empire?"

"The Saurons believed they could, obviously. And if they are here—" The Russian's shrug was different than the Finn's had been, more expressive. "They must have."

"You asked for another alternative," Ikola countered. "I think there is one. A second explanation for the Saurons being here, if they are, and a third alternative for us. Seventeen standard years is not so long. Would it be long enough for the Saurons to defeat the Imperial Fleet, and the Imperial Marines? I think of the young Finns who joined the 77th. They were roughnecks, most of them, and adventurous. And mostly they were not the big-mouths, while those who were, were more as well. They were the youths who liked brawls, and who more often than not won their fights. I think the same was true in other states, and probably on other worlds.

"And when, after training, they came home on leave, they had changed. They were still tough, but proud with a different pride than before. Pride in their regiment, their division. And they walked differently, moved differently. They even spoke politely to their parents! They knew discipline. In a tavern they might not show it, but they knew discipline where it counted."

He paused to let the interpreter catch up, for as he'd warmed to his subject, he'd spoken faster. Now he changed tack.

"Suppose the Navy beat the Saurons. What do you suppose would happen then?"

Demidov frowned, pursed his lips. "If they defeated them, really defeated them— They would surely destroy Sauron, their home world. And everyone on it. But to do that, they'd have to destroy the Sauron fleet, first."

Ikola nodded, saying nothing, leaving Demidov to carry his thoughts further.

The Russian shrugged again. "I suppose the Saurons, what were left of them, would scatter. And the Fleet would pursue them, try to eradicate them to the last ship, the last man. And woman." He frowned. "What you want me to say is that the Saurons who've come here, if they have come here, are a ship of refugees."

Ikola nodded. "It seems more probable. The alternative, if the Saurons are really here—the alternative is that in just seventeen years they have destroyed the Imperial Fleet. And in those same seventeen years have spread through the entire Empire, occupying every world to the very last. And this world would be the very last, or one of them.

"I do not think all that could happen in seventeen years."

The two men hadn't realized that the rest of the table had fallen silent and was listening, the Finns to Ikola and to Anna's translation of the Russian, Migruder to his own interpeter.

It was Migruder who interrupted, his laugh half bark, half sneer. "Shit!" he said. "Saurons! No Saurons would waste their time with a crummy back-water world like this! Some pansy saw something and panicked. Over the radio. Some other pansies heard him squawk, and they panicked. Now you sad sacks of shit are flapping around ready to suicide."

Lytikäinen was sitting on the same side of the table as Migruder. He stood abruptly, his chair clattering backward onto the pine floor, and with two quick strides had the Nevadan by the hair, even as the man turned in his seat. Lytikäinen jerked him backward, and Migruder's chair went over, Migruder in it. The man scrambled to his feet ready to fight, but the massive Dufva was between the two, keeping them apart. Lytikäinen he'd shoved sharply backward, sending him staggering. Migruder's shirt he'd gripped with a massive left hand, twisted, and jerked him close. The Nevadan looked paralyzed.

"We will be polite here," he said in ponderous Americ. With a grin, his face in Migruder's. Demidov, himself startled breathless, realized he'd misread the quiet, smiling logging engineer. The man was not placid, simply amiable. He'd probably smile at you even while throwing you through the wall. Seemingly Migruder realized this too, realized something at any rate, realized that this man could gobble up both Lytikäinen and himself with little effort. He snarled non-verbally as Dufva freed him, and straightened his shirt. His interpreter had retrieved Migruder's chair and stood it up again.

The man from Minerals was on his feet too, tight-lipped. Demidov suspected the man would like to have done what Lytikäinen had, but still he was responsible for Migruder's mission here. Now it would be a miracle if the man didn't head back for Hautaharju; this could even result in a break in diplomatic relations. On the other hand there was no point in anyone's raising hell with Lytikäinen; the damage was already done. Demidov was glad he wasn't involved.

That's when the music was interrupted with another report. Morgan, Migruder's interpreter, gave the outlanders a running translation into Americ. "This is Radio Metsäjoki. We have just received a report from Weather Service radio on Iron Hill, broadcasting on emergency backup power. Severe explosions have erupted in the power plant at Kivikuilu. There is fire there, and heavy smoke, presumably radioactive, is drifting down the canyon toward the capital. Extra-atmospheric fighter craft have attacked both the city and the military base south of it. Great explosions have occurred over the government district and the military base. The very air appeared to explode; the center of the city has been flattened. Of the government district and the apartment blocks around it, hardly a wall is standing. There is no sign of anyone left alive.

"Immediately after we received the preceding report, the Weather Service personnel reported that a fighter craft was circling their installation. Transmission then cut off.

"We will try to keep you informed of anything further that happens. Meanwhile, we return you to our music program."

Someone—the cook or the tavernkeeper—turned the volume well down then, and for a long moment the room was silent. Demidov looked around at the Finns. None were moving, though he could hear someone's labored breathing above the muted music. It was as if they'd been turned to stone. Then Migruder began to chuckle, the sound escalating, becoming a laugh, at first harsh and bitter, then loud, uncontrolled, as if driven by some psychotic mirth.

Demidov stared. He expected someone to strike the man, but no one moved. When Migruder had choked back his laughter, he spoke: "You Finns! You goddamn ridiculous people! Now you see how weak you are! You're fucked now, fucked good!"

He looked around leering. Then Demidov was surprised to find himself speaking, his voice loud in the stillness. "Migruder, you are a fool!"

Migruder's head jerked to stare at him.

"Think, man!" Demidov went on. "Where have you been all day? Haven't you been listening? Do you believe the Saurons make war only on people you don't like? They've already destroyed the planet's major military bases. Now they destroy the minor ones. They're also destroying the power-generating plants of the planet, and the governing capacity. What do you think is left of your father's barony? Of the government district at New Reno? Of New Reno itself?

"Your father can't protect you from this. He can't buy you out of it. You're in a foreign land a thousand kilometers from home, except now you don't have a home. You're alone here in the midst of a people you've insulted repeatedly."

Migruder's eyes bulged, not with rage but seemingly in shock. The man is insane, Demidov realized. *Truly* insane. He's been walking around with insanity seething just below the surface, for who knows how long.

The Nevadan turned abruptly and strode toward the door. No one tried to stop him.

The rest waited for dinner. The cook continued cooking, and when the food was ready, the tavernkeeper served them. The only things unusual about it were the quiet, and that two of the Finnish passengers went to the kitchen and helped bring out the food.

The food, it seemed to Demidov, was as good as it would otherwise have been. He even enjoyed it in a detached sort of way: ate detachedly, tasted detachedly, and watched those around him detachedly. He didn't wonder about his father in Novy Petrograd, or his brothers or sisters; he knew. Knew all he needed to.

A question did occur to him though, and when he'd finished his main course, he turned to Anna Vuorinen. "I have a question for *Herra* Ikola." He looked at the Finn. "If the nuclear plant has been destroyed, how are the locomotive's storage batteries being recharged?"

"Beginning here at Sahakylä, the railroad's power comes from the dam at Rajakuilu. The power for the whole northeastern part of the country does." Ikola raised his voice then, enough to get everyone's attention. "Who here wishes to return south?" He didn't say south to Hautaharju; just south.

Three of the four men from Minerals raised their hands. Probably they felt compelled to seek their families. Demidov didn't know whether to be surprised or not when Anna Vuorinen didn't raise her hand. He was definitely surprised when Migruder's interpreter didn't; he'd been sure the man was from New Nevada, and south was the direction of home for him. Perhaps, Demidov thought, he intended to wait and see what Migruder wished to do.

Ikola's home was south too, in Hautaharju, but he hadn't raised his hand. Demidov thought he knew why: Ikola had mentioned that his wife worked in the Agriculture Ministry, and that they lived in an apartment almost across the street from it. At home or at work, she'd have died. Of course, there might be children . . .

"There is a reserve armory at Metsäjoki," the Finn went on. "There will be infantry weapons there, including mortars and rockets, along with officers and noncoms.

And field rations for two months. Field radios too, for as long as their batteries last. It will take about fifteen hours to get there by train. Or perhaps only eight or ten, if the conductor decides we need not stop for log cars." He turned to the conductor. "Personally, I think it would be futile to haul logs. Perhaps later, if it should turn out that the Saurons are just a rumor."

The conductor said nothing. Shortly the engineer came in to say that the batteries were recharged. Walking to the train, Demidov spoke again to Ikola through Anna Vuorinen: "You never told me your alternative to slavery or dying in combat."

"Ah," said the Finn. "The other is to survive free. Survive and wait." His eyes were hard. "I've read considerable history, of both Haven and Earth. The Russian people, like the Finns, are good at surviving, at outlasting their oppressors.

Demidov said nothing more as they walked. He was digesting Ikola's answer.

Migruder stayed on the northbound train, drinking. Demidov suspected that Morgan hadn't said anything to him about going south. Meanwhile the conductor had decided to follow standard practice; they stopped several times to drop off empties and take on cars of logs.

It seemed to Demidov that what had happened at Hautaharju had caught up with Ikola. Early on, the Finn had gone to the restroom and not reappeared for quite a while. When he did, his eyelids had been swollen and spongy looking, his face pasty pale. Now he sat as if dead, his features slack, and did not talk at all. Even Lytikäinen and Dufva left him to himself.

Vuorinen gave Demidov his first Finnish lesson: "*olen,* I am; *olet,* you are; *hän on,* he or she is. . . ." The language, Vuorinen told him, was so conservative, a modern Finn could read the ancient books. It came, she said, from the tradition of learning ancient verse verbatim, and from pronouncing everything the way it was spelled.

Perhaps, thought Demidov. *But at a deeper level it came from valuing the old, even while adapting to and living with the new.*

Six hours after they'd left Sahakylä, the conductor announced they were approaching the village of Susi-lähde, where they would eat again. About time, Demidov thought; his stomach had been grumbling. "Susilähde." *Susi*, Anna told him, was Finnish for stobor, although on Earth it had meant a different pack-hunting animal. *Lähde* meant a spring of water. He sat repeating the name to himself, to the measure of the wheels clicking over the expansion joints in the rails.

It was near noon when they arrived, noon in a forty-hour day, and it was warm, nearly hot. Walking down the graveled street in the rays of Byers' Sun, Demidov sweated. Migruder hadn't gotten off the train with them; hadn't eaten since Tammipuro, and presumably had puked up that. Or had it been nothing more than diarrhea? As he walked, Demidov drilled the verb to be: *olen, olet, hän on, se on; olemme, olette. . . .*

Inside the tavern was half dark. No light burned. The place seemed deserted. Demidov looked in past Ikola, who'd led off from the train and stood just inside the doorway. The Finn called a halloo in Finnish, and the tavernkeeper came in from a back room. Then they all entered. "We cannot cook," the tavernkeeper said simply. "There is no electricity."

"No electricity?" Ikola sounded more vexed than surprised. "Those Sauron bastards! There won't be any at the railroad either then. The engineer won't be able to recharge the batteries."

Anna interpreted for Demidov while the others cursed or stood silent.

"How did it happen?" Demidov asked, and Anna passed his question on.

"It's damned obvious!" Ikola said angrily. "The Sauron sons of bitches have bombed the dam at Rajakuilu! They can't leave anything alone! They want to send us back to the stone age!"

He turned to the tavernkeeper. "When did this happen?"

"Less than an hour ago."

"Can you feed us cold food?"

"*Limppu* and butter, cold boiled eggs, some cold meat . . . I might as well use the meat up; there's no refrigeration now. Uno and Arvo are digging a cold hole on the shady side of the tavern, like in the old days. When they're done, I can keep things in it. But not frozen; not in summer."

They went to the table and sat down in the half-dark. There were only seven of them now, the three Finnish forestry people plus one from the Minerals Ministry, along with Anna Vuorinen, Demidov, and Migruder's interpreter, Morgan. The tavernkeeper, who'd sent his cook home, went into the kitchen and clattered around. Meanwhile there was no radio—no music, no news bulletins.

The conductor came stamping in. "There is no power!" he said. "I cannot recharge the batteries!"

"Tell us something we don't know," growled Lytikäinen, and gestured at the wooden chandelier, lightless overhead.

"How far can we go on the charge left in the batteries?" Ikola asked.

The conductor shook his head. "I don't know. Not all the way to Metsäjoki though, I think. The engineer should be here soon. He'll at least have some idea.

They ate in a silence broken only once, by the tavernkeeper. "You really think they've blown up the dam?" he asked Ikola.

"I don't know it," Ikola answered, "but I feel sure of it. I've never heard of the power failing in Koillinen Province before. Not along the railroad, anyway."

The cook stared thoughtfully at an upper corner of the room, then brightened. "When I was a boy, there was a big wood range in the kitchen here, and a tall, wood-burning oven. My father made me split wood for them each day. I think they may be in Hietala's old barn. I could move them back in here." He paused. "But it wouldn't be worthwhile if the trains don't run. I wonder if they cut up the old wood-burning engines for scrap?"

Perhaps, Demidov thought, *the dam wasn't blown up. Perhaps somehow the power line was broken. True it was underground, but there might have been a landslide somewhere along the line, or a torrent.* He shook his head. *No. The dam is blown up.*

The engineer came in then, swearing. *"Saatana!"* he swore. "Those bastards have really done it to us! Now I can't recharge the batteries!"

"How close to Metsäjoki can we get without a recharge?" Ikola asked.

"What's the point of going to Metsäjoki?" the engineer countered. "There won't be any electricity there either. Take my word for it."

"The point is the reserve armory there."

The engineer said nothing for a long half minute. "You think the Saurons will come even here? To Koillinen Province?"

"Maybe, maybe not; we need to be prepared." Ikola repeated his question then. "How far can we get?"

"I'm not sure. We might get halfway."

"That's a lot closer than this," Lytikäinen said.

"Shit." The engineer looked dejected. "I'm only two standard years short of my pension. And now this! And Erkki"—he indicated the conductor—"is almost as close."

"Four and a half," the conductor said. He looked as if he hadn't considered that aspect of it before. "Those rotten bastards!"

The room was quiet then, except for the sounds of tableware and eating. When they were done, they left, but not until Lytikäinen and the conductor had each bought a liter of whiskey. Demidov wondered if the tavernkeeper would be paid for their meals, now that the trains had stopped. He also wondered if it would make any difference. Would the economy continue in some sort of clumsy fashion, adjusting as it went?

The sun shone as if nothing had happened. The radio had said the radioactive plume from the power plant was drifting south. At least they didn't have that to worry about. At least not yet.

Partway to the train they met Migruder coming down the street. He was drunk, and looked truculent. The rest went on while Ikola, Dufva, and Morgan tried to talk the Nevadan into turning around and going back to the train. Anna Vuorinen waited nearby in the shade of a steelwood tree. When Migruder insisted on eating first, Dufva and Morgan started with him to the tavern. They'd grab something he could eat on the train, Dufva said. Ikola and Demidov, with Vuorinen, began sauntering back toward the railroad.

They were eighty meters from the train when Ikola heard the howl of a fighter's heavy engines. Instinctively, without ever having heard the sound before, he sprinted for the cover of a cluster of trees near the street, the others a jump behind. A series of explosions stunned them, and the locomotive and passenger cars split apart where they stood, pieces of debris raining down for ten seconds or more.

Ikola was up and running again. After their heads cleared, Demidov and Vuorinen dashed after him.

Indeed the stone age! They were even destroying the railroad rolling stock.

They didn't find actual bodies, only what was left of them: the engineer's in the wreckage of the locomotive cab, the conductor's in the first car, Lytikäinen's and the man from Minerals in the second. By that time Dufva and Morgan had run up too, and within minutes there were some hundred townspeople as well. And Migruder. The Nevadan looked sober now, Ikola thought, sober and full of anger. Somehow Ikola's own anger had receded. *Migruder! I should tell him he saved our lives,* Ikola told himself. *He'd really be mad then.*

Susilähde had a reserve rifle platoon, with its own small armory that held nothing heavier than rifles. One of its radiomen called battalion headquarters at Metsä-joki. The armory there was intact; presumably the Saurons hadn't recognized it.

Within the hour, Ikola, a captain in the reserves, had signed out several surplus packsacks, canteens and sleeping bags from the supply sergeant, along with five assault rifles, magazine belts, and an automatic pistol. All of them, including Vuorinen, had worn heavy woods boots when they'd left Hautaharju. The tavernkeeper provided them with potatoes and turnips and a large block of cheese. It was 130 kilometers to Metsäjoki, with no guarantee what they'd find there, but there were two small villages along the way, and some logging camps. With luck they wouldn't have to sleep out in the chill of dim-day or the hard cold of true night.

Ikola had given one of the packs to Migruder and one to Morgan. Migruder was grimly determined to walk the thousand or so kilometers to New Reno. Like the others, he had a small stock of groceries, but supplemented with two liters of whiskey. He'd had a revolver in his luggage all along, and had salvaged it from the wreckage. Now it rode in its holster at his waist.

Finally they started for the railroad again: Ikola, Dufva, Demidov, and Anna Vuorinen. And Morgan; Morgan was going with the Finns. His mother had been Finnish—it was she who'd taught him the language—and he'd had a bellyful of Migruder.

They didn't know what the world situation would be when they arrived at Metsäjoki.

Migruder too walked to the railroad, but apart from the others and somewhat behind them. When they reached the right-of-way, Ikola told the others to go on, he'd catch up with them. Then he waited till Migruder arrived.

"Migruder," he said.

The Nevadan didn't answer, merely stopped and scowled.

"Good luck," Ikola said in Americ, and held out his hand.

Migruder stared for a moment, first at the hand, then into Ikola's face, and his hostility seemed to fade. Nonetheless he turned without answering or meeting Ikola's proferred hand. He simply showed his broad back and started south along the right-of-way past the string of log cars on the siding. Ikola watched him go, then turning, strode north past the wreckage.

The others had gone only a little way, glancing back. Now they stopped to wait. Ikola caught up with them, and together they hiked north along the tracks, past the railyard and into the forest.

The bunker shook once again as yet another Sauron missile found its mark on the surface two hundred feet above. Colonel Edon Kettler didn't quite stagger, just modified his brisk pace for a few seconds into the rolling gait which the inhabitants of General Cummings' field redoubt had come to call the "Sauron Shuffle." This time, it was two steps to the right, one back and three forward; but like most modern dances, one just sort of moved the way it felt right.

Like everybody else in Cummings' orbit, Kettler was running to an appointment. Formerly an officer of Enoch Redfield's Satrapy Air Force, Kettler was now more or less attached to the Fort Kursk garrison, since that day he had flown through the Sauron's initial orbital strikes to reach Fort Fornova with a request for aid and a rapidly contrived plan to strike back at the invaders. Even before his arrival, all contact had been lost with the Redfield Satrapy, and Kettler had come to accept the fact that his status as a sort of military "minister without portfolio" was now permanent.

General Cummings had agreed to his proposal for attacking the Saurons. Mostly, he had been impressed by

47

Kettler's apprehension of the invaders' plans, which had allowed a team of "volunteers" to target a missile at the last Sauron shuttle down to Haven, the shuttle which Kettler had reasoned would be carrying their senior staff officers. Monitoring the Sauron transmissions in the hours which followed the attack, it had turned out that Kettler—a career military man in a provincial air force on a backwater moon, who had never even seen a Sauron—had predicted their actions perfectly.

Well, Kettler admitted to himself, *almost perfectly*. They'd caught the shuttle, but there was no way to keep its pilot from guessing the tactic and maneuvering to break the missile lock.

Even so, Cummings had taken an instant liking to Kettler, and with no country of his own to return to any longer, it had been only natural that the dispossessed pilot would find a place here.

Kettler put his briefcase up under one arm and pushed open the heavy door before him. He thought again about almost catching the Saurons, and remembered what he'd been told about no one being able to shave a margin of success thinner than a Sauron.

And anyway, "almosts" don't win wars, he reminded himself, and trying not to think of his family as he entered General Cummings' briefing room, Kettler reflected that he would try to do better this time.

Cummings looked up as he entered, and though he looked tired, there was none of the bone-deep weariness that Kettler saw in the eyes and posture of the other inhabitants of this post. *He lives for this*, Kettler realized, and remembered that Cummings too had a family when this all began. *A wife he knows is dead, killed in the first hours of the invasion, a daughter he can hope was safe, but whom he'll probably never see again.* Kettler supposed that he probably looked much the same as Cummings, himself.

Kettler's home had been in the Redfield Satrapy's heavily industrialized Horne Valley district, an area which the last scouts had reported was now filled with a 12,000 rad-level dust cloud. It was, Kettler thought, a common bond for most of Cummings' command.

"Good morning, sir," Kettler greeted his *de facto* C-in-C. He was still surprised at how natural that felt, considering the past differences between Redfield and the Hamiltons. But he reminded himself that "past" was indeed the word; the coming of the Saurons had changed everything.

"Morning, Ed." Cummings idly brushed brick dust from the map he was studying; "Came rather close this morning, didn't they?"

Kettler shrugged. "The price of using these old tunnels so close to the power stations, General Cummings. Every time the citizens try to re-start a generator for one of the hospitals, they get another strike for their troubles."

Cummings nodded, looking up at the cracked ceiling. "If the Saurons thought we were down here, they'd put a nuke right into this room." A young lieutenant brought two cups of coffee. "Time to move on, anyway, Colonel," Cummings said as he looked into his cup. "We've almost run through the supplies in this cache. What have you got for me?"

Kettler spread his papers over the map. "Concentrations of tribesmen in the Northern Steppes and bandits known to have been operating in the Shangri-La before the invasion. The information includes remaining records of the Redfield Satrapy, Cracovia steppe patrols and Novy Finlandia Intelligence—"

Cummings interrupted. "They're Finns, Colonel," he reminded him. "They call their nation *Uussi Suomi*; they're rather touchy about people using the Russian version of the name."

Kettler grumbled to himself that everybody outside "Uussi Suomi" had called it "Novy Finlandia" for as long as he could remember. And there probably wasn't much left of the place, whatever they called it. Still, he assumed Cummings had a purpose for wanting him to amend his own patterns of address. Cummings seemed to have a purpose for everything.

Cummings became absorbed in the data before him.

Kettler watched, and waited. He knew that Cummings had fought the Saurons for a good long while as an officer of the departed Empire. Cummings knew his foe, without a doubt, but he still welcomed Kettler's input. Kettler had exhibited something of a knack for guessing what the Saurons would do in a given situation. Perhaps he was more than a little bit like them, but no one had yet been foolish enough to tell him so to his face. Kettler suspected it was his objectivity that Cummings valued. Where Saurons were concerned, the General was conspicuously lacking in that characteristic.

Cummings began without preamble, "We're changing our methods of engaging the Saurons." Cummings sat back with a folder on the horse-clans of the northern steppes, flipped open a pair of glasses and put them on. "I'd love to think we could stage a major confrontation with the Saurons, but I don't think we'd win it even with every Havener capable of carrying a weapon."

"That's a cheerful thought. Sir."

Cummings looked at him over the rims of his spectacles and smiled. "We were losing our wars against each other long before they came, Colonel. We'd fractured and polarized ourselves into a state of balkanization that made late twentieth century Earth look positively monolithic."

Kettler had no idea what "balkanization" meant, but he remained dubious about Cummings' assessment of Haven's societal decline. The Redfield Satrapy had been an extremely stable—if despotic—entity, and its major opponent in the last years before the Saurons was the depressingly resilient republic of Novy Finlandia—or Uussi Suomi, as Kettler was trying to think of it, now. Lots of Haven hadn't been getting on too well since the Empire pulled out, to be sure. Other parts had gotten along quite nicely, thank you. Better than ever, in fact.

Cummings went back to his notes. "Dispersal of the industrial base would have finished us off in a century. Haven just can't support its population at Empire levels with dispersed industry. So, while I'd like a united front against the Saurons, it's going to have to be established in rather an unorthodox way. You were a fighter pilot, isn't that correct, Colonel?"

Kettler cleared his throat. "I'm a qualified pilot, General; Mister Redfield insisted that all members of the Satrapy air force be able to fly."

Cummings watched him. "The Redfield Satrapy had enough of an aviation industry to make that worthwhile?"

Kettler nearly blurted out the standard security-conscious response, before realizing its absurdity. "Actually, we did have a surplus of aircraft, General. Frankly, though, we had a rather poor pilot-training program, in my opinion."

"And you would be qualified to judge," Cummings answered; it was not a rebuke, Kettler realized. Nor was it a question.

"Sir?"

"Colonel, surely you don't think I'd have welcomed you into my staff without checking you out? You were a staff officer of the Satrapy Air Force. You were, in fact, something of a fair-haired boy, Enoch Redfield's organizational genius. That was before you ran afoul of the heir apparent, however."

Kettler remained silent at first, but knowing an answer was expected, he finally said: "That was all some time ago, General."

"Indeed it was, Colonel." Cummings agreed. "It was, in fact, a different era. And it's as dead as Enoch Redfield and his up-and-coming-tyrant of a son. But what matters is that you *were* his air arm organizational expert. Weren't you?"

"Yes, sir." *Here it comes, Edon,* Kettler thought. *You've outlived your usefulness and if you're lucky, you'll be put out on the road to try and survive the wasteland of cratered destruction that Haven was becoming.* He'd seen something very much like it happen a dozen times under Enoch Redfield; it would have happened to Kettler, too, after the duel, had he not been just as useful to the old man as Cummings had noted.

But it *would* happen here. It would happen because Cummings had no loyalty to a Redfielder, after all; he had no need for a pilot, no food to spare to keep one around; but most of all, Cummings had no air force. Kettler's years of training and study and self-discipline at the Redfield Satrapy University had been to develop the one skill which, even as a youth, he perceived his fellow citizens in the Satrapy had lacked. He was an organization man, and in the world of guerrilla warfare which Cummings had mastered, Kettler's kind of organization existed to be disrupted.

"Colonel?"

"Sorry, sir." Kettler closed his briefcase. "Yes, General. My sole expertise is in organizational work. I suppose that's not much help."

Cummings blinked. "Colonel, I don't know what you're talking about; organizational work is exactly what you're going to be doing in the next few years. If you live."

"Sir?"

"The Empire *made* Haveners live together. But the Saurons will give Haveners the opportunity—even the incentive—to ignore or kill one another; either is to the Saurons' advantage. There has to be a third alternative, and I think you're the man to provide it. We're going to try unionizing." Kettler wasn't quite sure he understood what was being said, until Cummings added: "You're familiar with the phrase: 'Hearts and Minds,' aren't you, Colonel?"

Suddenly understanding, Kettler smiled. He still had a job, after all.

A BETTER KIND OF WAR

Don Hawthorne

Cyborg Rank Koln stepped forward onto a strip of naked stone which jutted out from below the walls of the Citadel. Here, in this lonely, windswept, frigid place, he was suspended between two worlds. Behind him and above, the sweeping spires of the castle whose towers soared above the valley floor, in graceful arches which belied their strength, but spoke eloquently of their purpose: Nothing moved between the valley and the steppelands beyond without the approval of those who held this fortress. And below, the debris-littered northeast expanse of the valley the natives called the Shangri-La, where the ruins of the *Fomoria* still glowed with enough residual heat to be visible to his genetically augmented vision. The pall of irradiated smoke above the Shangri-La Valley was still slowly rising, the last mark of the great ship's passing. The cattle had struck a blow—futile, of course; but impressive nevertheless.

From even higher than the towers overhead, the sonic boom of First Rank Diettinger's shuttle fell on the Cyborg's ears to no response but a faint sigh. Standing there on the brink of that precipice, at the terminator line separating the shadow of the mountains behind him from the sunlit valley before, Koln felt as divided as he looked. He was filled with a sense of impending conflict and yet, typically Sauron, even this was clearly divided into two clear choices: To turn, and re-enter the ranks of the society which must now be built? Or take a single, brief step out into that abyss that began ten centimeters from his boots and ended more than a thousand feet below? Cyborg Rank Koln sighed again, dispiritedly.

Alas, I would probably survive such a fall no worse than crippled. Koln's jaw clenched at the thought of such an injury, for surely it was now beyond the capability of such meager resources as the Saurons had brought to Haven to repair him. And then he would truly be a slave of the Breedmasters, who would be only too happy to have at their disposal—literally—a Cyborg whose only value was his seed.

Turning sharply enough to swing half his bulk out over that vertiginous gulf, Koln left the precipice and returned to meet the First Rank's shuttle. And although he was still six levels below the Citadel's landing pad, he could hear the cheers of greeting from the Soldiers above.

Climbing the steep paths cut decades before into the stone of the mountainside, Koln reflected that while he had turned away from one brink, it would not be long before he must come to another; and the step he took then would have far greater consequences than the death of one lone Cyborg.

Galen Diettinger sat before the assembled staff of his last naval command, the *Fomoria*—re-named the "Dol Guldur" as a *ruse de guerre* to initially persuade the Haveners that they were being attacked by pirates. Now the name seemed to be a sort of jest among the younger crewmembers; one which showed no sign of losing its appeal.

Around the table were an even dozen section heads of all the most important functions aboard a combat starship. Overnight, they had been transformed into governmental ministers. Yesterday they had been smoothly integrated members of a military chain of command, today they were counselors. They had not yet begun to explore their new capabilities of limited disobedience. But he knew they would, in time.

Nor had Diettinger avoided a metamorphosis of his own. His place at the head of the table was now the seat of the First Citizen of the Sauron State of Haven. The collar tabs that had borne the insignia of a First Rank— the stark, white bar on a black field—had been replaced with the single round gem studs that symbolized the ruler of all the Sauron people. Or at least all those known to remain alive, anyway.

The subtle changes in his uniform had been carefully engineered by his wife. Despite unanimous acceptance of his new status as First Citizen by the survivors of the *Fomoria*, the First Lady had left nothing to chance. A trained historian and behavioralist, Althene had been careful to combine elements of his new appearance which proclaimed his civilian authority while reminding all who saw him of its recent military roots; to the Sauron mind, its only possible justification.

Althene had not been able to find diamonds of the proper size for his collar tabs, but a Third Ranker had returned from a patrol with a captured set of Haven shimmerstones, and she had suggested that they might serve as well. Having enjoyed something of a vogue centuries before in the CoDominium era and the Early Empire, the stones were in fact far more valuable than mere diamonds. Better still, they were unique to Haven, and as such, Diettinger had decided that they were far more appropriate to their function than diamonds would have been.

All that remained of his link with the *Fomoria* was the "vessel" badge that had defined just what he had been First Rank of; a gun-metal pin over his left breast depicting a Sauron starship in profile over a five-pointed star. Scarcely two inches across, the pin was a subtle but striking reminder of his origins.

So the preparations for his first performance were complete. With none of the trepidation of a lesser actor, Diettinger took his first step onto the stage of state.

"This will be brief," Diettinger informed the officer ranks gathered in the newly-constructed conference room. "Deathmaster Quilland; the wreckage of the *Fomoria* constitutes a tremendous quantity of metal. Detail survey teams to ascertain the extent of radiation damage to its component materials. Cyborg Rank Koln."

"First—Citizen."

Diettinger ignored Koln's nearly imperceptible pause. "Radiation levels of the wreckage must be assumed dangerous to Sauron norms. Coordinate with Breedmaster Caius and detach sufficient Cyborg Pathfinder troops to Deathmaster Quilland's command to allow completion of ordered surveys in seventy-two standard hours."

The Lady Althene, Diettinger's former Second Rank aboard the *Fomoria* and now his wife here on Haven, scarcely contained her surprise. She flashed a glance at her husband that promised this matter would be discussed further, in private, and at length. Diettinger appeared not to notice.

"Weapons; status of aerospace equipment?"

"Twenty-three operational vehicles, First Citizen; nine shuttles and fourteen atmospheric fighters. Three shuttles are no longer capable of interplanetary operations, one has damaged engines, operating at eighty percent efficiency. Nine fighters have lost assured vacuum integrity and are not presently approved for supra-orbital operations. Six are repairable to full operational status, but parts will have to be fabricated. This may prove impossible, and will depend greatly on the condition of such local heavy industrial and high technology fabrication facilities as have survived our invasion."

"Ordnance quantities?"

"Lavish, First Citizen. Enough for several dozen times as many spacecraft."

Diettinger nodded. "Completely dismantle two shuttles and three fighters and cannibalize them for parts. Store any surplus; where practical, use such items as masters when fabricating replacements. Have the remaining eighteen vehicles at full operational status within seventy-two hours."

Weapons nodded. Aboard the *Fomoria*, when the First Rank had said "within," it meant as immediately as Sauron skills could bring it about, and to notify him as quickly. It was a matter of personal pride that Weapons' skills and those of his staff could bring about such things very immediately indeed, and he had no intention of letting such a record lapse in service to the First Citizen. Weapons looked up at Diettinger. "Also, First Citizen—"

"Proceed."

"Substantial amounts of indigenous aircraft have been captured intact by Deathmaster Quilland's patrols. We have many pilot-rated Soldiers who trained on similar aircraft; such equipment would increase our air capability substantially, in addition to being much easier to maintain and repair with available local materials."

"Very well." Diettinger turned to Quilland. "Also, issue commendations for those patrols, Deathmaster."

Quilland acknowledged the compliment, then spoke: "Request, First Citizen." Quilland was holding a datapad, the screen of which showed several maps with enhanced outlines.

"Speak."

"Pacification raids into the surrounding hillsides would impress upon the cattle that loss of our capital ship in no way alters our combat capabilities."

"Refused. Recovery of the *Fomoria* debris and securing the immediate zone around the Citadel are more important at present. Such raids will be postponed until Weapons Rank has fully restored our air strike capability."

Althene had to restrain herself at that; this was not the time or place to confront her husband. The First Lady was counselor to the First Citizen, no more. She certainly could not challenge him in front of his staff. But to give the cattle any breathing space at this juncture was, she felt, the height of folly.

Still, she said nothing. But she allowed herself a rueful little inward smile. *As Second Rank, I could have brought up the subject now, in the meeting. But I can wait,* the former Second Rank thought. *As First Lady, I will have to.*

She looked at her husband for a moment, and decided the trade had been worth it.

As the last member of his staff left the room, Diettinger stood and circled the table, unfastening the collar of his tunic as he reached his wife's chair. He kissed Althene—until three weeks ago his Second Rank, now the First Lady of the new Sauron chief of state—and watched her stand and cross the room to open one of the windows that looked down on the courtyard of the Citadel.

Earlier, immediately after the brief ceremony formalizing Diettinger's ascension to First Citizen, she had stood beside her husband and presided over memorial services for the Sauron dead, those fallen during the fortnight-long invasion of Haven and the seizure of the approaches to its Shangri La Valley. Like all humans, Saurons too required the rites of passage that allowed them to bury their dead so that they might return their full attention to the concerns of the living. From the window, Althene watched as Medical Ranks moved among the bodies of the Soldiers which lay in state in the courtyard, marking any remaining usable organs for collection, to be excised and stored for future transplant use. When they had finished, Breedmaster Caius and his aides took extensive genetic samplings for tissue cloning and embryonic production; what remained after that would pass on to the

Supply Ranks, to be rendered into fertilizer for the cultivations being planned for the spring.

"A Sauron wastes nothing and wants for less." She repeated the adage from her childhood, and Diettinger half turned at the sound of her voice.

"Hm? Why did you say that?"

Althene closed the window and went to her husband. "Just an expression; characteristic, I think, of the Race." She lifted her hand and traced with her finger the patch covering the empty wound beneath Diettinger's left eyebrow. "We should be sure to instruct them to save an eye for you."

Diettinger smiled. "Already growing bored with my piratical good looks?"

"Hardly," she smiled, stepping into his arms. "But the First Citizen can't have any weaknesses. Certainly nothing so strikingly noticeable—nor even so dashing—as an eye patch." She frowned, troubled by a new thought. "And there's no telling how much longer we'll have the technological capability for such surgery."

Diettinger put a hand in Althene's hair and tucked her head under his chin. "I'll talk to Caius about it in the morning. There's still much to do today."

They stood together silently for a moment, until finally Diettinger spoke again: "You want to talk about the meeting."

Althene stepped away from him, composed and ready. "Indeed. You have made two decisions which I regard as grievous errors."

"The Cyborgs, of course," Diettinger acknowledged, "And the other?"

Althene sat down, resting her elbows on the high arms of her chair and lacing her fingertips together before her. "The other can wait for the moment. The Cyborg issue alone is enough to bring everything to ruin."

Diettinger's expression did not change, but Althene felt positive he was smiling. He had always had an ironic, even mocking sense of humor. Among Saurons, he would have been considered flippant had his combat record not been so formidable.

But since the Fall of Sauron—Oh, how those words sound in my heart, she thought. *They capitalize themselves, making me feel we are still falling—but since that day, Galen's humor has been on the wane. Some remains; only now I fear it is changing into something grim, something bitter. Perhaps even hopeless.*

"Well?" Diettinger asked quietly, and Althene realized she had allowed herself to become distracted. That would not do. "Galen, you have made it clear that the Cyborgs are valuable to the future of the Sauron race. Surely you also realize that they constitute a dangerous challenge to your authority as First Citizen."

"Which authority has already been formally established." He never took his eyes away from hers as he answered; it was a gesture of respect, not a tactic of debate.

"Yet you endanger it by your actions as soon as you receive it. At this point, the stabilization of your status as First Citizen of this fledgling Sauron state is of far greater importance to the future of the race than maintaining a breeding stable of Cyborg Super Soldiers. You represent a link to our societal past. In time, the acceptance of your status as First Citizen and your establishment of a dynasty will provide us with both direction and focus for a societal future." She leaned forward, taking his right hand in both of her own.

"Galen; Saurons are soldiers. We even call ourselves that, as often as not interchangeably with the name 'Sauron'. And soldiers—*any* soldiers—require order in their day-to-day lives. The most innovative and self-reliant of them still needs the assurance that they operate within a chain of command and responsibility. Otherwise they cease to be soldiers, becoming instead merely people with guns. People with guns do not follow orders; they follow demagogues.

"And, quite simply, there have never been demagogues

such as the Cyborgs have the potential to become. To allow them any sort of activity which will draw attention to their abilities is to undermine your own status in the minds of our people. That status is at this moment beginning to change, from First Rank of the *Fomoria* to First Citizen of the remainder of Sauron civilization. The official change is complete, but the *perceptual* change in the minds of our population here is still going on; it cannot be forced by action on your part, lest you invalidate the process. First Ranks are assigned by the High Command, but First Citizens are chosen by the people."

Diettinger rose and poured himself a glass of water; at the Citadel's room temperature, it was barely liquid. "Your point being, then, that the Cyborgs face no constraints against simply declaring one of their own First Citizen."

Althene shook her head. "My point being that the very fact of Cyborgs operating in high-profile activities at this stage of the transition of power *obviates the need for a First Citizen at all*."

Diettinger actually blinked. "Clarify."

"To the average Sauron, Cyborgs have come to represent the ultimate expression of human evolution. Stronger, smarter, faster than we Saurons, who are ourselves stronger, smarter and faster than any other species of human. These 'super soldiers' are to us as we are to the human norms, whom none of us can help but regard with some measure of contempt."

Half-smiling, Diettinger raised his eyebrows and gestured to his patch. "Need I remind you that this was the work of a human norm? As was the surprise of their nuclear weapon strike against the *Fomoria*; an attack which was aimed, according to all the best evidence, against me personally, as was the eventual defeat and destruction of Sauron and virtually the entire Sauron race. I assure you, Althene, that had I ever entertained any notion of regarding human norms with contempt—

and I never did—I would be highly unlikely to do so again."

Althene softened. "Ah, but need I remind you, Galen, that you are unique?"

She sat back. "To those Saurons raised to equate the superiority of the Cyborgs with the genetic triumph of the Race, a First Citizen who is himself 'merely' a Soldier is a figurehead, at best. At worst, he is an obstruction to the future the Cyborgs represent.

"I spoke earlier of the chain of command and responsibility, of which every soldier needs to feel a part. The Cyborg Super Soldiers utterly invalidate that need; a Cyborg is, by definition, a superior being, beyond all conventional considerations of morality or obligation, and thus, utterly outside that chain of command and responsibility. Challenge that core of soldierly values with the presence of charismatic Super Soldiers, and no Sauron here on Haven—no Sauron anywhere—could hope to survive the conflicts which must arise from such a challenge."

Diettinger turned away, and spent a long moment looking out the window at the spectacular view of the mountains beyond. When he finally spoke, he did not turn back to Althene, but continued looking out toward the distant peaks. "And your other objection?"

Althene frowned. "Galen, please; you must see that your policy regarding the Cyborgs is dangerously permissive. You must find a way to utterly deprive them of any influence in the society we are trying to create, or they will displace you ... and instead of a new Sauron homeworld, we will have only a squabbling mass of feudal hierarchies, each Cyborg a warlord with as many Soldiers as will follow his banner. We would even be vulnerable to the cattle—"

Diettinger turned back to face her. "Yes. Thank you, Althene;" he said dryly, "I am able to grasp the concept. Your second objection?"

Althene paused, prepared to push her luck. But she

finally just let out a short, even breath, and said: "Refusing Deathmaster Quilland permission to mount full-scale pacification raids against the cattle is foolish."

She almost bit her lip; that had been very poorly done, indeed. Instead of a valid counsel, it had come out sounding like petulant bitterness.

But Diettinger only nodded. "Perhaps. But they will surely expect us to take such action after their missile attack on the *Fomoria*, and the numbers simply don't favor us at this time. I want to be sure the Citadel and the surrounding areas are secure, and I don't want to push these Haveners too far, too fast. I don't hold them in contempt, nor am I afraid of them. But the truth is, I don't feel I understand them yet, and I am sure that neither does Deathmaster Quilland."

He rose and went to stand at the window. "And until I do understand them, at least a little better, I don't want to do anything they are likely to expect."

Both of them were silent for a long time. Finally Althene rose and moved next to him. "Put that way, I understand your decision," she said. It was part apology, part request that he return to the issue of the Cyborgs and explain his stand on them as clearly, and Althene felt that she had made a perfectly reasonable first gesture of rapprochement.

But Galen remained silent. She knew his moods; he did not seem angry, only thoughtful. She suddenly had the feeling that he was thinking about something totally removed from the subjects of Cyborgs or pacification raids, or even of her.

She changed tack. "I'm going back to our quarters, then."

Diettinger only nodded.

"Are you coming?"

He turned and shook his head. "No. Go ahead. I'll be along shortly."

You are dismissed, Second Rank, she thought abruptly, and for a moment her years of service had overlain the thought, making it seem perfectly reasonable and proper. But only for a moment. She was no longer the Second Rank of the *Fomoria*; she was Althene Diettinger, she was Galen's wife, and he had neither cause nor right to simply dismiss her. And she knew herself well enough to dread her own outburst of righteous indignation, perhaps even outright rage—she could have a terrible temper. But not today.

Instead, she nodded and turned to leave, and to her own surprise only felt sorry for her husband. In her heart she knew he would never speak to her with any conscious intent to hurt her. For him to have done so, he must be dwelling on something troubling indeed. When he wished to talk about it, she knew that he would talk to her.

Althene had been gone for exactly one minute when the opposite door of the office opened quietly. Not turning from the window, Diettinger shifted his eyes to look at the figure in the doorway.

"You heard, then?"

"Clearly."

Diettinger raised his hands from the sill and folded his arms. "You will agree, then, that we have a great deal to talk about." It was not a question. Even so, when no reply was forthcoming, Diettinger turned his head and looked at his silent companion.

The figure stepped from the shadowed doorway, closed and locked it behind himself, then moved quietly into the room and sat down at the conference table.

"I agree," said Cyborg Rank Koln.

Sergei Kamov reined in hard, leapt from the saddle and pulled his horse Mischa down to the sloping ground in a single smooth motion. The animal, superbly trained and accustomed to such treatment, barely grunted as its ribcage thumped against the cold, dry Haven soil. It had been a long, thirsty ride, and though he could now smell water, Mischa lay still, his nostrils flaring once as he calmly placed his head flat against the earth. Sergei drew his carbine from its sheath and steadied it across the animal's ribs, then he, too, became absolutely motionless.

Looking down the sights of his weapon, he watched the Sauron patrol on the other side of the river as it moved along the rock face like a pack of lizards; it was wondrous to behold. They clung to sheer rock walls beyond the ability of the finest mountain peoples Sergei had ever seen or heard of.

Still, it cannot be all that easy for them, or they would surely have noticed me.

Sergei was in dense brush, but he had heard that Saurons could see into the infrared spectrum, giving them a tremendous advantage when seeking the warm bodies of enemies against the low background heat of Haven's terrain. Surely, then, the climb which was impossible for normal humans must at least be difficult for the invaders, to so command their concentration.

As if to confirm this hypothesis, one of the Saurons had reached the bottom of the rock wall, and instead of watching the opposite bank for threats—where, in fact, Sergei now lay—the Sauron turned back to check his comrades' progress.

It must be training of some sort, Sergei decided. He recognized the behavior in the way the Saurons were conducting themselves; each man concentrated on the task at hand while the Sauron on the ground—apparently their leader—concentrated on their performance. Sergei Kamov himself had once borne such scrutiny under the watchful eyes of a Sergeant Major in the Haven Militia, and as he watched the Saurons, it told him what they were about. *Their leader has spread them out across a rock face with no place to go should they be attacked,* he thought. *Which means they are not concerned with being attacked; which means they must have many friends nearby.*

Suddenly feeling colder than even Haven's chill could account for, Sergei Kamov considered his predicament.

Sergei calculated that with a quick re-mount, he could be a quarter of a mile away before the first Sauron got across the river. At forty years of age, and having been on Haven since he was ten, Sergei Kamov was no longer young; even so, he was known and respected among his people for the skills he now exhibited. Squeezing the trigger, he did not wait to see the Sauron leader's head explode, but tracked immediately to the highest of the five figures remaining on the rock face.

Another shot, but the top-most Sauron's descent had changed from a careful progression to an eerily graceful flow of limbs; he and all the others were out of sight almost instantly. There came a ripping crackle from across the river, and Sergei saw he no longer had targets. The remaining Saurons had simply *jumped* to the river bank, perhaps fifty feet below, and were now laying down suppressive fire along his side of the river. To his right, several square meters of brush were sheared off as if a scythe had passed through them, showering him with leaves and wood fragments.

They will see my horse! Mischa's body heat must look like a bonfire to them! Gripping his saddle's pommel, Sergei threw his weight back and half dragged the horse a full meter. Responding to the familiar command, Mischa grunted and scrambled to his feet as Sergei threw one leg over the saddle. Wheeling, the cossack was heading away from the river when his mount suddenly screamed and pitched forward, catapulting Sergei over the animal's head. Sergei rolled into a crouch, turning to see Mischa frantically kicking his front legs, trying to find purchase to stand. Disemboweled by a burst from a Sauron weapon, the horse's hindquarters dragged uselessly behind it, the ground all about a vast smear of red. Sergei aimed at the center of Mischa's head, and was about to fire when he saw a figure appear on the ridge directly beyond his dying mount.

Without thinking, Sergei lifted the barrel a fraction of an inch in automatic reaction even as he squeezed the trigger; by nothing but great good fortune, the bullet struck the approaching Sauron beneath the chin, doing what only cross-cut rifle slugs could do to a human skull, Sauron or otherwise. Sergei's next shot gave Mischa a merciful death, then he was down behind a rock, only beginning to realize that the Saurons had already crossed the river! He shook his head. *I never had a chance of killing some and then getting away....*

He could smell Mischa's blood from here. In a moment, he knew, his own blood would add to the scent, bringing tamerlanes and other Haven denizens down from the hills to feed; the rest of the Saurons would be on him any second....

"Pah dak. Ta ma kuhk sa." Patrol Sub-Leader Ogme barked the commands in the Battle Tongue. An ambush, and Patrol Leader Parland had been the first casualty! Ogme restrained an urge to shake his head in dismay. The probabilities had shifted against them; or, as First Citizen Diettinger was sometimes heard to say: "Bad luck." Either way, Ogme and the other survivors of his squad were in a very bad position. Ogme had watched as Blooder Wirren reached the top of the ridge along the far riverbank only to be cut down almost instantly.

The cattle must have seen Blooder Wirren crossing the river; which implied that they had marksmen in the high ground on the far side. The low number of shots Ogme had heard bespoke excellent fire discipline, to say nothing of impressive accuracy. Almost, Ogme wondered if his patrol had not blundered into another group of Saurons, but that was only wishful thinking.

Ogme was well-trained; abruptly finding himself in command of a unit which had suffered two casualties without ever seeing the enemy, he made exactly the proper decision based on what little information he had. Moving with the superhuman speed and grace possessed only by Saurons, he and his two men withdrew from the river. Skirting along the base of the rock wall in cover only they could have exploited, Ogme's unit was well away from the killing zone in two minutes. One minute after that, Ogme was calling in his report.

Sergei frowned. *Where were they?* He had chanced moving twice, and was now almost fifty meters away from the body of Mischa and the last Sauron he had killed. He had expected to be dead long since, but the hail of fire had not come. Sergei could not understand why the Saurons had not killed him already; he knew only that he would never see it coming. No Havener lived who could apprehend the approach of Saurons when the Soldiers chose to move by stealth.

Suddenly, inexplicably, Sergei was seized with terror. That was why he could not hear them! They were not rushing to kill him, they were closing in on him to take him prisoner! Through him, the Saurons would find his village and obliterate his people. Again, acting almost before he was aware of it, Sergei bolted away from the river. Only occasionally did he stop to look back, and each time he did so the very lack of evidence of pursuit convinced him that the Saurons were closing in on him. By the time he stopped running, it was deep into true night and he was near death, but he had reached the pickets of the camp made by his people on the plains of the Northern Steppes.

He had gone less than a hundred yards when a trip-wire caught his ankles, and he pitched forward onto the gritty Haven soil. Before he could roll over, a soft-soled boot was put against the back of his neck, and next to it he felt the pressure of a rifle barrel.

Kamov closed his eyes, thought of his family, and prayed.

"Now where would you be going in such a quick hurry?" The voice from behind the gun barrel asked in clipped Imperial Anglic.

And Sergei began to breathe again.

                    *   *   *

It had been three days since the last full staff meeting, but Diettinger could have waited a great deal longer for this news. He listened to Deathmaster Quilland's report without comment. In a way, he was almost relieved.

Had Patrol Leader Parland survived—and had we Soldiers to spare—I would have ordered his execution, Diettinger thought. The reinforcing squad had combed the area for signs of the ambushing force, finding only one dead horse and four cartridge casings.

Order Parland's execution? More likely I'd have killed him myself. Letting a single horse-nomad kill two Saurons from ambush! What in God's name had that fool been doing, exposing his squad on a rock face like that?

"First Citizen?"

Diettinger turned his gaze on Quilland. The Deathmaster very nearly flinched. "First Citizen, having confirmed the presence of a single Havener nomad, Sub-Leader Ogme took another squad out this morning and conducted an extensive reconnaissance of the surroundings area. The nomad was met by a foot patrol of six human norms. This party then proceeded north by northwest into the steppes. Sub-Leader Ogme believes he has found the tribe of horse-nomads this fellow came from."

"Why is a tribe of horse-nomads sending out foot patrols, Deathmaster?"

Quilland shook his head. "Unknown, First Citizen. Sub-Leader Ogme believes this patrol might have been one of the Roving Squads reported active in this part of the valley."

Diettinger was silent for a moment. While all organized Havener military operations had ended with the invasion, lately there had been increasing guerrilla activity, far too well organized to be simple resistance cells. A large cache of weapons had apparently been spirited away into the Shangri-La's trackless mountains, and was systematically finding its way into the hands of human norm tribesmen, where it could—and frequently did— wreak havoc on the occasional Sauron patrol caught unawares. Diettinger took the long view of his people's existence on Haven, and an alliance between horse-mounted nomads and any other surviving, efficient and well-armed Havener military units was too dangerous to tolerate.

"Estimated strength of these horse-nomads?"

"One hundred, First Citizen. Twice that many females and children. Four times as many mounts, all of those being horses. None of the indigenous muskylopes used by so many other nomadic groups we've encountered."

Diettinger considered that. From what the Survey Ranks had been able to learn, that made these people extremely wealthy, by the standards of Haven nomads. And Haveners who could live on the steppes and retain such wealth were extremely dangerous, by any standards. "Livestock?"

Quilland shook his head. "None, according to Ogme."

"Interesting," the First Rank said. "A strong band. Able to seize or demand in tribute the best mounts as well as food animals; having apparently no need for self-sufficiency." Which meant a strong band, indeed, if they could take whatever they needed from their fellow Haveners. "Structures?"

"None, in the conventional sense," Quilland answered. "Some two dozen large mobile tents; I believe they are called 'yurts.'"

Diettinger turned to Weapons. "Airpower status?"

"Two elements of atmospheric strike fighters are now operational. Fifty-six ground attack configuration rotary-wing aircraft have been acquired from indigenous military units. We do have pilots qualified to operate such vehicles."

Diettinger nodded, once. "Sufficient. Coordinate with Deathmaster Quilland to determine the location of these nomads. Capture as many of their women and animals as possible and bring back as many male prisoners as practical. Kill the rest."

Breedmaster Caius looked pleased at the order. The

implanting of local women with fertilized Sauron ova brought to Haven aboard the *Fomoria* had fallen behind schedule, and Caius wasn't sure how long his Breedmasters would have an operational birthing facility; sooner or later, technology on Haven was going to level off.

"First Citizen." Cyborg Rank Koln had precisely the same voice as did all other Cyborgs—or at least it sounded that way to non-Cyborgs. Rich and deep, it was an orator's voice, or perhaps an opera baritone's. It had been quite literally designed to command attention; few Saurons—and no human norms—were immune to its influence.

Diettinger was quite aware of the implicit challenge to his authority by the simple fact of Koln addressing him unbidden, and dealt with it accordingly: "Speak," the First Citizen said after a long interval.

"I point out that had the Cyborgs been conducting this reconnaissance, or had even one Cyborg been participating, such an ambush would not have been possible." Only a Cyborg could have made a reprimand of the First Citizen sound like a status report.

"I am aware of the efficacy of Cyborg senses," Diettinger's tone could have dropped the temperature in the room another ten degrees. "It is one of their assets of greatest value to the Breedmasters."

Which rather clearly puts you in your place, Althene thought with some surprise as she saw everyone at the table except Koln stiffen slightly. Deathmaster Quilland caught her eye and gave her an approving nod.

Althene knew that against the Empire, Quilland had been only too glad to have Cyborgs to commit to action. But he was as staunchly opposed as she to having them in charge of the Sauron society Diettinger would establish on Haven. Quilland had privately admitted to Althene that, in his opinion, the Cyborgs were out of touch with the realities facing that society.

"Be that as it may," Koln continued, "The Pathfinder Cyborgs are already in the field. On salvage duty." Even

Koln's soft Cyborg inflections could not mask the irony
in his tone. "They can be recalled from this and
remanded to those units of Deathmaster Quilland which
will conduct this operation. In addition, I suggest—
again—the full release of all Cyborgs from the authority
of Breedmaster Caius until all Havener nuclear weapon
stockpiles can be found and seized, and the military situation thus stabilized."

Which will be in perhaps a thousand years, if ever,
Althene thought. But no matter; Althene knew her husband, and by his wording, Koln had denied his own
request.

"Regrettably, Cyborg Rank Koln," Diettinger pro-
nounced, "it is the very instability of the military situation
which precludes the investment of Cyborg assets."

Althene blinked in surprise, permitting herself an
unprofessional reaction. *"Assets" is putting it rather
forcefully, indeed.*

"There are too few Cyborgs for the colony to risk losing," Diettinger concluded. "At least until Breedmaster
Caius and his staff have determined the prospects for
continuation of the genotype. Weapons Ranks now have
sufficient anti-missile stations to defend our colony here
against more such attacks, and roving patrols will keep
the surrounding mountainsides clear of other sappers.
The Cyborgs are to continue their salvage operations, but
you may rotate the personnel as you wish, subject to
Breedmaster Caius' approval."

Well, he's said it, Althene thought. *He used the word*
colony; *by definition a political institution, and thus
requiring, and subject to, political—not military—
authority.*

Though in fact, in Sauron society the two differed very
little from one another, the status of combat-dedicated
citizens like the Cyborgs was clearly subservient in a
political environment, however potent their reputation
among the citizens of that environment might be.

It's a step in the right direction, at least, Althene

thought with real relief. And Galen's decision to allow Quilland to deal decisively with these nomads was more good news. Still, Koln's persistence troubled her. She had the feeling that something unknown to her had just passed between Galen and the commander of the Cyborgs, that perhaps more battle lines had been drawn than were obvious. Or safe.

Diettinger concluded the meeting half an hour later, without any further comments from Koln. After the others had left, Althene watched her husband enter notes on his datapad, fold the cover down and only then look up at her.

"Satisfied?" he asked.

Althene inclined her head a fraction. "Although allowing the Cyborgs to rotate duties . . ."

Diettinger waved a hand in dismissal. "They can't be completely idle. In a sufficiently extreme emergency, they would have to be committed to battle. They must maintain some level of activity to keep in fighting trim."

"Yes. I am glad, however, that you refused to allow them to participate in the pacification of these horse nomads."

Diettinger shrugged. "It's necessary that they be elsewhere."

Walking alone through the quiet corridors of the structure the Saurons had christened the Citadel, Cyborg Rank Koln made many seemingly aimless turns, taking himself down several meandering passageways with no apparent destination. Frequently, he passed great open halls, blasted out of the rock by the former inhabitants, which were now being converted to storage areas, production or processing centers, even living quarters; a few such caverns opened out onto the side of the mountains, and these were being converted to hangar decks for the remaining Sauron aircraft and the new vehicles recently seized from the Haveners.

In these large chambers, Soldiers moved about with the same sense of purpose they had shown weeks earlier as they gutted the *Fomoria* of valuable equipment before sending the ship on her last voyage.

Fleetingly, Koln corrected himself: *Dol Guldur*. More and more of the troops were referring to the *Fomoria* by that name, lately; as if they had forgotten their true origins already.

Well. That's part of what this is all about, isn't it?

Koln entered one of the hangars and went directly to the opening; frigid mountain winds scoured the area, whipping ice crystals about his feet and legs. He of course took no notice.

"Cyborg Koln," the voice came from the rim of the cave just outside the opening. Koln stepped forward, knowing that anyone who addressed him without adding the designator "rank" was the sort with whom he would want to speak. He was not disappointed. Standing a few feet from the hangar bay's arch was Cyborg Sargun, a long-time supporter—some might say sycophant—of Koln's views regarding Cyborg mastery of the Sauron race. Koln joined Sargun and the two Cyborgs greeted one another in their identical voices.

A few Sauron-norms moved past them, shivering in the cold; up here, even Saurons could be miserable. Only another Cyborg would have perceived Sargun's grimace of contempt, and Koln did. "You don't approve of shivering, Sargun?" Koln observed quietly.

"I regard it as a sign of weakness."

"Quite the contrary. Mammals—and any other creatures which can—shiver to generate body heat. It is in fact a very desirable survival trait." Koln allowed a brief, severe spasm to ripple through his frame; it did nothing to alter his stature or balance, however. "You really should try it."

"I am not cold enough to be distressed, Cyborg Koln. Not yet. When I am, I will pursue less demeaning methods of warming myself."

Koln's eyes slid sideways to meet Sargun's gaze. "Such as building a fire, perhaps?"

"You understand me perfectly, I think."

Koln shrugged, and made a broad, encompassing gesture. "What would you use for fuel in a place like this?"

Sargun turned back to look down on the valley. Out to the horizon, great palls of smoke from vast fires could still be seen. Only the nearest were pieces of the *Fomoria*; the rest were Haven's valley cities. Most had burned out, but many still smoldered, or had started up once more in the weeks since the invasion. "There is always something which needs burning, Cyborg Koln," Sargun declared.

Koln said: "Yes. Cyborg Arndt is currently commanding the Pathfinders. You will relieve him for the next round of salvage patrols. Inform him that this is on my authority, and do not clear the re-assignment with the Breedmasters. Let Cyborg Arndt tell them of the order after you have already left."

"A *fait accompli*, then?" Sargun's tone clearly indicated his contempt for such indirect methods.

Koln turned to look at him, scrutinizing the other Cyborg's features with an attention that verged on the discomfitting. Finally he turned away abruptly. "I have learned that a large concentration of debris from the *Fomoria* may have been deposited outside of the Shangri-La Valley, in the steppes to the north. You will take the Pathfinders outside of the valley to investigate this. Pay very close attention to the attitudes of the other Cyborgs with the unit and report to me immediately on your return." Without further ado, Koln turned away and walked back into the hangar, where he was soon lost from sight amid the mass of Soldiers moving to and fro within.

Sargun waited a few moments longer, looking out on the valley. Rumor had it that a raid was to be carried out on the steppes, and soon; a raid in which Cyborg participation had been specifically prohibited. Sargun was no fool, but he was not entirely sure he fully understood Koln's purpose in placing him in this position. Still, he prided himself on his ability to watch, and learn.

After a while, when he was sure no one was watching, Sargun even shivered experimentally. Skin muscles, long gone from human norms, had been reactivated in the Cyborg DNA code, and the effect was to abruptly raise his body temperature several degrees, bringing an almost soporific sensation of pleasurable warmth. Sargun's mouth twisted in a sneer even a human norm could have seen.

"Pah." He almost spat. Comfort was for the weak.

"Village" was perhaps not the right term for the nomadic community Sergei Kamov's people had established since being driven out onto the steppes in the years of Haven's post-Imperial decline, ten years before the Saurons came. Still, though they moved in the nomadic cycles of their Earthly ancestors, they were more like a village than a tribe. A small community, the men of age met to vote on issues that affected the group as a whole. No one man was allowed to become too powerful, though the influence of individuals waxed and waned along with their popularity and prosperity. Sergei had been in the middle ground of the council members, a moderate voice seriously courted only when a swing vote was needed.

Now, however, his position was very definitely unenviable. A lost horse and saddle made for a very severe dent in a cossack's prosperity, and incurring the wrath of the Sauron invaders—took an even heavier toll on one's popularity. But being escorted into camp by outsiders— armed men in camouflage paint, soldiers from the very Shangri-La Valley communities that had dispossessed his people—that put Sergei—and his family—in a very bad light, indeed.

"And why should we let ourselves get involved with the people of the interior?" Oleg Yarmoloff paced about the circle of men in the great yurt of the tribe, addressing each of his fellows as he passed before them. "We are here on these steppes, living as our forebears lived, because we were not welcome in their Shangri-La Valley. We and others like us—the Dinneh, the Tartary nomads, the White Horsemen, even the Chin—" he paused to spit into the fire at the mention of their hated foe, "have survived, despite the valley city-states having driven us into this wilderness of thin air and poor land."

Yarmoloff ended his circuit standing before Sergei Kamov. "Now the peoples of the valley have been struck down—no small judgment, if you ask me," Yarmoloff delivered this over his shoulder, to murmurs of general agreement. "And in bringing one of our own back to us, they think this entitles them to draft us into one of their armies." The murmurs grew into scattered angry rumblings as Yarmoloff peaked. "Like the ancient tsars; they do not consider us fit to live in their presence until the wolves are at their gates; then we are welcome—as soldiers to shed blood for those who would not have us as neighbors!"

For a moment, Colonel Edon Kettler thought the shouting would subside only after the lynching of him and the four other men in his contact team, but the nine men of the village council finally managed to restore some measure of order, allowing him to speak. "As I said, that's no part of the deal. I don't represent any one city-state or nation of Haven. There are none such any longer. We're talking about fair trade here, for an end we both want: The destruction of the Saurons."

One of the older councilmen, a hard-faced veteran named Korolyev, leaned forward: "Why should we wish the destruction of these Sauron? We have no cities for them to bomb; no industry for them to steal, no technology they need fear." Kettler realized that Korolyev was not confronting him; the old man's question was straightforward and guileless.

He and Cummings had known that these people would

be the toughest, which was why Kettler had been determined to go to them first. The steppes cossacks allied to the cause would be very persuasive in rallying other outlanders to the banner. "They mean to rule here, *gospodin* Korolyev," Kettler answered as directly. "And Saurons will not tolerate anyone on a world they rule who is not submissive to their will."

One of Yarmoloff's cronies in the assemblage, a hard-eyed customer named Kuprin, pounced on this: "And so? All men must have masters, *nyet*? It is the way of things. You yourself say there are no more cities, and we have seen with our own eyes smoke higher than the walls of the Atlas mountain range, from the fires still burning within the valley. These Saurons have a starship and weapons and they have power. If we must have a master, better them than this Cummings, who fights from hiding like a highwayman."

Kettler shot a glare at the sergeant of his escort. He and his men had been hand-picked to keep Kettler alive during these negotiations, but they had fought under Cummings for a very long time, and each of them owed their lives and the lives of their kin to the General a dozen times over.

Kettler thought about the villager, Kamov, whom they'd met on the way into the camp. Chased by Saurons, claiming to have killed two; a nice guy, as far as Edon could see, and it was just too bad that he was probably throwing him to the wolves with his next remark.

"They might accept your servitude, *gospodin* Kuprin," Kettler presented the insult with fine diplomatic civility, "were it not for the fact that your stated willingness to be a slave has already been contradicted by the actions of *gospodin* Kamov, here."

Sergei Kamov kept his eyes on the floor, but his chest tightened beneath a steel band. Since returning to the camp of his people with this Kettler and his men, he had been waiting for the moment when the council would simply order them all killed. *And*, he thought, *that moment is perhaps now arrived.*

Kettler went on: "The Saurons have only the people they brought with them on their ship, and *gospodin* Kamov has killed two of them. Within the valley, they have obliterated entire villages in retribution for such an act. All males are summarily executed, all females transferred to their Citadel, and by the Saurons' own proclaimed policy of eugenics, there is no doubt as to what the purpose of such captives must be. This is the price of the lives of their soldiers. Do you expect they will do less to your own people, because you are here on the steppes?"

Kettler looked around the room as he spoke, trying to stay with terms these cossacks understood.

"The Saurons must breed a new generation of soldiers to completely conquer Haven, and it is only now, before they can establish such a program, that they will be vulnerable to organized resistance such as we propose. Every Sauron we kill today is a hundred Sauron soldiers our grandchildren need not face; a hundred soldiers who will not be demanding your wives and daughters in retribution for every act of resistance by men like *gospodin* Kamov."

"Give them Kamov!" Yarmoloff snarled, ". . . and his daughter, too, if they want women!" At which Sergei's oldest son Nikolai was off the floor, his sabre half out of its scabbard, before Sergei pushed him back down amid the shouting.

"Sure, of course!" Kettler shouted. "That's the answer! Give them Kamov today. And tomorrow, maybe they'll take *gospodin* Korolyev, or Kuprin; and how long will it be before they want you, Yarmoloff?"

Yarmoloff whirled on Kettler. "If they come, they come. If we die, we die. But we die our way, on our terms."

There was no cheering at that, and Kettler knew that Yarmoloff had dropped the ball. Kettler waited out the

silence, then spoke: "Better, I think, that if they come,
they die. Does anyone here agree with me?"

The council heaved a collective sigh, and began confer-
ring in hushed voices.

Finally, the nine members seemed to reach an
agreement, and Korolyev addressed Kettler. "You suggest
then, providing advisors to us, for fighting the Saurons.
What sort of advice do you propose?"

Kettler somehow restrained himself from giving Yarmoloff the finger in triumph. Instead, he cleared his
throat, and told them what he expected the Saurons to
do, and how they might be ready for it, with the help of
the resistance movement being organized by General
Cummings.

After a while, as the council and the other men of the
village warmed to the plans, Kettler tried to send a look
of apology to Kamov, but the older man met his gaze
without any expression whatsoever.

Can't say as I blame you, Kamov, Kettler thought. *But
I had to use you to shame them; I had to take the risk
to keep Yarmoloff from winning and maybe having you
killed anyway.*

Kettler reflected that Kamov probably understood, but
it didn't matter whether he did or not. If he had guessed
right—that the Saurons would track Kamov back to his
people, and what they would do once they found them—
they were probably all going to die, anyway.

Sergei Kamov gave a final cinch to his new saddle,
listening for the horse's grunt as she let out a breath and
settled into the feel of the harness. Anya was a sturdy,
intelligent mare, not so hardy as Mischa, to be sure, but
perhaps a bit smarter for all that. Oleg Sedov had joked
that maybe she was smart enough to keep Sergei out of
trouble, since he didn't seem to be able to do so himself.

Sergei grimaced in rememberance of the laughter of
the other men in Sedov's tack shop when he had said he
needed to trade for a saddle to replace his own lost gear.

He could tell that Sedov had been close to demanding Kamov's finest remaining stallion as payment, but had obviously reconsidered at the last moment. Such a rapacious act would have served notice to the whole community that Sedov was getting greedy, and there was always someone else among their people—even several someones—who would be happy to see him lose his dominance of the harness trade.

Still, the saddle-maker had gotten the better of the deal; Sergei had another mare due to foal in the spring, and the newborn horse was promised to Sedov as payment. There was nothing to be done; horses Kamov had, but good saddles could not be just picked up anywhere on the steppes.

Sergei shook his head in resignation. He had lost more than a mount in losing Mischa; he had lost face among the other men of his village. And, of course, he had lost a friend.

The vote to move the village had been unanimous, despite the fact that the grazing land they now occupied had only just been settled on a fortnight earlier. The women would make their lives hell, the men knew. Here they had found pasture for the horses, a fair-sized stream for fishing, even a small copse of trees in a hollow that would provide shelter against the winds that howled off the North Sea and down across the steppes. In short, it was as close to a perfect spot for wintering in as could be found, and Sergei's run-in with the Saurons had now denied it to them.

The motion to drive him out of the community and turn him over to the Saurons had failed to reach a vote, but only just. Privately, Kamov was sure Sedov had argued so strongly against it just to be sure he would get paid for the saddle.

The issue of Colonel Kettler and his proposal had not helped matters, either. Nor had Kamov forgotten the gamble the fellow had taken with both their lives.

He heard footsteps, and looked up to see his daughter Natalya crossing the yard from the door flap of their yurt.

And not just our lives, Kamov thought.

Despite her light step, the ground thumped beneath Natalya's feet like a drum. The water table was very low here on the steppe, and the higher permafrost formed a resonating shell in the fall and winter. Sergei did not know it, but there were more similarities than differences between Haven's steppes and the Siberia of his heritage.

"So, where are your brothers?"

Natalya nodded back over her right shoulder. "Lavrenti's hitching up the team; he's almost done." She reached up to push a wind-blown drape of golden hair off her forehead. "Nikolai helped him with most of it, and then he took the rest of our horses to the big herd; he should be coming back now."

Sergei nodded. "Ah, that's good." He looked up at his daughter; fourteen years old and tall for her age, Natalya Kamova had never passed through the awkward adolescent stage that was a father's last glimpse of his daughter's childhood. Natalya was going straight from the beauty of a child to the beauty of a woman; she would be married within two years—four at the most, he knew—and then there would be another man and another family on whom Sergei could count for the protection of his daughter.

That was just a fact of life on Haven, one that part of him prayed for and another part cursed, because however much his daughter's husband might cherish her, he might condemn her to death on their wedding night. For on this feebly-lit moon with the baleful Cat's Eye gas giant looming overhead for most of the year, men and women could build fires against the bitter cold, they could band together against the beasts of the hills and the evil of their fellow human beings, but the air was simply too thin, and every mother faced that insidious enemy alone. Valeria had given him two fine sons a year apart. The births had been as easy as could be hoped for on Haven, but four years later Natalya had come, and Valeria had nearly died. Though his baby daughter was his pride and joy, Sergei had decided he was no longer willing to risk his wife's life for any more children.

There had still been doctors then, doctors who would treat the steppes people for barter. But most were far away, remaining relatively safe behind the Atlas Mountains and within the Shangri-La Valley, and Sergei did not want to risk he and Valeria getting used to the little pills they could barter for, only to one day find them used up and no doctor about. Sergei had heard of a doctor in the Valley who could still perform a certain surgery on men, and because he valued the life and safety of his wife more than he did flaunting his virility in the face of Haven's killing thin air, Sergei had gone to see the doctor, four days' ride away.

It was two days after the surgery before he could stand without pain, and almost another week before he could even think about riding a horse without becoming ill. He returned sixteen days after he had left, to find it had all been for nothing; Chin raiders had struck while he was gone, Valeria had been run through by a lance, and the only mercy had been that she was dead before the Chins had raped her.

His sons, Nikolai and Lavrenti, had killed their first men that day—as well as their second, their third, their fourth and their fifth; the boys had evidently inherited their father's gift for marksmanship.

Sergei sighed. *A lot of growing up for one afternoon in the life of two boys of eleven and ten.* Natalya had been six years old then; her mother would have been thirty in another week. Sergei wiped his eyes and strapped his saddlebags to the harness.

The mare snorted as Natalya stepped up to stroke her nose, slipping something past the animal's lips. "Shh, big girl," Natalya spoke soothingly, though the animal only crunched at something contentedly.

"Hey." Kamov began the litany. "Don't waste sugar on

the horses." He had been saying the same thing in the same way since Natalya had been tall enough to tell rock candy from quartz; it had never done any good, and both of them knew the routine by heart.

"Sweets for the sweet," Natalya grinned, popping a second rock-candy crystal into Sergei's mouth and a third into her own. "Besides, Anya's been mine for a long time, Papa," Natalya resumed stroking the mare's nose. "If I didn't spoil her, she wouldn't recognize me."

Sergei Kamov grunted. "I'm sorry to steal your pet, Nat'ya." He looked at his daughter's face, seeing her mother's there, reminding him once more how fiercely he loved his children. And his wife as well, still, though Valeria had been dead ten years last spring. "But a Cossack without a horse—"

"—is a man without legs, yes, Papa, I know." Natalya smiled and hugged her father with a strength that had frequently surprised both her brothers and several over-eager boyfriends.

Sergei failed to suppress a grunt. "Oof! You want Anya back so badly, take her! I can't ride with broken ribs!"

Natalya giggled, snuggling into the warmth of her father's coat, and Sergei held her close and stroked her hair, then pulled the hood of her coat up onto her head. "Cover your ears, you'll get frostbite."

"Pah! You just don't want the boys to see my hair."

Sergei rolled his eyes. "Too true." He kissed her forehead and held her away. "Everything is ready inside?"

She nodded firmly. "Our ship of the plains is ready for sailing, *Kapitan* Kamov. All cargo stowed and secured." Back on the near-mythic homeworld of Earth, hundreds of years ago, Sergei's ancestors had been wet-navy captains, and Natalya found the family legends passed down by her father endlessly fascinating. She read anything about the sea—*any* sea—that she could get her hands on.

"Good. Go on back in and watch over the fire coals." Sergei swung up into the saddle and looked down at his daughter; the sun was behind him, and his shadow fell across her face as she made to go to the *yurt*. "Natalya—"

She turned back, her face out of shadow now and the sunlight blazing from her golden hair and blue eyes, and Sergei felt he could scarcely breathe. "*Da*, Papa?"

He found himself unable to speak. Just as Natalya's smile was beginning to fade to a frown of concern, Sergei cleared his throat, frowned, and said: "Try not to let the place get burned down, won't you?"

Natalya smiled again. "I love you too, Papa." she said quietly.

Sergei smiled back and tapped his heels against Anya's flanks to put the mare into a canter. He circled the yurt, inspecting it as he went. He was looking very hard for recent alterations he knew to be there, yet he could see nothing amiss. He knew the Saurons had better eyes than normal men, however, and he worried still. Leaning down from the saddle, he checked the suspension; the leaf-springs of the yurt's low wheels and axles were carrying a bit more than usual, but seemed to be bearing up well nonetheless. Kamov finally came around to the complex harness at the structure's front where the team of ten draft horses waited for the signal to move. As always, his sons had everything in perfect order.

Scattered about on the plain around them, several of their neighbors had already begun the exodus, and thin clouds of dust were being whipped away by the chill wind. Lavrenti was up in the driver's seat, the reins of the harness loose in his hand and a cloth-wrapped automatic rifle in a scabbard beside him.

"Hey," Sergei called. "What happened? Where's your brother?"

Lavrenti waved and gave his father a rueful grin. "I flipped a coin with Nikolai and lost; so now I have to drive first shift while he gets to ride."

Nikolai came riding around from the other side of the team with the grin that made Sergei despair for the virtue of his neighbor's daughters. "And a good thing, too," Nikolai called. "The best rider should always go first."

Immune to his brother's jibes, Lavrenti only rolled his eyes—a gesture picked up from his father—and grinned.

Sergei smiled. "Huh. Using that two-headed coin again, were you?" he asked Nikolai, whose brows shot up in mock protest even as Lavrenti's jaw dropped in feigned outrage.

Nikolai was suddenly serious. "Father—what is it? What's wrong?"

Sergei's face had twisted into a frown of concentration so severe he looked stricken. He thrust his hand out, a gesture his sons well knew commanded silence. Sergei turned his gaze back over his shoulder, to the south. In the vast ranges of the Atlas Mountains was the pass into the Shangri-La, and atop that pass was the old fortress where the Saurons had taken up residence, re-naming it the Citadel. Staring hard at the mountains, straining to listen for he knew not what, Sergei waited.

Suddenly his eyes caught movement, and dropping his gaze from the heights of the ranges to their base, he saw them. They looked liked dragonflies, wings glimmering as they emerged from the shadows of the mountain range into the light of Byers' Star and the Cat's Eye gas giant. As Sergei watched, the dragonflies grew, gained detail, and became helicopters.

"Raid!" Sergei pulled the flare pistol from his belt and fired in one motion. The danger rocket was a blinding cobalt blue, sharply contrasting with Cat's Eye's orange haze that overwhelmed the feeble glow of Byers' Star and made up the bulk of Haven's normal light. "Lavrenti, get moving, you know what to do! Nikolai, with me!"

Lavrenti had the yurt rolling in an instant; he kicked open a vent flap at his feet and shouted down a warning to those within. As the mobile tent swung about toward the other yurts and those riders already responding to Sergei's flare, Natalya clambered up through the flap, dragging a huge vehicle-mount machine gun behind her. Sergei and Nikolai cut across the yurt's path and made for the group of riders approaching them.

"Commander Air Group, do you have visual?"

Fighter Rank Stahler put his craft into a tight bank as he circled the vast plains below. Three other supraorbital fighters, each still bearing the flaming eye insignia that had falsely proclaimed them to be pirates during the invasion, maintained their loose formation around him, scanning the surrounding skies.

There was virtually no chance of the Haveners mustering any aircraft which could threaten the Sauron fighters—or so Stahler's squadron members had at first declared. He had corrected them by recounting his own experience with a squadron of Havener biplanes and a particularly determined pilot; an experience which had cost the life of his wingman, Fighter Rank Vil. That had sobered their attitudes considerably.

"Affirmative, Assault Group," Stahler answered. Three thousand feet below, long streams of dust trailed out from behind the circular black lumps that were the nomad yurts, and still more from their herds and the outriders of their mounted warriors. "Continue present heading. Beginning first pass."

Stahler's group would provide pinpoint bombing of anything that looked like it might threaten the assault group's aircraft. Not wishing—or needing—to risk the remaining shuttles, the incoming attackers under Assault Leader Bohren were all in the rotary-winged aircraft captured from Haven armories. Fast, heavily armored and well-armed even by modern Sauron standards, the "helicopter gunships" (as their manuals identified them) would land and put Soldiers on all sides of the horse nomads, then take off once more to prevent any of the herd or their mounted defenders from escaping.

The land was flat steppe all the way south to the foot of the Atlas Mountains, with only slight depressions to the north. A river flowed along the eastern border of the strike zone, with a small copse of trees bordering to the north. The weather here on the steppes was fickle, with the North Sea winds able to sweep unopposed across the miles of flatland, but the Meteorology Ranks had assured them that a storm currently out to sea would remain there for at least another day.

Blinking in a coded pattern, Stahler activated the optic-nerve link to his ground attack weaponry. Where his eyes went, the barrels of six gauss cannon swivel-mounted beneath his aircraft's wings turned to follow. Hands free, Stahler manipulated the vertical thrusters which would stabilize his craft for sustained firing on any ground position which might warrant such attention.

Coming up beneath him, along the northern edge of the nomad mass of horses, a large domed tent filled his vision.

All things considered, Stahler thought as his fighter swept forward, *it looks like an easy day's work*.

He would not have believed anything so apparently simple could go so horribly wrong.

Lavrenti watched the fighters bearing down on them with something like religious awe. He slapped the reins over the team, and stood up in the seat, shouting at them. Beside him, his sister Natalya was fumbling with the pedestal mount for the heavy machine gun she had brought up from the tent.

The yurts of Lavrenti's people were a far technological cry from their Asiatic forebears; anything the Mongols had done, the Cossacks declared they could do better. Scavenged vehicle axles, huge pneumatic tires and advanced suspensions made the mobile tents as fast as their horse teams could run—eventually. They still comprised a great deal of mass, and even at their top speed, compared to the Sauron fighter, they were still as stones.

Lavrenti kept turning to watch as the fighter approached. Dark shapes moved beneath its wings, and two yurts in its path exploded like puffer spores, scattering carpets, pillows, household utensils and human bodies from their tops in great gouts of dust and flame and blood. There was no flash from the weapons on the Sauron craft, no roar to be heard above the surrounding din. Lavrenti knew the magnetic-accelerator weapons of the Saurons were virtually silent, and though there was nothing subtle in this attack, the next fighter could come upon them with no warning at all. *If, of course, we survive the attack by this fighter*.

He heard a clanking beside him and his sister's shout: "Get down, L'asha!"

The long barrel of the machine gun whipped about, clipping his shoulder as he ducked, then it was going off a foot behind his head with an ear-punishing roar. "You crazy girl! You can't hurt that thing with a pop-gun!"

But he kept driving; if they were going to die, as he was now quite certain that they were, it would be good to die fighting.

Behind him and to each side, Stahler's squadron members were completing their passes. So far, all their attacks had destroyed the rolling tents with no damage to the teams pulling them. Such was the expertise of Soldiers and the quality of their equipment. This first strike was intended to deprive the cattle of much cover against the ground forces now landing all around them. In a moment, the assault ships would disgorge their cargoes of Soldiers, then return to the air to take over the air-support role now being provided by Stahler's squadron.

Before him, Stahler saw a flicker of light on one of the yurts, at the point where the team of horses met the dome of the tent. A faint tapping of shells against his canopy told him it was small-arms fire, and aborting his climb, he increased forward and vertical thrust, slowing his fighter to a virtual crawl. A machine gun on such a mount could provide a very unpleasant surprise for the ground troops now closing in on the position, and Stahler had no intention of leaving it intact.

His ground speed barely fifty miles an hour and his fighter effectively a floating tank, Stahler focused on the still-firing machine gun as he closed; there was a young man urging the team, and someone behind him firing the weapon. Matching speed with the yurt, Stahler focused on the youth; his ship's weapons would take both the driver and gunner in a single burst. The sighting-implant painted twin hexagonal reticles over his field of vision, converging patterns which closed over one another and abruptly shifted to green; the weapons were locked on to the target, and as Stahler blinked again to fire them, the gunner became visible. "Shit!" Stahler roared in reflex.

In all species of humans, the instinct to preserve the opposite sex is nowhere stronger than in normal males; in all males, it is nowhere stronger than in Saurons. In all species of humans, the reflexes of Saurons are without equal, and among Saurons, the reflexes of pilots are something almost beyond the laws of physics. Stahler was completely unaware that he had jerked his control stick back, lurching the nose of the fighter up, sending his fire harmlessly over the heads of the boy and girl on the yurt. The tent rolled on, passing out of his forward field of fire, its riders in a crazy exultation over the antics of the bobbing spacecraft behind them.

Stahler recovered control in a red haze of fury. Had he not been under orders to preserve the livestock and females of these nomads, he would have emptied every weapon pod on his ship into that damnable tent, its team and its cattle, too. Stahler did not indulge in slaughter of opponents; it was inefficient and pointless. *But dear God*, he thought, *startled by the pretty face of a female human norm at a machine gun?* He almost groaned. He would never live this down.

"What is he doing?"
Cyborg Rank Sargun did not answer, remaining as

motionless as only a Cyborg could be. Such stability was necessary to the function of the optical enhancer—mere binoculars would have done little to improve a Cyborg's visual acuity—which was feeding data directly into Sargun's optic nerve through the small receptor patches on his forehead. The effect was to place Sargun's point of view in any scene within range of the OpEn unit. Right now he was watching Stahler's fighter as it leveled off, recovering from the seemingly pointless gyrations to which he had subjected it in order to avoid firing on the cattle female.

Switching the OpEn unit to standby, Sargun drew a short breath and finally answered Cyborg Rank Stern: "Apparently he wished to spare the life of the gunner; a human norm female."

Stern considered this for a moment. "Priority for captured females is this high?"

Sargun made the ghost of a shoulder movement that was the Cyborg equivalent of throwing one's hands in the air. "Fighter Ranks tend toward romanticism. The violence of the maneuver suggests it was reflexive."

Stern's lips flickered in a suggestion that he didn't think much of the pilot. Looking back over his shoulder, he gestured to the other Cyborgs in the salvage team: *Remain in position; engagement occurring ahead.* All twelve Cyborgs were motionless shapes spread out in the grass behind him, all twelve gave the subtle hand signal acknowledging his order: *Understood; advise at discretion.*

The sounds of the battle were carrying across the plains to them now. They were perhaps three miles distant; a two minute run for Cyborgs should they choose to intervene, but Stern was not yet sure of Sargun's position on violating direct orders against committing Cyborgs to combat.

He decided to be patient.

Sergei and Nikolai had joined a dozen riders and made for the right flank of the herds. Helicopters were sweeping slowly over the fields beyond, dropping men from twenty feet above the ground, at speeds which would have killed human norms. The dark forms hit the ground running, leaving wakes in the steppes grasses as they came on toward the cossacks.

Sergei cross-drew a pistol and a long, curved sabre. On his right, Nikolai had drawn two revolvers of an indecent calibre. Having heard a rumor that the Saurons had two hearts, his son had acquired the pistols during the first weeks of the Sauron invasion, declaring his desire for weapons capable of removing both organs at once.

"At least the grasses are still high," Sergei shouted over the thunder of the charging horses. "They'll have to get close for clear shots at us; we'll be able to shoot down on them from horseback."

Yarmoloff was on Sergei's left side, carrying a short-ened paratrooper's carbine fitted with an absurdly huge snail-clip. He raised it to his shoulder and loosed a burst, the weapon barely moving as the body of the animal beneath it rocked in a gallop. "Horseback's not much of an advantage against Saurons," Yarmoloff shouted back.

Sergei leveled his pistol at a wake in the grass ahead, moving incredibly fast. Firing, he saw the wake first shift direction even as he squeezed the trigger, then cut back on course for him a split second later. *Mother of God*, he prayed; *I'll take any advantage I can get . . .*

Assault Leader Bohren's rotor-wing pulled up and back, giving him a clear view of the battlefield. *Not much of a battle,* he considered, but the match-up of infantry and archaic cavalry had always intrigued him in his stud-ies. *Too bad the equation will change once the helicopters begin providing fire support runs.* The plan he had effected under Deathmaster Quilland's approval was pro-ceeding with an efficiency that might have seemed dull to anyone but the Sauron soldiers whose lives now depended upon it.

Bohren's expertise lay in organizational control. As one

of the Groundmasters for the initial invasion of Haven, he had been a paragon of efficiency. And, like all Saurons, he was a Soldier of the first magnitude; as a command Ranker, he was expected to be—and was—competent for leading assault actions against human norms. His only weakness lay in the fallibility of pure organization as a technique for combat.

Bohren would have been amused to learn that the human norms used to say: "No battle plan ever survives contact with a Sauron." Had Bohren been a bit more imaginative, he might have been less amused by appreciating that that phrase, within the context of the conditions under which the Saurons now lived, implied a potential for disaster beyond any powers of organization to withstand.

"Natalya," Lavrenti shouted, steering the yurt toward three others which had reached the center of the herd, "On your right, in the grass—"

"I see them!" The tall grasses close by had been trampled and flattened by the horses and tires of the yurts, but less than a hundred feet away the tall steppe grasses waved in the wind like a yellow sea. And on the shores of that sea, Natalya saw figures emerging, leveling weapons at the riders as they circled and fired into the grass.

The cossacks were as brilliant horsemen as ever their ancestors had been, and their generations on Haven had made them warriors of the finest stripe. This kept their casualties low, but nothing could prevent death when facing Saurons, and very little could bring victory. Each second, Natalya would see another rider tumble from his horse.

She waited until *gospodin* Buyalev passed, then swept a long, low burst across the grasses behind him. The vegetation was scythed down for yards beyond, and a Sauron in dull grey battle dress went down with it.

"Hi!" she shrieked, Lavrenti cheering behind her. Natalya could feel her nipples tighten against the fabric of her undershirt, and felt an incongruous relief that she was wearing a heavy coat, preventing her brother from seeing her arousal. She dismissed the thought; she knew about boys, and from the constant rattle of the assault rifle from behind her, she was pretty sure that Lavrenti was just as excited in his own way as she was in hers.

"N'asha, helicopter!"

The Sauron gauss weapons were virtually silent, but the helicopters mounted conventional Havener weapons; more primitive, but no less effective at these ranges. The gunship swept over their yurt from behind, rotary cannons roaring as they sliced the horsehair-felt and wooden framework into a collapsing wreck. The helicopter went by and banked to pass in front of them, turning to bring its cannons to bear on Natalya and Lavrenti. As it came about, Saurons emerged from the steppe grasses beneath it, advancing in the wake of its fire. Swinging the machine gun around, she kicked open the tent flap at her feet, and shouted: "Now!"

Beneath her and to the right, explosive bolts detonated, sending a quarter of the yurt's side flying out and away to land smoking on the grasses. Two dozen men and women dressed in the butternut camouflage of Cummings' Brigades boiled out of the opening, supported by another heavy machine gun within. The same thing was happening throughout the rolling mass of yurts; wherever a Sauron troop carrier was disgorging a squad, a company was leaping out of a yurt to ambush them.

Not even numbers such as these would even the odds, of course, and all the Haveners knew it. But Kettler had promised them Cummings' support, and the survivors would pass the word that it had been given.

Supra-orbital fighters were one thing, but Natalya had dealt with helicopters before. It was no accident that she operated the heavy machine gun while her brother Lavrenti covered her with a mere assault rifle.

Natalya focused her vision on the gunship's forward canopy—though armored, it was still the aircraft's only weak spot—and keeping the sights over the gunner's position there, she fired a steady burst into the transparent armor plating.

In the rear pilot seat of the gunship, Fighter Rank Amar almost smiled. More cattle troops meant more prey for the ground forces. As for himself, having had a great deal of experience with the futility of chemically-fired projectiles against the canopies of Sauron fighters, he ignored the pretty little cattle gunner's fire and flew straight at her. Only as his gunner, Fourth Rank Hsien, was about to fire the helicopter's forward weaponry, was Amar reminded that this time he was not flying a Sauron fighter.

The transparent panel in Hsien's forward canopy abruptly crystallized, then blew inward in a flood of glass granules and tungsten-cored slugs, passing through Fighter Rank Hsien's head and into the lower torso of Fighter Rank Amar seated above and behind him, ending only as it tore through the engine and fuel cells beyond.

The helicopter exploded, dropping directly on a Sauron who had been advancing beneath it in perfect, if imprudent, combat procedure.

The blast lifted Natalya and Lavrenti from the seat of the yurt and threw them to the earth two dozen feet beyond. Fuel and ammunition ignited the grasses all around the helicopter, and the wind began whipping the flames south and east into the tall grasses.

Natalya sat up, her ears ringing. She could smell hair burning, and turned to see Lavrenti senseless beside her on the ground, his coat and hat afire. Patting out the flames, she felt something hot pierce the flesh of her hand, and removed Lavrenti's cap to expose a long piece of smoking metal embedded in his skull. Too angry for tears, Natalya groped about, finding her brother's assault rifle, and taking a fresh clip from his belt, she began crawling toward the burning yurt. All around her, the volunteers from Cummings' Brigade were falling, but

continued to lay down withering fire as they advanced
into the grasses, where the battle would ultimately close
to hand-to-hand.

A sudden brilliant flash of light made Sargun start.
"They have lost one of the rotary wing aircraft."

"Were there troops aboard?" Stern asked.

"Unknown; one was caught beneath it when it fell."

Stern decided to test the waters. "The human norms
have more advanced weaponry than suspected, and far
more troops. They could inflict serious casualties on
our—on *those* forces."

Sargun turned to him. "Indeed. But we are forbidden
to intervene in any military actions. By order of the First
Citizen himself."

Stern nodded. "Were we to close to a better observation point, we might at least provide long range fire support. Without actually engaging the human norms."

Now Sargun turned to look back at the figures spread
about in the grasses behind him. One wore the bulky
harness of a Mark VII manpack fusion gun. The weapon
had been released from stores after Sargun's insistence
that it might prove necessary for cutting up samples of
debris from the *Fomoria* should any be found; and had
it proved necessary to do so, the Mark VII was certainly
up to the job. No human norm could even lift the
weapon, and even Sauron norms wore a powered hydrau-
lic harness when taking it into battle—Cyborg Philomon
wore the weapon casually slung over one shoulder.

The Mark VII generated a contained fusion reaction,
then released the energy in a directed pulse; extremely
destructive, but precisely contained. Intended to destroy
with surgical precision, the Mark VII's contained fusion
effect did not even generate fatal doses of x-rays or
gamma rays. Not fatal, at least, to Saurons.

Nothing was wasted, and everything went into the
weapon's blast sphere, with the resulting swath of
destruction rivaled only by heavy artillery. Imperial

Marines who had faced Mark VII-armed Saurons on the streets of contested worlds had nicknamed it the 'blockbuster'.

Sargun secured the OpEn unit. "Your point is well-taken. We cannot make an informed decision from this distance." He gestured to the remainder of the squad behind him: *Forward; remain concealed; maintain fire discipline*.

Stern was pleased. Sargun seemed like just the sort he and his men had been waiting for.

"Urrah!" A man on Sergei's left had seen the explosion of the helicopter gunship and stood in his saddle to raise a fist in triumph. His head suddenly exploded and he fell back across his horse's rump, arms splayed to the sides.

Yarmoloff poured fire into the burning grasses; the blaze had spread rapidly, and the smoke was making it hard to breathe, let alone see the enemy.

"Bastards!" Yarmoloff shouted, his horse wheeling. As it turned, a shadow flew from the brush, then another, then three more. The last three simply ran on without seeming to pay them any notice, but one dark blur slowed enough to become a large man who grabbed Yarmoloff's reins and dragged his horse to the ground, spilling the harness maker from his saddle. The Sauron raised one foot and crushed Yarmoloff's skull with a single blow, then released the horse to stagger to its feet and run wild.

Meanwhile, one of the other Saurons had closed on Sergei, who wheeled his mount and held his sabre out before him and his other hand behind his back, out of sight. The Sauron glanced at the sabre and stopped, raised his rifle in a leisurely gesture and aimed at Sergei's head; the cossack looked directly into the Sauron's eyes. Beneath him, Anya continued her graceful pivot, bringing Sergei's other hand around and exposing the automatic he held in it. The weapon barked twice, and the Sauron fell dead with two bullets in his brain.

Kicking Anya into a gallop, Sergei charged the Sauron who had killed Yarmoloff, firing with the pistol and extending the sabre in the edge-up position for a killing run-through.

But this Sauron was the type to act, not react. He too charged, running toward Sergei and keeping himself behind Anya's head and out of Sergei's field of fire.

Cagey bastard, Sergei cursed. *Let's see how he likes getting trampled, then*.

Anya was a cossack's horse, and she had long since been trained out of any reluctance she might have held as regarded running a man down. She weighed over half a ton, and bore down on the Sauron like a judgment, preparing to put him under the hooves she had trampled a tamerlane with only a year before.

With an eerie grace, the Sauron sidestepped the charging animal, and dropping his weapon, reached out and grabbed Anya's front right leg as she passed; jerking upward and outward, he threw horse and rider to the ground with a single pull. Screaming, Anya rolled to the side, flailing her legs before her.

The Sauron bent over to pick up his rifle and as he rose he turned toward Sergei. An impossibly large hole suddenly opened in his chest; Sergei could quite literally see daylight through the Sauron, who fell over dead with a look of utter astonishment.

Nikolai galloped up on his horse Pyotr, the massive revolver still smoking in his hand. He looked down briefly at the Sauron. "Huh. So perhaps they have only one heart after all, *da* Papa?"

Sergei scrambled over to Anya, who had struggled to her feet and looked at him almost in embarrassment.

"Is she lamed?" Nikolai shouted, keeping Pyotr wheeling, his eyes searching the surrounding smoke for the next Sauron.

"*Nyet!*" Sergei shouted in relief and jumped into the saddle. "Bad girl," he grunted at Anya, "getting surprised like that." He called to Nikolai: "Where is the headman?"

"Dead; we are falling back to the center. It looks like the end, *Otetz;* Papa, we've lost at least fifty men already."

Sergei leaned down and swept up the Sauron's weapon as he rode by. Rising and settling into the saddle, he bit back a curse. "Christus, fifty men? Are you sure?"

Nikolai nodded. The lad was utterly without fear, Sergei knew, but he looked shaken now. "And almost all of the Cummings Brigade, though their heavy weaponry has killed many Saurons. These Saurons, Papa; they are like nothing I have ever seen. And I have never seen so many at once."

There was a roll of thunder as the explosion of another helicopter gunship reached them; Sergei and his son spurred their horses and headed for the center of the shrinking circle that had been their community.

Assault Leader Bohren was worried. Reports indicated that his forces had killed over fifty of the cattle males, at least twice that of the heavy weapons ambush troops wearing the butternut uniforms, and another thirty-seven females incidentally—every one of whom had been armed and extremely effective with her weapon—yet the cattle showed no sign of breaking. He had just lost one helicopter to a girl with a machine gun, and another had crashed when one of the cattle on horseback had thrown a lance into its tail rotors. A *lance!* At least there had been no casualties from that one.

"What are the casualty figures?" Bohren addressed the Communications Rank seated beside him.

"Seven Soldiers have been killed, Assault Leader. Signals indicate that a further nine have activated their rescue telemetry and can no longer be counted as combat effectives."

Bohren was aghast. *Sixteen casualties? And seven of those* dead? He had brought a force of one hundred Soldiers to make a simple raid on human norms, and so far his operation was suffering the highest exchange rate since the Sauron landing on Haven!

Operationally, things were not all that bad. If Bohren's forces had been any other race but Saurons, his losses thus far could have been considered acceptable. But for the Soldiers, with their finite population of combat-capable troops, it was a disaster. It had been expected that these particular cattle would be fierce opponents, but these losses were unacceptable. "Recall Fighter Rank Stahler's squadron," Bohren ordered. "Instruct the units engaged in the field to pull back and mount suppressive fire to contain the cattle. We'll allow the gunships and aircraft to finish them off."

"Acknowledged, Assault Leader. New information from Sensor Ranks."

"Speak."

"Environmental Sensors show a massive storm front coming in from the north."

Bohren frowned. "Relevance?"

"Storm front is due to arrive this area in twenty-six minutes. Winds estimated at fifty knots, with heavy rain and strong electrical phenomena."

Saurons were not an expressive people, but at that news, Bohren's jaw dropped. "Meteorology Ranks said that storm front was continuing out to sea."

The Communications Ranker nodded. "Yes, Assault Leader. But weather patterns on this world have not been fully codified by the Met Ranks, yet. The gas giant incurs unprecedented variables."

"Very well. Proceed with revised orders and inform the helicopter gunships to press the attack for fifteen minutes, then to break off, land and secure for storm."

Bohren raised a hand to his brow. He wondered if anything else could go wrong, today.

Sergei and Nikolai had rounded up several dozen other cossacks and ten survivors of Cummings' volunteers, the latter armed with rotary grenade launchers. Together they had begun a sweeping skirmish action against the major Sauron assault force. The Saurons were pinning down the cossack forces on three sides with fire teams concealed in the tall grasses, while the helicopter gunships made their circular passes, raking the cossack yurts and horsemen with their wing-cannons.

Along the fourth side of the defender's position, the line of Cummings' volunteers held, but only because every remaining yurt was gathered there, and each bore at least three heavy machine guns—one even sported a rocket launcher. Women and children were spread about around and on the surface of every yurt, and every one of them capable of firing a weapon was doing so. Diettinger's assessment of Sergei's people as being a very strong community had been accurate; if anything (as Assault Leader Bohren was now learning), the Saurons had underestimated the Don cossacks seriously. Combined with the completely unexpected firepower provided them by Colonel Kettler's intervention, the Sauron attack was beginning to bog down.

As Kettler himself had told Cummings: "They'll still win any attack they make against those cossacks, General; nothing can prevent that. But I can guarantee that they won't enjoy it very much." Nor were they.

The grass fires were spreading, whipped up by the steadily freshening winds from the north. Behind those winds, a towering storm front on the horizon bore down on the battlefield, coming closer with each passing moment.

"Papa!" Nikolai shouted, pointing. "Helicopters coming up on the right!"

Sergei turned in his saddle, wheeling Anya about into a hard right turn, directly into the approaching gunships. The horsemen were only staying alive by constantly moving, keeping the Saurons from pinning any of them down, forcing the Soldiers to fire at moving targets and closing with the gunships to give them as little time in their sights as possible. And each Sauron whose position could

be ascertained by his fire was met by a hail of heavy
weapons fire from the Cummings units. Even so, the
Haveners were doing very little damage to the attackers,
and cossack after cossack fell from his saddle to the
bloody grasses below. Smoke from the grass fires was
now spreading all around them, blinding to the human
norms and terrifying to their mounts, but impeding the
Sauron's fire accuracy not at all.

"We have to hold them off until the storm hits," Sergei
yelled to the riders about them. "Then we can cover the
withdrawal for the yurts and Cummings' Brigade."

One man, Putin, nodded and roared: "*Da*, but then
what? No more helicopters, but their ground troops still
have us surrounded."

Sergei kneed Anya's flank as he leaned to one side,
signaling her to change course even as he fired a burst
into the grasses to his left. He ducked and winced in
the saddle as one of the Cummings' Brigade SLaGs—a
shoulder-launched, guided missile—shot less than a
dozen feet over his head, lighting the faces of the men
around him as it leaped across the sky toward a Sauron
helicopter. Sergei's reply was lost in astonishment as the
helicopter ducked under the missile at the last second;
the Sauron pilots were not—could not be—human.

"Shit," Putin amended, "If they can fly like that, they
can keep their helos up in a storm, too!"

"Shut up!" Sergei roared, as a runner from the Cummings Brigade dashed up to the horses, shouting up to
him.

"When the storm hits those 'copters'll have to land;
you push hard against the line of Saurons at the yurts
. . . break out, we'll fire off the rest of our SLaGs and
destroy their helicopters . . . maybe then we'll have the
edge in mobility."

Putin barked a laugh at the plan, and Sergei knew he
was right; one look at Anya's frothing lips told him that
none of their horses could keep up this pace for very
much longer. What they needed was something that had

been in very short supply on Haven for a very long time. They needed a miracle. Even so, he nodded at the man on the ground who, he now saw, was leaving a red trail from a blood-filled boot.

"*Da,*" Kamov nodded at the volunteer, and without realizing it, he saluted before riding off.

Natalya Kamova had made her way to the Danilov's yurt. The Danilovs were all dead, but the two surviving Cummings Brigade volunteers within their yurt were laying down a withering crossfire from a twin anti-aircraft mount, and the area around the tent was a killing zone for any Saurons who had dared approach. Natalya only saw two Sauron bodies; evidently they learned as quickly as they moved.

The Cummings troopers—a husband and wife—had been only too glad to see Natalya, immediately thrusting a weapon into the young girl's hands. Now Natalya sat atop the yurt with a SLaG of her own, an old Imperial weapon called a Viper. Despairing of ever hearing the lock-on signal when matching the Viper against the counter-measures systems of the Sauron-modified helicopters, she had finally begun aiming by eye and firing; the Cummings volunteers had given her a considerable supply of rockets for the Viper; and judging by the roar of automatic weapons from beneath her, their own views on ammunition usage were just as liberal.

Natalya watched as one of the helicopters, buffeted by the growing winds, turned to bear down on the last small knot of her people's horsemen. Firing, she saw the missile close on the helo, which dropped to avoid being hit, and in so doing lost its aim; the horsemen passed safely under it.

"Ha!" she spat, quickly slapping in another missile. Returning the Viper to her shoulder, she began tracking it across the fields, waiting for another of the helicopters to pass in front of her field vision. She would have to get lucky sometime.

Over the din of battle, Natalya suddenly thought she heard a bird; then she realized it was the detection signal of the viper's radar. There before her, still miles off, was a slowly moving dot, then another, and another; eventually she saw that the four Sauron fighters that had opened the attack were returning, and three of them were being tracked by the Viper's targeting sensors.

Natalya didn't know why the Viper was getting through the fighter's counter-measures; she could not know that the Viper had been specifically designed to deal with supra-orbital fighters, particularly those whose emissions identified them as Sauron. Against the less-advanced designs of Havener helicopters appropriated by the Saurons, the Viper was hopelessly overqualified; it was, in effect, blind.

None of this even occurred to Natalya. All she knew was that she would have a wonderful surprise waiting for those fighters when they got in range.

Besides having reached the relative safety of the volunteer-held yurt, Natalya's greater piece of fortune was simply this: The Sauron fighters' counter-measures were not defeating the Viper's sensors because they were not operating. Stahler's squadron was getting low on fuel when Bohren had recalled them to take over for the helicopters, and having encountered nothing but small arms fire previously; Stahler's wingmen had seen no point in draining their energy supplies by running deflectors against such primitive—if robust—weaponry as these cattle had evidenced. Stahler, as a matter of course, was running his deflectors at full power. He had always been a cautious pilot, which was one of the reasons he was still alive.

"Units three and four," Stahler instructed, "Break right and slow to ten knots ground speed; destroy the remaining mounted force. Unit two, stay on me. Target that tent with the anti-aircraft unit." Stahler glanced at his long-range sensor screen. The storm front would be on them in minutes, and that would pretty much decide the issue. His fighters could not stay up much longer than the helicopters, but by the time atmospheric conditions were bad enough to force them to break off, Stahler's fighters could wipe out the Haveners completely.

Which only makes me wonder why the hell we didn't handle it this way in the first place, Stahler thought. But he knew the answer to that. The Citadel needed the women of these human norms, needed their horses ... and needed their men too, come to that. The Saurons lacked for nothing except more Saurons, but that was a lack which would doom them as a species if it were not remedied.

So we'll have to contain them while our men on the ground close in and take them prisoner in the rain, Stahler considered. For Assault Leader Bohren's sake, he hoped that could be done. Stahler did not have clear information on the status of the battle, but simple visual observation told him that in terms of captives gained balanced against Soldiers lost, this operation was already running at a deficit.

The yurt which Stahler and his wingman were approaching was the source of suppressive fire that was pinning the majority of the Sauron ground force. Stahler began blinking to activate his targeter, when he saw an impossibly familiar figure turn slightly toward him, then disappear in a cloud of smoke and flash of light.

"What in God's name—"

Fighter Rank Arias, Stahler's wingman, shouted something over the communications link that sounded like a denial, and then he was gone. An explosion along his starboard wing batted his fighter aside like a toy to smash it into Stahler's own craft.

The intakes on Stahler's machine whined, their pitch rising crazily as the stabilizers sought to keep his craft level on its vertical thrusters. They would have been equal to the task despite the damage Stahler's craft had suffered in the collision, but at that moment the storm hit.

The force of electrical storms on the steppes of Haven, and the ruination they are capable of visiting upon any known product of human endeavor, are best left to the imagination. No parallel exists for them on any world settled by man, and the destructive energies released at their height have made prudence in bad weather part of the steppes-Havener character—to say nothing of an intimate familiarity with the principles of lightning rods.

At least three dozen lightning strikes heralded the forward edge of the storm, nine of them within a half-mile area centered on the combat zone. One struck the wreckage of Fighter Rank Arias' craft, skipped across thirty feet of air and discharged into Stahler's fighter before scouring a thirty-foot diameter area of grass.

Stahler's fighter bucked, the engines whined and spurted again, and the craft plowed into the ground with a sudden burst of speed that ripped the craft and two yurts in its path to shreds. There was just enough kinetic energy left in the smoking mass of metal to overturn the Danilov's yurt, spilling Natalya to the ground for the second time that day and bouncing the inhabitants and their weapon mount off the inside walls several times before the tent came to rest, axles up, half covering the wrecked fighter craft.

Stahler no longer had to worry about living down the harassment of his fellow Saurons.

"Who is commanding this debacle?" Sargun asked in a voice that was very nearly a snarl. "If the First Ra— the First *Citizen* does not order his eradication, I will do it myself."

Eradication was the ultimate punishment in Sauron society. Not limited to the mere execution of the offending Sauron, it extended to the sterilization of his progeny and utter removal of his genotype from the societal gene pool. Valuable aspects of such a Sauron would of course remain, but the unique genetic combination of DNA molecules which comprised him and his offspring, which defined them and would have proclaimed their line's achievements to future generations, was gone.

Forever.

"Unknown," Stern answered, "But it is not going well."

Sargun signaled Cyborg Philomon to bring up the Mark VII. "Even for a Cyborg, Stern," Sargun announced in a jest only another Cyborg could appreciate, "that is an understatement."

Philomon was at his side instantly. "Cyborg Sargun."

Sargun looked again through the OpEn. The monstrous waste of Soldier assets he was now watching was a godsend to Cyborg Koln's position of release for the Super Soldiers from the Breedmasters' control. Whoever the First Citizen had assigned to this assault was botching it so badly that he was doing what might be permanent damage to the colony here on Haven. Surely the Cyborgs could not be blamed for intervention which could not fail to turn the tide and win the day?

He turned to Philomon. "The Mark VII is fully charged?"

"Yes."

"Move in and destroy the Haveners. Staggered series of three shots at ten meter intervals to break up their mounted formation as we close."

"Engagement parameters?" Stern asked for the squad.

"Deploy and kill at will."

The Cyborgs took no joy in such an order, no satisfaction; they had as much eagerness for the coming battle as they did fear of it. Which was to say, none at all. If they felt anything, it was relief from the boredom of their salvage mission. This was their true field of expertise, and like any intelligent creature, they were most content when doing what they knew best.

Sargun's unit of Cyborgs was one mile away from the

fighting. Less than a thirty second run before they would be in the midst of the Haveners.

The Cyborgs—taller, broader than their Sauron counterparts—rose up from the ground like wraiths in grey, moving so rapidly across the steppe as to appear squalls of the rain now flowing around them. In fifteen seconds they were halfway to the battle. In twenty-five, Cyborg Philomon discharged three shots in rapid succession from the Mark VII manpack fusion gun, each shot precisely ten meters apart, each shot a blinding, roiling mass of heat and light, carving into the body of cossack horsemen with a fury that the survivors would remember in nightmares for years to come.

Sergei and Nikolai watched the fireballs rolling toward them across the plain, each detonating closer than the last, one of which embraced two riders less than ten feet from them. Putin and his brother-in-law, Myasischlev, were suddenly lit so brightly they were a rosy pink, then an Earth-summery yellow-white through which Sergei could make out details of their skulls, their ribs, even the pocket watch Myasischlev carried under his left breast. Sergei and Nikolai saw the illumination increase until Putin, Myasischlev and their mounts were but the faintest outlines in the white sphere before them; then even the outlines were gone and the sphere dissipated almost instantly, leaving no sign that men or horses had ever been there at all.

Three seconds after the last shot from the fusion gun had detonated among the remaining cossacks, the Cyborgs reached the area where the first shot had impacted. Slowing, they were at the second impact zone five seconds after that, and some were noticing that the ground surface was doing something odd. In another five seconds, the Cyborgs, whose comprehension was as rapid as everything else about them, were aware that they had made a grave mistake.

From the command helicopter, Bohren had monitored the events of the past few minutes with growing apprehension, culminating in the awful moment when he recognized the blast signature of the Mark VII, and realized that a fusion weapon could only mean Pathfinder Cyborgs.

Bohren watched in amazed horror as the Super Soldiers charged across the burned-out, superheated steppe into the mass of surviving Haveners. He watched as they slowed to take up a circular formation which would, in typical Cyborg fashion, obliterate every resisting human norm or device it came in contact with.

And Bohren watched too, as the ground beneath the Cyborgs abruptly collapsed, dropping eighteen feet to the sunken water table as fast as it could fall, the surface suddenly darkening as the permafrost, melted by the heat of the fusion gun's discharges, turned the crumbly Haven steppe soil into a syrupy mass of slick, grasping mud, into which every Cyborg—and a good many fast-thinking Sauron regulars who had decided to follow up the Super Soldiers' advance—instantly disappeared from the chest down into a quagmire of their own making.

The Havener nomads were spared by the grim coincidence that those not killed outright by the Mark VII's contained-fusion effect were those outside its blast radius, and thus outside the perimeter of the sinkholes it had created. Cossack horses screamed in terror, partly at the savagery of the weapons all around them, partly from the shock of finding themselves suddenly standing at the crumbling edge of an abyss, and partly from the storm which was now upon them in all its fury.

Lightning strikes, far more severe than anything Bohren had experienced within the mountain-sheltered expanses of the Shangri-La valley, were tearing into the ground all about. Rain was coming down in sheets which utterly obscured vision and, Bohren could see from the sensor screens, was adding to the nightmare of the quicksand in which at least a dozen of his men—and all but two of those damnable Cyborgs!—were now floundering.

Messages were flooding his Communications Ranker's

screen; the remaining fighters were breaking off to escape the storm; the gunships which had landed to wait it out were literally being held down by their crews, as Saurons began tying down the aircraft to steel poles driven hastily into the ground; ground troops were reporting that the surviving Havener horsemen were becoming impossible to engage in the rain, and those Saurons trapped in the sinkholes began calmly requesting assistance, as the Haveners were riding along the crater rims, firing down at them to great effect.

Bohren was an organizational genius. So long as events remained within the parameters he had anticipated, he could deal with virtually any contingency. But, like many Saurons of his late-war creche, he could do nothing he had not been trained to do. And while Sauron training encompassed a great many variables, its emphasis for the last twenty years had been on dealing with Imperials on known worlds. Sauron contingency planning had always revolved around combat on worlds someone would actually want; it had therefore rarely anticipated fighting for an environment like Haven.

Faced with a situation obviously beyond his capacities, Bohren's training did at least tell him when to cut his losses.

"Order a general disengagement, all channels." He felt the command helicopter rock under him as a sudden gust of wind slammed into it; outside, Soldiers hurriedly re-set two of the stakes securing it to the ground. "All forces to extricate themselves by paths leading past those sinkholes to aid Cyborgs and Soldiers trapped there. Troops to continue onward and make for The Citadel."

He had to shout the last order several times, as the crash of thunder all around them was beyond even the Sauron ears of his Communications Ranker to overcome.

From a vantage point several miles to the north, General Cummings watched the battle, and Colonel Kettler watched General Cummings.

Four days, Kettler thought. *Four days riding dispatch horses, motorcycles and a stolen river-speeder, then eight hours of stark terror in a stolen rotary-wing at ten feet off the ground, just to spend another twelve hours driving like demons in a kidney-killing runabout to get to here.*

But as the self-appointed leader of Haven resistance, Cummings had been determined to see this first hand. The older man was silent as he swept the starlight scope back and forth across the distant carnage. Finally, he switched off the power pack and closed the unit in its case.

"All right, let's go," Cummings told Kettler. They slid back from the rim of the low hill and rose into low crouches, making their way toward two small four-wheel drive runabouts. The driver saluted as Cummings and Kettler climbed in; around them, six camouflaged troopers festooned with steppe grasses appeared from their firing positions and clambered into another vehicle of their own.

Cummings' runabout bounced away through the worsening storm, the driver seemingly oblivious to the near-zero visibility.

"Where will the nomads head next?" Cummings asked. He had to shout over the rattling of the vehicle and the roar of the wind, rain and thunder.

"They'll make their way north, to the sea, and follow the coastline westward. They should link up with the mobile aid station we promised them in about a week."

Cummings shrugged, sat back.

"You realize, General, that in a week, their wounded will probably have already died."

Cummings looked straight ahead. "There's not a lot of medicines available, Colonel. The strong will survive; the weak—" he looked out the window at the roaring downpour—"the weak will not."

"And does that include our own volunteers, sir?" Kettler asked. He noticed that the driver's eyes flickered to the rear-view mirror.

"Everybody dies, son," Cummings said quietly. "That's why they were volunteers."

Kettler didn't speak for a long time. "That's something a Sauron might say, General."

Cummings gave a short, mirthless laugh. "That's something every Sauron says, every day of his life, Colonel Kettler. That's why they'll win if we don't fight them on their terms."

Kettler turned to him. "And what will we win, General? In the end?"

Cummings fixed him with a long look. "We'll win a world without Saurons, Colonel Kettler."

Kettler nodded, and turned away, thinking: *I wonder . . .*

Sergei Kamov found his son Lavrenti, dropped from his saddle and fell onto the corpse of his boy, weeping in rage and grief. Nikolai wheeled his own mount in a circle, orbiting his father and brother, watching the casualty-strewn field of battle around them. A grim prosecutor, he was more than ready to shoot the first thing that moved.

A riderless horse galloped by, disappearing with an equine shriek as another bolt of lightning lit the scene around them. Through the rain, Nikolai heard shouts.

"*Pomogite* . . . help . . ."

"Who is that?" Nikolai shouted into the rain.

Shapes stumbled toward them, wounded men supporting their fellows. A Cummings volunteer in the distinctive butternut camouflage was being carried by two dismounted cossacks. A dozen more of Nikolai's people trailed behind.

"Look; it's Kamov!" one cried, and the mass changed direction and began shambling toward them.

Nikolai intercepted them before they could reach his father. "What do you want?" the youth shouted harshly.

"We need Kamov; the headmen . . . the council are all dead. He's the new headman, now . . . what should we do?"

Nikolai looked over his shoulder to see his father standing up from Lavrenti's body. Sergei took off the boy's coat and draped it gently over his son's face, then crossed the field toward them, rubbing the rain into his face briskly with both hands as he came. Nikolai rode up to him, and spoke in as low a voice as could be heard over the downpour. "Father; the council is dead . . . they are saying *you* are the new headman now."

Kamov seemed at first not to hear, then he nodded once as he reached the crowd.

"Gather whatever horses you can. Anyone who can ride, do so. Head north to the sea, and wait there. Anyone who cannot ride, stay behind with a weapon and cover the retreat of the rest." Kamov turned to Nikolai. "Find your sister, Nikolai. If she is a captive . . ."

Nikolai felt the blood drain from his face at his father's tone, at the words he was sure must come next.

Something shifted in Kamov's expression, and he finished: "If she is a captive, try to let her know we will ransom her."

Nikolai let out his breath, and whispered "*Da*, Papa." He galloped off as Kamov turned to the remnants of his people. The crowd had doubled already, with more arriving every moment, huddling beneath cloaks against the storm.

Kamov looked at the two were carrying the trooper in camouflage. "Who is that?"

"One of Cummings' volunteers, Sergei. He was wounded with us while—"

Sergei had stepped forward, gripped the man by the hair and lifted his face. The eyes stared forward sightlessly.

"He's dead." Kamov let go of the man's hair and turned away. "Leave him and start gathering those horses."

The crowd simply stood, unmoving. Kamov rushed at them, tore the volunteer from their grasp, and threw the body into the mud. "Go," Kamov added in a quiet, even tone.

✵   ✵   ✵

Seeking shelter from the fury of the storm, Natalya had crawled into the wrecked yurt. She thought her ankle was probably broken, but her hands were unhurt, so of course, she had picked up another rifle on the way.

Drenched and covered with mud, she worked her way back into the wreckage that included the ruins of the Sauron fighter. The interior of the yurt, she saw, was liberally coated with an interesting red paste of bones, flesh and weaponry parts—a mix, she realized, of the anti-aircraft mount and its crew, and the moment she was past it, she was violently ill. The sound of the storm outside was not quite so deafening here, and she was completely sheltered from the rain. The metal mass of the fighter, she knew, was a dangerous thing to be around with all the lightning, but she was simply too tired, cold, wet and miserable to care. Lavrenti was dead, she was sure Papa and Nikolai were dead, and she wished she were dead, too. In a few days, she thought, if the Saurons did not kill her outright, they would take her back to their Citadel, and there would be plenty of time to cry then. For now, she wiped her face, pulled a blanket toward her and tried to get warm.

The blanket was pinned in the wreckage, so Natalya shifted her position to get closer to its anchor point and so get more of it about her shoulders. As she did, she saw something moving in the dim light, and leaning over, Natalya saw swaying in mid air an arm, covered in blood that had dried much too fast.

Looking up the arm, she saw a shoulder, and a torso strapped securely into an acceleration couch. The top of a helmet, glossy black, was facing her, its wearer's head tilted forward onto his chest. The rest of the pilot's body was hidden in the wreckage, but it was clear to Natalya that he was securely pinned.

The helmet moved.

Thumbing the rifle selector to full automatic, Natalya

raised the weapon to her shoulder and centered the sights on the top of the helmet.

I will look him in the eye, she thought, *And let him see I am only a girl.* Then *I will kill him.*

Slowly, the head came up, showing a face covered with blood from a broken nose. Natalya's gaze flickered to a strange symbology stenciled across the visor:

The helmet came up against padded headrest, the bloody eyes fixed on nothing. The Sauron, Natalya saw, was a ruin. She blinked.

A moment later, the pilot's gaze roved about the interior of the shelter, the blue eyes finally meeting her own. As they focused, Natalya clenched her teeth, and said: "*Do svidanya, Sauroniki.*"

She began to squeeze the trigger, when she heard the pilot say: "*. . . prokrassny . . .*"

Natalya stopped. She'd often been called pretty, but never by someone she'd been about to kill.

The briefing room was quiet, the only sound the wind howling past the shutters outside. First Citizen Diettinger was dealing with his first disaster as political leader of the Saurons on Haven.

Fourteen dead, he considered, reading the report a third and final time. *Including two Cyborgs. In exchange for fifty-two female captives, seventy head of livestock captured and one hundred ninety-three enemy dead, the rest of the nomads having fled to the shores of the North Sea.*

He remembered, without conceit, an official commendation he had received for having never lost a battle when he had been in command. He also remembered recently having told Althene that martial virtues were not social ones, and he wondered if perhaps his new civilian career might present him with a string of such achievements as this; a bitterly ironic mirror image of his military record.

Ah, well, Diettinger concluded as he closed the datapad cover. *One cannot, after all, do everything.* Even allowing for the astonishing level of firepower the Haveners had accumulated for their ambush, the colloquial term for Bohren's level of error was un-recordable. He looked up at Assault Leader Bohren, standing at attention, meeting his gaze. Beside the Assault Leader stood Cyborg Rank Sargun, staring straight ahead.

"You are reduced to the ranks, Trooper Bohren, and restricted from combat duty until further notice. Cyborg Rank Sargun."

There was no answer.

"Cyborg Rank Sargun," Diettinger repeated with a tone that made Althene shiver.

"Sir."

Diettinger glanced toward Koln, then back to Sargun. "In addition to direct disobedience of standing orders, resulting in the deaths of two Cyborgs under your direct command, you are presently exhibiting contempt of command by your failure to address me as First Citizen." Diettinger watched a muscle in Sargun's jaw twitch, and every sense went on the alert. He continued speaking, addressing Koln: "Cyborg Rank Koln, as commander of the Cyborg forces here on Haven, I will consider recommendation from you as to the nature of disciplinary action in the matter of Cyborg Rank Sargun."

Koln's answer was immediate. "Eradication, First Citizen."

Sargun's lips parted; his shoulders actually slumped.

Diettinger showed no reaction at all. "Agreed. Due to the scarcity of Cyborgs here on Haven, sentence to be commuted to personal sterilization and behavioral retraining, effective immediately. Report to the Breedmasters, Ranker Sargun. Dismissed."

Sargun's head trembled as he left the room, somehow remembering to salute first.

"Permission to speak, First Citizen," Althene asked quietly after the door had closed.

"Denied," Diettinger said shortly. "This meeting is adjourned."

The rest of the staff filed out, leaving Diettinger alone with Althene and, she noticed, Cyborg Rank Koln, who stood by the window and stared out at the mountains beyond.

When the last of them had left, Althene glanced at Koln, then addressed her husband: "First Citizen."

Distracted from some thought, Diettinger's gaze flickered to meet Althene's. "Hm? Oh, yes, Althene. What is it?"

Althene's gaze indicated Cyborg Rank Koln, but Diettinger gave no indication there was any problem with his presence. "I should like to discuss the situation regarding the battle. May we consider this a closed meeting?"

Koln said nothing, and Diettinger nodded. "If you wish."

Althene collected her thoughts for a moment, then began: "The fact that a well-organized force of local militia was present with these nomads, apparently prepared for an ambush against our attack, indicates an ominous level of cooperation among the peoples here, one which we have not confronted previously."

"To say nothing of excellent intelligence on their part," Diettinger added. "Perhaps even a security leak in our own organization."

Althene swallowed. "What?" she asked quietly. There had never been a traitor in any operation involving homogeneous Sauron forces, throughout the entire history of the race. The concept was, quite literally, a contradiction in terms, and for a giddy second, Althene wondered if the catastrophe had unbalanced her husband.

"What do you think, Cyborg Rank Koln?" Diettinger called across the room.

"The possibility warrants investigation, First Citizen."

Althene was on her feet. "Galen. *What is going on?*"

There was a long moment when Althene felt she really did not know who she was, or where. But at the end of it, Galen had risen from his chair to stand beside her, holding her gaze with his own.

Cyborg Rank Koln had joined him, and said only: "It is almost certainly necessary that she be told." With courtly grace, Koln had bowed to Althene, and excused himself with an almost elegant: "My lady." He returned to the window, where he stood once more, motionless as the mountains he regarded.

Diettinger turned to Althene and said: "I once asked a young fighter pilot what we Saurons were. As a race. Do you know, he couldn't tell me."

Althene watched, and listened. In the past weeks she had been aware of some strange relationship growing between her husband and Cyborg Rank Koln. But Galen would not speak of it, and she felt that she was about to learn its nature, at last.

"He wasn't even able to voice an opinion, Althene. Utterly convinced that he was expected to *know the right answer*, he was incapable of even hazarding a guess. For that young Soldier, the problem was one of training. He had been educated—programmed—completely beyond any ability to exhibit intellectual initiative."

Diettinger went to the wall with its map of the Shangri-La and environs. "What sort of answer do you think you could expect to that question, were it asked of Cyborg Rank Koln?"

Althene considered a moment. "I believe Koln *would* have an answer, Galen. At least as the question applied to Cyborgs."

"And that answer would be?"

Althene shrugged, at a loss. "Koln would consider us the ultimate fighting man, I suppose."

Diettinger turned to her with a smile of triumph. "Exactly. And the tragedy, at least for Koln and all the other Cyborgs, is that he would be right." Galen crossed the room and sat beside her.

"What we are, Althene, we as a race, are a people dedicated to the proposition that the value of the universe descends directly from the result of man's ability to observe it. *Without man, of what use is the universe?* As the only creature in his experience with the ability to intellectually apprehend existence, man is the creature whose observation of the universe establishes all concepts of value, which he then applies to his observations of the universe as tests of their validity. As we exist, and are intellectually aware of such existence, it is our nature, and even our obligation, to dominate the universe which we observe, intellectually as well as physically."

"Galen, this is primary school indoctrination, basic philosophy as taught to every four-year-old Sauron child—"

He continued, seeming not to hear. "So, as man is the measure of the universe, he is obligated to achieve a state of intellectual, physical, and spiritual evolution commensurate with that responsibility. That is the basic premise behind the Sauron practice of eugenics. That is the answer to the question: 'What are we?', which that young fighter pilot could not answer. We are the guardians of the ongoing effort to make man worthy of his obligation—and his heritage—as master of his own destiny and the universe in which it will unfold."

Diettinger was quiet for a moment, waiting for some comment from Althene. When none was forthcoming, he continued: "So Cyborg Rank Koln would be right. He and the rest of his species are, indeed, the ultimate fighting men. And, insofar as mastering the chaos of war allows us, as Saurons, to master the universe, he is right."

"But martial virtues are not social ones," Althene recalled.

Diettinger nodded. "What many Saurons—and virtually all human norms—have forgotten, is that warfare is only a means to an end. A race such as ours, which masters it, has mastered only a small part of the fabric of human destiny. An important one to be sure, as such mastery teaches—or should teach—discipline in the face of chaos, the value of sacrifice, the wastefulness of suffering and the value of human life, norm or Sauron. Those are all lessons to be applied to the full range of human experience. But a species which can *only* fight, no matter how well it does so, has no capacity for further growth."

Understanding at last, Althene turned to Koln. "Do you agree with such an assessment, Cyborg Rank Koln?"

Koln turned to her. "The logic is irrefutable, Lady Althene. It has been said that 'Cyborgs exist only to fight, and they fight like nothing else in the universe.' The second part of the phrase is mere hyperbole. The first is the more telling; it is, in fact, a pronouncement of doom."

"And as a result, you have no wish to usurp the First Citizen's authority?"

"Of course I do, my Lady. As does every other Cyborg. By our nature," he glanced at Diettinger, "we are incapable of anything less."

Althene turned to her husband, who only nodded. "And what would happen in such a conflict, Koln?" Diettinger asked quietly.

"The Cyborgs would win."

"And then?"

"We would attack the Haveners."

"And win?"

"Every battle we fought."

"Until?"

Althene jumped in. "Until there were no more Cyborgs left."

"Precisely, my Lady," Koln said quietly.

"But knowing this, why—"

Koln shook his head, and for the first time, Althene recognized the underlying emotion that suffused every Cyborg she had ever seen: Fatalism.

"War is the only thing we know, my Lady."

"The Cyborgs are the ultimate achievement of human genetic engineering," Diettinger said. "The operative word in that sentence being 'ultimate.' They are as perfect warriors as it is humanly possible to create. But they are the product of only a few dozen generations of human ingenuity and imagination. They are no match for the continuously evolving states of existence which humanity must face as it spreads throughout the universe. They are, by definition, limited. And thus, they are an evolutionary dead-end."

"Then the preservation of the Cyborg genotype—?" Althene began.

"—is crucial, as I have always said," Diettinger finished. "Just as it is crucial we maintain a technological advantage in weaponry superior to that available to the cattle here. As knowledge must be retained regarding modern combat tactics, literacy, printing, the arts—and indoor plumbing. The Cyborg population here on Haven, like that of the Soldiers, must be carefully guided, perpetuated—"

Now it was Althene's turn to interrupt: "And culled."

Koln and Diettinger shared a look, and it was the Cyborg who finally spoke. "Yes. Sargun was given the patrol because of the very great likelihood he would engage the Haveners in combat. Assault Leader Bohren was put in command because his lack of combat experience would require those under his command to demonstrate great levels of initiative to survive the Havener ambush."

"You knew?"

"I guessed," Diettinger said. "That was the reason for the delay in pursuit after the engagement at the river. To give the nomads time to be contacted by one of the roving militia patrols our scouts have reported to be organizing guerrilla activity in the Shangri-La."

"But we lost fourteen dead . . ."

"Fourteen dead, including two Cyborgs, all of whom were, arguably, weak links in the chain we must forge here if we are to survive."

"Galen; Pyhrrus of Epirus is not a Sauron role model. Were our troops to kill a thousand Haveners for every Sauron lost in battle, we would still lose such a war of attrition."

Diettinger frowned; he was not used to Althene failing to understand him immediately. "That is precisely my point, Althene; we have no business fighting wars of attribution. The war we will fight here will be against Haven and ourselves. Captives such as those taken today, and local women given over to our Breedmasters in tribute for passage into the Shangri-La, will be the true war; success in cross-breeding Saurons with Haveners the true victory. Engagements like these today will keep the more bellicose elements of our new society occupied, particularly the Cyborgs. Eventually, there will be a revolt—"

Althene went white with shock. "What—?"

Diettinger shook his head. "It is inevitable, but with Cyborg Rank Koln and myself manipulating the ringleaders, it will be contained, with the outcome finally establishing civil authority in our society here."

Althene's head fairly swam; could this be the same direct, straightforward man she had fallen in love with? Was it possible he could be so calculating as to conceive of, let alone support, such a ruthless scheme? "Galen—why?"

"Because, my dear, as you said yourself: We have here a population of young wolves." He nodded toward Koln. "And, if you will, bears. But these wolves and bears have no competition worthy of the name to keep them wary, and hungry, and smart. None, that is, except each other. Haven is a fine crucible, but it will be generations before they appreciate that. For now, they must be prevented from turning all their attentions into a fruitless war of attrition against cattle which are very un-cattlelike, indeed. By shifting the focus of their competition toward each other, we strengthen the security of all. More, they will begin to compete with one another as breeders, even as fathers.

"To that end, we can all be guided toward battling our only real enemy on Haven: Infant mortality. We will mount a war against the Haveners, but one led by the Breedmasters. A war where the tally of names will be those of healthy Sauron children safely born; and not young men and women needlessly killed."

The First Citizen of the Saurons sat beside his wife, placing his hand against her flat stomach, a gesture of human protectiveness older than the race itself.

"And that, in the end, will make it a better kind of war, after all."

Sergei Kamov watched his daughter. For a month now, she had been tending the wounded captive, whom Kamov had been surprised to learn actually knew a smattering of Russian. And he had learned more very quickly.

When you've lost an arm at the elbow and a leg at the knee, Kamov reflected, *you probably appreciate the opportunity to concentrate on something else. Like a language.*

He looked at the Sauron pilot—Stahler, his name was—and how he looked at Natalya . . . *or a pretty young girl*, he amended his thought.

The Sauron had healed surprisingly fast, Kamov noted. So fast that he had been well enough to be handed over to Cummings' people at the rendezvous. But Kamov, new headman of Haven's Don Cossacks, had explicitly forbidden any of his people to even mention their "guest," and General Cummings and Colonel Kettler had returned to their valley empty-handed.

Sergei had not forgotten Kettler's gamble with his life and that of his family. Nor had he appreciated how long it had been before the medical aid facility which Cummings had promised had arrived. Four of their people that might have been saved had died of gangrene, and Kamov had begun to have very serious doubts about this policy of attrition advocated by Cummings and Kettler.

He watched as Nikolai went to check on Natalya and her charge; his son seemed to be getting along well with the Sauron. *And why not? He was just a soldier, doing a soldier's work. His part in what happened was, at least, honest.*

In truth, Kamov himself found it difficult not to like this Stahler.

He heard Natalya laugh; a rich, strong, woman's laugh. He saw the flush in her cheeks at something Stahler said as he leaned forward to point at Nikolai's legendary sidearm, and his arm brushed against Natalya's and stayed there a little longer than necessary.

His own people would put him in a breeding facility if he were to go back, Kamov knew from talks with Stahler. *Locked into a hospital bed for ten years or more until he died of boredom. That's no life for a man. And when he was better . . . well,* Kamov had known a great many one-legged horsemen, with less strength and physical ability than this Sauron, crippled though he might be. "A cossack without a horse is like a man without legs," Kamov mused aloud. *But a Cossack with a horse doesn't need legs.*

Nikolai had left them, and Kamov saw Natalya and Stahler talking in much lower voices, now. The blush was back, and Stahler seemed a bit reserved himself.

Good, Kamov decided. He had lost a son; he would take a son-in-law.

Cummings would go mad if he ever found out, of course, but what of it? It was his man Kettler who had given him the idea, after all. Hadn't he told them all that the Saurons wanted was Haven women to breed their next generation of Soldiers? *All right, then.*

Sergei Kamov watched his daughter lean forward, receiving and taking her first kiss from her future son-in-law, and thought about what mighty cossacks his grandchildren would be.

Two could play at that game.

Excerpt from the personal log of Master Chief Boatswain's Mate Timothy Ferguson, Imperial Navy (Retired):

Twenty years today since I received my retirement papers and headed home to Haven. I took a lump sum retirement in lieu of pension, knowing Haven was a long way from the nearest Imperial paymaster. I still remember the trouble I had getting back here. I'd taken passage to Friedland, having heard that the 77th was getting ready to pull out. I was hoping to ride deadhead on one of the troop ships going from Friedland to Haven. But they'd already left by the time I got there, and no one else was interested in going to Haven, so I spent the next ten years knocking around the Empire, pinching my pennies and working for my passages. When I finally got to Tanith Sector, it was another two before I found the old Sintax, a tramp freighter that had seen better days, better years in fact.

I remember how relieved I was to convince her master that there was still a chance to make money with a cargo of shimmerstones, and that my services as a liaison and guide were worth a free one-way trip. I spent what was left of my lump sum on trade goods, and off we went. Sintax was the first ship into Haven in four years, and as far as I know she was the last one out.

What little government Haven had under the Empire was virtually gone. I was lucky that my home town, Ellington, was in one of the more "civilized" areas. Lord knows what I would have blundered into otherwise. I had grown up in farming country, always pretty much self sufficient, and folks had banded together to form a reasonably democratic government and fairly strong militia. I used my trade goods to have a sturdy house built on a bluff overlooking the Jordan River, and other than dealing with some pranks and trespassing by local kids, have lead a fairly peaceful existence.

Peaceful but empty. I have no ties left here, no friends. I have no responsibilities, but no purpose either. Just killing time . . .

The Boatswain

A.L. Brown

The day the invaders came, we were crouched in the
bushes beside a secluded roadway, waiting for a call from
Suzy, who was down the road about a quarter mile. My
mouth was dry and I was scared.

As if he could read my mind, Doug grinned and said,
"Nervous, Jim?"

"Not really," I replied. I wasn't about to admit what I
was thinking. These weren't the kind of pals you shared
your innermost feelings with. Suzy's voice came through
a commset, "Here he comes. Do it now."

We all pulled stockings over our heads, and Tommy
raised his ax and made the final cut into the trunk of a
tree. It crashed down across the road just as the liquor
delivery truck came around the corner. The driver
screeched to a halt. Imagine how he felt when he jumped
out, trying to figure out where the tree had come from,
and saw the ten of us with our faces covered. His eyes
were as big as saucers.

I turned to look at Jack, our leader, and just about
crapped in my drawers. The driver wasn't the only one
surprised. Jack had pulled a shotgun with a collapsible

stock out of the canvas bag at his feet, and was aiming it at the driver.

Jack gestured with the shotgun barrel, "Over here and down on the ground."

The guy's eyes got even bigger, and he did exactly what Jack said. Doug tied his arms, put a sack over his head, and with Tommy, led him off into the woods. They were to bring the guy someplace it would take him a few hours to find his way out of, and meet us later.

The rest of us moved the tree out of the way and rode off in the truck. Everybody was laughing like fiends, everybody but me. I just kept thinking about that shotgun. A little vandalism and graffiti, taking cars for joyrides, even roughing some assholes up; that was fine by me. Being an accessory to armed robbery was a little much. Maybe there was such a thing as too much adventure.

We drove the truck to the old abandoned Radcliffe place and hid it in the barn. We were just getting started on one hell of a party when the song on our radio cut out, and an announcer started to scream about pirates invading from space. As if Haven had anything worth their time. We thought it was a joke until the horizon lit up and the earth shook as the first nuke hit Fort Fornova.

It was a strange moment. Sandra started to sniffle a little, and some of the others looked a bit sick, but Jack changed the mood by scooping up a bottle of booze and shouting, "All the more reason to party, for tomorrow we may die!"

Excerpt—Personal Log—BMCM Timothy Ferguson, I.N.(RET):

I was asleep, napping in front of the vidscreen. I was dreaming I was stuck on the ground on Tabletop, watching another mushroom cloud in the distance; a Sauron hellbomb, slipped through the point defense. I was helpless, stranded in a local hotel. I wished I was back on the ship. At least then I could be fighting back. I won-dered how the watch section was doing, fighting the ship shorthanded.

Suddenly my glass slid off the table and shattered on the floor. The noise woke me, and I realized I was on Haven, at home in my living room. But the aftershock continued, and when I stepped out on the porch, I could see the familiar mushroom shape rising in the direction of Fort Fornova. This was no dream . . .

After all I had done that day, I never expected to end up in church that night. Yeah, I heard the bells ringing, but I could have stayed back at the Radcliffe's barn with my bunch, sucking on some of our stolen booze, smoking euph leaf, and watching the fireworks. The planetary defenses continued to test the invaders, and streaks and balls of fire lit the night. At one point, a fireball lit the sky to the south; another nuclear strike. Everyone was excited—Jack, Sandra, Tommy, Nick, Suzy, Paul and Doug. They seemed convinced that this should be the party to end all parties. This was the wildest thing we'd ever seen. Nothing ever happened up here in the head-waters of the Jordan River; not to someone seventeen and wanting to see the worlds. Hell, most people's par-ents moved here because it was so quiet. We were all joking about the things we might never have to do; go back to school, get a job, and maybe not even be around in the morning to suffer the consequences of our partying.

I was keeping up with the best of 'em when I heard the bells. My first thought was how stupid it was to call on a God who had obviously abandoned us. Until I remembered Mom would be there, like she had been so much since Dad had died. It scared me to think how she must be feeling, the way she always worried. I started to feel guilty, and all of a sudden the bunch didn't seem so fun any more, so I slipped to the back of the group and over the hill. As I was walking, a tight formation of military jets screamed over, about 500 meters up. When I got to the church, everyone was already singing a hymn, and I slipped into the pew beside Mom. She looked like hell, with her eyes all red and streaks down her face. But the smile she gave me made me sure I'd done the right thing. I looked around the church. There was old Reverend Quinnel up front, looking as sour as usual, and a bit like he'd been sucking some booze himself. In the pews around me was a small and sorry lot. Young Mrs. Jackson; wife of a merchant seaman, pregnant with her first child. Three couples and their kids in farming clothes; the Carlsons, Lius, and Slimaks. Doctor Lampson; retired sociology professor. The two widows; Thomas and Alvarez. Nikko Tomek; the church's mentally retarded caretaker. And in back, with a face carved from stone; that bastard Ferguson. He was a retired Imperial Navy Master Chief Boatswains Mate, a cranky old gimpy guy. I'd hated him ever since I was twelve, when he'd caught me stealing apples from his orchard and knocked me out with a sonic stunner.

The song ended and the minister led everyone through the normal service, but skipped the sermon and gave a quick benediction. As he started to rush down the aisle, Ferguson limped out to block his path.

"Father," he said, making the title sound like an insult, "your flock needs some guidance."

I grinned. This could be interesting. These two hadn't gotten along from the day they met. The Reverend rose to his full height of one hundred seventy centimeters and almost growled at Ferguson.

"What do you mean, guidance? We are pawns in a larger struggle, one that our puny efforts cannot change. Our fate is in the Lord's hands"

"I figgered you'd think that way," snorted Ferguson. "Me, I always heard that the Lord helps those that help themselves. So I think we need to talk about what we can *do* to keep ourselves alive."

"And how," snapped Quinnel, "do you propose to do that?"

"Well," said Ferguson, turning so he addressed the rest of the congregation as well as the Reverend, "I've been usin' an old military commset in my den to listen in on both the invaders and our folks. These may be pirates, but this is no smash-and-grab raid. It seems they want to set up shop here on Haven, and that here at the head of the valley, we're sitting on top of real estate they want for their own. So if we want to live as slaves, we should all stay put. If we want to live free, we have to travel west, down the river."

"And where do you plan to go?" shot back Quinnel.

"Well," said Ferguson, "I thought that sister church of ours, Jacksonville Methodist, might be a good place."

"That's over five thousand kilometers away! It's almost all the way down to the escarpment on the Xanadu, south of Hell's-a-Comin.' Are you crazy?"

"Yeah, and I'm also alive and free, and plan to stay that way.

"I have no time for madness. These are pirates. If we all lay low and keep our heads, they will soon be gone," said the Reverend as he pushed his way toward the door. "The less you listen to this man the better."

As he left, all our eyes turned to Ferguson. He described his plan in a low raspy monotone. It sounded crazy to me. He wanted us to build a big raft out of egg tree trunks, build a shelter on it, and lash Doc Lampson's pleasure cruiser into it for power. If we kept on the move, Ferguson figured we could make it to the mouth of the river in time for the start of the next growing season, and hopefully find some measure of welcome.

Ferguson tried to convince us that even though the trip would be long and probably dangerous, it was better than the horrors we were likely to face at the hands of the invaders. He said no matter how far we got down the river, each kilometer we traveled would be another one between us and them. He warned us that what order was left on Haven was sure to break down, that people would start getting crazy and dangerous, and that we all needed to stick together. With a haunted look in his eyes, he told us stories from his Navy career; stories about assault landings on disputed planets, about pitched battles in space, and about atrocities against civilians.

The way he talked began to turn people around. I caught Liu looking at Carlson with a question in his eye. When Carlson nodded, the tide turned and soon everybody but me seemed to be on board. Me, I said no, speaking for both myself and my mom. I still wasn't sure we could trust the crazy old man. I didn't think Mom could make a hard trip like that, and besides, why leave a place where I had so many friends. I took Mom home, helped her to bed. Instead of going to bed myself, though, I slipped back out to find my bunch.

Excerpt—Personal Log—BMCM Timothy Ferguson, I.N.(RET):

I guess this log of mine may become more important. I remember what my last commanding officer, Captain Higgins, told me about his personal log. I had been up in his cabin on some disciplinary business when he confided in me that a log allowed him to feel like he was getting things off his chest, things that as skipper he had no business confiding in his crew. I never really thought much about what he'd said until now. But at this point I need all the advice I can get. Other than conning some orbital gigs, this will be my first taste of command. I hope I'm up to it.

Most everyone is falling into line without a problem. I have mixed feelings about the Schmidts, Jim and his mother, staying behind. He's an insufferable little shit, but a strong and capable one. If he did come along, I could probably break him to the yoke. After all, I've done it with enough recruits over the years . . .

The Radcliffe barn was on fire, and the heat dried my eyes as I peered into the column of orange light and heat. It looked like everyone was gone. There was a small bundle lying next to the spot where the bunch had been hanging out, surrounded by empty and broken bottles. As I walked closer, my heart went into my throat. The bundle was little Suzy, with her clothes torn up, still as a post; her bulging eyes stared blankly at the fire. At first, I wondered if the pirates could have attacked. But there were no laser or bullet wounds that I could see. She'd been beaten, cut up, and it looked like choked. I felt for a pulse but there was none. I realized that it must have been people from the bunch that had killed her.

I had never liked Suzy myself. She had always been too quick to jump from guy to guy, and enjoyed playing us off against each other. But nobody deserved this. I felt a tightness in my chest and a catch in my throat. Suddenly, I was on my knees, puking my guts out. After a few minutes, I got up and headed for home. As I walked, I thought. Maybe Ferguson was smarter than I gave him credit for. When I got home, I pulled out my dad's old hunting rifle, loaded it, and sat on the porch awake until a red and fiery Cat's Eye finally brightened the eastern sky. Then I got Mom up and we walked to Ferguson's house.

Excerpt—Personal Log—BMCM Timothy Ferguson, I.N.(RET):

. . . I spent the night refining my plans. There are a number of tall egg trees growing on the bank of the river below my house. I figure that a raft ten by twenty meters should be large enough to hold all of us. By taking apart my garage, we'll have enough lumber to build a shelter on it. We could dismantle the house, too, but somehow

that seems like a crime, to destroy a perfectly functional home on a world where so much has already been destroyed. I figure we can split the shelter into four or five rooms. Two large rooms, one for berthing men and boys, and one for women and girls. A small stateroom for me, one where married couples can take turns getting away (I wish we had room for staterooms for all of them), and maybe a small storeroom. We can tether to the raft what small boats we can gather. And I figure if we build a deep notch in the back of the raft, we can lash in Doc Lampson's ten meter cruiser to give us power and steering control. With its solar charged cruising motor, one thing we won't have to worry about is fuel. . . .

The building of the raft took two brightdays and two dimdays of hard work. We used Doc Lampson's pier as a base for outfitting it. Ferguson was a real bastard, and drove us like we were slaves. The little grey-haired guy was everywhere, following us all around with that slow shuffling walk of his. The first day things went slow, but when Widow Alvarez went home that evening to find a gutted house, it gave us all motivation to work as fast as we could. It seemed like Ferguson was right. Even though the pirates were nowhere near us yet, things were already going to hell. After that, Ferguson had us ferrying supplies from our houses to the raft in groups, with at least two armed people in each group. The stuff we brought from his house was amazing. Military gear of all types: two radiation suits, comms gear, infrared goggles, ration packs, three helmets, and more. A sonic stunner, probably the same one he had used on me five years ago. Other weapons of all types: a half dozen pistols, an assault rifle, two shotguns, a laser rifle and even a 20mm chain gun with 2,000 rounds of ammo. This guy was some kind of weird. Between that stuff and the hunting rifles most of the rest of us owned, we were going to be armed to the teeth.

On the second night, we started sleeping in the large

shack we'd built on the raft, and in Doc's cruiser, and posting guards on the pier. I bitched at the idea of standing watch, until in the middle of the third night a group rushed the pier. Mrs. Liu and I were on watch and fired over their heads, but they wouldn't stop, so we fired into them. A couple shots came back in our direction, but they didn't seem to be very well armed or organized, and soon fled into the night. I went out and found two bodies. One was our county deputy sheriff, dressed in regular clothes. The other was Tommy, from my old bunch. I guessed I wouldn't miss this place as much as I thought. Mom was horrified that my watch had put me in such a dangerous situation, but quieted right down when she realized that we all were all in the same situation, regardless of what we were doing.

On the fifth day, the first brightday of a new week, we finished the raft and loaded up. I was standing on the bank below Ferguson, and looked up and caught him grinning in what looked like pride. He saw me looking at him and the smile disappeared.

"What're you staring at?" he snarled as he pointed over toward the people handling lines. "Get over there and get busy helping them."

Excerpt—Personal Log—BMCM Timothy Ferguson, I.N.(RET):

. . . It looks like things are going well. But I can't let them know it. They're green and undisciplined enough that if I let up now, they'll just slack off. After all, it's just me and a somewhat motley crew of 19. Here's a chart of what I've got to work with . . .

Name	Age	Occupation
Carmen Alvarez	71	Retired widow
Carlson Family		Farmers
Kjell	53	Father
Sarah	39	Mother

Freya	16	Student
Jon	7	Student
Terri Jackson	20	Wife of merchant seaman (pregnant)
Doctor Mikhail Lampson	62	Retired sociology professor
Liu Family		Farmers
Arthur	33	Father
Nila	37	Pharmacist, mother
Heidi	18	Student
Christopher	11	Student
Samuel	8	Student
BMCM Timothy Ferguson	68	Imperial Navy (Retired)
Slimak Family		Farmers
John	61	Father, millworker
Ludmilla	55	Wife, farmer
Cindi	9	Adopted daughter
Schmidt Family		
Katherine	42	Millworker, mother (widow)
Jim	17	Student
Nikko Tomek	24	Church's mentally retarded caretaker
Sonya Thomas	56	Accountant, widow

Not a lot of able bodies. Widow Alvarez is competent as hell, and would be a real asset, if only she weren't so long in the tooth. The Carlsons are good people, but simple. Kids are cute, but like most kids these days, pretty useless. Mrs. Jackson could be a problem, since we won't have any of the type of things she might need if her pregnancy goes wrong. Lampson is a nice guy, real intelligent, but a thinker, not a doer.

The Liu family is a good bunch, always seem to be happy and smiling. Arthur is quite a farmer, known throughout the county for having a green thumb. Nila, as a pharmacist, has some medical training, although not as much as I wish one of us had. Their kids, although they're nice too, probably won't be much help either. The Slimaks are a quiet pair, who like to keep to themselves. And their daughter is a spooky little thing. That could spell trouble on the raft, where we'll all be living elbow to elbow, with no privacy to speak of.

Mrs. Schmidt is pretty frail. I'm afraid if things get rough, she won't last a minute. Jim Schmidt, like I've said, has potential, but it's mostly wasted. Nikko is dependable although he's more than a little slow. And Sonya Thomas is a shy little wallflower, Carmen Alvarez's roommate. I get the impression that Carmen calls the shots in that house.

Anyhow, not much to work with. With times on Haven being hard, most able bodies have gone elsewhere, leaving the old, young, and stubborn behind. I wonder if this is how Moses felt, when he dragged that gaggle of former slaves off into the desert . . .

Old Reverend Quinnel had shown up a couple of times during the building of the raft and had gotten into some ripsnoring arguments with Ferguson and the others. Each time he stalked off in disgust. But just before the raft was ready to leave, he showed up again with a paper bag in his hand. Ferguson went ashore, already turning red in anticipation of another confrontation. But after exchanging a few words with the Reverend, he turned and motioned us all ashore.

"Lissen up," said Ferguson, "the man has something to say."

"I won't even try to convince you to stay," said the Reverend, "but since you are so intent on killing yourselves, I just wanted to do something before you left."

He reached into his bag and pulled out his hymnal, a loaf of bread, a bottle of grape juice, and a plastic cup. He ran through the communion service quickly, with tears running down his face. Before long, everyone was bawling. With all the excitement and tension, the old words took on a meaning that I had never noticed before. We tried to convince him to come along, but he wouldn't budge. When we finally slipped our lines and moved out into the channel, our last sight of home was old Quinnel, standing on the shoreline alone.

It made me feel funny. I never even liked the guy, but I thought I would miss him.

Excerpt—Personal Log—BMCM Timothy Ferguson, I.N.(RET):

. . . Well, we're off. I hate to say it, but I feel bad for Quinnel. I'm not sure he's putting his faith in the Lord as much as he is just scared to do something risky. The communion ceremony made me realize something funny. This is the first time in my life I'll be sailing on a vessel where my religion is the prevalent one. I spent over thirty years in the Navy with them trying to push their state-sponsored version of Christianity on me. I guess that's one of the things that made me go through the trouble of shipping back to Haven when I retired. Like I never really felt comfortable with a different religion, I never really felt comfortable anywhere else . . .

If I thought Ferguson was an asshole at home, it wasn't half as bad as he was on the raft. He spent all his time telling us what to do and how to do it. Watch lists and work lists were all the guy seemed to come up with. And when we weren't busy with that, he was running us through drills. Fire drills, collision drills, attack drills, navigation drills. He had us practice pushing the raft upriver with the cruiser, even though the direction we wanted to head was down. Even little seven year old Jon Carlson had a post for the drills, and jobs to do. And to my surprise, the older people just went along with all this like a herd of sheep.

"Trust him, Jimmy, he knows what he's doing," my

mom would say. I couldn't believe someone didn't just pop off and deck the little jerk.

It finally came to a head between me and Ferguson on our sixth day out. Doc Lampson and I were coming off watch, and Ferguson and Kjell Carlson were coming on. I decided to stay up to watch Cat's Eye set, and snuck into the pantry to get myself a little snack. When I came out with a candy bar in my hand there stood Ferguson, hands on his hips.

"And just what do you think you're doing?" he snarled.

I was in no mood to take any shit. "Nothing that's any of your business."

"Like hell it's not," he replied, "We don't have enough food to get us half way to where we're going. And that candy is the kind of thing we want to save for an emergency."

I didn't even answer, just tried to push past him. Before I even knew what hit me, I found myself on my back with his knee in my chest and an arm across my throat. I tried to tell him to get off, but all that came out was a wet gurgle.

"Lissen up, you little shit, and lissen good," he hissed. "You think you're too smart and too good to cooperate with anybody. I've got twenty people on this raft to keep alive. And if I have to make a choice between that and making a spoiled brat like you happy, you don't even have to guess what I'll choose."

He got up and went to put the candy bar away. I went at him again, but got a fist in my groin. As I went down gasping, he said with a nasty grin on his face, "I can keep this up a lot longer than you can, boy."

He was close enough, so I took one more shot. This time he got me in the nose, and I went down hard, my eyes stinging and my face feeling like it was on fire. I didn't really decide to stop at that, but he walked off, and that was the end of it. No one had seen us and he never mentioned what happened to anyone. When I showed up at breakfast with a mashed up nose, and Mom asked me what happened, Ferguson chimed in to suggest that I must have slipped on my way to my rack. And when the new watch bills went up, I found myself on watch with Ferguson.

Excerpt—Personal Log—BMCM Timothy Ferguson, I.N.(RET):

. . . Had my first run-in with the Schmidt boy today. Not sure we even have enough food to survive, and here he is munching on a nice little snack. Gave me a chance to prove who's boss, though. Have to keep on him. He's got potential, I just have to pick through the shell he's got built up around himself . . .

Our progress in those early days was slow. We moved only on dimdays and during bad weather. Ferguson claimed that was the hardest time for the invaders to spot us. During brightdays, we stood out like a sore thumb. And he claimed that during the chill of truenight, we'd stand out to anyone with infrared or night vision equipment. Problem was, the times we were hardest to see were also the hardest times for us to navigate. The riverbanks tended to blur into the surface of the river, and it was hard to tell where we were, even though we had nightscopes of our own.

At the other times we pulled into side channels or tried to pull up near steep banks where trees hung over the river. We even cut down trees to lash to the raft and help us blend in better.

The older people had it toughest. Especially my mom. She'd always been a little frail, and I was afraid some of the others, especially the farming families, resented how little she was able to help out. I tried to help her when I could, but my own duties kept me pretty busy.

But despite how hard it was, we soon fell into the pattern of our new life. Our days were controlled by our watchstanding; who we spent time with, what we did.

Ferguson continued to drill us constantly, and we learned a new language, one he claimed hadn't changed for hundreds of years; heave around, avast, lively now, port and starboard, up behind, belay that. We learned to pronounce things the way Ferguson wanted us to; forward became for'ard, forecastle became fo'c'sle, and boatswain became bos'n.

Weather became one of our most important topics of conversation, especially with winter coming on. Weather is your life on the river. Rain is misery, especially with wind. Cold bites you to the bone. And clear days and nights are like heaven. The water surface became a guide to us. Every ripple had a meaning; a bar ahead, an eddy in the current, a change of wind. We learned to pole the raft past sand bars, and more than once had to free ourselves from a snag or reef.

The banks of the Shangri-La Valley rivers are still mostly wilderness, forests and fields with only an occasional house or farm. It just shows you how undesirable Haven is. Even after 500 years, the most hospitable part of the planet is still mostly empty. It was a good thing for us it was, though. The one thing we wanted was to be left alone, and fortunately, most others we saw seemed to have the same idea.

Excerpt—Personal Log—BMCM Timothy Ferguson, I.N.(RET):

. . . Starting to make some progress. Our first major hurdle, passing Falkenberg, went without a hitch. We shut everyone into one of the bunkrooms, and sealed it off as best we could. We set up a fan and filter to bring in air that was as clean as possible. I got in one of our antiradiation suits and sat on the bridge of Lampson's cruiser to conn us through. I put John Slimak in the other suit and stationed him on top of our raft with the chain gun ready. He'd had some militia experience, and

*during drills had shown some aptitude with firearms. I
hoped that meant he'd be able to fire if he needed to.*

*We went through the city at night, using infrared gog-
gles to see. Wanted to go though at twilight, but we
needed to see ourselves. I pushed the cruiser's engines as
hard as I dared, and we cut through the water about as
quick as such a bulky craft could. The city wasn't in as
bad a shape as I thought it would be. At least most of
the waterfront buildings were still there. It looked like
the city had been hit by tactical neutron weapons—
kill the people and leave the buildings for plunder. I
prayed to God that the plunder hadn't started yet, and
that we'd be left alone. We didn't see a soul, and I suspected that the rapid click of the radiation counter on
my suit indicated why. Within a few hours we were west
of the city, and John and I unbuttoned the others. I
left him to answer all of their questions about what had
happened, and stayed on the bridge alone. I was still
shaking from the adrenalin. Mrs. Alvarez came up and
handed me a cup of cocoa. When I tasted it, I found it
was laced with alcohol. I smiled at her, because that was
exactly what I needed at that point.*

Maybe there is hope for this bunch after all. . . .

It was thirty-seven days since our journey had begun,
and ten since we'd passed Falkenberg. I was still upset
at Ferguson for locking us up. I had really wanted to see
what was going on. But it was hard to be upset on such
a nice day. It was beautiful and the sky was clear, with
Cat's Eye up along with the sun to form the double
shadows that used to fascinate me when I was a kid. We
were moored to the shoreline of the river, our lines
secured to the thick conifers that lined the bank. I was
lazing on the foredeck daydreaming about Freya Carlson.
Even though Heidi Liu was older, she was a fat little
busybody, a real goody two shoes. Freya, on the other
hand, was a fine looking little thing that smiled at me in

a way that made me suspect she kind of liked me too. I wouldn't mind . . .

Suddenly the watchstander's whistle began to blow, short blast after short blast. Attack drill. I turned and was running for the fantail where my rifle was racked up when the shooting started. I dove for the deck and stared in surprise at a hole that had appeared in the bulkhead beside me. The whistle stopped short and someone started to scream. I turned to look at the shore, and saw a bunch of people burst out of the woods and jump onto the raft. I was too far away from the fantail, so I reached up and grabbed an ax that was racked up next to me. Ferguson came bursting out of his cabin with his laser rifle firing in short bolts. Mrs. Alvarez poked her head out of another door, an automatic pistol bucking in her hand. A young guy came at me, leaping off the cabin, and I caught him in the belly with the ax. Blood spurted from his mouth, and he looked surprised as he fell into the water, taking the ax with him. I picked up the hunting rifle he had dropped and tried to lever another cartridge into the chamber. The damn thing was jammed so I reversed my grip on it like Ferguson had showed me, and used it as a club. I bashed another guy in the head as he tried to jump aboard. Suddenly there was a gigantic crash and I was pushed into the water, my ears ringing.

By the time I struggled back on board it was over. The crash had been a grenade or explosive shell hitting the cabin, smashing a good portion of it to bits. There were bodies and blood everywhere. Nila Liu was working with the wounded, but some were beyond hope. I saw Ludmilla Slimak with the side of her face blown away, her husband John near her with a hole in his back the size of a plate, and Heidi Liu almost torn in half by the explosion. I started to scream when I looked into the cabin because my mom was in there, torn to bits. Arthur Liu and Ferguson passed me, stripping weapons and ammo from the bodies of our attackers, and throwing

the bodies over the side. Mrs. Alvarez came over and
tried to shush me, and I buried my head against her
chest and bawled like a baby.

Before I knew it we were under way again. They
brought those of us who had lost someone into the bunkroom to get us out of the way and calm us down. Mrs.
Jackson was so shook the other women thought she might
have her baby right there and then. Somewhere along
the line, somebody handed me little Cindi Slimak to
hold. And I thought I had it bad. The kid was only nine
years old, and had just seen her parents ripped to shreds
before her eyes. I held her and rocked her until she
cried herself to sleep.

Excerpt—Personal Log—BMCM Timothy Ferguson, I.N.(RET):

*. . . I may as well have pulled the trigger myself. There
are at least a dozen things I could have done to prevent it. . . .*

We never did find out who the people were who
attacked us or why they did it. They weren't soldiers,
that was for sure. That kid I had put an ax in was no
older than me. We figured they must have seen the raft,
and decided we had something they wanted. Our party
had been reduced from twenty to fourteen in about ten
short minutes. Besides Mom, John and Ludmilla Slimak,
and Heidi Liu, who I'd seen, John Carlson was dead
from a stray bullet, and Sonya Thomas had been killed
on the fantail. It was her blowing the whistle that had
warned us. When we stopped the next day to bury them,
Ferguson had some special words to say about Sonya
dying at her post. I hadn't seen him cry before that, but
his voice caught when he talked about it.

We all approached our drills with a new and grimmer
sense of purpose. Two things had convinced me that
Ferguson knew what he was talking about. One was the

way an old fart like him knocked the shit out of me without even breaking a sweat. And the other was the way we operated when the bunch attacked us. Without Mrs. Thomas doing what she did on the fantail, and the rest of us at least trying to do what we were assigned to, we all would have been dead. Ferguson might still be an asshole, but at least he was an asshole who knew what he was doing.

Excerpt—Personal Log—BMCM Timothy Ferguson, I.N.(RET):
. . . One thing I stopped having to do is rag on people to stay on their toes. After the Slaughter, as they have come to call it, no one complains about watches and drills as much. But even still, I'm keeping on them more than ever. Hard work can be therapeutic. . . .

A few weeks later the river started to ice up on us during the nights. Ferguson checked the charts and found us a creek with high banks, shaded by trees. We brought the raft in and moored it securely, and hauled Doc Lampson's cruiser up on shore by rolling it across a bunch of logs. Before long we were iced in firm, and we stayed that way for nearly two months. As bitter as Haven was, we usually didn't have such hard winters as that one was. Ferguson said it was because of all the nukes throwing dust in the air, and seemed worried as to how long the winter was going to last.

It was a tough time for all of us. We tried to keep busy, but there wasn't much to do. Me and some of the others did get out to do some hunting, ice fishing and scouting around, but mostly we just stayed cold and hungry, and got on each other's nerves.

It was during the second month of being iced in that Mrs. Jackson went into labor for real. She had not been doing too well in the last few weeks, crying that she would never see her husband again, and that her baby wasn't going to have a father. They cleared us out of the big bunkroom, and for a long time all we could hear was hushed voices and her moaning and crying. Then suddenly it was silent. Ferguson came out and said simply, "We lost them."

We couldn't dig a grave, so we cut a hole in the ice and buried her and the baby in the river the next day, and there were only thirteen of us left.

Excerpt—Personal Log—BMCM Timothy Ferguson, I.N.(RET):

. . . The winter is a hard one. I feel bad about Mrs. Jackson and the baby. It is less of a burden on all of us, though, not to have a new child to care for.

I keep worrying about nuclear winter. I remember reading about the "years with no summers" on Earth after the Great Patriotic Wars of the 22nd Century. I've been trying to listen to the commset, but not getting much. The nukes have hosed up atmospherics that were already marginal at best. I heard a fragment of a conversation the other night that might have included the word "Sauron." I hope I'm mistaken. If it is Saurons who have invaded, I'm worried that the rest of us won't make it even under the best of circumstances. I guess we'll just have to trust in the Lord. . . .

The days finally started getting warmer, and the ice began to break up. It was nasty work in the cold, but we soon got Doc Lampson's cruiser launched and were on our way. But even though we were making good progress again, Ferguson had been getting jumpier for days. The Sergius Narrows were coming up, and he'd picked me to act as his helmsman during our passage. From what he described, it was going to be nasty. The riverbed cut through a rocky area, and even though the river was wider than at any other point along its course, the channel was a twisting passage lined with rocky outcroppings. Ferguson had spent hours of my off watch time testing me on steering commands and navigation drills. Finally I'd had all I could take.

"Shit, man! You've done this all your life. How do you expect me to learn it all so fast?" His eyes narrowed for a second, and I thought he might take a swing at me. But then he just smiled, his eyes twinkling at me from underneath his cap brim.

"Son," he said, "you seem to be forgetting just what kind of navy I was in. No bobbing around like a cork for old Ferguson. I was in the Imperial *Space* Navy. Vacuum welding in free fall, working with monocables, repairing docking collars, and conning orbital gigs; that's what a boatswain in the space navy does. You want to know how I know all this stuff about the river? Well, here it is."

Ferguson reached into the chart table, pulled out an ancient dog-eared book and tossed it to me. I looked at the cover. "The Haven Practical Navigator," I read, "Originally Written by Kapitan (Vtorogo Ranga) Nikolay P. Prokofiev, CoDominium Maritime Guard, 2069 A.D. Eighty-seventh Edition. As Updated by Imperial Maritime Navigation Bureau, Haven Contingent, 2612 A.D." The book fell open to a section in the middle. "Chapter Twelve–Navigating the Rivers of the Shangri-La Valley."

I looked up at him. "You mean ... we've been ... you get it all from a friggin' book?"

"Sure do," he said.

"But aren't you worried you'll make a mistake? You act so sure of yourself."

He sat down in his seat and shrugged. "Would it help anyone," he asked, "if I let them know I was afraid?"

I looked at him with new eyes. The lines I saw on his face weren't anger, they were weariness. But as quickly as the moment came, it passed. He stood up again and picked up the book. The arrogant grin I had become so used to pulled at his mouth and he winked at me.

"And that," he said, "is our little secret."

And it stayed that way.

Excerpt—Personal Log—BMCM Timothy Ferguson, I.M.(RET):
* . . . I took a risk today. I had to. Otherwise I may have gone to pieces. It's been getting harder and harder to hide the strain. The boy has been pretty good lately, and I really needed to unload. But I keep telling myself to keep my distance, from him and the others. There is too much at stake here for me to ruin it by being weak. . . .*

A couple of nights later I found out that Ferguson didn't have just one secret. Shortly after the evening meal, Mrs. Alvarez opened the door of Ferguson's cabin to bring him some laundry. I don't know how she forgot to knock, but I guess it doesn't matter. She dropped the linen she was carrying and screamed. I was just around the corner, and one of the first to get there. There was Ferguson in his underwear, with two metal legs lying across the table, one opened and partially disassembled with a tool kit beside it. He gave a small sad smile to those of us who clustered around the door. His face was red as a beet and the light of his red night light glinted off a sheen in his eyes.

"They say that if you fight someone long enough, you become like your enemy. I guess the Saurons aren't the only ones who are half man and half monster, are they?"

Mrs. Alvarez and all of us tried hard to apologize, but he shooed us out. It was a few days after that before we saw much of Ferguson. And none of us ever worked up the courage to talk about it again.

Excerpt—Personal Log—BMCM Timothy Ferguson, I.N.(RET):
* . . . They know. I'm not just a retired sailor, I'm a crippled one, half a man. But what is strange is that they don't seem to care. I expected revulsion. Or I expected*

pity. What I didn't expect them to do was treat me the same, to continue to respect me, and listen to me. Keeping the secret took more out of me than what I've faced since the secret got out. Funny . . .

The passage of the Narrows had proven to be easier than we had feared. Or maybe we had spent so much time preparing and planning for it that it just seemed easy. I had spent the days since then poring over the navigation book. One morning, while we sat in a side channel, I asked Ferguson, "What was a CoDominium?"

He grunted with surprise. "Didn't they teach you any history in school, boy?"

"Sure," I said. "Two semesters of it. One on Imperial History, and one on Haven. But I don't remember that."

"Hell, kid. It was the CoDominium that first colonized this sorry little planet."

"Really?" I asked. "I thought it was the Harmonies, searching for freedom of worship. Who were these CoDominium people? Were they from Earth, too?"

Ferguson snorted. "The CoDominium was an alliance of the two greatest nations on Earth, Russia and the United States."

I began to realize that I wasn't going to win this one, but I was still curious. "What States were those United ones?"

Ferguson rolled his eyes. "If the Saurons hadn't done us in, we would have done it to ourselves." I guess he could see I was getting red, because he continued, "Hell, kid, it's not your fault. Can't know what the assholes didn't teach you. History's a hobby of mine, 'specially military history. Want to learn some yourself?"

I agreed, and it was the smartest thing I had done in a long time. Ferguson was full of stories, and once I'd asked, used them often to while away a boring watch. I learned that Falkenberg and Lermontov were more than just names of cities, about the Patriotic Wars, and about the wars that brought the Empire together. He told me the stories of ancient warriors of the Earth; Hannibal, Mao, Caesar, Nelson, Sun Tzu, Napoleon, Lee, and more. He told me things I'd never known about the Empire, and the difficulties they'd had even scraping by in the early days after the wasting of the Earth. And he could hold out for hours on the history of the Imperial Navy.

Soon I found myself pumping both him and Doc Lampson for information, and reading what books we had, hardcopy and disk. I had always hated to read, but out here on the river, with no vids or anything, there wasn't much else to do. And daydreaming about Freya Carlson, my other favorite activity, lead to nothing but frustration. I found reading was a way I could forget my own problems and get away from it all for a while. And when I got depressed, I could think of all the things that the old-timers went through. I mean, if those old farts could face the kind of troubles they did and get by, then so could we.

Excerpt—Personal Log—BMCM Timothy Ferguson, I.N.(RET):

. . . I just realized the other day that it's been weeks since I worried about Jimmy Schmidt. When I didn't trust him, I didn't get much of anything out of him. But now, the more I load him up, the better he does. In fact, he's become a real pleasure to spend time with. Even with Castell City and the dangers of the other nuked cities coming up, I feel I've got someone I can depend on. Makes me wonder if maybe my own attitude was holding him back as much as anything else.

It's a good thing he and everyone else are doing well. I've been feeling pretty poorly lately. I don't think it's sick as much as it's nerves. After his performance in the Narrows, I'm seriously thinking of letting the kid take us through Castell. . . .

*   *   *

It was a dead dark truenight, cold and clear. Nila Liu and I were on the bridge of the cruiser, bundled into our two antiradiation suits, and using infrared goggles to see and trying to navigate the raft as best we could. Despite the cold, we were sweating our butts off inside the heavy suits, uncomfortable as hell. We wanted to make as much time as we could getting past the radioactive ruins of Castell City. The rest of our crew were sealed into their cabins to reduce their exposure. The city had been hit real hard, even harder than what Ferguson had described to us about Falkenberg. At one point, the river flowed through a crater, forming a large circular lake. After that it narrowed down and started looking normal again.

Just as the radiation counter indicated it was safe, and we started to pull off our hoods, the raft lurched to a stop. We ran forward to find a giant chain with links almost half the size of a man stretched across the river at water level. Beams of light bracketed the raft from each side of the river and an amplified voice boomed out.

"Lay down any weapons and stand by to be boarded, by the order of the Free Shangri-La Militia."

A boat came putting up with a skinny guy at the bow, dressed in a brown uniform with gold bars on his collar. He was flanked by two grim faced men in undecorated uniforms of the same color, each with a laser rifle held at high port. He stepped aboard and strutted up to me.

"The State of Free Shangri-La has established a complete embargo on unauthorized river traffic. Who are you, and why are you ignoring our rulings?" he demanded.

A firm voice came out of the darkness by the shack. "I think," it said, "that you should be addressing the question to me, son."

A figure stepped out of the darkness and I had to fight hard to keep my eyes from bugging right out of my head. It was Ferguson, but he didn't look anything like our Ferguson. He was dressed in crisp khakis with

mirror-shined shoes and a black-visored hat with a gold
anchor on the front. His chest was covered with bright
ribbons, and a gold cross on a black ribbon was suspended around his neck.

"Master Chief Boatswain Timothy Ferguson, Imperial
Navy," he said, "And whom do I have the pleasure of
addressing?"

I wasn't the only one whose eyes were bugging. The
skinny officer was amazed. "Lieutenant Art Lamont, at
your service, sir," he stammered.

Ferguson was in rare form. He gave that officer a story
about a secret Imperial mission with such a serious face
that even I started to believe it. Within five minutes he
had the Lieutenant apologizing to us and writing out a
safe conduct pass to help us in the event we ran into
any of their patrols downriver. It seemed that down here
on the Xanadu, there was still some semblance of a government left, a fact that might allow us to make time
without worrying so much about being attacked. The officer took off in his boat and they dipped the chain enough
for us to slip over it.

I looked hard at Ferguson, whose face was poker calm.
"How the hell did you do that?" I asked.

"Son," he said, with his face finally splitting into a grin,
"any chief worth his salt can get what he wants from a
shavetail officer, and leave the officer thinking it was his
own idea to do it that way in the first place. The secret
of the relationship between officers and chiefs is that
even though we chiefs run things, we let them think
they do."

*Excerpt—Personal Log—BMCM Timothy Ferguson,
I.N.(RET):*
. . . It was the kind of moment you live for . . .

After we passed Castell City, we found a lot more
signs of civilization. The "State of Free Shangri-La," as

they called themselves, had kept order pretty well. We even found ourselves able to pull alongside the river at some of the small villages along the way and trade. But we didn't stay anywhere too long. We found that our raft, and especially Doc Lampson's cruiser, attracted the envy of the people we traded with. Although there was no violence, we did have to pull the cover off our chain gun on at least one occasion to intimidate some people. But even with the strain of these contacts, we began to feel safer than we had since we had left home. Our biggest problem was that some of us, especially Mr. Carlson, began to push to end the journey. His wife, Sarah, had never really recovered from losing her son, Jon, during the Slaughter, and she had been getting pretty sick lately. But Ferguson continued to insist that we keep going until we reached the Jacksonville people, down near the escarpment. It was kind of hard to argue with a man who had so much experience with war, so most of the rest of us just kept out of it.

Excerpt—Personal Log—BMCM Timothy Ferguson, I.N.(RET):

. . . Mrs. Carlson worries me. But I'm not sure what good stopping will do. I'm not even sure the Jacksonville people will welcome us, even with the ties we already have with them. If we stop up here, we probably won't mix with anyone else, and 13 people is just too small a group to survive on their own. So we press on, and I'll have to shoulder the responsibility. . . .

I was lying outside on the bow, trying to get some sleep. My recurring nightmare had come again, the one where I kept seeing the kid I'd killed during the Slaughter, his face frozen into a grimace of pain, and his guts streaming from his open belly.

I wasn't too surprised I had my dream. We were all pretty depressed. Mrs. Carlson had died during the day.

She'd been bedridden for weeks and finally just faded away. Freya was a wreck, and had cried herself to sleep. It made my heart ache to see her in such pain. I wished I could hold her and tell her things would be all right.

All of a sudden, I heard a shot, and bolted upright. I hollered to get folk's attention, and ran for my battle station. I looked around to see where the shot had come from, but didn't see anything. The others were rushing around, too, but it was soon quiet as everyone came to a stop at their stations, scanning the night.

Then a scream cut through the night, and all hell broke loose. It was Mrs. Liu. She'd just found Kjell Carlson. He'd taken one of the pistols and put a bullet through his head, falling across the body of his wife. Now there were only eleven of us left, and Freya, whose parents had been spared up till then, had lost them both in just a few short hours.

Mrs. Alvarez went in with Freya to comfort her and hopefully get her back to sleep. Ferguson, for some odd reason, decided that the rest of us should work through the night to fix some things on the raft. It was a darkday, so after a light breakfast, I bunked out alone in one of the cabins. Just as I was dozing off, I felt warm breath on my face, and Freya slipped into my sleeping bag with me. If she was wearing anything, it wasn't much. I tried to say something, but she put her hand over my mouth and then pulled it away and kissed me hard. I started to kiss her back when something smacked me in the back of my head. I was so tangled up with sleeping bag and girl that I could only turn my head. It was Mrs. Alvarez, shining a flashlight into my eyes.

"You should be ashamed of yourself, Jim," she scolded. "This poor girl is vulnerable, and here you are taking advantage of her."

She looked at Freya. "Honey, I know you're hurting, but this is no way to make that hurt go away. Get dressed and I'll let you stay with me."

Freya started to cry as she put on her robe and slipped

out the door. Mrs. Alvarez turned to me again. "Before you think of trying anything again, think of how we had to bury Terri Jackson. We can't afford to have little Freya pregnant."

I laid there a long time awake. My guts were churning and my head was spinning. Now that Freya was gone I felt kind of funny. It was not something I admitted, especially with the bunch I used to run around with, but I was still a virgin. I had a basic idea of what was supposed to happen, but I almost felt relieved that Mrs. Alvarez had saved me from showing my ignorance. And I couldn't believe what Freya and I were going to do just a few hours after the death of her parents. All the stupid deaths. I began to wonder if any of us would make it to the end of this journey.

Excerpt—Personal Log—BMCM Timothy Ferguson, I.N.(RET):

. . . More deaths, and worst of all a suicide. Suicide is like poison on a ship. It might as well be a contagious disease, the way it spreads depression and hopelessness. And in the midst of all our other problems, a goddamn romance seems to be brewing. This is going to take some thinking. It's a no win situation. If we break them up, they'll both be moping around for weeks. If we don't break them up, they'll be mooning around for weeks. Either way, the boy who is fast becoming my right hand man is going to be an emotional basket case. . . .

The next day, as we came off watch, Ferguson pulled me aside.

"Jim, Mrs. Alvarez had a little talk with me. I need you to be real careful with Freya. She really likes you and I know you like her, but it's not a good time for you two to get serious.

"But if you do, and you feel like it's time, I want you to remember that anything worth doing is worth doing right," he said as he tucked something into my shirt pocket.

I pulled Ferguson's little gift out that night and looked at it.

It was pill case. Inside, with a rolled up informational brochure, were twelve thirty-day sperm inhibiting contraceptive tablets all lined up in a row.

Excerpt—Personal Log—BMCM Timothy Ferguson, I.N.(RET):

. . . Under normal circumstances, I wouldn't dream of it. Carmen Alvarez will kill me if she finds out, but these are different times. I feel like the two kids getting together is inevitable, and Carmen is right about one thing, we don't need the girl pregnant. Besides, with all the deaths, who knows how long any of us will last, and who am I to deny the kids what happiness they can find in the mean time. May God forgive me if my decision is a wrong one. . . .

We passed Hell's-a-Comin' a few weeks later. Again, we slid through ruins that stretched for miles. It was so quiet it was spooky. No plants or trees were to be seen. No birds or insects moved. The shores were lined with blackened ruins and melted rock. We had a little party the next day, because the last major city on the river, and hopefully the last nuclear target the invaders had hit, was now behind us. Because of the prevailing westerly winds in this part of the valley, we no longer had to worry about the unseen threat of radiation.

The population on the riverbanks began to thin out again, and we were alone for as much as two or three days at a time. We were too wary to let our guard down, but we began to hope for perhaps the first time that we could make it where we were going.

By now the river was an old companion. It was no longer a surprise when the clear water from a stream refused to mix with the muddy waters of the Xanadu, sometimes even for miles downstream. The way we could read a snag in a ripple in the water, the way we could guess at our best route by following the trend of our leadline readings, the way we could smell bad weather a day ahead of time: all this and more built our confidence. Ferguson was backing up on discipline a little, and we began to sing and play around in the warmer weather.

Excerpt—Personal Log—BMCM Timothy Ferguson, I.N.(RET):

. . . Well, we all learned a lesson about lax discipline. We clipped a rock the other day, and bent the hell out of the prop on the cruiser. We can still run it in a pinch, but the vibrations from extended running could blow the shaft seals, and then we'd really be in trouble. This will add weeks to our trip, just as we were coming to its end.

The trouble is I'm sick and tired of being the Old Man. I don't want to keep cracking the whip, even though I have to. I just want to relax and go along with the crowd, and rest. . . .

I was on watch on a slow Sunday afternoon. It was holiday routine, and the church services which were our only planned activity on Sundays were long since over. The day was beautiful, a hot lazy brightday. Ferguson sat silently beside me on the cruiser's bridge, staring into the distance. With the engines off and the raft drifting with the current, it was one of those watches where your hand wants to rest lightly on the wheel, and it's hard to focus your attention, even though you know you have to.

"Why did you do this?" I asked suddenly.

Ferguson squinted at me under the brim of his cap. "Do what?"

"You know, help us out, come along. You were set up to do pretty good all by yourself."

He was quiet for a few minutes. A terran eagle

swooped down and pulled something long and slippery out of the river ahead of us. But before it could get too far, the thing looped itself around the wings of the eagle, and they both hit the water ass over teakettle. A few moments later the eagle struggled out of the water alone, and flew off sputtering.

We both chuckled for a moment. "Well?" I asked.

Ferguson grimaced. He wasn't one to talk, but he also wasn't one to try to weasel out of giving people an answer.

"All my life, I had the Navy. But it wasn't just the Navy, it was the people. When they retired me, I didn't know how to make ties to anybody, how to get along. Not without the Navy. But when the invaders came, I couldn't stand the thought of dying alone. People are like playing cards. They can't stand up by themselves, it only works if they lean on each other."

I didn't know what to say back to that, so we finished the watch together in silence.

Excerpt—Personal Log—BMCM Timothy Ferguson, I.N.(RET):

. . . Even with the engine casualty, we're only a couple weeks out from our destination, which is giving us all a funny feeling. The journey has lasted so many months that the raft and river are our home now, and you can see everyone acting awkwardly as they realize that our lives will soon be changing. There is a feeling of relief, too. Being past the most thickly settled parts of the river, we are in much less danger from the people of the shores. And most important, we're thousands of kilometers from the invader's base at the head of the valley. It's funny, but I'm almost sad the trip is over. Not that I'm glad all this has happened, but for the first time in my life, I am with a group of people who care about me, and I care about them. Even in the Navy, as much as I felt at home,

there were still barriers: religion, language, customs. Here
I can finally be myself, can be at peace. . . .

I guess I'll never figure out how Ferguson knew what
was happening that night. He did have our night vision
binoculars, so maybe he saw a glint in the moonlight. Or
maybe heard a distant sound . . .

It was the middle of truenight with the musky smell of
spring in the night air. Ferguson and I were out hunting,
crouched in a makeshift blind by a game trail, waiting
for something to blunder into us. We were silent and
watchful, armed with two laser rifles we had found in a
wrecked military aircraft a week before. The raft was
moored in a creek about half a kilometer behind us.

Suddenly, Ferguson stopped sweeping with the binoculars. He flinched and hissed at me through clenched
teeth.

"Jim, get out of the blind and into that stream behind
us. Roll around in the water to reduce your infrared
signature and then set up in as dense a cover you can
find to fire in front of the blind. When the time comes
to shoot, don't hesitate or you'll die."

"Wha . . . wha?" I stammered. I had no idea what was
going on.

He repeated his instructions. "Jim, we don't have
much time. Just do it," he said, and gave me a crooked
little smile, "and take care of yourself and the others."

If I'd learned one thing during our journey, it was that
when Ferguson told me to do something, I was best off
doing it. So within half a minute I was soaking wet,
huddled behind a bush, with my cheek against the stock
of my laser. Before I had any time to wonder about what
had spooked him, I saw a dim form moving down the
path, gliding silently through the night. Suddenly, as if it
could see, it turned and fired a laser into the blind. Ferguson's own laser fired wildly toward the sky. I fired
myself and my beam slashed across it. It spun and fired
back even as its guts spewed out, and my shoulder

exploded with pain. Then, as suddenly as it began, it was over. The forest was dead silent except for my panting. I walked over, giving the body another hosing with the laser as I moved forward. It was a man, but strange looking. I wondered if this was one of those Sauron supermen we'd heard rumors about from people we had passed on the river. His face bulged over the eyes, which glittered in the starlight. As I leaned over him, though, I realized that the bulge was some kind of night goggles. I pulled them off and saw what looked to be just an ordinary man. But he was also in a full combat uniform, carrying an advanced laser rifle, and the way he had moved indicated military training and experience. It seemed that we had run into some sort of military scout, one who shot first and asked questions later.

I moved into the blind and checked on Ferguson. He was a mess. There wasn't much blood, because a laser cauterizes the wounds as it makes them, but his face and chest were a twisted ruin. Now there were only ten of us left.

I blinked back tears as I put the guy's goggles on myself. The forest around me snapped into view, almost as clear as day. I didn't see any other sign of movement, but my throat was dry and my heart beat fast. This was top of the line military equipment. If this was a lone scout we were all right. If not, we could all be dead in minutes. In any event, we had to get out of here and fast. I crouched and slung Ferguson over my shoulder. I couldn't leave him out here, lonely in the dark.

When I got back, folks didn't seem to believe what had happened. They were confused and began to argue with each other. The only thing anyone was doing that made any sense was binding the laser burn on my shoulder. I tried to get them to realize the danger we were in, but they just kept arguing about who should be doing what. Finally I'd had enough.

"Quiet!" I yelled. Surprisingly, they all hushed up and

looked at me. Quite a different bunch than the ones that left on our journey so long ago. Gaunt and hard looking, but still not hard enough to cope with the loss of our leader. Suddenly I realized what Ferguson was getting at when he told me to take care of them. I remembered watching him during sleepless nights, the concern in his eyes when we faced a dangerous situation, the secret of our book and how little he really knew about the river, the way he agonized over each of us. The weight of those words fell around my shoulders like lead.

"He left me in charge," I said, stretching the truth a little. "We're facing what might be the worst situation we've faced yet, and we've got to face it ourselves. Now Freya, Nikko and Art, you get the lines ready to slip. Doc Lampson, I want you in the cruiser ready for a fast push. We might need those engines, vibrations and all. And the rest of you, break out our arms and get to your battle stations."

They all began to bustle around purposefully. I backed up to lean heavily on the wall of the shack. I was exhausted, but I had to smile at the way they all were so willing to take orders from a skinny 17 year old. Suddenly I realized that Cindi, the little Slimak girl, was staring up at me. My smile disappeared.

"What're you staring at?" I snapped, and pointed over toward the people handling the lines. "Get over there and get busy helping them."

We never saw another thing that night, and other than a brush with some rabble who tried to collect a toll from us, and a few more of the tense moments we had whenever we passed other vessels on the river, we didn't have any more trouble at all. We made it to the community where our sister church lay two weeks later. I led Mr. and Mrs. Liu, the only ones left who knew these people, up a dirt road from the river until we reached a large newly-built stockade. We hailed them and were able to come in, but under close guard. They were pretty surprised once they recognized who we were. Like we figured, they were not keen on bringing in new mouths to feed. But they considered our journey to be something of a miracle, and couldn't bear the thought of turning us out after all we had done to get there. Between that, the Liu's friendly nature, and the use of some of the "convincing skills" that Ferguson had taught me (a little bluster and a lot of bull), we soon found ourselves members of the Jacksonville Methodist Freehold and Commune. Our travels were finally over.

Epilogue

It's a long way up the hill. At times the path is so steep, and the grass so slick, that the mule almost loses his footing, and I end up bracing my feet and hauling on the bridle to keep him moving. He struggles under the load that so many other people in the commune thought was a fool's errand, the task that kept me busy through two winters. But I have someone to visit, and a debt to repay.

We climb through the long and sweaty afternoon, and at last reach the top. I pull the load off the mule's back and drag it into place at the head of the grave. My job is done, my conscience is at ease, and I can go back home to Freya and the baby. I step back to look over my handiwork and read the inscription I carved into the stone:

**Master Chief Boatswain
Timothy Ferguson,
Imperial Navy**

———

**Any man can make a rate,
but only God makes Boatswain's Mates.**

It was one of his favorite expressions. I hope that, wherever he is, he sees it and it brings him a smile.

Deathmaster Quilland allowed himself the brief luxury of a sigh wile he indulged in an even more uncommon Sauron activity: reverie. Looking out his casemated lancet window, he leaned his chin on his palm and considered the trickle of distant, milling specks that moved through the pass beneath the Citadel. That traffic was the end-product of the new Sauron reality: an endless round of tribute patrols, Havener guerrilla retributions, responsorial pacification campaigns, and then a brief period of uncertain calm—before the whole cycle began once again.

Quilland shook his head, returned to the hardcopy dossier in front of him, scowling at the coarse sheets upon which it was printed. Hardcopy instead of heads-up displays or, at the very least, computer screens: that he had lived to see it all come to this was unthinkable—which was why Deathmaster Quilland tended to repress every faint tinge of reverie that threatened to intrude upon his thoughts. But on some days, the recollection of things past was too strong to be fully dismissed. And the dossier in front of him was not helping matters.

Senior Assault Leader Ashcroft's young, promising life was summarized in the statistics that reeled out in

seemingly inexhaustible streams upon the papers before
Quilland. Written commendations supported the conclusion implied by the young Soldier's service record and test
results; he was upward bound into the command ranks.
One of the Race's brightest progeny, he was a bold young
challenger ready to meet the heartless universe on its own
terms—but with only Haven and its insufferable cattle as
the whetstone upon which to test the sharpness of his
nascent skills. Quilland shook his head again and closed
the dossier with a careless sweep of his hand. A Soldier
such as Ashcroft—the youngest officer on the *Fomoria*
when it had jumped into the Byers' System—should have
been able to look forward to a life of bright opportunities
and demanding challenges. But here on Haven—

A set of hard knuckles rapped three times against the
10-centimeter timbers of Quilland's door. The Deathmaster pushed the dossier aside, straightened, and resisted one
last urge to sigh. "Come in."

The door swung open swiftly, easily, belying its impressive mass—which Quilland knew to be in excess of two
hundred kilos. Ashcroft—fair of skin and hair—entered
with three long, sweeping steps that simultaneously suggested the grace of a dancer and the lethality of a martial
artist. "Senior Assault Leader Ashcroft reporting as
ordered, Deathmaster Quilland."

Quilland nodded. "Be seated."

Ashcroft curtly nodded his acquiescence and thanks
and slid into the severely-constructed straight-backed
chair that faced the Deathmaster's desk. Quilland noted
the fluidity of the Soldier's motion, thought, *He's aware
of his skills—enough to be proud and appreciative of them,
but not enough to be cocky. Once, years ago, had we had
another battalion of lads like him, we could have held that
beachhead on*—but that was history now, events and memories as dead as the comrades left in the brambles of that
long-forgotten landing zone on a long-forsaken world that
was untold parsecs and years distant.

"Deathmaster Quilland?"

Quilland started, found that he had been staring straight into Ashcroft's almost achromatic grey eyes. "Yes?"

"Are you—quite well, Deathmaster?"

Quilland brushed past the inquiry. "Senior Assault Leader, you are to report to your century's quartermaster for equipment assignment. You will complete requisitions for rwo platoons worth of materiél—D-grade equippage."

Ashcroft's brow rose and then fell. "An independent command—with D-grade outfitting?"

Quilland refused to show his sympathy. "Your question suggests that either your hearing is impaired or that you are disposed to questioning orders, Senior Assault Leader."

Ashcroft straightened. "Neither, Deathmaster. I was simply—surprised."

And with good reason; a young turk with your potential has every reason to expect a reasonably equipped unit for his first command. But this is Haven, and First Citizen Diettinger has other plans for you, I'm afraid. Quilland's voice and eyes retained their tenor of indifference. "You will be collecting your unit in ten hours. You will have two T-days to prepare your troopers for your mission. You are advised to spend at least one day going through full-unit drills."

"May I inquire why, Deathmaster?"

It gets worse, my poor, proud eaglet. "Your unit has not worked together prior to this assignment, Senior Assault Leader. The sixty-eight troopers have only been reorganized into a field-duty unit within the past week."

Ashcroft looked genuinely baffled. "I don't understand, Deathmaster."

"Your unit is comprised of"—Quilland almost winced as the euphemism prepared to pass his lips—" 'reassigned personnel.' " *Meaning you're getting the dregs from the bottom of the Sauron barrel, Ashcroft. Genetic preference ratings of D-3 and less, fertility ratings of seven and worse, lower bell-curve performance in terms of strength, dexterity, intellect, creativity. All the troopers of your command were once functionary types with marginal roles, such as clerks, data processors, and even maintenance assistants for now-extinct technologies: all roles that no longer exist. Of course, they are still Saurons for all of that, but—*

If Ashcroft was disappointed by learning the nature of his first command, he did not show it; he nodded once. "I understand, Deathmaster. And my mission?"

Quilland pointed over his own shoulder to the hardcopy map behind him. "You are to conduct a general reconnaissance of the mountain passes located at the juncture of the Miracle and Girdle of God mountain chains. These passes are called 'The Knots' by the cattle. You are to carry your reconnaissance through The Knots and into the tidal plain beyond. You are to follow this river"— Quilland traced the east-running blue line with his finger—"out of the pass and to the coast. There, you will assess the shore regions for general habitability, current settlement status, and natural resources."

Ashcroft blinked at Quilland's sudden conclusion. "And then, Deathmaster?"

"And then you conquer the region. You have another task in mind, perhaps?"

"No, Deathmaster."

"Very good. Yours is the first team that we are sending into this region. Shortly after beginning your mission, you will pass through the area formerly belonging to the Redfield Satrapy. You may augment your unit's basic equippage by commandeering suitable materiél from the locals there." *Assuming they have anything left that's worth commandeering—which I doubt.*

Ashcroft only nodded once. "I understand, Deathmaster."

Do you? Do you really? Do you understand that Diettinger is giving you the dregs in the hope that you'll turn them into a better unit—but also because, if your recon team is waylaid and slaughtered out in that trackless mountain wilderness, it will only be a minor military loss—and a further refinement of the overall Sauron genetic pool? Quilland returned the young officer's nod. "You have your orders, Senior Assault Leader Ashcroft. You are dismissed."

Another nod and Ashcroft rose and smoothly strode toward the door. Quilland watched the young Soldier's back, appraised and approved of the broad shoulders and otherwise rangy build that was the new model—the Haven model—of the Sauron Soldier. A promising officer—a rocket still early in its steep, rising trajectory—but flawed. *Will you reason it out, my young eagle? Will the knowledge catch you quickly, before you leave on your mission? Or will it come to you later, on some lonely grey mountainside of treacherously damp slate? Can't you guess why Diettinger is willing to risk you on such a low-priority mission, Ashcroft? Are you so truly the Sauron ideal, so willing to obey, to trust the wisdom of your superiors, and never once consider what your orders imply about how those superiors see you—that they might know more about Senior Assault Leader Ashcroft than he knows about himself?*

Ashcroft's grey uniformed back disappeared around the doorjamb. Quilland sighed, opened the young officer's dossier, looked down at the Breedmaster's report one more time. Brave young Ashcroft; always in the thick of it, even as a young trooper. Always where the action was hot—and the radiation intense. Breedmaster Caius was not certain whether it had been the repeated battlefield exposures or some other problem—such as a xenovirus—but the fertility results were indisputable.

And because we're on Haven, they're also unalterable— which was why the results were suppressed. Ten years ago, Ashcroft, we could have given you back the posterity resident in your own genes. But now, there is no chance of it. You are another victim of our exile on Haven, another grand ideal lost forever, flawed only in your inability to recreate that ideal in the form of a successive generation. And because of that, my bold young eagle, you are relegated to the level of a tool— a thing we will use and consult and call comrade and even Deathmaster (maybe, someday). But you and your legacy are already dead to us, as are the sons and daughters who might have been yours, but for a few too many rads on some inauspicious day several years ago.

Quilland scowled at the documents once again and closed the dossier slowly. He turned and looked out the window at the lilliputian rivulet of tribute that meandered slowly past his eyrie and into the Shangri-La Valley. He sighed again—but didn't even realize it.

THE GIFT OF THE MAGI
Charles E. Gannon

Perhaps the night had suddenly grown darker, or perhaps he was blacking out due to blood loss; whatever the reason, Emmanuel Knecht felt himself lose balance and fall forward. As he hit the frigid ground, the pain in his left shoulder surged and then burst beyond its former periphery. The pain washed down through his left lung, and a taste of bitter copper rose into his mouth. Emmanuel was mildly surprised to discover that he was able to trace the progress of each new sensation with an almost luxurious detachment. He didn't even flinch when the crossbow bolt in his left shoulder grated against the frozen earth and pushed through another centimeter of muscle and sinew: that was a bad sign.

The woman was the first to reach him. With a strength that seemed incongruous in her spare frame, she grasped his right upper arm and rolled him over. He closed his eyes as his entire weight was momentarily poised upon his left side; he felt the splintered ends of his shattered collarbone brush against each other. As those conductive points of pain made their brief contact, he felt rather than saw an excruciating, absolute whiteness. But part of his mind remained far away from that actinic agony—a part that kept asking, *Why doesn't it hurt more?*

Then Knecht felt the earth against his back and the pain faded, but the brightness grew. Emmanuel allowed his eyelids to open slightly; the woman's lantern—mostly covered—shone in his eyes. He calmly thought, *She'll get us all killed,* and then clawed at the light with his right hand, trying to knock it away.

His hand refused to respond as intended. His attempt to slap aside the lantern manifested as a weak, sweeping gesture, as though he was merely trying to ward off the illumination. However, this feeble effort produced the desired result; she lifted her cloak to cover the lantern. But not before he saw her face more clearly, more proximally, than he had thus far: high, slightly weathered cheekbones framed by sandy blond hair faintly streaked with grey—well-preserved, considering she was a woman in her early twenties.

A *woman* in her early twenties; ten years ago, some recidivistic male bureaucrats—willfully clinging to their socially-incorrect ways—still insisted upon calling women in their early twenties "girls." And, ten years ago, there was a certain physiognomic logic to their choice of words; back then, most women of twenty-five were fresh-faced and smooth-cheeked, their bodies graced with sweeping curves that bespoke a healthy mix of fat and muscle. But all that was before the arrival of the Saurons. Now, childhood was over before it had a chance to begin; girls were women by age fifteen.

Above her flesh-taut cheekbones, the woman's eyes roved back and forth, watching Knecht for signs of consciousness. Hers were sad eyes, he thought; they were grey-blue and bracketed by crow's feet, each talon-like crease a *memento mori* of something forever lost. Parents, siblings, friends, virtues: their passings were recorded where her tears had mourned them.

The man who travelled with the woman approached

and looked over her shoulder at Emmanuel. "He alive?" the man asked her.

She nodded. "But not by much. We've got to stop."

Emmanuel shook his head; they both started. "I'm still conscious. Help me up."

The woman hesitated but the man moved forward and took hold of Knecht under the left armpit. Flaring pain engulfed Emmanuel's left lung, arced up his neck and then into the left temple. The woman came to support him on the right side, and, swaying between the two of them, Emmanuel straightened his legs. He smiled and nodded. The man and woman stepped aside. Emmanuel thought about taking a step, but someplace between the thought and the first motion, the surrounding darkness folded in upon him and the starry sky spun like a celestial pinwheel. Knecht fell, tried to get up again, but he couldn't; the woman was holding him down. "Be still now," she told him. There were tears in her voice.

The man walked off, muttered a single word: "Damn." It was clear to him that Emmanuel was not going any farther. When the man spoke again, it was in a tight, still voice. "They're going to find us—find us and kill us."

"Be quiet," the woman whispered.

His response was hushed, but obstinately grim. "They're going to kill us."

Emmanuel swallowed, noticed how dry his throat had become, and turned his head away. So close, so close, and still no way to get help. But maybe that was a blessing in disguise. This way, he could not be tempted to disregard the secrecy protocols, could not expose the others who were awaiting his return. Knecht had run out of the easy answers to which he might succumb—the kind of easy answers that had gotten him into this predicament in the first place.

Knecht had spotted them just as dusk was closing in: a man and a woman setting up camp. Even at a distance, Emmanuel could see that they were haggard and weary, and all his training—and instincts—told him, *Don't stop. Don't get involved with a pair of doomed refugees that you can't help anyway. Don't take stupid risks; you're almost home.* But when she looked up, saw him, and waved—*waved*—Knecht could not help himself; he had to go to them. He could have been anyone or anything: a Sauron, a bandit—hell, there were even rumors of cannibals in the area. Nevertheless, she had offered Knecht a timeless human gesture of greeting. It marked her as a good person—and too ingenuous to survive in outlands roamed by petty warlords, marauders, and, possibly, Saurons. She and her travelling companion were just bodies waiting to be harvested—unless Emmanuel intervened.

So Knecht made his first mistake: he joined them. He helped them light their fire (using a flint striker; the waterproof matches would come later—if they seemed to be the right sort of people), and asked them where they were bound. The man's vague answers and largely inaccurate geographical references informed Emmanuel that this couple really didn't know where they were going. And that meant—in the darkest sense of the idiom—that they were going nowhere fast. Maybe, if they had been mean-spirited or rude, Knecht might have moved on, but instead, they offered him an equal share of their food and invited him to camp with them for the night. Emmanuel accepted the food with genuine gratitude—and a gnawing sense that he was now obligated to help them.

That's when he made his second mistake—when he saw, and opted for, the "easy" answer, thereby violating every bit of wisdom that four years on Haven had imparted to him: he offered to travel with them for a day or two. He did not mention how close he was to his home, what that home was, or that he was hoping that maybe—just maybe—they could become a part of his community. All he offered them was his fellowship and another mouth to feed, but they welcomed and agreed

to his offer. Good people, all right—too good to survive
very long on their own.

As the blackness of truenight grew thicker, he listened
to their story. They had started as a group of fourteen,
the only survivors of a Sauron raid upon their town. For
several months, they bounced from one site of semi-
civilization to another, running before the continually rising tide of famine and disease that characterized the
third year of the Sauron occupation. In the end, they
decided to abandon the Shangri-La Valley entirely. They
struck for the east coast: a dangerous journey, but one
which they felt would put them beyond the scope of the
Sauron depredations. They followed the River Jordan to
Little Crater Fork, a craggy cleft where the Madigan
River joins the outflow from the mountain-bound Crater
Lake. Saurons and sickness had reduced their number to
nine by that point. Two more were lost in the narrow
ravines flanking the Madigan River's northeasterly
upstream course. Two hundred kilometers south of that
source, the survivors left the ravine network and
ascended into the rugged, rolling highlands that were
known as The Knots. Two months and three more of the
refugees were lost as they navigated those winding
passes, the Miracle Mountains soaring towards the clouds
on their right, the peaks of the God's Girdle jutting
upward on their left. The last four survivors eventually
came to the humble upland source of the Widebay River
and began a twisting descent to the east coast. Slippery
footing near a waterfall claimed one refugee, and the
cliff lions got another. The last two—the man and the
woman—had pushed on until, four days ago, they topped
a bluff carpeted with wireweed and saw the sun rising
over a distant ocean: the Eastern Sea—and their
destination.

Emmanuel smiled, nodded, thought: *How can I tell
them that their destination has doom written broad
across its untamed tidal flats? That it's teeming with land
gators, covered by swards of deadly firegrass? That its*

coastline is a wild, wind-blasted heath, haunted by the banshee-like cries of carrion-seeking stobors? All that, and winter is following hard upon their arrival in this dubious paradise. What word of hope can I offer them? An assurance that the Saurons aren't interested in the east coast? True for now—but what about next year?

And that had been Emmanuel's third and critical error: to assume that he—or anyone—could ever assert with any accuracy what the Saurons were and weren't interested in.

Two hours after sunset, they heard horses approaching. Because they *could* hear the horses, Knecht knew that it was already too late to do anything constructive. However, the male refugee apparently had not yet learned the basic facts about night combat. So, when he rose up brandishing his spear, Emmanuel sent a palm-edged chop into the back of his right knee. The man crumpled backward, spitting out a curse—which died in mid-utterance; less than thirty meters away, a rifle barked. A bullet whispered through the space the man's torso had occupied only a moment before.

Three, possibly four, seconds later, a Sauron with an assault rifle emerged from the darkness, the weapon's barrel sweeping back and forth with the regularity of a cold, grey metronome. Another Sauron galloped in shortly after, leading his partner's horse by the reins. Theirs had been a standard Sauron tactic, one that Knecht had seen many times before. Under the cover of darkness, a single sniper silently insinuated himself into close range. Then, the main body—in this case, the horseman—began a slow, noisy advance. When the enemy's leaders and combat-capable personnel started to react, the sniper went to work, trying to eliminate as many as possible.

As the second Sauron began to dismount, the sniper took a particular interest in Emmanuel; the black abyss of the rifle's flash suppressor had centered on his chest. Knecht sat very still, letting his loose black robes obscure and thereby diminish his round-muscled frame—a frame that would have told a Sauron observer: *This one eats well and regularly, even better than you do*. The sniper's attention remained on Knecht a moment longer, and then the barrel began to drift in the direction of the male refugee, who had—unwisely—glanced at his fallen spear. The rifleman took a frost-crunching step forward, and Emmanuel, feeling himself momentarily unobserved, conducted a rapid assessment of the tactical situation.

Two Saurons. One armed with a six-millimeter assault rifle, currently at seven meters range and closing. The other, at eleven meters range and tying the horses, was currently unarmed, although a readied light crossbow was hanging next to his saddle. Both Saurons had enough gear on their horses to support brief independent operations, but not enough to suggest that they were living off the land. That made them advance scouts—outriders for a larger unit. However, that unit was probably on a low-priority mission; there was only the one primitive, small-calibre firearm between the two scouts—well beneath standard Sauron ordnance ratios.

The sniper took another step, the frozen wireweed crackling like broken glass under his boot. Emmanuel felt a bead of sweat trickle out of his armpit, snake wetly down his side; he had to act. Not for himself, not for the refugees, but for the people at home: the people who were depending upon him to ensure their safety by protecting their secrecy—even at the expense of his own life. Knecht waited for the Sauron sniper's third step, waited for the frost to crackle. As it did, Emmanuel thumbed back the hammer on the revolver he held concealed within the folds of his travelling mantle.

The hammer's metallic *clik-clak* blended into the shattering of the wireweed, and the sniper, ears filled with his own noisy progress, did not pick out the sound. However, his comrade started, made a half-turn in Emmanuel's direction, and then spun back toward his horse, his

hand an eye-defying blur as he lunged for his crossbow.
The sniper—hearing his partner's swift, combat-paced
movements—froze, alert but obviously perplexed.

Emmanuel felt time slow down as he raised his hands
toward each other. His left palm locked into place
beneath and behind his right-handed hold upon the
revolver. He had to get both of the Saurons: otherwise,
they'd discover everything. They'd discover that the
revolver was of recent die-cast manufacture. They'd discover that the barrel was cold-rolled, that the propellant
was nitrocellulose based. In short, they'd discover that
their campaign of technological expunction had missed
at least one community capable of creating weapons
which could challenge their domination of Haven.

Even as the revolver's hammer was falling, Knecht saw
that the sniper's head was already turning back in his
direction, the muzzle of the assault rifle trailing slightly
behind. The roar from Knecht's pistol obliterated all
other sound and the 11-millimeter magnum hollowpoint
slug opened up a red crater just to the right of the Sauron's sternum. The Sauron wobbled but the assault rifle
continued to swivel toward Knecht.

Emmanuel's second shot wasn't as clean. Fighting
against the resistance of the uncocked hammer put his
shot high; it punched a gushing hole through the Sauron's upper left lung. The assault rifle started chattering,
but Knecht's hit had rocked the Sauron backward; the
muzzle rose, bullets whining overhead into the darkness.
Emmanuel leaned into the revolver, exhaled, and
squeezed the trigger sharply; the top of the Sauron's
head disappeared. Then the body toppled backward, the
assault rifle stuttering fitfully for one last moment.

Emmanuel swung toward the second Sauron—who
locked eyes with him over the taut, drawn arms of a
loaded crossbow. Knecht heard the weapon's string sing
and the shuttle slap forward—just as the rim of his
revolver's muzzle superimposed itself upon the Sauron's

chest. Knecht snapped the trigger back—and felt, as well as heard, the world explode.

The detonation was in his left shoulder. He tried to breathe, couldn't. Heard someone running toward him, then realized it was the sound of his own feet kicking against the ground as he told himself *Get up Get up Get up*—but couldn't. Then he could breathe again. Did so and almost passed out when the crossbow bolt grated against a splinter of clavicle. That triggered a second detonation of all-consuming pain: a silent detonation, this time—except for a scream which, he realized a moment later, was his own. Then another gunshot, this time from the assault rifle. He raised his head, dizzy from the pain that the movement produced in his shoulder. The woman was standing over the crossbowman, the assault rifle aimed down at his inert form. Then the male refugee grabbed Knecht, helped him up, and told the woman not to waste ammunition: a revolver shot to the heart and a rifle shot to the head had to be lethal—even to Saurons.

Emmanuel remembered insisting that they throw the first Sauron's body on the fire and then drive off the horses. Lacking the strength to explain why, he waved off their questions and took his first stumbling step into the darkness—and toward the sea. They called after him, surprised, worried; "Where are you going?"

He turned, almost fell, croaked, "Home." He started to run again. A moment later, he heard their footfalls join the cadence of his own.

They had covered eight kilometers since then. Emmanuel was sure of that much: he could hear the sibilant rush of the Widebay river from where he lay. But that still left at least five kilometers to the coast, and he couldn't make that distance under his own power. No way to build a litter: nothing but wireweed nearby, and nothing but the stobor-infested darkness beyond that. And after the Saurons finished tracking the two horses, their main body would be in hard pursuit. Emmanuel looked at the woman, discovered that she was looking at him again, her eyes deep and unreadable. "Help me to sit up," he requested.

She put down the lantern, placed a hand behind both of his shoulders and drew him toward her. Emmanuel felt the bolt shift, but it did not scrape against any of the shattered bones. As she removed her hands, he allowed himself to sag forward slightly, letting his waist bear the weight of his torso. He looked up, saw that the man had squatted down alongside the woman. His eyes were wide, bright, restless. The woman's gaze remained steady, as though she was waiting for Emmanuel to say something.

Emmanuel cleared his throat. "I have a plan." The man's eyes quickly focused on Knecht. "It is a plan that will save some of us, but you must be prepared to do whatever is necessary in order for it to work."

The man's eyes widened for a moment, then his jaw set and his eyes narrowed; "If it's necessary, I'll do it."

Good, thought Emmanuel. *He may not be much of a thinker, but he has courage enough to be prepared to offer his life in exchange for ours—or at least, for hers.* Emmanuel looked at the woman, who had not yet responded. She nodded slowly, her voice low and hoarse, "Yes. I'll do what must be done."

Emmanuel sighed, nodded, produced a thimble-sized plastic container from within the folds of his cloak. He unscrewed the top of the container and shook four small, cream-colored spheres into his palm. The woman's eyes grew large; evidently, she knew what she was witnessing and understood its larger significance. Knecht swallowed the home-made aspirin in a single gulp, aware that the woman was now following his every movement with keen interest.

The man held out a battered canteen; "Here. Pills go down easier with water." He had not noticed what his travelling companion had; that the pills were not of pre-Sauron manufacture.

Emmanuel waved the canteen away. "Thank you, but I'm fine. In order for this plan to work, I have to tell you a story—"

The man's mouth fell open. "You have to *what*?"

"Tell you a story."

"With the Saurons right behind us? We don't have time to listen to any—"

The voice that cut in was the woman's; "Shut up." The man stammered, and then fell silent. The woman inclined her head, but her eyes never left Emmanuel's. "Please," she said, "tell us your story."

Emmanuel resisted the urge to lean back as the pressure of poignant memories gathered in his chest. Closing his eyes, he sought for words that would relieve him of that crushing weight. . . .

Vera ran a hand down her leg, spreading the sweat of a two-kilometer jog into an even, shiny (and not unattractive, thought Knecht) thigh-coating layer. A second pass—this time with a towel—removed the gleam and brought Knecht back from the edge of an undefined sexual fantasy. Vera, noting his rapt attention, smiled and reiterated her question—which he had obviously not heard. "So why *should* anyone want to live on Haven? I'd think that people would rather live here instead."

"Here? On Ayesha? Where we get our food, our air, and our warmth from machines?"

"And what's so bad about machines?" Vera's tone had become slightly more severe, but her brow was still smooth, her eyes animated and almost . . . playful?

Knecht felt his brow wrinkle while his mouth smiled— an incongruous combination that reflected his puzzlement over Vera's seemingly contradictory social signals. "There's nothing wrong with machines—when they're operating properly. But if they cease to function and one is completely dependent upon them, then—"

"—then one calls a repairman."

"Yes—if there's a repairman around to call. The war with the Saurons—"

"—is far away from here. Nothing is going to happen to us outbackers, Emmanuel. Byers' System has nothing that the Saurons want. Besides, the Imperium will win: it must."

Knecht shrugged. "Perhaps. But even if it does, how much of the Imperium will be left when the war is over? Will there even *be* an Imperium? You've heard the latest stories, Vera: whole worlds have been cut off from Imperial contact and are backsliding into a second Dark Age—worse than the one which occurred after the break-up of the CoDominium."

She nodded, some of the mischief gone from her bright eyes. "Yes, I've heard those stories, Emmanuel—but perhaps that's all they are: stories."

"I wish I could believe that, but I can't. I don't see how anyone can. Particularly you."

Vera's brow furrowed. "What do you mean?"

"Well, I hear that even you pilots are having repair and maintenance problems, now."

Vera's light blue eyes sharpened, studied his face closely. "Where did you hear that?"

Knecht brushed past her inquiry. "From what I've heard, over a third of Ayesha's tankers and shuttles are currently grounded due to 'primary failures.' Do you deny that?"

Vera looked away, then shook her head: no.

Knecht continued gently. "Where, then, are the spare parts you need for repairs? On back order, like everything else around here."

"The spare parts are coming with the next supply shipment."

"So said the captain of the last Imperial transport that passed through. And that was—what?—almost ten months ago? That makes the current supply ship almost half a year overdue."

Vera would not look directly at him now. "What are

you saying, Emmanuel?" Her voice was small, nearly lost within the faint hum of the motors which kept the spin gym—a massive rotunda—turning at a stately two revolutions per minute.

Knecht shrugged. "I am saying that it makes no sense to wait and see if the Imperium will come apart; it's already starting to do so. We haven't been able to get replacement parts down in life support for almost four years now. And don't believe what the administrators are telling you about 'integral ecological viability;' hydroponic self-sufficiency is a failure—at least insofar as establishing a closed bioloop is concerned." Without thinking, Emmanuel put his hand atop Vera's to add emphasis to his conclusion. "Don't you see? One day, the Imperial ships will stop coming—and on that day, we will all begin to die."

Knecht saw his argument affect her—or rather, he saw that Vera was affected, and assumed that her response was caused by his argument. Vera, who was staring down at Knecht's hand, raised her eyes back to his. "But, Emmanuel, how could Ayeshans survive down on Haven? It's cold, inhospitable—and crawling with bandits. And what about the gravity? How long do you think I would last?" She drew her hands away and placed them on her unusually slim hips—a physiological trait common to most persons who had been born and raised in low-gee environments.

Knecht resisted the sudden impulse to place his hands on hers once again. "You were raised in a half-gee; living on Haven would take some adaptation, but you'd make it."

"Would I? Here I am, exhausted by a ten minute jog in a one-gee environment." She swept her hand around to indicate the entirety of the spin gym. As she did, the entrance—an iris portal located in the rotunda's hub—dilated, admitting three individuals in sweat suits. The shortest one was an almost ghost-thin woman. She was laughing loudly, assertively, head tossing back, a

tightly-braided pony-tail swishing in a raven blur; Janine
Chattaburray. In almost every aspect—physiognomy, per-
sonality, politics—she was Knecht's outspoken antithesis.
He refocused his attention on Vera.

And found that she had followed his gaze toward Janine Chattaburray. She smiled faintly; "A friend of yours?"
Her voice indicated that she knew otherwise, but there
was another, subtler, tonal component that suggested—
what? Uncertainty? Concern? Maybe even rivalry?

Knecht merely uttered a cross between a grunt and a
laugh. "I'd expect that she's much more your friend than
mine. Janine is not fond of my views—or of me."

Vera looked back at Janine, who seemed to have
noticed Knecht from the corner of her eye, but did not
look directly at either him or his companion. "Janine—
my friend?" echoed Vera dubiously. "No, I think not."
When she turned back to face Knecht, she wore a small,
enigmatic smile.

Knecht, perplexed by Vera's response to Janine, simply
bored back into the core of their conversation. "Even
people born here on Ayesha, in less than point one-five
gees, could survive on Haven. Or, to be more specific,
they could survive at Castalia, where there are neutral-
buoyancy tanks specially designed for low-gee—"

"Emmanuel, you speak of Castalia as though it actually
exists." A look of mild incredulity evicted a little of
Vera's smile.

"Castalia does exist. I—rather, *we*—have documenta-
tion that shows it to be—"

"—a pie-in-the-sky pipe dream," finished a new
female voice.

Emmanuel did not have to look up to identify the
speaker: it was Janine. But—as he always did—he looked
up anyway. The wispy zero-gee worker had approached
to within a few meters, hands on hips, and flanked by
two much-larger male friends. Knecht nodded, acknowledged her with a single word: "Janine."

She didn't even look at him, but concentrated her

brown-black eyes on Vera. "I thought you had more sense than to waste your time with Ayesha's most prominent 'evangelist of the absurd.' " There was an extra measure of archness in her tone—apparently aimed at Vera herself. "Has he tried to recruit you into his precious 'Castalia Society' yet?"

"No," Vera answered, her enigmatic smile returning. "Not yet."

This response seemed to irritate Janine. "I had thought better of you, Tekla." She spat out Vera's family name as though it were a curse.

Vera's smile broadened. "Whatever you might think of me, you obviously approve of my taste."

Janine's chocolate-brown complexion darkened. "Your taste? Tekla, the only taste you seem to have is a taste for humiliation—and self-destruction. Do you know what the rest of the piloting staff will say when they learn that you've been listening to this mumbo-jumbo Castalia crap?"

"Frankly, I don't care what they say."

Janine leaned forward sharply, aggressively, her voice lowered to a sharp hiss. "Tekla, I don't think you're getting the message; I've got enough political connections to make *sure* that you care what the other pilots are saying." Janine leaned forward another few centimeters, the tip of her nose only a few millimeters away from Vera's; the challenge was unmistakable.

Knecht rose and stepped forward, crowding Janine back. "That's enough." He had meant it as a command; it came out as a snarl. Janine turned, eyes bright and fists clenched, but there was a quality to her facical expression that Knecht didn't understand, an eagerness that seemed oddly reminiscent of arousal.

The two of them stood toe to toe for the better part of a second. Then the thinner of Janine's male companions shoved forward, trying to interpose himself—but, not being accustomed to a full-gravity environment, he overcompensated; he tumbled toward Knecht. Knecht foresaw the unintentional contact and brought his hands up—reflexively—to steady himself—but he also foresaw the misunderstanding that would surely follow. Janine saw it, too; over the thin man's shoulder, Emmanuel saw her expression change. Excitement transformed into dread and her eyes shaped a clear message of regret; *No—I didn't mean for this to happen.*

The thin man bumped solidly into Emmanuel, who used his hands to ward off some of that impact—a response that Janine's protector felt as a retaliatory shove. For a moment, there was indecision in the zero-geer's eyes—indecision regarding Emmanuel's intent, indecision about how to respond. Then Janine's companion abandoned the uncertainty of thought for the clarity of action; he swung a haymaker at Knecht.

Knecht ducked the blow easily and straight-armed the man in the abdomen. The zero-geer went down, but his larger friend was already in motion: he dove forward and bore Emmanuel to the ground. As they landed, the attacker's left elbow sank deep into Knecht's gut. Then, with surprising swiftness, his right fist came around and slammed into Emmanuel's left cheekbone.

Knecht's world flickered and became uncertain. Women were shouting. Another voice—a male voice that he recognized but could not place—was saying *Stop I'm warning you Stop*. Knecht saw the big zero-geer's fist draw back again, cocking like the hammer of a pistol—

But the poised fist did not fall; another hand had locked around the zero-geer's wrist. That new hand pulled, twisted, and wrenched the fist out of sight, around and behind the zero-geer's own back. The big man emitted a grunt of pain, rising to a crouch as he tried to wriggle out of the armlock, thereby giving Knecht a clear view of his rescuer: Owen Trainor. Knecht smiled; Owen's presence meant that the fight was going to be brief—very brief.

Evidently, Owen's reputation was not universal knowledge amongst zero-geers. Knecht's first assailant regained his feet and angled in toward Owen, fist back for a blow—but Owen moved first. He rose up on the ball of one foot, half spun, and swept his other foot out, up, and around; toe angled inward, Owen's boot plunged deep into the zero-geer's solar plexus. The slap of the impact was accompanied by a whoosh of expelled air; the thin man crashed to the floor, wheezing for breath.

Then Emmanuel was aware of Vera kneeling at his side, her face close to his, her breath warm and sweet and so pleasant to feel that he didn't notice how much his head hurt when she helped him back to his feet. Owen released the large zero-geer with an outward twist, sending him back toward Janine. Owen nodded at her. "Why don't you and your friends move along, Ms. Chattaburray?"

Janine answered with a defiant glare. "Why blame it on us, Trainor? We didn't start anything. But your friend is a little oversensitive—particularly when it comes to his precious Castalia."

"He's 'oversensitive'?" Owen's response was as flat and sharp-edged as slate. "Maybe your memory needs a little refreshing, Chattaburray. Emmanuel's father died searching for Castalia—left him without any family to speak of. That makes him the last direct descendant of Castalia's founder, Jonathan Knecht. For good or for bad, Castalia's shaped his whole life, so you tell me: is Emmanuel really 'oversensitive'—or are you just *in*sensitive?"

Janine opened her mouth for a retort, but first, she stole a quick glance at Knecht. At the mention of his father, Emmanuel's eyes had gone blank—as blank as a dead man's. Janine closed her mouth slowly, stared at Owen, at Vera, and then motioned for her two protectors to follow her out of the spin gym.

Owen turned to look at Emmanuel. "You okay?"

Knecht shook off the memories of his father and nodded—which hurt. "Yeah, I guess."

Owen shook his head. "This has got to stop, Manny. You're making trouble for all of us."

Knecht nodded again. "Yes; I know."

"Emmanuel did nothing wrong." There was indignation in Vera's voice. "She—Janine—came over to us, looking for a confrontation. With me."

One half of Owen's mouth curved into a smile. "Oh?" He and Vera looked at each other for a long moment, then she smiled and looked away. Owen let his partial smile spread to the other half of his mouth and nodded. "I see. Well, Manny, maybe this is a special case. So don't sweat it. But you've got to be careful where—and how loudly—you get on your soapbox. Overdo it, and you'll undermine everything we're working for." Owen took a step back, raised a hand. "I'll see you—both of you—later on." He smiled again—almost as mysteriously as Vera, Knecht thought—and then left.

Vera, looking after Owen, asked, "What did he mean, 'undermine everything we're working for?'"

Emmanuel sighed. "This is not the first time I've gotten into a fight because of my—beliefs. And when I get into a fight, that causes problems for the other members of the Castalia Society."

Vera leaned her head to the side. "So what is this 'Castalia Society?'"

Knecht smiled. "I'm surprised you haven't heard of it, considering you've been on Ayesha for almost four years now."

"Five; almost *five* years. I've heard of Castalia, but this is the first time someone has mentioned a 'society.'"

"Well, we're not exactly popular with other Ayeshans, so we don't advertise a great deal. Sorry; that's a misleading understatement: we don't advertise at all."

"You mean you're some sort of secret society?"

Knecht laughed. "We couldn't be 'secret' even if we wanted to. One of our membership requirements is that each of us spends at least twenty hours in the spin gym each week."

Vera stared. "That's four times the standard requirement."

Emmanuel nodded. "Yes. So if you see a muscle-heavy person in the spin-gym every day of the week, it's a good bet that he—or she—is a Society member. But I guess we have become somewhat insular, even reclusive, over the years. Not because we want to, but because other Ayeshans don't want to hear what we have to say."

"Which is?"

Knecht sighed; moment of truth. Well, what was the worst that could happen? One more scornful rejection could hardly make a difference. And yet, it was different with Vera; it was important to him—*personally* important—that she did not consider him a crackpot. Aware that his hands were trembling slightly, he clasped them together and forged ahead. "The Castalia Society feels that we—the entire population of Ayesha—should relocate to Haven: in specific, to Castalia. That wasn't how we started out; for years, we just wanted to rediscover Castalia's location, maybe go back and visit. But then the Imperium showed signs of coming apart, so the Society started thinking that, maybe, the time had come to move back to Castalia."

"You really think that your ancestors lived in this legendary Camelot-under-the-sea?"

"I don't think it; I know it. We have journals, letters, other documents which prove that Castalia did—does— exist. We even have evidence that some of our forefathers continued to visit Castalia as caretakers up until a hundred-fifty years ago."

Vera nodded. "And you think that Ayeshans—even the zero-geers—would be better off down there if the Imperium collapses?"

"Absolutely. That's why Castalia was founded in the first place—as a refuge for the workers who were forced to abandon the CoDominium's fueling station here on Ayesha. When the CoDominium fell apart, those Ayeshans faced the same problems we're facing today: no way to guarantee life support, food, essential natural resources. So they went to the only place where all those

things are available; our sister moon, Haven." Emmanuel
nervously touched one of Vera's hands to add emphasis.
"I know it sounds like an extreme solution, maybe even
a crazy one, but it worked for my ancestors. It saved
their lives—and I'm sure that if we can rediscover Castalia's precise location, it can save us too."

Vera's response was a slow smile—the most enigmatic
one yet. "How quixotic," she said. Then she put her
other hand on top of his. "Tell me more."

The woman shrunk deeper into her mantle. "I thought
the Saurons destroyed the fuel station before landing
on Haven."

Emmanuel's responding nod was shallow. "They did."

"Then did you leave Ayesha before they attacked?"

"No."

"Then how did any of you survive?"

Emmanuel smiled. "We owe our lives to mechanical
failures. A year before the Saurons came, our interplanetary transmitter died; our radar had gone even earlier.
So when the Saurons arrived, they didn't detect any signs
of a spacefaring community on Ayesha."

"What about your small craft operations? And your
power generation?"

"They hit us when we were half-way through a one-
week maintenance cycle. Life support was being drawn
from battery reserves while we refitted the fusion reactor.
And the small craft—those few that were still operational—were being refurbished."

The man drew his eyes away from the surrounding
darkness, fixed them on Emmanuel. "I heard that the
Saurons used a nuke on the station. So whether they
knew you were there or not, it shouldn't have mattered
much; you should have been slagged along with everything else."

Emmanuel shook his head—carefully, lest he jar his
shattered collarbone. "The fueling station itself was not
on Ayesha. It was at the end of a thirty-kilometer tether.

We cracked and purified the hydrogen on Ayesha, then pumped it through tubes up to the station. That way, the big ships could take on fuel directly, which was a lot faster than shuttling tankers to and from the surface of Ayesha.

"So, when the Saurons hit, they only targeted the automated station at the end of the tether. My guess is that they probably thought the ground facility was automated too, so they didn't bother to hit us."

"You all survived?" The woman's slightly widened eyes hinted at a tentative measure of hope.

Emmanuel was sorry to disappoint her. "No. Even though the Saurons vaporized most of the station, there was still plenty of debris—and most of it landed right on top of us . . ."

"Say again your last message, Knecht. You're breaking up."

"I am approaching the bulkhead now, Control. I see no signs of excessive structural damage. I should be able to reestablish pressure integrity in this section. Over."

Knecht's repeated message had even less success getting through than the original. There was a crackle of static, and then, "Knecht? Please copy, Knecht; over."

"I copy, Control. Are you guys reading *me*?"

Evidently, they weren't; there was a long pause before Control's next message. "Knecht, if you can hear me, turn around; we are not receiving your transmissions. I repeat; return to section R-17 and unsuit. You've done everything you can."

Emmanuel turned off his vacuum suit's helmet speaker; no use listening to orders he wasn't going to obey. Fixing broken bulkheads was only part of the reason he was out here, anyway. He launched into a long, gliding leap that carried him within a hand's breadth of the flickering overhead fluorobars. He drifted toward the emergency bulkhead, where hazard lights were pulsing red, rapid, and desperate—like a racing heart. There would have been a loud klaxon to accompany the strobing lights—had there been air enough for the sound to reach him. As his long lateral fall brought him closer to the bulkhead, he could see why it hadn't closed all the way; a dark mass was jammed between the edge of the massive pressure door and the groove designed to receive it.

A discordant, two-toned chime sounded in his helmet. Knecht sighed; he might be able to turn off the radio, but there was no getting rid of the air depletion alarm. He hoped he wouldn't need more than five minutes to unjam the bulkhead, or else he might—

The overhead fluorobars pulsed once—a sharp spasm of painful whiteness—and then they went dead. Knecht pawed at his left gauntlet, fingers fumbling to find the control stud for his helmet lights. One of the zero-geer vacuum techs could have hit it on the first try, but they virtually lived in their suits. Knecht—and the other Society members—had been excluded from full-vacuum work details for more than a year now: more proof that they were being relegated to the status of second-class citizens.

Knecht finally found the control stud; a single luminous shaft cut through the dark and painted a blue-white circle on the rapidly approaching bulkhead door. Knecht reached out a hand, dragged it along the wall; his rate of approach diminished. Five meters away from the bulkhead, he half-rolled and reached out a hand toward the dark object obstructing the bulkhead. The mass was irregular in shape, but not angular. Although primarily a dark maroon-brown, there were other colors evident: patches of white, red, and green—the texture of which suggested some sort of fabric. He reached out, locked his hand around a stumpy brown protuberance, and tugged; the protrusion came off with a brittle snap. Knecht brought the object up into the light. Despite the bulbous distortion, despite the seamed and ruptured surface, despite the almost pumice-like texture, Knecht immediately realized that he was holding a young child's arm.

A rainstorm of putrid globules—his own vomit—splashed off the inside of the helmet's visor as he hurled the little limb away. He clawed at the wall, pulling himself backward, heart hammering, breath loud and rapid in his ears. Then he felt the deck come up softly under his buttocks; Ayesha's feeble gravity had pulled him down. He let himself fall all the way back, let himself lay flat while he told himself that everything would be all right. He just had to take it easy, take it one step at a time. He'd finish this bulkhead, get a new charge of air, and then he'd continue his search for Vera. Or maybe she had already called in. Or had reached the pressurized levels while he was out looking for her. Anything was possible—anything except the thought that she might be among the dead. Surely she was not among the dead. That simply *wasn't* possible. He wouldn't *let* it be possible. He wouldn't.

The persistent, two-toned air depletion alarm was what finally brought Knecht back to an awareness of his surroundings. He rose into a sitting position, studied the mass that kept the bulkhead from closing. Now that he knew to look for it, he could see that it was comprised of at least five separate corpses. Flesh pulped by exposure to vacuum, they had frozen into a tangled melange of bloated torsos and limbs, brown-black from deoxygenation and dehydration of blood and tissue. Riven shirtsleeves and pant legs offset the gruesome organic components.

Knecht drew his legs under him and pushed slightly; he floated slowly toward the shattered mass of humanity. Reaching around, he removed a pry-bar from the brace of tools mounted on the side of his life-support unit. As he came within a meter of the mass, he drew the pry-bar back for the first chop and thought, *Just as long as I don't see a face.*

It took Knecht four minutes to clear the jam—four

minutes of which he retained almost no memory, other than imprecise, half-formed images. He remembered hacking at purple and taupe lumps until the pressure door was mostly free. He recalled the bulkhead laboring to close—crushing, splintering thin shards of frozen Ayeshans before it finally established a seal. Then, the intermittent tone in Knecht's helmet became more rapid; three minutes to air depletion. Knecht turned, hopped, pushed his heavy soles back against the sealed bulkhead, and then kicked. Launched by the dual pistons of his legs, he arrowed back down the passageway.

By the time he reached section R-17, he had run out of air. A pair of fellow Society members helped him cycle through, told him that a few more survivors had turned up—some badly wounded. With long, gliding strides, he ran toward the now-stationary spin-gym, which was being used as a combination triage site and town hall. He tumbled through the hub accessway, head turning from side to side, eyes probing the clutter of faces, looking for—

Vera emerged from the crowd, pushed hard against him and held herself close, both arms locked around him as though she was fearful that something might tear her away. "Manny," she whispered, his name broken into pieces by her short, rapid sobs. He closed his eyes and breathed deeply; it was all right now. Everything was going to be all right.

The incoming flow of survivors and emergency maintenance teams pushed the two of them gently along, carried them away from the hub and toward the open area usually used for martial arts and gymnastics. There was a meeting—or was it a confrontation?—developing at the center of that space. Keeping an arm around Vera, Knecht wiped the vomit from his face and sidled forward through the thin crust of spectators ringing the *ad hoc* arena.

Vance Trainor—Owen's father—towered over Janine Chattaburray. His eyes were cool and grey, like the twilight sky that Emmanuel's father had talked of seeing on

Haven. Janine's were bright black marbles, stabbing up at Vance and then sweeping across the gathering crowd—before darting back toward Vance once more.

"We don't have the time to discuss insane schemes," she snapped, waving her hand impatiently. "We have to get to work—and quickly—if we're going to save this community."

Vance—twenty-five years her senior—shook his head. "Ms. Chattaburray, no amount of work is going to save this community. And you know it."

Her eyes and voice flared. "Hydroponics is still intact. So are the two lower levels. We can make it."

Vance nodded. "Yes, for a few months; maybe even a year. But what then?"

Chattaburray rolled her eyes. "By that time, we will have rebuilt—and the Imperial Navy will have arrived. As soon as they find and eliminate the Sauron bastards who did this, they'll send a rescue mission here."

Vance smiled. "And what if there is no Imperial response, Ms. Chattaburray?"

Janine snorted, looked away. "Don't be absurd."

Vance's smile flattened into a grim, thin-lipped line. "Imperial visits to this system have been declining steadily for the past ten years. The last military ship through here was the *R.D. Spaulding*, four years ago—and we weren't even their destination; they were just passing through as a part of their redeployment." Vance half-turned toward the growing crowd. "Let's face it, folks. We are not at the top of the Imperium's priority list. Hell; I don't think we're on that list at all. It's been a year and a half since the last ship—a broken-down subsidized freighter—came through. Why should we expect them to send a task force now?"

"Because there are Saurons in-system," retorted Janine. "Because even if the Imperium doesn't care about us, it will track down its foes and eliminate them."

Vance shrugged, grinned. "Is that so? Well, I served three two-year tours with the Marines, ma'am. And let me tell you, unless things have changed a great deal in the past twenty-five years, the Imperium will do what it can, when it can—and forget about the rest." He turned to face the crowd fully. "It's no secret that success against the Saurons hasn't exactly been a foregone conclusion. Imperial forces have been getting stretched thinner and thinner. That means they're going to husband their remaining assets carefully, protect their essential resources—and accept marginal losses." He paused to look around the group. "We, ladies and gentlemen, are a marginal loss. Even if the Imperium knows that the Saurons are here—and note that I emphasize the word *if*—they probably can't afford to do anything to help us. So we'd better start finding our own long-term answers."

Janine scoffed. "Such as Castalia? What a brilliant answer that is: to descend to Haven—into the laps of the Saurons themselves—to search for some mythical under-sea paradise. And until we do 'find' it, how do we eat? How do we evade the Saurons? And how do we even get planetside? We only have one atmospheric interface craft; all the lighters and tankers are designed for work in vacuum. They'll never survive a planetfall."

Knecht was surprised to hear Vera's voice, loud at his elbow. "That's not necessarily true. The non-atmospheric craft have a good chance of making it through a single planetfall; they just won't be able to lift off once they're down."

Janine responded with a sardonic smile. "A 'good chance' of making it through a planetfall?" She looked around the gathered listeners. "My, doesn't *that* sound encouraging?"

Vance's voice was loud and sharp. "Sounds better than starving, freezing, or suffocating to death here on Ayesha. Vera's right; non-interface craft should be able to make a one-way trip. That's how the first group of Castalians managed to get down to Haven in the first place. If they could do it, so can we.

"And we have a number of advantages that they

lacked. We don't have to build a community; it's already there, waiting for us. We know that it's located somewhere near the mouth of the Widebay river—"

"—give or take a few thousand square kilometers," sneered Janine.

"—and we also know that, as of a hundred-fifty years ago, the undersea habitation domes and their life-support systems were still in prime condition."

Janine shook her head. "But what about the Saurons? Their fighters are probably buzzing around the stratosphere like angry hornets. They'll see us coming and blow us to pieces."

Vance smiled at Janine. "That's why we don't go immediately, Ms. Chattaburray. They'll pull their fighters in when they're done destroying Haven's industrial base. So we wait for a month—or longer, if that's possible."

"And what about the cruiser itself? I suppose the Saurons are going to pull that in, too?"

"Yes, Ms. Chattaburray, that is precisely what they're going to do."

Janine gaped. "You *are* mad, Trainor. How in hell do you expect that the Saurons are going to land that mountain of metal?"

"With great care. But rest assured: they're going to try to land it—just as soon as they feel that they can do so safely. That cruiser is a gold mine; not only of technology, but heavier metals and electronics. As soon as the Saurons have decided on a place of permanent residence—which is almost sure to be in the Shangri-La Valley—they're going to try a controlled deorbit of their battlewagon."

"What's to stop them from keeping it in orbit and using it as a stand-off platform for bombardment, observation, and communications?" The question came from a gawky teenager with his arm in a bloodstained sling.

Vance smiled at the young man. "That's good thinking, Willy, but from what little we can see and hear of their operations, the Saurons are not here to conduct a raid;

they're here to stay. And that means they're looking beyond immediate military advantages; they're looking for sustainable modes of operation. Without a spaceport, and without extensive technical support, routine transfers to and from orbit are not a viable long-term option. Nothing puts wear and tear on interface craft like punching into and out of a point nine gee gravity well that's coated with a Terran-normal atmosphere. So we've got to assume that the Saurons aren't going to make routine orbital transfers an integral part of their long-term plan. And since they can't keep the cruiser operational without those transfers, their only logical alternative is to deorbit the hull and cannibalize its metals and surviving subsystems."

Janine put her hands on her hips. "And once we've made planetfall, how do we keep even an occasional Sauron aerial patrol from spotting our own grounded craft?"

Vance looked her square in the eye. "By putting down in the water, Ms. Chattaburray."

She laughed, swept her gaze across the growing audience. "How many people would like to volunteer for a nice swim on Haven? Raise your hands. Nothing to worry about, of course; it's not as though our non-atmospheric craft will be smashed to pieces if they attempt a water landing." She turned dark, smug eyes back to Vance.

His chin came up slightly. "I won't deny that there's considerable danger involved."

Janine laughed again. " 'Considerable danger?' Is that a new synonym for 'suicide'?"

The momentary silence was broken by Vera; her voice was small but firm. "What Mr. Trainor suggests is risky, but not suicidal. Almost certainly, we will lose some of the non-atmospheric craft, but not more than two, maybe three."

Janine turned to glare at Vera. "How very cavalier, Mrs. Knecht—but what if you or your husband should happen to be on one of those less fortunate transports?"

Vera's tone did not change. "That's the chance we have to take—along with everyone else. And as a pilot, the statistics indicate that if my boat does go down, I'm the most likely to die: the cockpit is the most dangerous place to be during a failed deorbit attempt."

Janine looked at Emmanuel, then looked away and snarled, "This plan is madness; you Castalians are going to get us all killed."

Before he was aware that he had an urge to do so, Emmanuel stepped forward into the informal debating arena. "Your fears are justified, Janine." She turned to look at him, surprised—and worried. Emmanuel faced the crowd. "But we can be sure of this; if we stay on Ayesha, we *will* die. I know a lot of you think that we Castalians—myself in particular—have some pretty strange ideas. But you also know that I'm a good life-support technician—and that I'm not a liar.

"So here's the truth; the self-sufficiency hydroponics aren't going to work. Ever. We could have done it if we had access to the right technology—but that was too expensive. Now, to make matters worse, two-thirds of our community has had its pressure integrity compromised. We've lost a huge quantity of air and moisture out of our bioloop, and we're never going to get that back. We can't be sure that the fusion plant can be brought back on line; a number of the support systems have been damaged. And we can't make new fuel for it or our own spacecraft: the ice-crackers and hydrogen purifiers were ruined when the debris from the fuel station smashed through the two upper levels."

He paused, looked into the tense faces surrounding him. "What I'm saying is that we can't stay here. Even if Castalia is a pipe dream, even if some of us don't make it down to the surface of Haven, that's better than certain death on Ayesha. If any of us are going to survive, we've got to make planetfall."

Most of the on-lookers were nodding slowly, somberly. Janine blinked, her eyes bright, and then she walked out

of the circle. Vance was already button-holing community
leaders to discuss evacuation strategies. Vera glided over
to Knecht and circled his waist with her long, slender
arms. "You did the right thing for us, Manny."

He shrugged. "It's not the way I wanted it to happen,
but I guess the two of us will find out what it's like to
live on Haven."

Vera looked up at him, smiled, shook her head; "No,
not the two of us, Manny; the *three* of us."

At first, he didn't understand what she meant. Then,
joy washed through him; but that happiness was harried
by the image of a small, frozen limb—bloated and ruptured from exposure to vacuum. Confused, Emmanuel
leaned into Vera and buried his face in her shoulder.

"How many of you survived the attack?" The woman's
tone was quiet, respectful.

"About four hundred, not counting those whose
wounds were mortal. We never found most of the six
hundred who died; most of them were pulverized when
the debris hit, or they were sucked out into open space.
A lot of the casualties were low-geers; they tended to
live close to the surface, close to their work."

The man hugged his knees with his arms. "You must've
lost a lot of your spacecraft, too."

"Actually, we were pretty fortunate in that regard.
Almost all our boats were in the repair bay, which was
located almost a kilometer away from the main base and
the refinery."

"How long before you abandoned the base?"

"Almost three months. We waited until the Saurons
had settled down in their new home. We knew that if
they detected us making planetfall, they'd spare no
expense in exterminating us; it was easy to guess that
they weren't going to brook any technological rivals."

"Which is exactly what you've become." The woman
smiled faintly.

Knecht said nothing. He just stared at her.

Her smiled faded. "You're a Magi, aren't you?"

"I'm a what?" Knecht suppressed a grin; *a* Magi. Haveners had foregone the correct singular form— Magus. "Magi" was the label some unknown Havener had conferred upon the mysterious wanderers who started showing up a year after the Saurons arrived, wanderers who occasionally helped an outlying community with a tidbit of scientific knowledge or medical insight. The name had stuck. So now—whether one or twenty were being spoken of—the term was "Magi." "I'm a what?" Knecht repeated.

The woman's eyes never left his. "A Magi. You know what I'm talking about."

Her companion interrupted with a snort of derision. "The Magi are fairy-tales, made up by people who want to believe that the Saurons don't hold all the cards—by people who don't want to face facts."

She didn't bother to turn toward him as she offered her rebuttal. "Didn't you see his revolver? His pills?"

"Yeah, so? They're holdovers; there's plenty of old technology left laying around."

"That revolver isn't old technology; the barrel is too heavy, the frame too large. It's post-war manufacture, just like the aspirin. Didn't you notice? His pills were little, uncoated spheres; they weren't flat and shiny like pre-war pills." She nodded at Emmanuel. "I'm right, aren't I? All you Ayeshan refugees—you're the Magi, aren't you? You rediscovered Castalia, found the old machines. That's why people are starting to think you're wizards—because you're still producing technology that the Saurons have wiped out everyplace else."

Emmanuel shrugged. "We try not to use it unless we have to."

The man leaned back on his hands, slowly processing Emmanuel's indirect affirmation of the woman's hypothesis. "So you *are* a Magi."

Knecht smiled.

"How many of you are there?"

"Not as many as we'd like."

The woman leaned forward. "Did you lose a lot of people during planetfall?"

Emmanuel felt darkness threaten his vision again, fought it back, nodded. "Yes. We modified the spacecraft as best we could, but they were all in need of repair and replacement parts that we couldn't provide. So we—we lost a lot of people when we deorbited."

"How many?"

Knecht sighed, closed his eyes. "Too many . . ."

They were initiating the third and final turn; a long, sweeping arc designed to eat up forward velocity. The tanker's modular hold had grown uncomfortably warm; it wasn't designed to handle the heat of atmospheric reentry.

Down below, Emmanuel saw a dappled sheet of choppy grey water, occasionally occluded by clouds. Then the window's blast covers slid into place and there was nothing to look at but the ashen, frightened faces of his fellow passengers, who were cocooned in mattresses and lashed to what had once been tankage baffles. The only sound was the rushing of air and intermittent whimpering—not all of which was coming from the children.

Emmanuel turned his head all the way to the left, looked at the small round accessway that was just out of his arm's reach: the passage to the cockpit module— and Vera. The faint chatter of intercraft communications which leaked out of that accessway was becoming more frequent; they were approaching the landing zone. Knecht closed his eyes, concentrated on making out the incoming messages—

"—reported multiple electronic failures just before Garvey crashed. So keep a gentle hand on your retros, everybody. The control circuitry wasn't built for this kind of heat."

"Any survivors from Garvey's lighter?"

"Negative, Johnny; he broke up at four thousand meters, airspeed still over three hundred fifty kph."

Vera's voice broke in. "Flight leader, what are your recommendations if we start losing retros?"

Silence for a moment, then: "Vera, are you having trouble?"

"Just a little, Vance." Emmanuel felt his pulse increase; for Vera to admit any problem at all meant they were in deep trouble.

Vance's tone suggested he understood that as well. "You losing retros, too?"

"Not as completely as Garvey, but yes. The main thrusters are failing, also; I don't have enough kick for another pass. Besides, I don't think the hull could take it."

"Airspeed?"

"Two-sixty kph."

"Rate of descent?"

A long silence. "Unpromising, Flight leader." Vera's voice was utterly flat. "What do you suggest?"

"Bring your nose up; take her in at a forty degree incline—and pray that your stabilizers hold. And before you hit, try—" There was a burst of static and then silence. Vera's copilot swore.

"What happened, Roy?"

"The tight-beam's orienting gimbal just fried and died. We're on our own."

"We always were, Roy. Let's bring the nose to thirty-five degrees; give me forward retros at seventy-five percent."

"You've got 'em." A persistent tremor crept into being along the belly of the tanker. "How are we doing?"

"Not good enough; give me another five percent."

The tremor increased—and was abruptly succeeded by a muffled metallic screech and a vicious portside wrench. The rush of air became a howl and Emmanuel felt his stomach try to push its way into his ribcage. They were falling—fast. One or two of the passengers' whimpers became wails of panic.

Roy's voice cracked. "Shit, what was—?"

"Portside stabilizer has sheared off. Give me full portside retros."

"Aye—" and then Knecht was rammed back into his mattress. His stomach lost interest in his ribs, dove down to press against his intestines.

Vera's voice was tight, sharp. "How much time do we have left on the portside retros, assuming full burn?"

"About fifteen seconds—but, Vera, I've got red lights all over that board; we've only got fifty percent function with those retros. The rest burned out."

There were two long seconds of silence before Vera murmured, "Cut the forward retros back to thirty percent."

"Thirty percent? But, Vera, that will bring our nose down."

"I'm aware of that, Roy; just do it."

"But with our nose down—"

"Roy, if we come in with our nose *up*, our aft end will hit the water and swing us down into a high-speed bellyflop. But, at one hundred fifty kph, we'll have too much forward momentum to just stop and sink; we'll start cartwheeling across the water—and we'll wind up looking like modern art. But if we go in nose first, the cockpit module will absorb the brunt of the impact—enough to help the cargo module dig into the water. It'll roll once—maybe twice—before it starts to sink, but the passengers should be able to survive it."

Emmanuel could hear Roy swallow—a constricted gulping sound—before he replied. "But if the cockpit hits first—"

Emmanuel painted the picture in his mind. The transport's dome-eyed, wedge-shaped head—the cockpit—plummeted toward the water, the thoracic tankage section stretched out behind it. For a moment, the whole ungainly structure leveled off and sped above the choppy waters, the swells reaching up toward it—and then the head pitched down. There was a white explosion of steam and spray, a screech of tortured titanium as the narrow neck joining the cockpit and the tankage section snapped. The decapitated cockpit flattened under the impact, the dome-shaped eyes shattering inward, the rush of water smashing the precious contents of that metallic skull, smashing—

"Vera!" Emmanuel shouted as he began unbuckling his makeshift harness. No; not nose first. And not Vera. Anything else, anyone else—but not that, and not her. "Vera!"

Emmanuel heard her voice, but the words were not meant for him; Vera was speaking in the utterly calm tone she used with Roy. "Seal passenger section for impact and immersion."

Knecht undid the last buckle, struggled out of the mattress that enfolded him, jumped towards the cockpit accessway. "Vera! Don't—" The pressure-rated cockpit door slammed sideways across the accessway. Knecht pounded on the door with his fists once, twice—

Then the floor fell away from him; the nose was dropping. Knecht had his mouth open to scream, but he never got the chance to do so. The tanker hit the waves; the cockpit door seemed to leap at him. He rebounded off that surface and was thrown back into the tankage area. Then the door buckled, burst, and a jet of water rammed into the hold. The flume hit him square in the chest and sent him tumbling the length of the tankage section. Screams and rushing water filled his ears but all he could hear was a voice inside his head, a voice which sounded like his own—a voice which kept repeating the only thing that mattered: *Vera Vera Vera* . . .

"How did you survive?" asked the man.

"We were all wearing vacuum suits; when we hit the water, we sealed up and swam out."

The woman's eyes were lowered, her voice low and gentle. "How many people did you lose?"

Knecht cleared his throat, cleared an image of Vera from his mind. "Seventy-one. Most of those went down with Garvey's lighter. We lost another sixteen on my transport, mostly people who were knocked unconscious when we hit; they drowned in their harnesses."

"So you refounded Castalia with only three hundred thirty people?"

Knecht shook his head. "Less than that. We lost another twelve before we actually found Castalia."

"Low-geers?"

"Only four died because of gravity-related medical problems. The rest—well, that's how we learned about the stobors." As if to emphasize his point, a banshee-like yowl rose in the distance, wavered, and then fell in a warbling diminuendo. A moment later, a pair of similar cries answered it.

"They've caught the scent of the Sauron we threw on the fire." Knecht nodded. "That's good."

"Good?" The man sounded skeptical. "If the Saurons follow the sound of the howling, they'll find our campsite—and our tracks—pretty quickly."

Knecht nodded. "Yes, but by the time they find the campsite, the Sauron I killed will have been torn to pieces by the stobors."

"So?"

The woman answered for Emmanuel. "Once the stobors have started in on the Sauron's corpse, no one will be able to tell how he died—at least, they won't be able to determine that he was killed by high-quality, home-made slugs."

Knecht nodded. "The stobors will hinder the Saurons more than they'll help them. If a good-sized pack descends on the campsite, they should obscure our tracks—even cover my blood trail as they drag off pieces of the Saurons' bodies."

"Okay," said the man, "but we've got to get moving—and soon. Are you just about done with your story?"

Emmanuel nodded, smiled. "Almost . . ."

Knecht was the third person to enter the facility, behind Owen and a wide-eyed Janine. Their helmet lights played about the dome-like room, their misty breath showing up as bright wisps of fog.

Knecht advanced, following the wall; his palm brushed through cold droplets of condensation. He felt for cracks in the internal surface; a smooth, icy surface met his touch. "Hull integrity seems pretty good," he remarked.

"It may be," responded Janine, "but the air is terrible."

"After a century and a half, that's no surprise." Owen played his helmet light across the floor, moved toward the rows of lockers that protruded from the far wall. Before reaching them, he came upon a small table and stopped; there was some kind of demarcation line painted on the floor in front of it.

Janine joined Owen, looked down at the line's yellow-and-black diagonal crosshatching. "Hazard marking?"

Owen nodded. "Yeah. Probably indicated the periphery of the mandatory dress-out area."

"Dress-out?" echoed Janine. "Why would the founders have been worried about radioactive contamination?"

Emmanuel angled away from the wall, came to join them near the table. "Not just radioactives. The founders tried to be prepared for everything: biochemical agents, marine microorganisms, unknown viruses. They were pretty thorough."

Owen reached down toward the table. "Speaking of thorough"—he picked up an old-style hardcopy clipboard—"take a look at this." He handed it to Emmanuel.

Knecht shined his helmet light down on the ancient yellowed paper and read:

WELCOME TO CASTALIA

Instructions for limited base restart:
Proceed to circuit box (labelled A-lb) located
    four meters due north.

Knecht turned, lights sweeping along with his gaze,
until he had turned ninety degrees to his left. A large
grey box—power conduits running from it both laterally
and longitudinally—was spotlighted at chest height.
White stencilled characters identified it: "A-1B." He
turned back to the instructions.

Locate rheostatic control (color coded red) at
    extreme upper left hand corner of circuit-box
    A-1b's internal control panel.
    Adjust red rheostatic control to a setting of .065.

Knecht looked at Owen, who was reading over his
shoulder. Owen shrugged. Knecht responded with a similar gesture and crossed over to the box, dripping cold
Haven seawater as he went. He took firm hold of the
box's hinged cover, yanked—and almost fell to the floor
when the cover swung back easily.
    Janine approached, surprise in her voice. "No rust?"
    Knecht squinted, ran a finger along the edge of the
cover. "Nope; coated with grease—must be a couple of
millimeters thick." He slowly tilted his head upward, illu-
minating the length of the circuit box's control panel. As
advertised, a red rheostatic dial was located in the upper
left hand corner; it was already set to .065.
    From behind, Owen mumbled; "Those old bastards
didn't miss a trick."
    Knecht nodded, checked the next instructions on the
clipboard's cover sheet.

Locate square green button ("power up") at the bot-
    tom of the control panel. Depress button. If button

illuminates, riverine hydroturbine function has been successfully initiated. In the event that button does not illuminate, consult electro-magnetic gauge immediately to the right of the "power up" button. If the needle shows any activity, hydroturbine function has been successfully initiated, but the bulb within the "power up" button has failed. Replace as per maintenance annex code X:117-b3.

In the event hydroturbine function is not initiated, all efforts should be made to restore full function to this power generation system. Aforementioned riverine hydroturbines are located at the mouth of the Widebay river (map coordinates B17.6 × AA4.1; low-tide depth of 7 meters).

Knecht looked up; the green button stared back at him. He raised his finger, stopped.

Owen came closer. "What's wrong?"

Knecht kept the quaver out of his voice. "What if, after all these years—"

Janine interrupted. "Go ahead, Emmanuel. Just go ahead; it'll work."

Knecht depressed the button. A faint tremor went through the walls, the deck—and the green button illuminated. But only for a moment: with a sharp flash and a loud pop, the green glow vanished as rapidly as it had appeared.

Owen's voice was calm. "Bulb gave out—but we've still got power." He tapped the electromagnetic gauge. "Needle rising to nominal."

But Knecht was already flipping greedily through the sheets on the clipboard, his eyes roving from one tantalizing extract to the next:

"To restart main fusion plant, bring L-Hyd/LOx fuel cell banks to 500 kilowatts output and—"

"In the event that your base reactivation team is being pursued by hostile forces, a ready armory is available, located in dressout lockers A1-L3 and A1-L4. Ready weapons have been inundated with TLX micrograin polymer lubricant and sealed in ready-for-use plastic pouches. Ready armory consists of: 15 M78 NeoValmet semiautomatic rifles with 10 20-round clips per weapon; 30 CT-T2 thermite grenades (6 second fuses); 1 M78A NeoValmet automatic squad support weapon with 10 100-round linkable belts; 30 NeoColt-brown Ultra-Power semiautomatic pistols with 5 19-round clips per weapon. Main armory stores are located in habitation module B2, and have been fully disassembled (and immersed in lubricants) for long term storage. Main armory inventory includes—"

"Emergency dehydrated food stores are located in water-tight canisters bolted to the foundation of habitation module AI (this module) at those sites indicated in Figure 2.b, below. Average temperature of surrounding water is 4 degrees centigrade, ensuring long-term preservation. Emergency foodstuffs are comprised of (by mass): 38% dried fruits, 42% assorted grains, 8% unrefined sugar, 12% protein/vitamin concentrates. Distilled water is available in reserve tanks C3 through C14—"

The typewritten cornucopia of riches continued to flood past Emmanuel's widening eyes; better than even he had dared to imagine. He let the welcome words of technological plenty jump out at him: medical supplies, machine shops, centrifuges, hydroponics, catalytic separators, laboratories, pressure suits—and of course, the founder's own library.

The last page differed from all the rest in that it was hand written; a brief note that read:

Welcome to Castalia.

   *It is our hope that this facility and its resources will
never be needed again, and that therefore, this letter will
go unread. However, those of us who have maintained Castalia over the years need only consult the annals of founder
Jonathan Knecht to confirm that humankind's periodic pro-
pensity for self-destruction is a cyclic certainty.*
   *Castalia can provide you with the means whereby you
may endure this period of destruction. Use its resources
cautiously and sparingly. Avoid all unnecessary contact
with other communities on Haven. You will be tempted to
provide overt aid to distressed populations, but you are
counselled not to do so; although such contact may save
lives, your technological wealth is likely to foster curiosity,
envy, and greed in those whom you help.*
   Good luck.

   Dagmar Knecht, Caretaker

Dagmar Knecht: Emmanuel's great-great-grandfather.
Janine drew close, looked up briefly; Knecht was only
vaguely aware of her as he continued to stare at his
ancestor's signature. "You were right, Emmanuel." Janine's voice sounded strangely distant—and soft. "You—
you've got a lot to be happy—to be proud—about."

But the bliss that Emmanuel should have felt—standing at last in Castalia—refused to rise up. He put the
clipboard down, underlined his great-great-grandfather's
name with a wet forefinger, and thought; I wish Vera
could have seen it. I wish—

Emmanuel's vision blurred. Drops began to spatter on
the desiccated paper, the ink dissolving and running
wherever it was touched by his tears.

"So the whole base is still operational?" The man's
voice rose to the marginally higher pitch that often
accompanies incredulity.

"Hardly. Only the hydroturbines are producing any appreciable power levels."

"The fusion reactor?"

Knecht shook his head. "Scrap metal. A century and a half of deterioration—even though it was literally in 'cold storage'—is too much for us to refurbish. Same with the fuel cells."

"What about the other systems—the labs and machine shops?"

"We've got about forty to fifty percent of the systems back on-line, but I don't know if we're ever going to do much better than that. Still, we're averaging about ten kilos of cordite per week, and last year we produced our first batch of antibiotics."

"I'm glad to hear it—but why are the two of us hearing about it at all?"

Knecht waited until the man met his eyes. "I'm telling you all this so that you'll have to go there."

The man blinked. "To Castalia?"

"Where else?"

"Listen; I don't *have* to go anywhere."

Knecht smiled at the man's reflexive obstinance; it was surprising how many adults insisted upon behaving like overgrown adolescents. "Of course you have to go to Castalia—now that you know what I am, and that Castalia exists. Consider your other options. You can leave me here, but you'll always wonder 'What if the Magi didn't talk? What if the Saurons didn't learn enough from him to locate Castalia on their own?' You think they're simply going to stop looking for the place that I—and my revolver and aspirin—came from? No; the Saurons will follow, using the only clue they have:"—Knecht raised an accusing finger—"your trail. They'll track the two of you for months, if necessary. And how are you going to evade them? They've got horses, firearms, and senses that are twice—even three times—as keen as yours.

"Your other option is to kill me here and now. But

unless you know of some way to prevent the Saurons from discovering my body—and your tracks—you're still in the same predicament; they'll come after you to discover who killed their outriders, and how it was done. Face it; if you want to survive, you're going to have to disappear—and there's only one way to do that: you have to go to Castalia."

The woman's voice broke the split second of silence that followed Knecht's argument. "You mean 'we'; *we* have to go to Castalia."

Emmanuel smiled at her, which was the closest he could bring himself to expressing his gratitude. "No: I can't make it—and you know that."

"But—"

Knecht held up an admonishing finger. "You said— *both* of you said—that you were prepared to do whatever was necessary in order for some of us to survive. Were you lying?"

The woman opened her mouth, then closed it and hung her head. The man kept looking at Knecht, his face betraying a strange collision of emotions: admiration, disorientation, and personal relief.

Knecht tried to smile. "It's just as well, you know. The Saurons are going to need a scapegoat, a body. They've lost two of their outriders, so they're going to insist on finding—and punishing—the responsible party. If we all disappeared without a trace, they wouldn't leave this area. They'd keep searching. Eventually, they might find some telltale sign of Castalia—a bootprint, a spent cartridge casing; something. And that would be the beginning of Castalia's end. The Saurons would come back with a larger search party, and then an even larger assault team—whatever it would take to wipe us out."

Knecht drew the revolver from under his travelling cloak, held it out to the woman. "Take this. Give me the rifle." She complied silently. Knecht checked the assault rifle's magazine; nine rounds left. Enough to give a good account of himself, to compel the Saurons to shoot to kill. He turned out the many hidden pockets lining his dark garments, gathering the small, significant arcana that marked him as a Castalian Magi: waterproof matches, vials of aspirin, chloroform, antibiotics, several dozen rounds for the revolver, flash paper, a cigar-length roll of cordite, a small surgical kit, a palm-sized abacus, a mirror-backed compass, and several small handbooks cluttered with chemical and physical equations. He motioned the woman forward and deposited this strange collection in her hands. Then he reached into his last unemptied pocket and produced a small parabolic reflector with a foldable tripod. He handed it to the man. "Inside the compass cover, you'll find a number of phosphor fuses; they'll fit into a groove at the center of this reflector. That's how you'll signal the people at home— at Castalia." Knecht felt the darkness close in again, realized that the pain in his shoulder had stopped; in its place there was a strange, spreading cold.

The man cleared his throat. "Where should we—"

"Follow the river east. To the coast. Then follow the shore south. Two kilometers. Set the reflector on the beach and—and light a phosphor fuse. Then wait."

"How long?"

"Until they come. They'll come. They always do. Tell them"—Knecht looked at the woman, thought that her eyes reminded him of Vera's—"tell them that I sent you. Tell them—how it was."

The woman rose, a liquid glitter in her eyes. "I'll tell them—everything." She bent down and her lips grazed his cheek. Then she rose, turned, and headed for the river. The man lowered his eyes, nodded awkwardly, and stumbled after the woman.

Emmanuel checked the assault rifle, snapped the safety into the "off" position and waited, thinking of Vera.

They had been sitting under the cover of a frond-like bush for two hours when she saw the trail of bubbles approaching the shore. The faint, effervescent line advanced toward the small headland where they had placed the glowing reflector and had watched it beam its pinpoint message of light out over the dark waters. The woman rose and began walking down to the ocean's edge. As if in response to her movement, a head and torso emerged from the grey-black swells; instead of a human face, a pressure suit's broad, gleaming visor stared back at her.

As her companion bundled their packs together, a wave stretched its frothy length upon the scree, sighing slowly into silence. Before the next swell began curling over upon itself—burbling and rushing as it came—there was a moment of almost perfect stillness.

In that moment, she heard a distant tattoo of small-calibre rifle fire—which was quickly drowned out by a sustained sputtering of heavier weapons. Then silence. She felt a tear run down her cheek, brushed it sharply away, willed the next wave to obliterate the silence.

Before it could, the stobors began to howl.

Assault Leader Mav was that rarity among Saurons; a man with no discernible sense of humor.

Mav took everything with deadly seriousness; one of the reasons, he was fond of telling his men, why he was not dead. To which his men invariably replied: "How can you tell?"

At which point Assault Leader Mav would run them through another training exercise designed to reduce Saurons to sweating masses of cramping, quivering muscles and bruised bones. Or, to put it another way, to kill anybody else.

But Mav only did that when he couldn't exact his favorite revenge on his squad: Patrol duty. Today, Mav had got his first choice. Mav had volunteered the squad for a special pacification mission as conceived by the Survey Ranks.

And it was a beaut, his men had agreed.

Lancer Dolman carried his squad's support weapon, usually requiring him to engage the enemy at a distance. This morning, however, he sat on a rock with the rest of his fireteam, he and each of the other eight Saurons looking into their pack mirrors and grimacing.

"Argh." Dolman said. No, that wasn't right. He tried again. "Aragh." He turned his head to one side, tried a snarl. "Argh-arrh . . . Arh." He finished with very little confidence in his acting ability.

Around the circle described by Dolman and the other members of the squad, Assault Leader Mav stalked like a panther held at bay only by a campfire's feeble glow.

"Fierce!" Mav exhorted the men of his squad. "Make sure they see you. Get in their faces with a snarl that'll freeze their blood. The Survey Ranks have established that these Havener indigs are especially tough. Their bush fighters are tougher still, but they'll be depending on support from what's left of the cities. The survivors of our invasion who are still in those cities will, therefore, be the weak link in the resistance. Our job is to impress each and every one of them that we can be more savage than anything they've ever seen on this mudball moon they call a home."

Mav reached out and grabbed Dolman's chin and turned the young Soldier's face up to him. "You call that a snarl?" Mav jerked Dolman's jaw around to point it at a line of animal corpses laid out on the rocks. Each beast's head was facing the members of Mav's squad; each beast had been killed by Mav personally since yesterday, and each beast was as savage an example of Haven fauna as Mav could locate in one night's hunting. Dolman thought it was a pretty good cross-section of things to avoid.

"Look over there, Dolman; the locals call that thing a tamerlane. See those teeth? You should have seen its eyes in the light of Byers' Star. And that one's a cragspider— you've all seen what they'll do to a muskylope—has an almost human face, hasn't it? Those 'borers with the shiny teeth are the worst, though; they chew through *stone*. They don't even notice when a man's guts get in the way. Think about that, all of you. Use that, and let's put the fear of God into the next batch of cattle we find cowering in the ruins of their cities; ruins *we* made!"

Dolman sighed. It was tough enough trying to follow

the Survey Ranks' orders to present a "fierce face" to the Haveners without Mav's biology primers and amateurish exhortations to non-existent Sauron "primal instincts."

The biggest problem was that Dolman, like almost all other Saurons, simply did not have any *idea* of how to be "fierce" in battle. Human norm propaganda to the contrary notwithstanding, Saurons were not killing machines; they were civilized men and women who were the very best at what man, as a species, excelled at. They made war, and "making war" was a function of intellect and intelligently applied force.

"Ferocity," on the other hand, was a function of *ego*, and Saurons had long since perfected a concept unique among all human civilizations: The subjugation of the ego to the battle plan. A Sauron at war was a perfect Soldier executing his training in as ideal a manner as could be hoped for in an environment of chaos. Exhibiting "ferocity" in such a situation was, by definition, a waste of energy and a detriment to concentration. It was, therefore, counter-productive to the mission. Other, lesser peoples needed some outside impetus to charge themselves with adrenalin; Saurons were *born* with the conscious ability to control such combat-enhancing glands.

The Survey Ranks, therefore, weren't trying to tap into some lost capability of the Sauron psyche; they were trying to get blood from a stone

Dolman caught a look on Mav's face that was very like despair. He felt badly for the Assault Leader, he really did. But Mav should have known that his men were incapable of endangering the mission by "play-acting" at children's games when they were working. . . .

Surprised at his own thoughts, Dolman blinked. "Assault Leader Mav," he called out.

"What is it, Dolman?"

"What's our mission, Assault Leader?"

Mav put his hands on his hips and stared at him. "What?"

"The mission's objective, Assault Leader; what is it?"

Now Mav blinked; after a moment's consideration, during which Dolman realized that Mav himself had simply accepted the Survey Ranks' imperatives without analyzing them, the Assault Leader spoke: "To impress upon the cattle of this world that Saurons, as a race, are the most utterly ruthless and dangerous opponents they have ever encountered."

There was a nearly imperceptible sussuration as the squad exuded a collective sigh of comprehension.

"Terror tactics, then, Assault Leader?" one of the other Soldiers asked. "Pointless cruelty, occasional decimation of captives; the odd atrocity?"

Mav thought a moment, and Dolman could see his mind working in the expression on his face, which said: *Could that be what the Survey Ranks meant? Why hadn't they just said so?*

Mav looked up. "Yes," he said. He sounded as if it were a revelation. Satisfied to at last receive comprehensible instructions, the squad went back to their mirrors.

Dolman looked into his own, and snarled.

"Whoa," he said, taken aback. He'd actually startled himself. The tamerlane and the cragspider looked positively cuddly compared to the visage that stared back at him.

Not bad, he decided. *Not bad at all.*

A LITTLE BEASTLINESS

Edward P. Hughes

Summer on the Haven steppe is little more than a
state of mind. The ambient temperature rises minimally.
The permafrost softens. The ice sheets shift a verst or
two polewards. And, for a few hours around noon in
sheltered spots, hardy characters may discard outer
garments.

A man and a woman crouched on the hillside above
the river *Karsts Udens,* binoculars focused on a line of
figures snaking out of the railway valley below.

"They look like Saurons to me," grunted Captain Janis
Klimkans. "Bounding along like that, full of piss and
vinegar."

Corporal Linda Berkis studied the forms climbing
towards the old fuser plateau. Her stomach contracted.
Since the invasion, the Saurons had become bogeymen.
"What are they doing out this way?"

The captain eased the straps of a wicker basket from
his shoulders, and placed it on the ground beside his
pack. "Looking for anything they missed from orbit, I
imagine." A flutter of wings came from within the basket.
He grunted. "The bird's restless. Must be the heat." He
pushed open his visor. "These frysuits are too damned

219

hot for yomping around in the summer. Galdins has a nerve, sending us out here to exercise his bloody bird."

Linda Berkis opened her own helmet, and dabbed her brow with the tail of a scarf. Janis was right: it was too warm inside the chameleon suits. "I expect that's why they're called frysuits," she commented. "Just the same, I wouldn't care to be out here long without one. We'd freeze before lightfail." She sighted her DZ7 rifle experimentally on the figures below. "Do you think those superswine know there used to be a fuser here?"

The captain studied the foe through his glasses. Legend had it that centuries ago the plateau by the river had been the site of a CoDo fusion plant. Only mossy humps and holes remained of any structure the CoDominium Engineers might have erected. Of the pipe bridge which had supposedly crossed the river taking power and hot water to a Tartar metropolis, no trace lingered.

Klimkans grimaced. "The Saurons may have heard rumors. I hear they're destroying any power sources they locate. If they discover there's a fuser in Refuge, we can start worrying."

She made a face. "If they follow the river it'll take them straight to the Gullet."

Through the Gullet lay the only way into the Vale of Refuge. Thirty versts downstream, *Karsts Udens* foamed through a gorge, spilled over a cliff and spread itself in a lake. The fuser stood on the cliff edge, its feet in the cooling river water. Surplus heat from the plant, transferred to the lake, warmed the valley and rendered Refuge habitable. The lake, via submontane courses, drained into the sea beyond the mountains, warming those frigid waters and providing icefree access to the trading post of Icedge.

"If they hope to eliminate every power plant that survived the bombing, they'll check everywhere," the captain told the corporal. "If they decide to go down river, we're in trouble." He refocused the glasses. Twenty-one figures climbed towards the fuser ruins, the rear two hauling a truck loaded with equipment. All of them carried weapons. No doubt of it, they were the dreaded Saurons. Probably from the ship which had crashed in Shangri-La Valley. It would wise to assume they had heard of Refuge and its fuser. Too much traffic passed between Udenspils and Castell City for the valley's existence to remain a secret.

Linda Berkis licked her lips. "We could pick them off from here, boss."

He frowned. "Corporal, would you mind not addressing me as 'boss' when we're playing at soldiers?"

She grimaced. Military service was compulsory for both sexes in Refuge, but Linda Berkis could not get used to addressing her employer as "captain" on their annual service.

He added gently, "Twenty-one moving targets would take some picking off. And I wouldn't call us crack shots!"

She patted her DZ7. "I reckon I could manage them with this."

"You bloodthirsty beggar! What about the bodies?"

She stared at him, eyes round and innocent. "Couldn't we chuck 'em in the river?"

He frowned at her. "And foul our valley drinking water?" He shook his head. "Besides, those monsters will be telling HQ every move they make. Stop those reports, and HQ knows something's wrong."

She chewed a lip. Janis Klimkans could be irritatingly logical at times. "So we just watch them, and hope they go away?"

Klimkans wasn't listening. "If only there was some sort of bridge!" he muttered. "We could have lured them onto the steppe . . ."

Across the river the tundra stretched for miles. Berkis thought she detected a smudge of muskylopes on the horizon.

"We could lose them out there," Klimkans mused.

"Lose Saurons? You're dreaming!"

He sniffed. "Oh, they're not invincible. They can be outsmarted. They're soldiers. Trained to act, not think. Get 'em confused so they don't know what to do for the best, and you can lick 'em—unless they have a cyborg with them."

Her eyebrows went up. "A Cyborg?"

He nodded. "A sort of super superswine. Half man, half machine, they say. Nothing baffles *them*."

Her eyebrows climbed even higher. "Where did you get all this dope about the Saurons?"

He shrugged. "There's a tech in Udenspils who was mixed up in that Redfield fracas. He reckons he's fought against Cyborgs."

"And survived? He must be smart."

"He's smart enough to stay home while we fart around out here on our own."

She peered at the enemy through her binoculars. The Sauron patrol had almost reached the plateau. She lowered the glasses. "Hadn't we better start outsmarting those buggers, boss? We don't want them heading down river and locating Refuge."

He rolled onto an elbow to scan the slopes behind them. Apart from a few rock rats basking in the warmth of Cat's Eye and Byers', they were alone on the hillside. "Hold onto your muskies, Corporal," he told her. "A whole Sauron platoon will take some bamboozling."

She squirmed closer to the ground, binoculars propped before her in the heater. "Can they see us from down there?"

He shrugged. "Lord knows what sensors they have. You're supposed to be invisible in a chameleon suit, so long as you don't radiate any signals. Keep your head down, and stay off the air."

She pushed down the aerial on her backpack. "I'm mute, boss, 'till you give the word. Hadn't we better get rid of *putns*? We don't want to be lumbered with excess baggage if that patrol sees us."

He contemplated the basket. "Galdins wanted me to

take it as far as the old railway cutting. And he wanted snow. He's keen to see if they can find their way home in poor visibility."

She pouted. "He'll get no snow here in summer. Him and his pigeons! If the Commissar knew what you get up, you'd both be cashiered."

"I wouldn't mind," Klimkans said comfortably. "I'd be able to get on with my job."

Janis Klimkans resented time spent on military service. In his civilian persona, he blasted terraces out of rock slopes to provide spaces for expensive homes. Currently he was opening a way into an adjoining valley to make room for Udenspils' expanding population.

Corporal Berkis sniffed. "And I could go back to my drill, I suppose?" Corporal Berkis as a civilian bored holes for Janis Klimkans' explosive charges.

He grimaced. "I believe you'd sooner drill on a barrack square then in the mountains!"

She shrugged. "It makes a change."

He shook his head. "I don't get it. What's so hot about playing soldiers, Berkis?"

The corporal flushed. She picked at a patch of heather. If Jan Klimkans couldn't work it out for himself, there was no way Linda Berkis would confess what drew her to army life.

"Well, enjoy it while you can!" warned the captain. "Anyone captured by Saurons can forget about going home. According to that tech from Redfield, they treat their prisoners like cattle."

Sometimes Janis Klimkans could be hateful. Linda Berkis turned her back on him, and focused her attention on the figures below.

The lead trooper had reached the foot of the old fuser mound. He squatted, then leaped straight up onto the plateau. In turn, each man emulated the leap. One trooper stayed at the base of the mound with the equipment.

The corporal squealed. "Did you see those jumps!

They're not men—they're bloody grasshoppers! We don't want them in Refuge!"

Klimkans closed his eyes at the sight of those Sauron athletics. He saw his home in Udenspils, the oranges, vines and figs growing in his garden—all threatened by these grasshoppers. Did Corporal bloody Berkis realize that whoever attempted to keep them out of Refuge would be running a considerable risk in the process?

He tucked his glasses back into the case. Simply watching them wasn't going to stop a Sauron invasion of the valley. Steps would have to be taken. Captain Janis Klimkans didn't consider himself particularly valiant, but one's duty was one's duty. He swallowed a large lump in his throat. "We'd better let the bird go," he told the corporal. "It can take a message back for us. Maybe the Pirmais can cook up a welcome for that lot if we can't stop them."

He scribbled in a note book, tore out the page, and rolled it into a cylinder which he tucked it into a tiny plastic tube. He unstrapped the basket. "Grab the bird," he ordered. "Hold it while I fix this to its leg."

Canister fixed, he took the pigeon in one hand and hurled it high. The bird fluttered in circles for a few minutes, then took off in a westerly direction. Shading his eyes, Klimkans watched it out of sight. If it reached home, Galdins would be warned of the Sauron patrol. And the general could try to organize a way of dealing with the threat. Meantime, his two sacrificial goats would do what they could to render the warning superfluous.

Klimkans unbuckled his helmet, and wriggled out of his chamsuit. "Get your rig off, Corporal," he ordered. "We'll have to hide all this stuff."

She looked at him startled, her face blank. "My suit? Whatever for? You want me to freeze?"

He straightened his coveralls. "Don't be silly, Corporal. It's midsummer, and nearly second noon." He glanced skywards: Cat's Eye glowed low in the west. "We have at least ten hours to lightfail. You'll be warm enough without a suit for a while."

"But I'm comfortable as I am."

"Who's worrying about comfort?" he demanded. "We can't let the Saurons learn we have outfits like these."

"Who cares what the superswine learn!"

He gritted his teeth. "Listen Corporal, I was forced to take a woman on this outing because female frysuits are different from male frysuits—different sizes, different plumbing, and so forth. I chose *you* because we've worked together, and I had an idea you were intelligent. So don't start acting stupid. We have a chance to do something more sensible than forming fours in a Udenspils barracks. Don't you want to help?"

"But we don't *have* the technology to make chameleon suits," she protested. "Jekabs Ozols got them in Castell City. They're imported from Frystaat."

"The Saurons don't know where the Commissar shops."

She flushed. "Well, he won't be pleased if we leave two of his smart suits out here. They cost three thousand crown apiece."

Klimkans shrugged. "Ozols can afford to lose a couple of them if it helps us keep the Saurons off his neck." He eyed the impedimenta scattered around. "We'll take the bows. We're steppe dwellers. We've been hunting rock rats. Horn bows aren't too technically advanced for simple nomads."

Her eyes grew large as saucers. "We will . . . *what*?"

He managed a smile. "Be brave, Berkis. We're going down there to reason with the bastards."

As captain and corporal dropped to the trail, the Sauron by the truck turned, weapon raised. Klimkans promptly elevated his arms. Berkis followed his example. Sauron and Orfanians faced each other.

The Sauron wore body armor, a star on each shoulder. His visor was raised, his eye cold. Klimkans glanced up at the Saurons probing the fuser detritus. Did they have a Cyborg with them? What did a Cyborg look like? Would he know one if he saw one? The motionless confrontation continued. The Sauron levelled his weapon. Klimkans went cold. Was this bugger going to shoot?

"Better do something, quick, Captain," murmured Corporal Berkis.

As if released from paralysis, Klimkans threw away his bow, got to his knees, and bumped his forehead on the ground. He called in Americ, "Don't shoot, lord!"

The Sauron lowered his weapon. "What do you want, creature?"

Klimkans whined. "Lord, we have hunted all day without success. Would your honor have food to spare?"

The Sauron frowned. "Why should I have cattle food with me?"

"Please, your honor, we've eaten nothing today." Klimkans risked a quick glance up. The creature still held his weapon ready.

Berkis whispered. "Call this reasoning, boss?"

He whispered from the corner of his mouth. "Get down before I knock you down!"

She got to her knees. "I'm going to be sick."

The Sauron frowned. "What is all this grunting?"

Klimkans restrained an impulse to throttle his corporal. "Herd talk, lord," he babbled. "The female says you have a kind face and she hopes you will give us something to eat."

The Sauron contemplated the bows lying on the ground. "Where is the rest of your herd, creature?"

Klimkans made a sweeping gesture. "Out on the steppe, lord."

The Sauron's trigger finger moved. The trail bubbled at Klimkans' knee, and began to fume. "Be more precise, beast," commanded Authority.

Janis Klimkans swallowed bile. Heat from the molten pool in the path penetrated his coveralls. "I—I can't be more exact, lord," he stammered. "We are a nomadic people. We rove the steppe."

The Sauron turned a cool gaze on Berkis. "Perhaps the smaller beast can help?"

Linda Berkis had felt the warmth radiating from the bubbling puddle at Klimkans' knee. Her temper rose. Did the superswine think a souped up laser could overawe free Orfanians? Well . . . perhaps it could. She stammered, "How—how do you mean, lord?"

The Sauron raised his weapon. "For the last time, creature, where is your home?"

She was suddenly shaking. Janis thought he could reason with this arrogant bastard? A creature who liquified rock just to intimidate people. Who would probably liquify her if she refused to answer him. Linda Berkis was ready to die for Refuge—but not in such an ignominious way! She glared at the creature. "We followed the river . . . lord."

The trail bubbled beside her. She felt heat on her leg.

"Are you unsure of my status?" queried Authority.

She tried to still a trembling jaw. "N—no, lord."

"Sure?" Lightning flashed again. A puddle boiled in the trail before her. A wave of heat washed her face. She bowed her head. "My home lies down river, your highness."

"Ah! Veracity at last." The Sauron looked pleased. "How stubborn you cattle can be! Small beast, can you think of a reason why I should not incinerate you now?"

Was the bastard serious? Civilized people didn't talk like that. "We could be useful," she gambled, hoping Klimkans concurred.

"Lord?" prompted Authority.

"We could be useful, lord."

"In what way?"

She couldn't stop trembling. Bubbles still appeared in the path before her. "Beasts can pull burdens, lord."

"And what burden do you envisage pulling?"

"Your truck, lord?"

"Ah!" He seemed pleased. "An intelligent response! Little beast, that carrier's powerpack has failed. The unit is no longer self mobile. Are you suggesting that I let you deputize for a useless power unit?"

"It would save your men pulling it, lord."

"Do not worry about my men, little beast. Do you think you can tow an equipment carrier?"

"We could try, lord."

Authority spoke briefly into its helmet. The trooper by the vehicle stood back.

The Sauron gestured. "Pull it!"

Linda Berkis approached the carrier. She gripped the attached harness, and heaved. The vehicle moved an inch.

"The little beast finds the task difficult?" inquired the Sauron. He turned to Klimkans. "Help your companion!"

Klimkans got to his feet. He looped the harness across his chest, leaned into it, and pushed. The carrier rolled after him.

The Sauron commander lowered his laser. "You have won a reprieve, little beast. You and your fellow animal would be useful draft beasts. You may pull my equipment. Let us see now where this river takes us." He spoke into his helmet. The rest of the Sauron platoon bounded down from the plateau, and dressed a line before him.

Klimkans scowled at Berkis. In their own tongue, he muttered, "I guess you just saved our lives, Corporal . . ."

She smiled tremulously. "Think nothing of it, boss."

His mouth twisted. ". . . but someone else may have to foot the bill." He saluted the Sauron Commander. "Ready when you are, lord."

Authority eyed him gravely. "I do not tolerate insolence, beast. Whether you are ready or not has no significance." He spoke briefly into his helmet. The platoon turned on its heel, and set off along the trail. Klimkans and Berkis followed with the equipment truck.

*   *   *

General Andrei Galdins, stood on his balcony. By leaning over the parapet he could see his ground floor colonnade reflected in the waters of Lake Nesalst. High overhead, tilted slats admitted a cooling breeze to the valley. On the wall behind him, birds clucked in cages. Galdins stretched luxuriously. Refuge was a fine place to live in. As Deputy for Defence, he had time for his many interests. A flutter of wings caught his ear. A bird circled overhead. Recognizing it, he hurried indoors for the seed jar. His birds were precious. The one circling above descended from a pair imported decades ago from Roossia-na-Terra. He strewed seed on the parapet. The bird swooped. General Galdins captured it with practiced ease.

"Welcome home, *draugins*," he murmured.

The pigeon clucked contentedly. The general examined its leg. "What have we here? Has friend Janis sent us a note?"

He removed the canister from the bird's leg, and tipped out the paper cylinder. Spreading the paper amid the bird seed on the balcony, he donned his spectacles.

"*Suds!*" he muttered. "This is catastrophe!"

Breathing hard, General Galdins thrust the bird into a cage. Sometimes one's job had to take priority over one's hobbies.

Jekabs Judeiks Ozols, twenty-third Pirmais and hereditary ruler of Refuge, despite epicanthic eyefolds betraying a Tartar ancestry, boasted of direct descent from the legendary Orfan who had given his name to the first valley dwellers. Perhaps the blood of a certain Cham Khokuts, who, weary of a freezing yurt, declared peace on his Lettish neighbors and moved in with them, had diluted the original Orfan ichor. The Pirmais could be as sly and lazy as any Tartar. But, unlike his forbear, he wished to be loved as a benevolent despot. Refuge tradition, requiring him to appoint deputies, thwarted any aspiration towards tyranny, absolute or otherwise. Jekabs

Ozols knew what was good for his subjects. Trouble was, his subjects often disagreed with him. He waved the paper, foul with seeds and traces of guano, at his Deputy for Defence. "What is this rubbish, Andrei?"

General Galdins twitched. The Pirmais evidently intended to be difficult. "Sir, as you know, in pursuit of more secure means of communication, I have been experimenting with pigeons for the transmission of messages—"

Jekabs Ozols raised an admonitory finger. "Don't beat about the bush, Andrei. I know you've been up to something. I scent lese-majesty here, and I warn you, I take a dim view of it."

Galdins paled. Jekabs Ozols didn't joke where the Pirmais' dignity was concerned. The general gulped. "Please read the message, Pirmais."

Ozols frowned. "What message?"

"On the paper—in your hand, sir."

Ozols gave his deputy a cold eye. "Why did you not say, *nederigums?*"

Galdins swallowed the insult. "I am a fool, sir," he mumbled, feeling there were grounds for that opinion.

Ozols held the sheet of paper as far away as he dared. The pencilled scribble danced before his eyes. He muttered a Russki blasphemy. "This man's hand should be cut off. Can *you* read this scribble, Andrei?"

Galdins took the paper. In a quavering voice, he read aloud, "Have spotted a Sauron troop near the old fuser mound. Suspect they are looking for power installations. Will do our best to entice them away from Refuge. Try to think of something in case we fail."

Ozols paled. "A Sauron troop, did you say?" he queried.

"That's the message, Pirmais."

"And who is this 'we' who have spotted Saurons?"

"Captain Klimkans is a reserve captain in the Pioneers, Pirmais. He is the Klimkans of Klimkans Construction which is currently extending Your Excellency's realm.

When he was due for military service I decided he should try out our new chameleon suits. Corporal Berkis, one of his employees, is testing the female garment. I sent them up the *Karsts Udens* trail as far as the railway cutting."

The Pirmais looked down his nose. "I hear the suits were modified, Andrei. Let's hope they work properly." He nodded at the paper in the general's hand. "Where do your pigeons fit into this tale?"

The Deputy for Defence traced a pattern on the carpet with a delicate toe. "Sir, you know I believe that pigeons can be useful as message carriers in wartime. Unless they are physically intercepted, no one can pry on information transported by pigeon—"

"Which wartime are we discussing?" interrupted Ozols coldly.

Galdins' exposition floundered before the Pirmais' attack. "Sir," he gabbled desperately, "think what this report implies. If those supermen discover our valley . . ."

Jekabs Ozols sat down, the delights of tormenting his deputy forgotten. He propped an elbow on an ornate table imported from St. Ekaterina, and dabbed his forehead with an embroidered handkerchief. "Can we deal with a Sauron invasion, Andrei?" he asked.

Andrei Galdins seated himself without permission, relief tempered by fear of the Saurons. "There is no doubt we could cope with a single troop of the creatures, sir. But we have to remember their main force. If a single warship can render Haven's defences nugatory, what chance does our army have? We have the chameleon suits, of course. But not all the high-tech life support equipment is fitted. They make our soldiers practically invisible and bulletproof, but I can't claim they'd enable them to defeat supermen."

Ozols sighed. "Does that mean we must surrender, Andrei?"

Galdins sat to attention. "No, sir. But it means we must devise a way to keep them out of the valley."

"Easier said than done," grunted Ozols.

"Don't be despondent, sir. Our dusty sky vents baffled their satellite cameras. Refuge's existence might still be a secret."

Jekabs Ozols chewed on a thumb nail. "Assuming prisoners don't talk," he grunted. "What if this Sauron patrol follows the river to the Gullet?"

"If they do not suspect the valley exists, they might miss it." Galdins forced himself to sound cheerful. "I'm sure Captain Klimkans will do what he can to steer them away."

Ozols was not impressed. "What would Orfan Pirmais have done in my shoes?" he asked. Jekabs Ozols yearned to emulate the first ruler's wisdom and statecraft.

"A good question, sir." Galdins kept his voice cheerful. "He'd surely have found a way of outwitting the Saurons. But then, the first settlers were giants."

Pirmais Ozols looked up, his eyes bleak. How easily this prosy numbskull assumed the improbable! "The first settlers were ordinary men and women, like us, Andrei," he snarled, "with their backs to the wall."

"Yes, sir," acknowledged his deputy hurriedly. The Pirmais obviously didn't want to be cheered up.

The Commissar got to his feet. "Get me Zeltins," he ordered.

Linda Berkis had reached the limit of her endurance. Her back ached. Her knees were rubber. The palms of her hands chafed on the harness straps. Her existence had become a nightmare in which her only purpose was to drag this Sauron truck up and down the twists and turns of a rocky *Karst Udens* trail. Klimkans plodded beside her, heedless of her suffering. Around her, Saurons trotted like automata. She wiped perspiration from her face, stifling a sob.

Without warning, the platoon halted. Klimkans dug in his heels, his back against the carrier, and brought it to a stop. Grateful for a respite from hauling, Berkis stood and waited. The Sauron Commander appeared, arms akimbo. "The little beast is tired?"

She nodded, too weary to speak.

"Rest," he ordered. "I have commanded a halt."

Shaking with relief, she sank to the ground.

Authority turned on Klimkans. "You rest also, surly beast!"

Without a word, Klimkans slumped.

The Sauron commander patted her shoulder. "Remember, little beast—you volunteered to pull my equipment."

"I'm not complaining, lord." Her throat was dry. She found it difficult to speak. She croaked, "Will there be anything to drink, lord?"

"Refreshment will come," he promised. "Someone will bring you food."

The corporal stared tiredly at her boss. Had he been listening? Janis must be as hungry and thirsty. Did his silent back show his opinion of collaborators?

A trooper wearing chevrons on his sleeve opened a locker in the carrier's flank. He tossed two packages to Berkis.

She retrieved them from the dust. Klimkans' back was still turned to her. "Janis?" she whispered.

He sat motionless, unspeaking.

She tugged at the plastic wrapper of a package. "*Ludzu, Janis!*" she pleaded in the old tongue.

His face remained averted. "*Ko tu grib'?*"

She pushed a pack towards him. "There's a place ahead where we pass a steep drop to the river."

"So?"

"We could lose the carrier, there."

He picked up the Sauron food. "What use would that be?"

She examined her package, seeking a way in. "If they lost this truck, they might call off the patrol."

"Why should they do that?" He jerked a tab, and peeled back plastic. His pack began to steam.

She found the tab on her own pack, and tugged. "They'd lose their equipment, wouldn't they? That must make a difference. They wouldn't have brought the damn thing if they didn't need it. Some of the stuff on it must be essential."

He eyed her sourly. "What's essential to a Sauron platoon?"

Her pack began steaming. Her mouth filled at the delicious odor. "How should I know? Platoon gear."

He opened his package. "Like?"

She shrugged. "Ammunition? Tents?"

"You could be right." He sniffed at the food. "This smells like 'lope."

She tasted hers. "Could be vulpe." Uncaring, she began to eat. "Do you think it's worth a try?"

His eyes glinted. "That superswine will make puddles of us."

She shrugged. To be incinerated for sabotage was more dignified than being wiped out as a nuisance. Any true Orfanian should jump at the chance to sacrifice herself.

"I'd risk it," she told him. "If it forces them to abandon the patrol, it would save Refuge from being invaded."

He chewed reflectively for a moment. "Okay, Berkis. We'll give it a try. When I shout, drop the harness. I'll see the truck goes into the river." He grimaced wryly. "And if that bastard liquefies us, I'll recommend you for a posthumous decoration."

She grimaced. "I've always wanted a medal."

"Me too," he assured her in a voice lacking conviction.

General Teodors Zeltins studied the floor gloomily. "There must be a way to stop them," he muttered.

Jekabs Ozols peeled a citron grown in his own garden. "Have we no army, then?" He watched the general. Zeltins' wriggles were often as entertaining as those of Galdins'.

"It isn't that, Pirmais." The general fingered his tiers

of medal ribbons. Why couldn't the Pirmais keep his
nose out of military matters? Given time, a man could
think up ways of handling these superswine. But with
Ozols' beady eye watching every move ... The general's
gaze lingered longingly on a well padded armchair: only
the paramour had been invited to sit.

"Then what is it, man? Are my soldiers not eager to
kill Saurons?"

"Sir," began Zeltins hesitantly, "if this patrol finds our
valley, there'll be a Sauron fighter overhead within half
an hour dropping nukes on us."

"So?" The Commissar heaped peel on a plate. "You
listen to too many radio reports, Teodors. Do you really
think we are worth nuking?"

The general shot an appealing glance at the other
Deputies present. Neither spoke. People grew wary in
the Pirmais' company. Galdins caught the eye of Victorija
Budina. The Commissar's mistress, he suspected, was
laughing at him. "It's safest to assume they would use
nukes," he growled.

"Then," said Ozols, waving a citron segment, "this
patrol must not be allowed to discover our valley."

"That should be our aim, sir."

"So we set an ambush for them, and wipe them out!"

Zeltins licked his lips. "It isn't that easy, sir. Those
Saurons are better armed than our soldiers. Remember,
a single Sauron cruiser neutralized all Haven."

"So?" Ozols swallowed a segment of fruit, and wiped
the back of his hand across his mouth. "They missed us,
General. And this platoon has no cruiser with them. Send
in a few of our fliers. They should have no trouble."

General Zeltins clenched his fists. Attack first and
repent at leisure. This idiot had all the finesse of his
Tartar forbears. "Sir," he assured the Pirmais, "we can
destroy the Sauron patrol without much difficulty. It is
how to prevent them reporting the existence of the valley
which bothers me."

Jekabs Ozols looked down his nose, mouth twisted into

a tart rosebud. "Are you telling me that is beyond your ability, General?"

Zeltins detected the threat in his master's voice. His shirt grew clammy on his back. "I've said, sir—there *must* be a way."

Greta Vitolins, Deputy for Interior Security, intervened bravely. "I think Teodors means the Saurons must be prevented from finding the way through the Gullet."

The Pirmais smirked. "How? Do we paper over the crack?"

Zeltins closed his eyes. Ozols' juvenilities irritated him. "That would be quite a task, sir," he said patiently. "But we do need to find a way of concealing the gorge's entrance."

The woman lounging on a divan, exercised a paramour's privilege. "That shouldn't be too difficult, General dear."

Ozols whipped around, fingers spraying citron juice. "You have a plan, Vicky? Do tell us!"

Victorija Budina clasped slim hands behind an elaborate coiffure. "If the Saurons are not allowed to reach the Gullet, they will not be able to discover it."

Ozols nodded. "Very true, my love. But how do we achieve this desirable state of affairs?"

She told him.

The Pirmais fingered his chin. "The idea is attractive. Can we muster enough people to fill the relevant roles?"

Zeltins clutched at a provident straw. "You may leave that to me, sir."

Ozols shot him a nasty look. "Sometimes I feel I might do better to leave as little as possible to you, Teodors." He glanced around the room. "And the equipment we shall need?"

Greta Vitolins said, "We have plenty of props in store, sir."

Ozols' eyes glittered with sudden exultation. The Budina's plan offered him the opportunity to act out a long nurtured fantasy. "By the blood of my ancestors!" he shouted. "We'll do it! And I, your Pirmais, will personally conduct the enterprise."

Linda Berkis staggered under the strain of dragging the heavy carrier. The temperature had dropped in the last hour. Her breath hung visible in the air. She whimpered. *"Man salst, Janis."*

"Freeze, then," he responded, rejecting the intimacy of their mother tongue. "I can't do anything about it."

She bit her lip. Her numbed feet skidded on rimed rock, stiffening harness chafed her skin. Could she endure it much longer?

A tall shape moved beside her. A hand took the weight of the harness. A voice said lightly, "My little beast tires?"

Tears trickled down her cheeks. Were these creatures telepathic? "I'm cold, lord," she whimpered.

"You came unprepared for the night?"

Was the bastard being solicitous? His tone sounded amiable. The corporal thought regretfully of a warm frysuit secreted versts back on a hillside. "We didn't expect to stay out so late, lord," she lied.

The Sauron spoke into his helmet. A trooper pushed Corporal Berkis aside, and took her place in the harness. The Sauron commander tugged a sheet of plastic from the carrier, unfolded it, and draped it over her shoulders. "This will keep out the cold."

So his concern was genuine! Teeth chattering, she clutched it around her like a cloak. "Thank you, lord."

"The other animal does not feel the cold?" he asked.

"I think he—it—does, lord."

The Sauron commander raised his voice. "Do you want a sheet, surly beast?"

Janis Klimkans turned his head. His face was white, his lips blue. "If you please, lord," he mumbled, shamefaced.

The Sauron dragged another sheet from the carrier, and tossed it to Klimkans. "You were a fool to hunt inadequately clad. Where is this base of yours?"

Klimkans surveyed the trail before them. The mountains harboring Refuge should be visible around the next turn. "We will see it soon, lord," he muttered. Numbed fingers tried to spread the plastic without ceasing to press his chest against the harness. The Saurons made no attempt to help him. Arrogant bastards. It had been a mistake to think he could talk them into anything. Making the most of a free-wheeling moment in a declivity, he got the sheet around him. The warmth cheered him immediately. The light was fading. Would there be a chance to escape in the darkness? Tethered to a truck, with a Sauron beside him, the matter was debatable. Especially if they really could see in the dark.

The Sauron commander frowned. "Your base comes no nearer, beast. Is it on wheels?" He paused, listening. "Point reports there are tents out on the steppe. Do cattle use tents?"

"Lord?" Klimkans faltered.

The Sauron commander said patiently, "My man at point can see what appears to be a number of tents pitched on the steppe. Do cattle dwell in tents?"

Klimkans' brain spun. Tents? On the steppe outside Refuge? Was this a Galdins dodge to divert the Saurons?

"I—I—" he stammered.

The Sauron commander patted Berkis' shoulder. "I seem to be taxing your companion's abilities, little beast. Can you answer my question?"

She was just as puzzled. Who was crazy enough to camp on the steppe after nightfall?

"Are there many tents, lord?" she asked.

The Sauron consulted his radio. "At least a hundred," he told her. "And many campfires. Also carts, and beasts like you among them. Also the beasts which walk on four legs."

Berkis' mind raced. It sounded like a Tartar settlement. But no Tartars lived on the nearby steppe these days. Her pulse pounded. What if it were a mock camp, set up to deceive the Savrons for some reason? She feigned surprise. "It sounds as if you've found our base, lord."

He patted her encouragingly. "What else does my little beast tell me? May we ford the river here?"

Whoever had built the bogus camp, must have crossed *Karsts Udens*. She muttered in her own language, "Boss, how deep is the river here?"

Janis Klimkans' back stiffened. "This two legged creature wouldn't know, Corporal."

She eyed him patiently. No doubt Klimkans resented being addressed as "beast" by an arrogant bastard who only distinguished between men and muskylopes by counting legs. But what did Janis expect? He had been quick enough to call the Sauron "lord" at their first encounter. "Come on, boss," she urged. "No one likes being considered a 'beast.' You have to put up with it. Can these bastards cross the river here? Is it too deep?"

"Not deep enough," Klimkans muttered.

The Sauron commander patted her arm. "No herd gabble! Speak Americ!"

Janis Klimkans swallowed his anger. Displaying so many lights, the builders of the encampment must want to be noticed. Why try to avoid what was now inevitable? He recalled previous forays. "There is a ford, lord," he said. "But the lord must be wary. There are gaps, and the water is deep."

The Sauron commander gave him a puzzled look. "Your behavior improves, beast. Lead the way!"

Darkness was complete. Cat's Eye and Byers' had set. They rounded a bend and saw a swarm of fireflies flickering on the steppe. Klimkans caught his breath. Someone definitely didn't intend to be overlooked.

The Sauron pointed. "Observe the largest tent, beast!"

Klimkans peered into the night. "Lord," he apologized, "this creature sees only lights."

The Sauron frowned. "You have defective vision?"

"No, lord," murmured Klimkans. "Just beastly optics."

"Watch your tongue," cautioned Authority, "or you may be lamenting its absence."

Janis Klimkans clamped his jaw shut.

The trail descended the last slope. But for the darkness, the entrance to Refuge would be visible a few versts ahead. Could the Saurons see that far with their infrared vision? A little distraction might help. Klimkans licked his lips. "Permission to speak, lord?"

"What is it?" snapped the Sauron.

"This creature can no longer see the path, lord."

The Sauron spoke into his helmet. Torches illuminated the trail underfoot.

"Thank you, lord." The dazzle of the lights made the surrounding night darker. It might help to obscure what lay ahead. He plodded on, watching for the path the camp builders must have used.

Within minutes, he found it. Pointing, he called, "There, lord!"

Lights swung to illuminate a well-trodden track leading riverwards. Frozen ruts and hardened footprints obliterated any sign that the trail led elsewhere.

Without orders, Klimkans turned onto the new trail. The platoon halted, then followed him like sheep. He plodded on, exultant. These supermen weren't so goddamn smart. And, whatever lay across the river, they had been turned away from Refuge.

A spidery structure loomed out of the shadows. Klimkans recognized the lattice work of an army bridge he had seen bolted together many times on maneuvers.

The Sauron commander unholstered his sidearm. "Beast, what is this? Why did you not inform me there was a bridge?"

Janis Klimkans' mind went blank. There had been nothing over the river when he and the corporal had left Refuge that morning.

Beside him, Linda Berkis froze. Unless Janis found his tongue, their captor might use that laser. And Klimkans seemed struck dumb.

She plunged in, tongue thick in her mouth. "Permission to speak, lord?"

The Sauron swung round. "What is it, little beast?"

"The bridge is new, lord," she gabbled. "It must have been built after we crossed this morning. Our khan must have decided to make our return easier."

The Sauron inspected the structure. Its newness was unarguable. Fresh paint shone on the pontoons below. He slid his weapon back into its holster. "You have a considerate leader, little beast."

She started to sweat. "My lord is too kind."

He eyed her speculatively. "Let us meet this considerate leader of yours."

The banks of *Karsts Udens* were already freezing. The Sauron tested the ice with a wary boot. "The water hardens fast," he told the corporal. "In another hour this structure will not be necessary."

Her head spun. Did he expect her to justify the bridging of a freezing river? Why couldn't Klimkans dig up some excuses? "We were expected back before nightfall, lord," she improvised. "And the ice cannot be trusted to bear much weight."

"Let us see if we can trust this flimsy structure," he said.

"Perhaps we should cross singly, lord?" she ventured.

"That will not be necessary." The Sauron grasped her arm, and led her onto the bridge. The plastic floor creaked and boomed beneath them. She thought of the heavy equipment carrier following them, and walked faster.

"You are concerned for my welfare, little beast?" queried the Sauron. "Even though I have forced you to haul my equipment?"

"I wouldn't like to see you drown, lord," she told him.

Faced with such a happy event, she reflected, one could always close one's eyes.

He showed surprise. "You creatures are capable of loyalty?"

"We do have feelings, lord," she admitted.

"But your companion is less amiable."

"He has much on his mind, lord."

The Sauron frowned. "The surly one has a mind?"

They were challenged a hundred paces from the angle of tents and transport. The sentry wore soup bowl helmet and padded jacket. He carried a strung bow, a scimitar dangled from his belt. Berkis shrank back: as a child she had been scarred by Tartar tales.

The sentry let an eyelid droop.

She caught her breath. What was Karlid Vittenbergs doing here in that rigout? And would the Sauron be deceived?

Authority eyed the bogus sentry. "Out of my way, beast!"

Karlid Vittenbergs remembered instructions. He stretched his bow and aimed an arrow at the Sauron's breastplate. "Who goes there?" he demanded. "Friend or foe?"

Linda Berkis smothered a giggle.

Authority unholstered a deadly side arm. "Do you wish to become carrion, animal?"

Vittenbergs, who, when not being a Tartar, sold vegetables from a barrow in Udenspils market, hastily lowered the bow. "The khan invites you to visit his yurt, sir," he gulped.

The Sauron holstered the side arm. "Your khan chooses hospitality instead of hostility? How original."

Vittenbergs unnocked his arrow. "Follow me, chief."

"Proceed, creature," ordered Authority. "And the correct mode of address is 'lord.'"

"Yes, lord," gurgled Karlid Vittenbergs.

Ducking under a canvas awning, Berkis recognized the marquee used for Udenspils carnivals. Floored with cushions, and draped with hangings normally the property of Udenspils Operatic Ensemble, it made a convincing yurt. As she and the Sauron commander entered, a glittering major domo she had last seen fining traffic offenders, stepped out. He raised a hand. "No females!"

Authority halted in mid stride. "The little beast is with me. You will allow it to pass."

Berkis smirked. It would do Peter Arajis no harm to learn that the customer was not always intimidated.

Major domo Arajis clutched the jewelled belt supporting his ornamental scimitar, and pondered the wisdom of overdoing the act. He had heard tales of Sauron brutality. Perhaps the Pirmais would permit some relaxation of the rules. "The lord wishes the woman to accompany him?" he queried.

The Sauron commander eyed the mock major domo with ill-concealed enmity. "Must I repeat myself, beast?"

Arajis stepped back. "That will not be necessary, lord. Please proceed. No one will impede the lady."

"Lady?" queried the Sauron commander, staring about him.

"The—er—little beast," explained Arajis delicately.

A helmet bobbed in comprehension. "Ah, yes—of course."

They entered in triumphal procession. Fake Tartars made way for authentic supermen. Sauron and captive proceeded along a red velvet carpet, and halted before the great khan himself.

Like an unfolding flower, Jekabs Ozols rose from his cushions. He bowed. "Welcome to my humble yurt," he declaimed.

The Sauron commander ran his gaze over the marquee. "Is this your domicile, beast?" he demanded.

"While the grazing lasts," confirmed the counterfeit khan.

The Sauron's lips compressed. "Do you know who I am?"

Ozols blinked. For the sake of his role, he had discarded his spectacles, but one would be myopic indeed to be unaware of his interrogator's identity. "We have heard of you," he admitted.

"And you bid me welcome?"

Ozols shrugged. "You have conquered our world. We would be foolish not to face facts."

The Sauron commander raised his eyebrows. "Another reasonable beast? Life is full of surprises. Beast, I am addressed as 'lord.' You will answer some questions."

Ozols concealed his uneasiness. "Ask away . . . lord."

The Sauron glanced at Berkis. "That bridge was built this morning?"

Ozols hesitated. The superswine must be referring to the flimsy structure the army had flung across *Karsts Udens* that morning to facilitate moving props onto the steppe. Why was this creature interested in a bridge? Behind the Sauron's back, the female corporal looked sick. Jekabs Ozols suspected his response might be a matter of importance. The Pirmais examined the roof hangings for inspiration. What had the corporal told the superswine? It would be safest to opt for the truth—but the truth precisely, and not a syllable more than the truth. "It was not built this morning, lord," he said.

Authority pondered. The surly beast had been veracious! Perhaps these creatures were incapable of deceit! "When was the bridge built?" demanded Authority.

Ozols tried to catch the corporal's eye, but Berkis' head was lowered in what looked suspiciously like prayer. How could a man respond correctly when he didn't know what untruth was required? Ozols sighed. "It was built this afternoon, lord." He waited for the explosion.

The Sauron commander nodded: the beast's accuracy was commendable. "And why build a bridge?" he asked.

Ozols swallowed. By keeping strictly to the truth, he seemed to have avoided disaster so far. He glanced at the corporal, seeking further inspiration.

Linda Berkis refused to look up. The Commissar was a better fencer than either she or Janis.

Ozols perspired. Why build the bridge? Tell the truth, and ruin his scheme? No way! But why else build a bridge? South of *Karsts Udens* there was summer pasture. Grazing might be an excuse. But he had told the Sauron that the bridge had only been built that afternoon, and the creature would have noticed evidence of traffic on the far bank. Jekabs Ozols cudgelled his brain. Invention was the daughter of necessity. "There was a previous bridge which collapsed, lord," he gabbled. "We salvaged the remains."

He waited, sweating. The Sauron nodded his head. "You construct bridges quickly, beast."

Ozols damned the army and all its works. "It only needed bolting together, lord," he choked. "We have done it before. It is the only way to get our 'lopes over to the south bank." The Pirmais clamped his mouth shut, and defied the lightning.

The Sauron commander glanced around the marquee. "You say you are nomads," he observed, "yet you are profligate with light and heat?"

Ozols untangled his tongue. Breathing easier now they had got off that bloody bridge, he said, "My yurt is heated by a portable power source, lord. Some of my people rely on solar power packs, and batteries for the night. Others use windmills, or fuel cells. I believe it is even possible to suck heat from frozen ground, but we don't have the equipment to do that. Each yurt is responsible for its own comfort."

"And why camp on the edge of the steppe?"

Ozols ventured a shrug. "The grazing is rich here in the summer, lord. We give our 'lopes a treat."

Authority reflected. "I am minded to give you a clear bill of health, beast. You do not appear to be a threat, although there could be questions about your power source. I have orders to destroy all power plants I discover."

Ozols remembered he was an uncultured barbarian. He clasped his hands. "Lord, I beseech you, be merciful. Without our plant we would freeze during the night . . ."

Linda Berkis choked. Jekabs Ozols had missed his calling. He would have been a riot on the stage.

Authority deliberated.

Ozols pressed on hurriedly. "Would your highness not share our meal before deciding?" The Pirmais clapped his hands, not waiting for a response. "*Ludzu, pusdienas!*"

Female slaves appeared, bearing bowls as big as cartwheels. Berkis recognized one flimsily clad serf as a waitress from her favorite snackbar. The bowls, she realized, were trophies from the Folklore Museum. A steaming dish was set before the bogus khan. Ozols waved an invitation. "Be our guest, lord!"

The Sauron commander eyed the food suspiciously. Jekabs Ozols knew the value of sacrificing a pawn. He jerked a thumb at Berkis. "We do not permit the animal that speaks to eat in male company, lord."

Authority removed its helmet, a frown on its aquiline features. "The little mare is an honorary stallion," the Sauron announced.

Ozols subsided into his cushions. "As your honor decrees." He indicated the dishes set around them. "Will you permit us to offer meat to your men, and the other prisoner?" He dipped into a bowl, fished out a dripping gobbet, and popped it into his mouth. Jaws working, he stared blankly at the Sauron commander.

Authority closed its eyes, for a moment looking sick, then spoke into a comm unit. The thud of feet on Udenspils' Opera House carpet, the rumble of wheels, announced the arrival of the Sauron platoon. The trooper sharing Klimkans' burden dropped his section of harness, removed his helmet, and joined in a rush to the nearest bowl.

The Sauron commander tugged off metalled gloves. He stared warily at the bowl before Ozols. "What is this?"

"'Lope stew, lord," mouthed the Pirmais, fishing for further tidbits. "Thickened with a little barley, and maybe a carrot or two."

The Sauron sniffed at it. "Nothing else?"

"We have nothing else," lied Ozols. "Vegetables are costly."

"Hardly a balanced diet," commented the Sauron.

Ozols wiped fingers on his thighs, probed a pocket, and placed a bottle on the nearest cushion. "Try one of those, lord."

The Sauron examined the offering, eyes doubtful. "Pills? What are they for?"

The bugger was softening. Ozols scented victory. "Vitamin pills, lord," he murmured confidentially. "They help to keep us fit."

The Sauron commander put down the bottle unopened. "Manufactured in Castell City, I see." He dipped a cautious finger into the stew. "You nomads certainly travel around."

Ozols kicked himself. Showing the pills had been a slip. Next thing, this cocky bastard would be wanting to know where he did his shopping. He belched, allowing a rivulet of gravy to run down his chin. "We buy where we can, lord." He nodded imperturbably at the carrier thawing out on a borrowed carpet. "Why do your men pull that?"

The Sauron commander licked his fingers. The stew was tastier than anything he had eaten recently. He decided to overlook this Tartar's prying. "The power pack does not function," he grunted.

Superswine was definitely mellowing. Ozols risked a reproof. "Perhaps it is repairable, lord. Would your highness permit one of my technicians to examine it?"

Linda Berkis blinked. Had Ozols gone mad?

"No one meddles with my equipment," grunted Authority, fishing deeper into the bowl.

"I do not suggest meddling, lord," larded Ozols. "My technicians are experts."

Janis Klimkans murmured. "I suspect his highness may be suffering from a gimp coil burnout."

The Sauron suspended mastication. Was the surly

beast actually trying to help? "What is a 'gimp' coil, beast?"

Klimkans shot a glance at Ozols. One didn't steal the Pirmais' thunder with impunity. "You—you may know it by a different name, lord," Klimkans stammered. "But, a burnt out gimp coil means the carrier's power pack won't work."

"You are the expert?" asked the Sauron mildly.

"No, lord." Klimkans pointed to Berkis. "She is the expert."

Corporal Berkis blushed.

The Sauron commander stared. "*You*, little beast?"

She bowed her head modestly. "I have some expertise, lord."

The Sauron frowned. "Where did you learn about power packs?"

Panic gripped her. To explain that she was normally neither soldier nor nomad, would reveal the existence of Refuge. "I studied books, lord," she improvised.

"And you believe you can repair the carrier?"

"If you will permit, lord, I will try."

The Sauron waved a hand. "Let the little beast look at the machine. Give her what assistance she needs." He turned to Klimkans. "Help her!"

They found the power pack cell. Berkis pulled out a rack. The circuits resembled those which powered her drills. Maybe the Saurons shopped in Frystaat too! She located a blackened area where current had grounded, and prised out the dud coil. "Do you carry spares, lord?" she asked.

The Sauron commander raised his eyes to the chevroned Sauron. A quick exchange followed. "We have no spares, little beast," the Sauron told her.

Had the army used her drills to build that bridge? Best not enquire. Any talk of such technology might lead them to Refuge. But where else find a gimp coil substitute? Chameleon suits? Hers was tucked under a rock some thirty versts back along the *Karsts Udens* trail!

Berkis dropped into Latvian. "Any chance of getting hold of a frysuit, boss?"

"*Kapec?*" he demanded.

"Gimps in the powerpack."

He shook his head. "No way we can risk letting this superswine know we have chameleon suits."

She brushed hair from her eyes, feeling tired and defeated. "What do we do, then?"

He stared at her. "Don't Sauron suits use powerpacks?"

Her eyes lighted. "And they'll have spares!"

He glanced at the Sauron commander. "He'll tell you. You're his pet."

She got up, burned out coil in hand. "Lord, I need a replacement for this. May I look in the powerpack of one of your suits?"

Sauron eyes narrowed with suspicion. A queasy feeling told her she was treading on dangerous ground. "It is only a suggestion, lord," she said hurriedly. "We have nothing here that will do the trick."

Authority spoke rapidly. The chevronned Sauron rummaged in a carrier locker, and produced a small box edged with knife blade terminals. He gave it to the commander, who passed it to Berkis. "Is this what you seek, little beast?"

She took it, astonished at his compliance. "It could be, lord. Permission to open it?"

He dipped unconcernedly into the bowl. "Do as you wish."

She prised open the pack: a row of gimp coils lay inside.

"Jesus!" swore Klimkans. "And we hauled that damn truck for thirty versts!"

Working quickly, she transferred a coil to the carrier's powerpack, then buttoned everything up. She motioned the nearest trooper. "Try it please, lord!"

The soldier looked for permission, before climbing into the driver's seat. He flipped switches. A hum of power filled the yurt. He moved a lever. The carrier trundled along the carpet.

Berkis flushed at the applause.

"Well done, little beast," growled the Sauron commander. "You have remitted yourself and the surly beast from servitude. Our equipment is no longer your burden." He contemplated her, his meal forgotten. "I could use a technician with your talent. Will you work for me?"

Berkis caught her breath. Was he serious? No Orfanian could ever agree to serve in a Sauron unit. She lowered her eyes. "If the lord will forgive me . . ."

Authority actually laughed! "Understood, little beast. You are not disposed to volunteer." He turned to Ozols. "Did you tell me that vegetables were expensive?"

The Pirmais shifted uneasily. Another motiveless question! When would this nuisance be satisfied? "I may have mentioned the matter, lord," he admitted.

"Expensive in cash?"

Ozols scented a trap. "Er—yes, lord," he quavered.

The Sauron showed magnificent teeth. "And your vitamin substitutes are bought in Castell City. Tell me, devious beast—where do nomads obtain such appetizing food?"

Ozols gulped. He had lied about the vegetables to authenticate a supposedly Tartar meal. He dared not reveal that the stew had been prepared by a team of top chefs. That Udenspils stores teemed with home grown produce. Ozols clutched his head. It was that bloody bridge all over again! Icedge would have to take the blame.

"Lord," he said. "To the north, there is a hypermarket where one may buy imported delicacies."

Sauron eyebrows rose. A boreal hypermarket was evidently a novelty to the superman. He frowned. "This market is distant?"

Ozols shrugged. "Getting there takes about sixty hours, lord."

"Riding the four legged cattle?"

Ozols swallowed. "Yes, lord."

"And how quickly do the fourlegs travel?"

"We reckon six or seven versts an hour, lord."

"And your hours are the same length as those in Castell City?"

"The horologists insist on it, lord."

The Sauron was in no mood for humor. "The fourlegs cover six or seven versts *every* hour?"

"They walk in their sleep, lord."

"And the length of a verst?"

Ozols shrugged. "A verst is about a kilometer, lord."

The Sauron calculated. "Then it is some four hundred kilometers to this hypermarket?"

"If you say so, lord."

The Sauron commander glowered. "Did you not hear me say so?"

Ozols squirmed. "Figure of speech, lord."

The Sauron scowled at him. "Seek precision, beast! Communication is difficult enough without needless obliquity."

"Yes, lord." Jekabs Ozols swallowed some needless indignation.

The Sauron stood up. "In which direction is this hypermarket?"

The Pirmais rose too. "Due west, lord. Keep the mountains on your left and you can't miss it." He paused. Best supply a reason for the warmth of the sea, too, or this bugger would start looking for power plants again. "The market is in a settlement called Icedge, lord. It's built on a bay which does not freeze. We believe the sea is warmed by vulcanism."

The Sauron swallowed the fiction without a blink. "Does the river flow into this benevolent bay?"

Blast that bloody river! It was like an arrow always pointing to Refuge. Ozols cleared his throat. "The river disappears into a mountain gorge, lord."

Sauron eyebrows went up. "And thence?"

The Pirmais shrugged. "I couldn't say, lord. We steppe dwellers dislike poking our noses into enclosed spaces."

The Sauron sniffed in disdain for claustrophobia. The concept of a heated sea seemed to intrigue him. He donned his helmet. "I thank you for your hospitality, beast. First Rank insists that I check all population centers. I will look into this place called Icedge."

Tongue firmly in cheek, the Pirmais bowed. "Will you not stay to enjoy our hospitality, lord? We had hoped to display our dancing girls for your entertainment."

"Capering cattle hold no attraction for me or my men," snapped the commander. He spoke into his helmet. As if worked by a switch, the platoon came to its feet.

And good riddance, reflected Pirmais Ozols, watching them prepare to go. They didn't deserve to see Victorija and her ladies flaunting their underwear. He bowed. "We wish you a safe journey, lord."

"What could harm us?" smiled the Sauron. "Have we not subjugated your planet? Be glad we let you live in it."

He made a sign. The platoon faced left. At another signal they marched off, followed by the equipment carrier. As he passed Corporal Berkis, the Sauron commander bent to whisper in her ear.

Jekabs Ozols kicked a cushion clear across the tent. "Thank Hecate that farce is over!"

Teodors Zeltins unbuckled his sword belt, and let it fall. "Congratulations on a magnificent performance, sir. You surely saved our valley from the Saurons."

Ozols dabbed his forehead with a crocheted exhibit from Udenspils folk museum. "You think so, Teodors? I know my tongue is stuck in my cheek. I haven't told so many lies since my wife suspected that my friendship with the Budina was less than platonic."

Zeltins grinned. "They were very convincing lies, sir. Thank goodness the Saurons do not share your good lady's suspicious nature."

Andrei Galdins doffed a Tartar helmet. "I take it we can we all go home now, sir?"

The fake cham yawned. "That's not a bad idea, Andrei. The prospect of sleeping in a comfortable bed allures me."

Janis Klimkans coughed respectfully. "I wouldn't get too hooked on the idea, sir."

Jekabs Ozols paused, arms outstretched. "And why not, Captain?"

Klimkans swallowed. "Those Saurons will be back."

Ozols blanched. "Who says so?"

Klimkans smirked at Berkis. "Tell the Pirmais what that boss man said to you on the way out."

She paled. "He said he hoped to change my mind about joining his platoon . . . *when he returns*!"

Jekabs Ozols stood petrified.

Berkis peeped timidly at the First Citizen. "I didn't promise him anything, sir."

The Pirmais clapped a hand to his brow. "Will I never be rid of the monster! Did he say when he'd be back?"

Berkis trembled. "No, sir."

Klimkans' arm crept around the corporal. There was no need for the Commissar to pick on Berkis.

General Teodors Zeltins recovered his sword belt from the carpet. "We mustn't risk him finding the yurt dismantled, sir." He buckled the belt around his waist. "Perhaps it would be advisable to resume our Tartar roles?"

The Pirmais poised, legs astraddle, hands on hips. "Are you advising me to stay here until that bloody Sauron returns?"

Zeltins elevated innocent eyebrows. "It might be expedient, sir."

"I must agree with the general," murmured Deputy Galdins, getting an oar in. "For the security of Refuge, we ought to maintain our cover as Tartars."

The Pirmais vented his resentment on another cushion. "So I am to rusticate here until that pest deigns to show his face again?"

General Zeltins covered a grin with his hand. "I'm afraid so, sir." He glanced at the trembling Berkis. "There might be another solution, Pirmais."

Jekabs Ozols eyed this slippery general with suspicion. "Which is . . . ?"

"Send the corporal after the Saurons. Let her join them. Then there's be no need for them to return to see if she's changed her mind."

Ozols chewed his underlip, pondering.

Klimkans watched, incredulous. Surely the Pirmais wouldn't be tempted by such a calculating ploy!

"And if she refuses?" Ozols challenged.

Zeltins scowled. "She will not be permitted to refuse."

Linda Berkis' world dissolved in confusion. The Pirmais and General Zeltins debating her future as if she were a chattel! She opened her mouth to protest, but no sound emerged.

Klimkans blurted, "Sir, you can't do this to the corporal!"

Ozols' eyes grew opaque. "Can I not, Captain? When did I forfeit the ability?"

Klimkans set his jaw. He and Berkis had hauled that faulty Sauron equipment wagon for thirty versts, over rough ground, bodies numb with cold, sweat freezing on their eyebrows. And this plump parasite was prepared to hand her over to the Saurons in the hope of evading a few hours' discomfort. Captain Janis Klimkans began to boil. "Sir," he warned, "if Corporal Berkis joins the Saurons, she may be forced to transfer her allegiance."

The Pirmais' eyebrows went up. "Does that matter?"

"She could tell them about Refuge."

Ozols' eyes bulged. He spluttered. "She—she wouldn't dare!"

Klimkans coughed diplomatically. "She might have no choice, sir. We don't know what methods the Saurons use to extract information."

Ozols swung on Zeltins. "Is Captain Klimkans correct?"

The general's blood was already chilling. Had he slipped up? The Pirmais could be ruthless with people who made mistakes. He coughed. "Captain Klimkans may possibly have a point, sir. The Saurons might decide to torture her—since she is no more than an animal to them."

The Pirmais' lip curled. "Then your solution is flawed?"

General Zeltins flinched. "Perhaps I spoke too hastily, sir." His straightened his Tartar costume. "But we must get the corporal out of the way. That Sauron fellow will be looking for her."

"So where do you suggest we send her, Teodors?"

Klimkans had an inspiration. He risked interrupting the Pirmais again. "Our chamsuits ought to be brought back, sir. We hid them near the old fuser ruins."

Jekabs Ozols stiffened. "You have been leaving my expensive chameleon suits around? At three thousand crowns apiece?"

"I don't imagine the rock rats will steal them," muttered Klimkans.

Jekabs Ozols' piggy eyes glinted. "You must retrieve them, Captain. The treasury cannot afford to abandon six thousand crowns to rock rats."

Klimkans swallowed a smile. "Shall I take Corporal Berkis with me—to keep her out of the way?"

Ozols lowered opaque eyelids. "Perhaps you should. You may need her help to locate those suits." The Pirmais tugged at his lip, cogitating. Klimkans held his breath. Important matters were plainly being considered. "It will be a long walk," resumed the Pirmais. "And chilly without your chamsuits. We suggest you take Generals Zeltins and Galdins along. They will retain their Tartar cover . . . for the security of Refuge." The Pirmais smiled.

Janis Klimkans saw two high ranking jaws sag. A Pirmais upset was a Pirmais implacable.

"They will be able to advise on any problem you encounter," added Ozols. "They are good at that."

Klimkans saluted. "I'll see about lights, sir. It will be difficult following the trail in the dark."

"Do that," agreed Jekabs Ozols. "We wouldn't like to think of anybody stumbling around blindly."

The Pirmais smirked at his deputies.

General Zeltins glowered at General Galdins.

General Galdins avoided General Zeltins' eyes.

Captain Klimkans smiled at Corporal Berkis.

Corporal Berkis stared at her captain with unalloyed admiration.

Anton Quilland frowned.

From Deathmaster of Troops aboard the *Fomoria*, Quilland had become the *de facto* Commander in Chief of all Sauron Soldiers on Haven. But the span of time to reach this position ... years, years. Thirty of them since the *Fomoria*—Diettinger's ship, by God, and damn the day they had changed her name to that ridiculous *Dol Guldur!*—since the *Fomoria* had first come to Haven. He looked across the room to a holoplate of First Citizen Galen Diettinger on the wall, flanked by a pair of banners that bore the flaming eye insignia of the Saurons on Haven.

Quilland considered that, for all the woes facing the Saurons these days, things at least were more like those heady, early years. The Pacification; the establishment of the Tribute systems; Diettinger's Great Gate and the first true allies it brought the Saurons from among the violent, disparate peoples of Haven: A tribe so abused by their fellow Haveners that Diettinger had easily convinced them of the wisdom of joining their fortunes to those of the Saurons, who now held the pass between the Shangri-La and the Steppelands.

It was a long road that had brought them here, and like all long roads, loneliest the nearer its end. There was a knock on his door and his aide entered to announce that Breedmaster Caius was waiting in his anteroom to see him.

Quilland was pleased; he and Caius had never been close, but they were *ka-ch'k;* "old comrades" in the Battle Tongue. They had been through times together that were already legends among the young Blooders heading out on their first patrols.

Over the years, the Breedmasters passed on their knowledge of Sauron progeniture to increasing numbers of students. As their ranks grew, they had grown in influence, and now, with the new generations of Saurons finally maturing, they had all the power of genetic Inquisitors. All Saurons respected them, many revered them, but few liked them. Breedmasters presided over every birth like evil fairies, bearing the genetic judgments that were their responsibility and greatest power. Breedmasters decided at birth if a Sauron child was left with its parents or cast out—literally—from the Citadel.

None of them pretended to enjoy their status as occasional murderers of children, any more than Saurons in combat enjoyed killing; it was simply their responsibility. All Saurons knew their place in their society, so no blame was levied against fellow Soldiers carrying out their duties to that society. No blame—but no parent, Sauron or human norm, could help but treat the Breedmasters with dread. About their children, Saurons were as human as any human norm.

But Caius and Quilland, at least, were friends, *ka-ch'k* from the First Days, as Sauron historians were already calling them. *As if the Sauron homeworld and its war against the Empire—which brought us all here—had never been,* Quilland thought.

"What brings you here, Breedmaster?"

"I have a report regarding Daborah."

Quilland was silent for a moment. "Daborah" was the

code name for a project Caius and he had worried about from its inception: The return of selected female Soldiers to active combat duty.

"Speak." Quilland spoke in a low voice. It was not a command; more a supplication.

"There have been complications," Caius said.

"Unexpected?"

"Only in degree. A Soldier from Angband Base waits in my quarters with news of an unauthorized raid against the town near Angband; the natives call it Tallinn."

Quilland lifted an eyebrow. "This man is your spy?"

Caius nodded. "A perennial Fifth Ranker; a plodder. Perfect for such observations as were required."

Quilland reflected the areas where Project Daborah was being tested; all were very far indeed from The Citadel, and purposely so. The dispersal was intended to limit the chances of any disaster spreading to the main Sauron outposts in the central Shangri-La; a wise precaution, as it now seemed.

"Angband is six thousand kilometers from here; how soon can he make his report to us?"

"Immediately, Deathmaster; he is here."

Quilland was rarely surprised; rarer still did he show it. "He came here?"

"Two days ago, he stole a rotor-wing from Angband and flew all night to the eastern Shangri-La transportation hub at Firebase Twelve. From there he stowed away aboard a tribute lifter."

"Why didn't he simply demand transport in your name?"

"He was accompanied by a human norm. A female."

"What? In God's name, why?"

"He brought her as a witness."

Quilland remained silent for a long time. "It's that bad?"

"It could hardly be worse."

"Send for him."

Caius produced a small rod from his tunic and spoke

into it softly. Minutes later, the aide ushered in a Sauron
Fifth Ranker and a human norm woman; elderly, with
eyes that had seen their share of hardship, but unbowed.
Good, solid peasant stock, Quilland thought to himself.
Only a few centuries ago she'd have fit right in among
the colonists of Sauron itself.

That raised a disturbing implication in the back of his
mind; one he didn't care to dwell on.

"Do you speak Americ?"

"Some." The woman spoke in a voice low with barely
checked terror; still, her eyes were clear, defiant. Quilland
gestured to his aide, who produced a chair for the human
norm female.

Cattle, he thinks of her, Quilland thought. It was a failing
the Saurons were only now beginning to train out of their
young Soldiers; no one who'd ever seen a stampede treated
real cattle with contempt.

"Are you hungry?" Quilland asked, attempting to put
her at ease.

"Always." There was in her bearing before she spoke a
hint of contempt for the question.

Good, Quilland thought. Brave. Another gesture sent
his aide off to fetch her food and drink. "I want you to
tell me, in your own words, what happened to your village
of Tallinn."

The woman watched him for a moment, then asked:
"Why?"

Caius was taken aback by the woman's effrontery; his
spy was openly astonished. Quilland waited a moment,
then his face split in the wolfish grin for which he was
known.

"You mean 'what difference would it make,' don't you?"
the Deathmaster asked. The woman's expression did not
alter, and Quilland continued after a philosophical shrug:
"Perhaps none. After all, you and the rest of the people
of Haven are going to have to live with us as overlords.
You don't have to like it; you don't have any say in it."

He leaned forward, conspiratorially: "Then again, we're

not stupid; we can create more trouble for ourselves than you can create for us. Removal of elements such as the Saurons who attacked your village—against orders, by the way—can only strengthen our position, and yours. Tribute women we can already have, by the hundreds. Productive villages to trade with are harder to come by."

Quilland shot a glance at Caius, remembered some of their fears concerning Project Daborah, and took a chance: "And one witless banshee with a laser is not going to endanger productive relations between Haveners and Saurons, nor is she going to be allowed to lead my men around by their balls. Not without answering for it, she isn't."

Quilland watched the old woman's face as she listened, and knew that he would hear it all, and all of it the truth. Not because the old Havener cared a whit for "relations between Haveners and Saurons"; certainly not because Quilland's standards of discipline were being compromised.

She will tell it all for the sake of simple, raw hatred, Quilland knew.

The old woman began to speak, her voice gaining strength as she convinced herself she was signing the death warrant of at least one Sauron, perhaps more. It was an account of almost ludicrously inept brutality, which had nevertheless convinced her that she at least knew how ruthless Saurons could be.

Quilland felt no need to tell her that the female Sauron in question would almost certainly be lobotomized and relegated to Walking Womb Status; a hardy crucible for birthing Saurons until her insides withered from the mileage of dozens of Soldiers—or one Cyborg.

Ruthless? Thinking about the uses to which Caius would put the offenders, Quilland decided that the old woman didn't know the meaning of the word.

THOSE WHO LOSE

Harry Turtledove

The chilly air of Tallinn Town was thick with the stink of woodsmoke. The onion dome of the Orthodox church swayed, toppled, crashed down through the roof. Two still forms lay in the street outside the church. One, a black-bearded priest, would never again be anything but still; blood from a dreadful head wound soaked the dirt beneath him and soiled his embroidered robe.

At the crash of the collapsing dome, though, the other figure stirred, twisted, slowly sat. Svetlana Mladenova gazed upon ruin through half-focused eyes. She held her head in her hands. Her heavy body swayed back and forth in mourning older and deeper than conscious thought.

How long she stayed there, rocking, keening, she never knew. She looked up again at a shout in a language she did not know. This time, the world looked clearer. That clear sight only made her long for the previous blur. Tallinn Town had truly fallen, if one could speak of a fly falling when the swatter came down on it. She listened for gunfire, but the Saurons must have mopped up the last hopeless fighters while she sprawled senseless in the street.

The shout came again, closer now. She turned her head toward it. The motion made everything spin sickeningly for a moment, but then the world steadied. She got her first good look at a Sauron Soldier. Before, the invaders had been nightmare figures in their aircars, in the combat vehicles that laughed at anything mere hunting rifles could do to them.

Rather to her surprise, the Sauron seemed an ordinary man, not a fork-tailed devil. He was taller, leaner than most of the men of Tallinn Town; his tight-fitting gray uniform, exactly the color of the smoke he strode through, emphasized that. But his sandy hair, his light eyes were no different from those of the half the townsfolk.

He looked startlingly young. Thinking that, Svetlana found she was laughing at herself. Her granddaughter stood at the edge of womanhood, so the whole of Tallinn Town looked young to her.

Then the Sauron moved. Svetlana thought her eyes were playing more tricks on her—one instant he was *there*, the next *here*. *Here* was right in front of her. She looked into the barrel of his gun, saw her own death there. What was one more, added to so many?

The gun barrel gave a peremptory jerk. "Get up, old woman," the Sauron said in Russki so bad, so Americ-accented, that Svetlana needed a couple of seconds to understand. They almost cost her her life. "Get up," the Sauron repeated. "If no—" He did not say what would happen then, but the gun pointed at her face once more.

She was not sure she could get up. But she was sure that if she failed, this fresh-faced conqueror would kill her as she stepped on a cockroach, and would worry more about the round he'd wasted than her corpse. She heaved herself upright, stood swaying.

The Sauron gave her no time to steady herself. He gestured with the gun again, sideways now. "Go along. That way." Again, she could hardly follow his accent, but the gun barrel made the meaning plain enough. She managed a step, another, a third.

"Where are you taking me?" she asked.

"Shut up." That phrase came out clearly, as if the Sauron had had practice using it. Likely he had.

He cocked his head at every house he passed. Once, he walked over to one, kicked down the wooden door, went inside. He was back in seconds, herding two townsfolk in front of him. One of them, a boy of about fifteen T-years, staggered along white-faced, clutching an obviously broken arm to his chest.

His sister was a little older. She might have been pretty, were she less frightened. She started to cry when she saw Svetlana. "What will they—?"

The Sauron cut her off. "Shut up." In what might have been chivalry, he deigned to point with a finger instead of his weapon. "That way, cattle."

A few houses further on, he broke down another door. The boy with the broken arm bolted. A single shot rang out. The boy pitched forward, fell on his face. The Sauron peered out a window. Grinning at the old woman and the young, he tapped his ear. "You try run, I hear you." He disappeared again, returned with more captives.

Had he heard them too, Svetlana wondered, moving inside their house? She'd heard nothing, but her ears were not what they had been. Still, she doubted any normal man's hearing could have filtered such tiny sounds from the chaos that filled Tallinn Town. What was the Sauron, then? Only one answer came to her: *the new master here.* She shuddered, shambled on.

Tallinn Town was not a big city, not even by Haven's modest standard; the Tallinn Valley did not yield enough to support a big city. A few minutes' walk took Svetlana and her fellow prisoners outside the last of the houses. In the beetfields by the edge of town, people were herded together like ... *like cattle,* Svetlana thought uneasily, remembering the word the Sauron had used.

Men stood here, women there. She wondered why

they did not mingle. For that matter, since only a handful of guards stood in the field, she wondered why some did not try to run. Then she saw the coils of razor wire that sparkled with deceptive cheer under the light from Cat's Eye and Byers' Star, turning fields into holding pens.

The gate to the women's enclosure was more razor wire, strung between a frame of posts. Before the guards let her inside, they felt her more intimately than even her late husband had been in the habit of doing. One pulled the crucifix off from around her neck, but when he saw it and its chain were only brass, he tossed it back with a snort of contempt. She scowled at him, blackly as she could. Immune to her hatred, he laughed and grabbed her backside again. She squalled in outrage, fairly leaped into the pen to escape such unwelcome attentions.

"Mother!" "Grandmother!" Hit by embraces from two directions at once, Svetlana staggered, almost fell. Tears cut hot tracks of joy down her chilly cheeks. After a bombardment worse than anything she'd imagined, after seeing so much death and casual destruction, she'd given up hope that Olga and Yelena still lived. But here they stood hugging her, hardly even hurt. She crossed herself over and over, sending up prayers of thanks to God.

"Are you all right, mother?" her daughter Olga Ryzhkova asked. She was a solidly built woman still of childbearing years, capable-looking rather than pretty: what Svetlana had been twenty T-years before. "Did the *nemtsi*—" The word, which literally meant *tongue-tied*, had come over the centuries to apply to Germans. It fit the Saurons like a glove.

"I am alive; to be alive now is to be well enough," Svetlana answered. She pointed over to the men's pen. "Have you seen your Sasha?"

Fear filled her daughter's blue eyes. "No. I do not think he is there. The last I saw of him was when he took his gun to fight. Since then—" She shook her head, unwilling to go on.

Yelena said, "But Yuri is in the men's pen, mother. He was skipping about as happily as if it were his birthday."

"Your little brother was only nine T-years, Yelena," Olga said. Under the brave front she kept up for her daughter's sake, she sounded worn and fragile, as if she were running on the last of her reserves. But somehow she managed to smile, and continued lightly, "To one that young, everything—even a pen—is a game."

Svetlana hoped her grandson would be able to keep thinking that, though she knew how forlorn such hope was. A little more of it died every time the Saurons brought fresh prisoners out of Tallinn Town to the pens. For one thing, the women's pen filled far more quickly than the men's. For another, all the townsfolk, women and men alike, looked dazed and tattered and—*beaten* was the word she found at last. The Saurons, by contrast, strode about on their errands as if they thought themselves God's anointed.

Olga scowled when she said that aloud. "More likely the Devil's mother," she said, reproof in her voice. Svetlana thought her daughter was surely right. Yet she had prayed to God, and what had it got her? The holy church fallen in on itself, Father Pavel stretched in front of it with half his face gone, and Tallinn Town . . . she tried not to think about what would happen to Tallinn Town in time to come.

Hours slid past. Byers' Star crawled slowly up the sky. The Saurons did not feed their prisoners, or make any other provision for them past ensuring they could not escape. When Svetlana needed to relieve herself, she had to squat in an already befouled patch of mud. It was on the far side of the enclosure from the men's pen, so the bodies of her fellow captives shielded her from that shame, but nothing shielded her from the gaze of the Sauron guard a few meters away on the other side of the razor wire.

He had more Russki than did the fellow who'd

captured her. Grinning nastily, he said, "Cover yourself, old woman. I've seen far better than you."

"*Metyeryebyets*," she snarled, the first time in her life, so far as she could remember, she'd ever called anyone anything so foul. The Sauron just laughed at her. She did not know whether he'd understood.

After some nameless stretch of time, new prisoners stopped coming. A Sauron marched arrogantly out between men's and women's pens, shouted in Russki: "Hear me, cattle!" The voice was brassy and high, high enough to make Svetlana stare. Sure enough, those were a woman's breasts pressing against the field-gray tunic. A woman Sauron! Somehow for Svetlana, it was one abomination too many.

"Hear me!" Woman or not, this Sauron sounded fierce as any other. "You belong to the Race. You had better understand what that means, if you want to live a little longer. I don't care one way or the other—it's up to you."

The Devil's anointed indeed, Svetlana thought. She believed the Sauron witch absolutely. Too many men, women, children lay dead in the ruins of Tallinn Town for her to doubt. And even were that not so, the scornful amusement with which the Sauron spoke carried conviction of itself.

"You will obey us in all things," she said, as if setting forth a law of nature. "If you fail in obedience, you will be punished. If you raise your hands against us, you will die. You may as well see now that we need no guns to enforce our will." She walked over to the men's pen, pointed to the biggest, strongest-looking fellow she saw. "You—go the gate. The guard will let you out. Here is your chance for revenge if you can take it."

The word flicked Misha Sikorsky into a trot. He was a brown-bearded bear of a man, fifteen centimeters taller than the Sauron woman, fifty kilos heavier, and twice as wide through the shoulders. He was also, Svetlana knew, the best wrestler in Tallinn Town.

The Sauron said, "You want to kill me, don't you?"

He did not have to answer; one look at his eyes was answer enough. She laughed a taunting laugh. "Come ahead and try. None of the other Soldiers will stop you, I promise, and I have no weapons. I am yours for the taking." She shifted her stance, spreading her legs slightly. "For that matter, you can take me as you like if you beat me. I would give myself to you; your genes might aid the Race."

"I wouldn't dirty my prick with you," Sikorsky said— and as he spoke, he sprang. In normal times, he was not the sort to strike a woman even when he was drunk, which made him a minority in Tallinn Town. Now, though, he went after this one as if she were any other foe—and why not, with the ruin her kind had dealt out in Tallinn Town, and in which she shared?

He was powerful, he was quick—and it availed him nothing. Cries rose from both men's and women's pens as he roared toward the woman Sauron. Svetlana shouted with the rest, a prayer to the God who did not seem to be listening. The woman merely waited, flat-footed and relaxed. She ducked under his grab as if he'd warned her it was coming, slid behind him, grabbed. She had the same deadly speed the Sauron who'd caught Svetlana had shown.

The townsfolk's shouts cut off as if sliced away by a knife. Misha roared, in surprise and anger. But he was a veteran of too many brawls to panic at the unexpected. He reached round behind him, bent his knees to roll forward and over, to crush the Sauron woman with his greater weight.

Before he could—long before he could—she jerked back. He let out a startled squawk as his feet left the ground. Without visible effort, the Sauron woman lifted him over her head, slammed him to the cold, hard ground. He groaned, tried to rise, faltered; he shook his head as if it were filled with fog. Blood ran from his nose and the corner of his mouth. Grinning, the Sauron woman walked up to him to finish him off.

He snaked a hand round her ankle, yanked. She went down, an expression of absurd surprise on her face. Svetlana's ecstatic scream was lost among hundreds. No longer pretending to be more dazed than he was, Misha pulled the Sauron toward him.

She kicked him in the ribs with her free leg. He groaned. She grabbed his right arm, twisted cruelly. He screamed then, and clutched his shoulder. After that, the fight was no longer a fight but a beating. When the Sauron woman stood up after a couple of minutes, no one in the pens could doubt her victory had been no fluke.

The woman ran her hands through her hair, the first even slightly feminine gesture she'd shown. She delivered her verdict: "He was better than I thought, but not nearly good enough." Beaten yet again, this time through their champion and by one who looked to be the weakest of the Saurons, the prisoners sagged in despair.

The woman barked, "Now you've seen. We don't *need* weapons against the likes of you. But we have them, too, and what isn't here we can call up from the Citadel. Revolt and you die, and die for nothing, for you can't hurt us. Do as we say and you'll manage well enough—better than before, maybe, for the steppe nomads will never dare trouble Tallinn Valley again."

"The Saurons are worse than any nomads," a woman close by Svetlana said, looking back toward the ruins of Tallinn Town.

"But they are stronger," another woman answered, as if that mattered. In a way, perhaps it did. Folk of the Russki blood demanded strength in a master above all else, even kindness or fairness. Strong the Saurons were. As their spokeswoman talked (and as Misha Sikorsky still lay unconscious), they gathered round her like a pack of stobor satiated for the moment but ready to kill again if the whim struck them.

The woman Sauron said, "We have also a Breedmaster

among us. Babies will die needlessly no more, nor mothers."

Remembering her own travails at birth; remembering friends of her youth now long T-years dead in childbed; remembering, as those of Tallinn Town did, the medical techniques those of Tallinn Town no longer commanded, Svetlana thought the Saurons could have had Tallinn Valley for the asking on the strength of that promise alone.

The Sauron woman showed her teeth. It was not a smile—more a warning. "Of course, we do this for ourselves and our purposes first. This is a matter you had best not misunderstand. You are ours."

"What will they do to us?" someone said, soft and fearful.

"Did you not hear? Whatever they want," someone else answered.

What the Saurons did seemed benign enough: they opened the prisoner pens. "Men, find your women. Wives, find your husbands," the Sauron woman called. "Do it quickly, for we have other business to attend to here."

Under the guns of their conquerors, the two crowds, male and female, mingled. And even under those guns, glad cries rang out as couples crushed each other in embraces the more fervent because they'd thought they would never embrace again. Olga charged into the thick of the men, shouting Sasha's name. Svetlana and Yelena both hung back; neither had a partner waiting.

As pairs formed, the Saurons separated them—and any attached children—from the rest, until they formed a distinct group of their own. A line of Soldiers, weapons at the ready, screened them from the men and women (more women than men, two or three times as many; the fighting had been fierce while it lasted) who remained solitary. Svetlana's heart sank to see her daughter not far away. Sasha had gone down, then. One more anguish on top of all the rest.

The woman Sauron said, "All right, you families can

go back to your town. Start putting things together again, make sure your crops grow. We'll be putting in perma- nent fortifications over there"—she pointed east, across the Tallinn River from the town—"and we have first claim on your produce. Anything you raise over what we take, you get to keep. So if you intend to eat from now on, you know what you have to do."

One of the men was bold enough to ask a question: "Suppose we don't raise even enough for you?"

"We figure one of two things in cases like that," the Sauron woman said with another of those dangerous smiles. "You might be lazy, in which case we kill you and bring in harder-working cattle. Or you might be holding out on us, which is treason to the Race—in which case we kill you and bring in cattle who know better. Anyone want to know anything else?"

Glum silence from the crowd. Several Saurons ges- tured with their gun barrels. Svetlana had seen that peremptory motion so many times in the past few hours, and each so nearly identical to all the others, that she wondered if the Soldiers practiced in front of a mirror.

A few at a time, the intact families shuffled toward Tallinn Town. All but a handful of the guards turned back to the men and women—mostly women—they still held. Svetlana did not like the expression on their faces. Again they reminded her of stobor, a pack of stobor sitting in a circle around a calf they'd cut out of the herd, waiting for the moment when they'd all leap together and tear the little animal to pieces.

The woman Sauron nodded to a man who came up beside her. It was not exactly a salute, but it was a defer- ential nod. He was older than she, and wore fancier collar tabs—his had four stars and a stripe, while hers bore three stars only. He said something in shrill Americ which sharpened that—hungry—look in the Saurons' eyes. A couple of them let out quickly stifled whoops. The—officer?—spoke to the woman Sauron.

She turned his words into Russki: "Base First Rank

Shagrut tells me to inform you of what will happen next. You are spoil of war, as should be obvious to you. Now you will be awarded."

Awarded. It was a word without any particular flavor. Svetlana found out in moments what the Base First Rank—*pompous, outlandish title,* she thought before those moments passed—meant by it.

He spoke in Americ. The woman Sauron translated: "Assault Leader Uldor, you have first choice among the cattle women, as reward for having saved two comrades' lives in hand-to-hand fighting."

Uldor stepped out from among his fellows. The pack of them bayed, once more like stobor, then fell silent in eager, animal anticipation. Uldor was older than most of the Saurons, a rather weather-beaten man with gray at his temples and bags under his eyes; had he not worn field-gray, he might have been a farmer or, more likely from his broad shoulders and big, powerful hands, a smith: no one to notice in particular.

But he wore field-gray, and was noticed. The women shrank from him as he strolled slowly through their number, all but a couple of brazen wenches who cast sheep's eyes at him because he was a conqueror. Soft questions and guesses ran through the crowd of captives: "What will he have us do?" "Cook his food—?" "Wash his clothes—" "Go to his bed—?"

"Hush!" three women said at once. "Don't give him more ideas than he has."

Uldor already had all the ideas he needed. He walked up to a young woman, reached out and gave her breast a considering squeeze, as if he were contemplating the purchase of a pig and was trying to decide what sort of hams it would yield. The woman—Katerina Katushova, her name was—had been free a few hours before, and did not yet grasp what slavery meant. Crimson with indignant fury, she knocked his hand away.

Without change of expression, without particular malice, but with Sauron speed and strength, he hit her in the belly. She took two stumbling steps backwards, folded in on herself as she did so, hit the dirt hard, and lay there struggling to breathe. Uldor took no more notice of her, but went on to examine another girl. When he fondled her, she stood quiet and submitted, however much she trembled. Among the women, that was the instant when fear crystallized into terror.

Uldor strode on, looking at this woman, groping that one, until he came to Olga Ryzhkova. She was not as young as most of the others for whom he'd paused, being close to his own age. She glared at him when he touched her, but did not pull away—as if that would have done her any good. Perhaps he felt her up for something other than mere amusement, for as he took his hand off her bosom he said in bad Russki, "You have had childs." It was not a question.

"Two," she admitted, forced by his stare to reply.

"Young enough for more," he said. With no more ceremony than that, he shoved her to the ground, jumped on top of her. When she screamed, he hit her, not as hard as he had Katyusha Katushova, but as a warning he could do worse—much worse—if he cared to. She struggled as hard as she could, but she might as well have been Tallinn Town fighting the Sauron aircars. He hiked up her skirts, tore off her drawers, dropped his field-gray trousers far enough for what was needed, shoved himself into her. She screamed again, but he ignored her now.

Svetlana screamed too, curses fouler even than the one she had directed at the leering Sauron guard. She threw herself at the man atop her daughter. Had the other women joined her, Uldor might have had a bitter time, Sauron though he was, before his comrades could free him. But Svetlana leaped alone. Fear held her friends frozen.

And the Assault Leader remained a Sauron, too. Hardly interrupting the up-and-down motion of his hairy buttocks, he leaned up on one elbow, caught Svetlana in the side of the head with the point of the other. The impact was like a bomb going off. She lay on the cold ground, dazed, while Uldor finished raping her daughter.

By the time Svetlana's senses returned, Olga and Uldor were back on their feet, the Sauron matter-of-factly zipping up his fly. Olga tried to tear herself away, but he held her with fingers like iron. He said something to her. She shook her head. He hit her, hard enough to snap her head back. She bent over and vomited. He waited till she was through, then hit her again.

"Hear me, woman," he said. Maybe he spoke louder, maybe Svetlana's head was clearer, but now she heard him, too. "We do. We do like just now if you fight, we do nice if you good. But we do." Now he took her head, made her look at what was going on all around. "You think you—how you say?—special? You not special. Others same like you. You cattle, you belong to Soldiers now. You *ours*."

The Saurons were busy proving that to the people of Tallinn Town in the most literal way imaginable. Half a dozen of them mounted the women they'd chosen. More screams mounted to the deaf sky. And more Saurons prowled through the captives, choosing new victims.

Olga's shriek rang through the rest. "Not Yelena!" she screamed. "Not my daughter. God have mercy, Uldor, I'll do anything you want, but keep that man from my daughter. She is too young."

Svetlana followed her daughter's trembling finger. She had already died a hundred times since Byers' Star crawled up over the horizon. Now she died a hundred more, for a Sauron stood thoughtfully before her only granddaughter. Yelena's eyes were wide as dinnerplates, as if she did not, could not, believe what they were taking in.

With a single motion, quicker than a cave lion's leap, the Sauron ripped her blouse, baring her small young breasts to the chilly air. She turned and tried to flee. He was on her before the motion truly began.

And Uldor told Olga, "You do what I want because I want. Is enough."

So this is what slavery means, Svetlana thought numbly. When her husband was still alive, he'd sometimes hit her if things did not suit him. She'd thought her lot very hard. She would have thought it harder yet, were that not the way of most husbands in Tallinn Town—common misery is easier to bear than misery unique to oneself. Now all of Tallinn Town had more misery to bear than she'd ever dreamed of.

The Sauron who had leaped on Yelena grunted, twitched, got to his feet. His cock was smeared with blood; more blood stained the girl's inner thighs. The Sauron said something in Americ. His comrades, those who weren't busy enjoying their own crimes, laughed heartily.

Yelena's little brother Yuri screamed: "You son of a pimp, you hurt my sister!" He dashed at the Sauron. "I'll kill you for that!"

Two or three people had a chance to grab him. Somehow, they all missed. Face white and determined, small fists flailing, he did his best to make good his threat. But the Sauron was not only a man grown, he was a combat veteran with genetically engineered strength and reflexes. He lashed out with a booted foot. The hard toe caught Yuri under the chin. His neck bones parted with a noise like a dry board broken over a knee. His body as limp as a sack of beets as he fell, and Svetlana knew he would never get up again.

Yelena had not screamed while her maidenhead was ripped asunder. She screamed now, and went for the Sauron with nails like talons. Laughing, he caught both her hands in one of his. She tried to kick him, with no better luck. He bore her to the ground and methodically set to ravishing her a second time.

Olga's face went white as curded cheese, but she did not leap to her daughter's defense even though her own new master's grip on her was for the moment light. She'd already begun to learn the lesson the Saurons were teaching, the lesson and the futile, bitter taste of slavery.

Svetlana was learning also, though she did not fully realize it. She knew she could not fight the Sauron, knew what she'd got for trying once, knew she was likely to get worse if she tried again. And so she stood, hating herself for her weakness (another lesson of slavery), swaying back and forth as she had in front of the ravaged church. The church, though, was only wood and metal and paint. It might, God willing, be rebuilt. But how to go about rebuilding a ravaged girl? It was a question without answer, or hope of answer.

Hope? Hope was ravaged, too.

Svetlana looked around at the people who had been townsfolk but now were only fellow slaves. The Sauron woman straddled Misha Sikorsky, rocking up and down on him, raping him as shamelessly as any of the other Soldiers violated women. Svetlana had never imagined such depravity. That men, who securely fancied themselves the lords of creation, who prayed their thanks to God for not having been made female—that they could be used as callously as the tenderest maid left her even more dazed and confused than he had been before. Now *everything* on Haven seemed topsy-turvy.

Not all the Saurons resorted to public rape with the women they chose for themselves. Those who did, in fact, were a distinct minority. But they made quite clear the fate that awaited any girl who thought of resisting. When a Sauron picked someone, she came with him. Her eyes might be numb with horror, but if she had a brain in her head she did not try to make matters worse than they were. As Uldor had said to Olga, they could do it nicely or rough, but if a Sauron wanted to do it, he would.

And already some of the women began to measure their status in terms of their new masters'. Not far from Svetlana, a pretty young thing sneered to an older woman, "Your Sauron has blank collar tabs. An officer wanted *me*."

The older woman opened her mouth, no doubt to curse her tormentor, but closed it again without saying anything. If she angered the pretty girl's master, how could she be sure a simple trooper could protect her?

There were more captives than Saurons. Several picked a second wench for themselves; the Sauron woman, having wrung poor battered Misha Sikorsky dry, chose another stalwart man. Before long, only the rest of the single men and a few old *babushkas* like Svetlana remained unselected.

The Base First Rank spoke to the woman Sauron. She had not bothered to put her trousers back on, but strode around careless of both cold and decency. Still half naked, she translated for her commander: "You men, gather in a tight group over there." The bachelors and widowers obeyed her gesture, moving about fifty meters away from the Saurons and the women who were now theirs.

If the Base First Rank gave a signal, Svetlana never saw it. But a dozen Soldiers together opened up with their hand weapons. The single men went down like winnowed barley. The women screamed, but the Saurons took no more notice of them than if they'd been so many kermitoids croaking by the riverbank.

The woman Sauron said, "Single men are dangerous— as dangerous as any cattle, anyhow. They have a habit of doing stupid things like plotting, and will try to kill without caring what happens to them or to anyone else afterwards. We see no point in exposing ourselves to any risk, no matter how small. The Race does not breed fools."

What the Race bred, Svetlana thought, was monsters. But they were strong, deadly strong, monsters. Tallinn Town had fallen to a small detachment. All Haven had to lie under the Sauron's grip now. What choice was there to obey, at least until God granted that the mighty but wicked fall?

Her mind formed the question without realizing it might have another answer. After a moment, though, she saw one: she could die.

The woman Sauron said something in Americ. Whatever it was, it had no visible effect on the Soldiers to whom she spoke. She turned to the Base First Rank, asked a question. He looked over toward Svetlana and the other old women. His eyes were flat and blank and cold as the night sky with both Byers' Star and Cat's Eye gone from it. Under those merciless eyes, Svetlana felt cold herself. She could indeed die. Finally, to her relief, Shagrut turned away with a shrug.

The woman Sauron switched to Russki: "The Race is not wasteful, either, nor would Haven let us be even if we cared to. We see little point in feeding crones who cannot breed—and no Soldiers seem to want them. So—"

From too far away to hear what she said, Svetlana saw Olga urgently talking to Uldor. The Sauron laughed and shook his head. Olga persisted. He backhanded her; the blow was not hard enough to knock her down, but blood trickled from a corner of her mouth.

A few Saurons moved away from their slaves, started drifting toward the *babushkas*. Svetlana knew she should scream, knew she should run. What point, though, when screaming would gain her nothing and running perhaps another second or two of life but surely no more? If she was to die now, she would die with dignity, for her own sake if nobody else's. She stood where she was, began to make her peace with the God who had so hideously betrayed Tallinn Valley.

In spite of the slap from Uldor, Olga kept talking. He raised a closed fist in warning, but she persisted, and with more than talk. She set her hand on his crotch, let her fingers close round the cock that had so recently ravished her. And she pointed toward Svetlana.

Uldor laughed again. Svetlana knew she would die and was glad, glad she would not have to see what her daughter was forced to sink to. Now that fate had rolled over her, rolled over all of Haven, like an avalanche, better that she not live among the ruins and miseries the Saurons would leave her people. But when God summoned her before His golden throne, she intended to give Him a piece of her mind.

Resigned to death, she scarcely noticed Uldor pat that obscenely groping hand and step away from Olga. When he came toward her, she merely expected him to kill her himself and pile more sorrow on her daughter. Instead, he studied her with the same intent seriousness he had used in choosing a younger woman to rape.

She stared back, without hope and thus without fear, ironically drawing strength from her absolute weakness. Uldor did not look like a monster. But then, only the young thought looks matter for much, and Svetlana felt as if a thousand T-years weighed on her bones.

"Old woman," he said in his halting Russki, but the bald, rude words were not a tithe of the age Svetlana knew inside. "Old woman, you can work?"

"I can work," Svetlana said. What was life but work? As soon as she could walk, she'd worked in the barns and the henyard and the garden plot. She'd swung a scythe at harvest time, singing songs that went back to ancient, legendary Earth. She'd cooked and cleaned and swaddled and washed and sewn and chopped wood and . . . Of all the questions the accursed Sauron might have asked, she'd never expected one to make her laugh in his face.

He reached out to feel her arms, her shoulders, her back, as if she were a muskylope he might buy. Whatever he found must have satisfied him, for he said, "You can cook?"

"I can cook." When she said those words, she began to think she might live. She knew one thing for certain: having seen death up close, she would never fear it again. For a slave, that was knowledge more precious than gold.

Very well, the Saurons could kill her—but they could do it only once.

Uldor kept looking at her. All at once, he made his decision. He took her by the arm in the same unbreakable grip he had used with Olga when Yelena lay spreadeagled on the ground, dragged her away from the other *babushkas*.

A couple of Saurons pointed at Svetlana, laughing and rocking their hips forward and back. Even in the midst of catastrophe, she felt her weathered cheeks heat. Uldor growled something and made a fist. After that, the filthy jeering stopped.

The woman Sauron pointed to the rest of the old women, asked a question. Though it was in Americ, Svetlana could guess what it meant. "Anybody else want one?" No one seemed to. The flat, harsh cracks of rifle fire began behind her.

She staggered as if the bullets pierced her own flesh instead of her friends'. Had it not been for Uldor's strong arm, she would have fallen. He frogmarched her back to where Olga stood. By then, the gunfire was over. There hadn't been that many *babushkas,* and how was an old woman even to try to run?

Uldor let go of Svetlana. She stumbled forward into her daughter's arms, the two women clung to each other. "Olga, I should have died. I was ready—you should have let me die? Why should I go on living now?"

Olga's tears mingled with hers. "I wanted to die, too, when Uldor, when he—" She had to stop; she was crying too hard to talk. "But if I die, mother, who will look after Yelena. The Sauron who—" She broke down again, but Svetlana knew what she meant. A man who found sport in raping a virgin who was barely a woman—what could her granddaughter look for from such a man but more abuse as long as she lived?

"But what you did, to get Uldor to come for me." Svetlana shook her head. "Better to die, better to die."

"I didn't think so." Olga Ryzhkova had a stubborn

streak as wide as her mother's. "What I did—what could I do? I have only my body to give. What else is there? Should I have held back and let them murder you?"

"Yes."

"No," Olga said. "No and no and no. We live. We have to go on as we can. I'd just lost Yuri. I couldn't bear to lose you, too. This is what happens after wars to those who lose. I would have done the same had the steppe nomads taken Tallinn Town, I'm sure I would."

"This is what happens to those who lose," Svetlana repeated dully.

"Enough talk. Too much talk," Uldor said. He gave his new women a shove toward the higher ground across the river where the Sauron fort would go up. Their heads bowed, they trudged off in the direction he had set them.

Deathmaster Quilland sat at his desk and thought. Nothing moved but the slow rise and fall of his chest, and an eyeblink every thirty-seven seconds. If a fly had landed on his face, the skin would have twitched to dislodge it with equal precision.

"Enter," he said.

The noise outside his office would have been impossible for a human norm to detect; but despite the age that had turned him bald and gaunt, Quilland was still a Sauron and in complete command of his facilities. When his system finally wore out, it would do so from simultaneous failures and the process would be swift.

Cyborg Rank Marln came through the door and sat. He raised a brow imperceptibly.

"Security level One," Quilland said. Marln nodded and waited. "You are to proceed to Angband Base and oversee the restoration of discipline and the completion of the facilities."

Marln nodded again, the same slight jerk of the chin. Angband base was over ten thousand kilometers away, commanding a valley at the far end of the Great Northern Steppe. It was the last and latest of the string of bases

the crew of the *Dol Guldur* and their descendants had
built to stake down that area in the two generations since
they'd arrived, fleeing from murdered Sauron. It was
intended to control Tallinn Valley, one of the rare areas
outside the Shangri-La lowlands with air thick enough
that women could give birth in relative safety.

"There were grave breeches of discipline," he pointed
out. "Counterproductive actions with regard to the
human-norm cattle of Tallinn Valley."

"You have full authority," Quilland said. Almost redun-
dantly; Marln was, after all, a Cyborg. He went on: "Fur-
thermore, you are to evaluate the situation in the area to
the south. Records indicate that the Eden Valley could
be a valuable acquisition, if it can be acquired with a
minimal commitment of resources."

Logistics made a large expedition impossible. Founding
Angband had strained the reserves of Firebase Ten, the
nearest Sauron outpost to Tallinn. Eden was more than
seven hundred kilometers further.

"If Tallinn cannot be held?" Marln said.

"Then it must be neutralized as a possible base for
attacks on our positions further north and east. Extermi-
nate the human-norm population, destroy all capital works
such as irrigation canals, and evacuate the garrison to
Firebase Ten."

Marln asked a question with a subvocalization. Quilland
showed his first expression of the interview, a smile that
would have made a human-norm blanch.

"In that case," he explained further, "I will handle the
reassignment of the personnel involved in the failure
personally."

In which case, Cyborg Rank Marln thought, *they would
probably envy the cattle of Tallinn*.

He rose, his mind already methodically reviewing the
data.

KINGS WHO DIE . . .

S.M. Stirling

"Humans?" the Sauron subvocalized.

His companion raised slightly from his prone position and peered into the truenight.

"Possibly," he said.

Even to the gene-enhanced vision of the Soldiers, there was little to see in the truenight darkness. Byers' Sun was down, and so was the Cat's Eye, the gas-giant planet that Haven circled; not much starlight was getting past the high overcast of ice particles and windborne dust. It was very cold, minus thirty celsius at least, and what breeze there was was from behind them, so they could not scent the intruders. There was only a set of faint wavering lights, reddish, the IR heat-signature of life. That might be from a pack of stobor down from the foothills and making a try at Tallinn Valley's livestock.

"Doesn't matter shit, either way," Under Assault Leader Uruk said. "We'll see 'em off."

He stood, clicking the safety on his assault rifle. There was no reason to be more cautious. The Soldiers here had marched all the way from the Citadel, the great fortress of their people at the eastern entrance to the Shangri-La Valley. That was better than ten thousand kilometers, fighting all the way—and nobody had been able to seriously hinder them. First Citizen Diettinger himself had seen them off, drawn up in field-grey ranks. Nearly two thousand, then; most had been dropped off at the bases along the northern slopes of the Atlas mountains as they marched west. Fifth Company was the last and best, selected to found Angband base and tie down the westernmost end of the line.

Uruk brought his rifle to his shoulder, aimed, and stroked the trigger.

Crack. A scream of pain; humans, then. Uruk had not expected to miss.

He had not expected to take return fire, either. Few humans had firearms any more, and none could see well enough to shoot accurately in this dark. Muzzle flashes spat out of the night at them; he dove for the earth a fractional second before the first bullet hit. One pounded into his shoulder, another into a hip, a third into his side. He willed away fear and pain, commanded blood vessels to clamp down, took an inventory. Collarbone and pelvic bone broken. Major internal injury, kidney gone. A glance over at his companion; one of the hollowpoint bullets had removed the top of his skull, and another had smashed their communicator. Well, the noise would bring reinforcements. There was a whistling in his ears as he took cover behind the body and raised his rifle one-handed. Whistling, and shooting stars.

"Rhodevick's hit!"

"Shmuel, patch him up—come *on*, get that fire-lighter working!"

Miriam van Reenan snapped the orders lying on her back, holding out her arrow. A bullet pecked at the crumbled adobe of the sheep-pen wall above her as the Sauron assault rifle fired again. The man beside her was pumping a hardwood plunger in a cylinder that held tinder and punk. He shook the embers out on her arrow. Flame blossomed, caught on the wad of oil-soaked muskeylope underdown wrapped about it below the head.

"And keep that bliddy arse-cutter Sauron's head down, Yigal!" The fire felt indecently warm on the eyeholes of her facial mask, where frozen breath clung to the down around her mouth.

Rhodevick van Reenan lay curled about himself, the night-sighted rifle lying beside him. Miriam felt a stab of grief and anxiety at the sight of her half-brother; if Rhodevick died . . . *Mother and Aunt Ruth will both kill me. Then Pa will do it again.* Shmuel was busy with bandages. He could help if anyone could, he was son to old Allon himself. Ten meters down the wall her brother Yigal duckwalked to a new position and then came smoothly to one knee. *Crack-crack-crack-crack*, and he fell back to slap a fresh magazine into his New Aberdeen 7mm. At least all the ancient ammunition was still working. . . .

Miriam rose. Pushed out of her mind the thought of a Sauron prefrag assault rifle round punching into her, tumbling through flesh and cutting bone. The bow rose in her hands, the bright beacon of the fire scorching her gloved hand as she drew to the ear. The pulleys on either end of the stave clicked; four hundred meters, very long range, but she was half of the blood of Frystaat, and the bow was a heavy one. So were the other six archers on either side of her, her brothers and sisters.

whirt. whirt. whirt. whirt. whirt. whirt.

The fire arrows arched through the night. Miriam's eyes were nearly as dark-adapted as a Sauron's, even if she could not see heat. To her the shafts were bright as beacons, outlining the huge conical shapes of the grainstacks as they descended. *Whunking* sounds as they thudded home. Another arrow was pressed into her outstretched hand. It slid through the cutout in the center of the handle, smooth pull of cold-stiffened muscle as she drew, waiting had been the hardest—*whirt*. Again, again, and the fire was catching in the straw now. Little reddish caverns of fire, broad-winged scarlet birds taking perches on the top and flapping. No use thinking how much human sweat had gone into that barley; only Saurons would eat it now, if they left it.

"Enough!" she shouted. "*Gut genoegh!* Good enough, now move it. *Trek.*"

"Well, the young *sklem* will make it, eh?" Piet van Reenan said with relief, sinking back in the hot-spring water. *Or so Allon thinks.* If anyone knew, the gentle old *mediko* would. Rhodevik would limp, perhaps, which was cheap enough when you considered what one of those Sauron bullets could do to a man.

Piet had seen that, more times than he liked to remember. Back when the Saurons landed his first wife Sarie had been killed in the initial strafing; he had seen her dead, with their twin daughters. *Sarie, the girls, too many friends. Now my son.*

"Oh, but they owe me a debt," he whispered.

Ruth nodded, the smile-lines on her face turning bleak a moment. There was scarcely a living human on Haven who could not make that claim, and no need to say who the debtor was.

She sighed. "I'd never have thought Rhoddie would *do* something that stupid," she said.

"He's my child as much as yours," Piet said sourly, caught between pride and anger. "*I* was certainly an idiot at his age. And Miriam put him up to it—put all of them up to it—or I'm a *hotnot.*" He drew a deep breath and controlled his anger; rage brought on the chest pains, nowadays.

"How are *you*, darling?" Ruth asked in sudden anxiety.

"Not bad, for a dying man," Piet said. His wife winced and turned away, swallowing.

Piet stood, shrugging to hide his own pain. That was more of the spirit than the body, as yet. There was no mirror in the fieldstone room that held the bath; just a small window covered with thin-scraped stretched hide.

Faint winter light came through it, pale and cold in the
steam-mist rising from the hot-spring's water. But he
needed no mirror to see the first signs, or to feel them.
He was a tall man for one of Frystaat's race, 170 centimeters, thick in the arms and legs, massively broad in the
shoulders. The folk who settled Frystaat had adapted well
to their planet, to crushing gravity and poisonous metal-
heavy winds, to the flaying heat of the F5 sun and the
constant menace of an alien ecology older and more
energetic than Terra's.

So it was normal for him to look gaunt, little subcuta-
neous fat over the strong thick bones and massive muscles. It was not normal for him to look *this* gaunt, nor
for the heavy spatulate fingers to tremble. Even slightly,
even occasionally. His heart pained him sometimes, when
he exercised hard. The hair of head and close-cropped
beard was nearly all silver against the teak-dark color of
his skin, only streaks of the original butter-yellow . . .

And Frystaaters do not live long lives, he thought
grimly. If the planet did not kill them young, the adapta-
tions did. Hearts beating too strongly, swift nerves slipping over into filibration . . . *and this is not even Frystaat.*
Haven was an easier world in some respects; only .91
standard G's, as opposed to his birth-planet's 1.75. The
climate was miserable—Haven was the chilly moon of a
gas giant planet, barely terrestroid—but too cold rather
than too hot. Frystaaters had little defense against cold;
they lived in the polar zone, which was the only area
cool enough for Terran life. On Frystaat, the equator
went over the boiling point of water every day. So it was
a minor miracle he had lasted this long, nearly sixty full
T-years.

"It's the way of things, my heart," he said to his wife,
gentleness in the tone if not the words. "And a miracle
I've lasted this long, considering all the people who've
tried to kill me."

Ruth gave him a shaky smile and handed him the
towel. Piet smiled for a moment, lingering over the

contact of their hands. *Quite a woman*, he thought. Thirty T-years, and still as straight and slender as the girl of sixteen he'd taken down from her father's iron cross. Lines around the eyes and streaks in the seal-brown hair simply made the face look lived-in, a better home for the spirit within. There had been little romance in their union to start with; he had saved her life and helped her to power among the Edenites, because his own followers needed the Eden Valley, fertile and low enough that women could bear to term there. They had married to unite ex-marauders of the Band and the Edenite farmers; much the same reason he had earlier taken Ilona ben Zvi to wife, when the Band took in the survivors of Degania.

Thirty years and seven children had made it more than a political match. Three decades, hard work and fighting, quarrels and reconciliations, famine and war and shared grief at two small graves . . .

"Well," Ruth said, brushing the back of her hand across a cheek, "it's going to be a busy enough day. There's Miriam's case to decide. That girl takes after her mother—only much worse." Ilona van Reenan's work of choice had always been with the Band's military side, and her daughter had quite a following among the younger hotheads. "Unless you think I should disqualify myself. People might misunderstand."

Piet grunted as he finished with the towel and pulled on fleece-lined sheepskin trousers. Nobody had ever appointed Ruth as Judge . . . it had just happened, with more and more people bringing her their quarrels and troubles.

"Nie," he replied. "Nobody will think you're partial. Hell, Ilona wanted to burn her butt," Piet said, smiling again.

"Piet, this is *serious*," Ruth said, crossing her arms and glaring at him. "She may have started a *war*."

"Maaks nie, my love, we're *already* at war with the Saurons," he said. "It's attacking them against orders that bothers me."

"Husband, the granaries she burned were all that stood between the *Tallinnayska* and starvation. Do you think the Saurons will hesitate to collect their taxes twice, because she destroyed the first set?"

He pulled the heavy wool tunic over his head and shrugged into his jacket, a whole sheepskin with the fleece turned in. Saber and pistol went over that, the feeling as natural as the shiny places the belt had worn on the glazed leather.

"Letting them consolidate in the Tallinn Valley is a menace to the People, Ruth," he said with rare formality. "Mercy for the *Tallinnayska* may be . . . more than we can afford."

Base First Rank Shagrut did not pace. He would have *liked* to pace, but one did not waste energy before a Cyborg. The visiting panjumandrum from the Citadel was not expected to be at Angband base long; he was on a general tour of the outposts. While he was here, his authority was as absolute as that of First Citizen Diettinger himself.

They were seated in the temporary commander's quarters of Angband Base. The square stone fort was still a-building, mostly by gangs of forced labor from the Tallinn Valley to the west. Through the unglazed window he could see the rolling benchlands of the valley floor, grey-white with sparse snow or loess soil, speckled with pale barley straw; it was bright trueday, with the sun and a full Cat's Eye both up. Sauron vision was sharp as binoculars; he could see the eternal snowpeaks of the Iron Limpers beyond it. Much of the snow would be CO_2 . . . The air had the absolute purity of midwinter on Haven's steppes, too cold to bear moisture or much scent.

"Resistance has been much greater than anticipated by Intelligence," he pointed out to the visitor from the Citadel. It was not an excuse—Soldiers did not make excuses—but it was an accurate observation.

"This is often the case," the Cyborg replied.

The face above the *totenkopf* collar-tabs was nearly as skull-like as the insignia. Cyborg Rank Marln *did* stand, turning and looking out through the unglazed gap where double-panels of glass would one day stand. The temperature was minus 10 Celsius in the warmth of midafternoon sixty hours after sunrise, nothing either of them was much bothered by, given wool field uniforms.

"Nevertheless, this base is seriously behind schedule," he continued.

"Cyborg," Shagrut acknowledged.

Maybe he's past it, he thought. Even the biomechanical implants and extra genetic engineering of a Cyborg Rank had to fail sometime; entropy won all wars. Marln was one of the old ones, the generation that had come with the *Dol Guldur* to Haven, fleeing ruined Sauron. He had been born on Homeworld, the only one of the Soldiers at Angband Base not born locally. Shagrut had been nurtured in a Havener womb, although the fertilized ova had been produced on Sauron; most of his command were crossbred, part of the eugenics program that was to turn Haven into a new Sauron in time.

Time. We need time.

"Time," he continued aloud. "Destruction of supplies and foodstocks has altered the time parameters. More Soldiers will not cure the problem; we cannot feed them. Likewise, we cannot increase levies of either food or labor from the cattle tribes without counterproductive losses from famine and increased rebellion."

"Amplify your report," the Cyborg said.

"Initial conquest was within estimate," Shagrut said; not without a trace of pride. A battle that went according to plan was a considerable victory. "Examples were made at the first sign of resistance. The cattle became convinced that further struggle was futile, and we made it plain that enough resources would be left them to ensure survival."

Just barely, but anyone who had lived through the past thirty-four T-years on Haven was a natural-born survivor.

Seventy percent of those living when the fleeing Sauron ship *Dol Guldur* arrived had died in a single decade. Some quickly in a blaze of nuclear fire, others more slowly of famine, disease and the chaotic violence as the lucky ones fought over scraps.

"The cattle to the south were the causative agents," Shagrut continued, clamping down on a dull blaze of anger. "They slipped in a party of infiltrators and burned much of the stocks." Grain was usually stored still in the straw, and threshed as needed. "The sabotage was confined to stocks already levied as tribute. Their replacement required pushing the cattle to the edge of starvation; many escaped and are being harbored by the cattle to the south, in the Eden Valley and surrounding areas. We have had to allow others arms in order to hunt native wildlife for supplemental food, but some of these have deserted to the enemy."

Marln nodded. "And if we bring in reinforcements, the supply situation will become worse still," he said.

Unspoken was the thought that the Citadel's surviving aircraft could probably solve their problems with a few strafing runs. It would not be risked; there was always the chance that an Imperial antiaircraft missile survived somewhere. And if any did, it was probably among the troublesome cattle of the Eden Valley.

"Give me a further report on the ringleaders of the rebellious cattle community in the Eden Valley," he continued.

"Yes, yes, of course I'll bloody see them," Piet said grumpily, settling into the armchair. His sword was hung by the entrance—symbol that force was obedient to law, within the Band—but he shifted the pistol unobtrusively to his lap; old habits died hard.

The *Kapetein's* house was the best in the town of Strong, and the living room doubled as a meeting-place. It was long but fairly narrow—timber for rafters were rare—with an ingenious earth stove at one end making it fairly warm, and a rugmaking loom pushed into a corner. The walls were whitewashed adobe, the floor brick covered in colorful muskeylope-hair carpets, and a stuffed cliff-lion head barred its overlapping rows of fangs from the wall amid racked tools and weapons. A meal of courtesy had been laid out on the table, round loafs of rye and barley bread, beer, hot eggbush tea, cheese and meat. Luxury foods as well, stewed clownfruit in brandy, fried potatoes, geffish. Piet wore quilted trousers and sheepskin jacket despite the fire and thick walls; Haveners sweated at what he considered comfortable, and it was bad manners to insist, besides being a waste of coal.

The visitors from Tallinn looked at the food longingly as soon as they came in. There was a smell of poverty about them anyway, visible in the raggedness of their clothes; that and desperation in their eyes.

"Come, friends," he said. "Sit, eat. We will talk."

He spoke in slow, accented Russki; that was the common tongue in Tallinn, as Americ was in the Eden Valley, although many of the Band spoke Hebrew or Lithuanian, or Piet's own native Afrikaans.

There were three of the foreigners. Others followed them. Ruth and Ilona, Piet's wives. Ruth was Judge, too, of course, and Ilona was head of Company van Reenan. Several of his elder children; Andries, the boy was shaping well . . . *Have to stop thinking of him as a boy*, Piet reminded himself. *He's a man with children of his own, now.* His daughter Miriam and her gang, she was scowling and turning her shapeless felt hat in her hands with well-merited apprehension. The heads of the Companies, mostly younger men now, though the units still bore the names of his old comrades from the wandering years after the Saurons came. All of them settled in; the *Tallinnskaya* were visibly restraining themselves as they struggled not to bolt their food.

Walking arguments, Piet thought, eyeing some of the Church elders. Even after a generation there were still many among the native Edenites who disliked the Band.

The last Prophet—Boaz, Ruth's father—had been a complete lunatic towards the end, and the coming of Van Reenan's Band had been as much liberation as conquest. And Bandari leadership had made all the difference as the Eden Valley and its dependencies struggled to survive in a world without the machine technology the Saurons had smashed. Still, the Band were overlords of a sort, and mostly heathens or Jews at that, among Edenites who were all of Americ descent and followers of the same sect of the Edonite Church. The men from Tallinn were a welcome reminder of possible alternatives much worse than the status quo. Tallinn had never been rich by their standards; the Eden Valley was larger, lower and much more fertile. But they had not starved either, before the Saurons established a garrison there.

"Let's get the meeting under way," he said. "Not you, Miriam bat Ilona—nor the rest of you young fools. You stand until we need you to answer questions."

"Lord *Kapetein*," the Tallinn ambassador said, as the others sank into their seats.

Piet winced slightly; he had never liked the way his rank was becoming a ruler's title. *Captain in the armies of a fallen empire*, he thought mordantly. Sparta's forces had withdrawn decades before the *Dol Guldur* came, exiling one retired officer from Jaarsveldt's Jaegers behind. Haven had heard little of the struggles that followed. The Sauron homeworld had been smashed, but the effort had wrecked the Empire and the surviving fragments had fallen into civil war, that was obvious. The mere fact that no interstellar ship had entered the Byers' Sun system for thirty years was proof.

"Lord *Kapetein*, we throw ourselves on your mercy."

Mercy of an ex-bandit. Although that had been in desperation, not choice. There had been no other way to survive, or him and the followers he collected. Haven had been a rural backwater under the Empire, but still half the population had lived on protocarb synthesized at the fusion plants, and agriculture had rested on fertilizers and machines.

"The Saurons are grinding our bones for bread! Our children are dying; they devour our substance like land gators."

Piet nodded; a Soldier ate more than an unmodified human, the metabolic price of increased strength and endurance. Angband base held a full company, plus their women and the servants needed to support their specialized warrior existence. The burden was cruel, the more so as essential labor was diverted to build the fort.

Ruth leaned forward. "We're prepared to take more of you in," she said gently.

There were nods and murmurs around the table. The Bandari lands had come through the hard years and out the other side. There had been years when everyone went hungry to keep the seed grain and the breeding flocks, but now they could produce more as soon as they had hands to work vacant land and tend the animals. The Tallinn farmers were good sorts, not like the wild and violent Muslin herdsmen who peopled most of the high steppe of this continent.

The Tallinn men scowled; the youngest blurted out:

"We came here to ask for your help in war, to free ourselves, not to beg a place as hirelings!"

"Better hired hands in the Pale than serfs to the Saurons," Ilona said with brutal practicality.

"Slava Bogdu! Easy for you to say, Jew bit—"

The young man sat back abruptly, pulled back and cuffed across the side of the head by his compatriots. The older man by his side spread his hands at the cold glares of the Bandari.

"Forgive Mikael, your honors," he said. "His father and brothers were killed when the Saurons came, and they took his sister for a tribute maiden."

Even Ilona murmured something; the young man hid his head in his hands and wept with an awkward barking sound.

"It's true we owe you help as good neighbors," Piet said slowly. "Also, your troubles have been made worse by actions, hmmm, actions for which we're responsible."

Miriam and her siblings shuffled and stared down at their hats, or the toes of their scuffed leather boots.

"So." Piet's hand closed on the pewter cup full of tea. "Then again, we don't want a nest of *soldati* only three weeks' travel away, no indeed."

"Piet," Ruth whispered, touching his arm. He started, then forced his hand to relax; the thick metal had been bending under his grip as if it was butter-soft. Slightly embarrassed, he shifted his grip and squeezed it back to circularity.

"On the other hand, we can't declare open war."

"Why not?" Sergei Tamasaare said. He was brother to the *knyaz* of Tallinn, and led the exiles.

Piet throttled back a snarl. "Because we haven't the strength!" he snapped: *You fool*, went without speaking. "There are three hundred fighting men in Angband, every one of them better than our best—and they have automatic weapons with plenty of ammunition. Possibly Gauss guns or energy weapons, but certainly assault rifles, machine guns, mortars."

"You outnumber them many times over," Tamasaare said, running a hand through his thinning flaxen hair. "You've . . . the Bandari have never been defeated, not since my father's day!"

That's right, remind me how bloody old I am, Piet thought. *At least I've never gotten senile enough to believe my own legend.*

"Nothing would please me better than to kill every Sauron in Angband," he went on with massive patience. "Fewer than two hundred of our forces have modern firearms. The rest have bows and flintlocks—" and reinventing the flintlock had been a technical feat; when the computerized machine-shops died under the EMP of Sauron nukes, blacksmithing had had to be redeveloped

from scratch "—and not all that many of those. We could
mobilize three thousand or a bit more—"

"Three thousand, three hundred twenty-seven, counting first, second and third echelons," Ilona said.

"Thank you, my dear. That's *including* farmers with
pikes and scythes, nursing mothers, and sixteen-year-old
girls with hunting bows. It's *probably* enough to hold the
passes into Eden long enough for hunger to make the
Saurons leave—we've put a lot of effort into fortifying
them. On the attack, against their walls and minefields?
Suicide. The reason we haven't been defeated while I
lead us is that I never attack unless I'm stronger, not
because we're magicians."

Tamasaare's face crumpled. "Then ... you can do
nothing?"

"Nothing?" Piet said. Suddenly he grinned like a stobor, a shocking expression. "I didn't say that at all. I'm
just not going to make a public announcement of my
strategy."

"Andries, I'm disappointed in you," Piet said. The family business had been kept for last, and there were no
outsiders in the big room now.

"Ah, Pa—" the younger man said awkwardly. "I didn't,
that is—"

"Didn't go haring off into enemy territory yourself,"
Piet said. "Thank *God* for small mercies. You may be too
old to spank, boy, but tell me you didn't know anything
about it and I'll *kick* your butt." He paused, long enough
to let the agonized embarrassment sink in. "I thought I
could trust you; now I'm not sure. I won't recommend
that the Company leaders elect a man I can't trust, so
you'd better start earning it back before I die."

Triple-level fear and shame; Piet paused again before
concluding: "Get out."

Just as he was opening his mouth, Piet thought. It
was almost unfair—he had two generations' experience
in handling men—*but all in a good cause.*

Miriam's head sank further into the collar of her jacket as her eldest brother crept away. She was a solid-built young woman; brown skin and bronze-streaked hair from her father's blood, curved nose and dark eyes from her mother. She launched a preemptive attack:

"It worked, Pa."

Piet paused, nodded. "It did at that; which is all that stopped me from having you at least run the gauntlet for indiscipline—believe it, girl."

Miriam lost color and swallowed; that was one of the Band's heaviest punishments, running between a file of your comrades stripped to your underwear and being flogged with the buckle-ends of their belts.

"Even when we *were* a gang of bandits, we didn't act like that," Piet went on. He halted for a full half-minute. "Since I'm not going to make it a discipline matter, let the Judge decide your sentence."

"It was for the honor of the Company," young Sarie blurted.

The other van Reenan children gave her glares, and she subsided. *Even the bloody words keep changing on me,* Piet thought. He had divided his followers into companies originally, because it was sensible and he'd been a career soldier, once. Now they were turning hereditary; he suspected that the word meant something more like "clan" in the younger generations' mouths.

"You are *not* too old to spank, so bloody shut up," he said. *God, how do they grow so fast,* he thought, looking at the sullen defiant young face. Remembering the tiny girl-child they laid in his arms, or a toddler stumping toward him as he rode into camp and demanding to be swung *high, pappa! high!*

Ruth cleared her throat. "I've been thinking on this matter," she said formally. "Miriam, since you are responsible for your brother's injury, you can work in the infirmary for ten cycles." The young woman winced; that meant bedpans. "Sarie, your weaving is a disgrace, so—"

She plowed on, ignoring the wails of protest.

*   *   *

"I don't think Miriam and the others are going to like that *at all*," Ilona said, rising. The room seemed emptier with the children gone.

She limped slightly as she walked to the sideboard and poured two glasses of clownfruit brandy, raising an eyebrow as she looked at Ruth. The younger woman shook her head and patted her stomach; she was two months' pregnant, and it was best to be careful, particularly with a late pregnancy that was the last chance for another child. Ilona nodded. She was a tall woman for Haven, with a long braid of greying black hair down her back, lean and weatherbeaten and ageless in worn leather and wool. Most of her last thirty years had been spent out on the high steppe to the west of the Eden Valley. That was by unspoken agreement; Ruth for the valley, she for the high country and Piet to share his time between both. Most of the Bandari proper—the descendants of the original Band of refugees who had followed Piet—were herdsfolk now, moving with the seasons and the grass, although a few were craftsfolk here in the valley. Herders brought their flocks down in the winter, and pregnant women past their third month stayed there as well.

"You don't think I was too hard on them, dear?" Ruth said, slightly anxiously. Four of her children had been involved, and three of Ilona's.

"Nu," Ilona replied, sinking back into her chair with a sigh.

The stiff leg was a legacy from a brush with the Azeris who lived north of the Pale—had lived north of the Pale, before they tried rustling Bandari sheep. The heavy burn-scars on one side of her face were much older; that had happened when Degania was overrun and the *Ivrit* settlers joined the Band for vengeance, before Piet ever came to Eden.

"Nu," she went on. "It was fiendishly subtle—humiliation and dirty hard work, *those* aren't going to make those wild chaverim heroes to the youngsters. *I'd* have sent Miriam through the gauntlet and given her a martyr's crown.

"So," she went on. "What *is* your strategy, Oh Khan?"

Piet sipped at his brandy, refusing to rise to the bait. *She knows I hate being called that even more than* Kapetein, *the way they mean it these days.*

"Miriam's little escapade suggested it, and what Ruth said," he mused.

Ruth raised a brow. She had fought in the *coup* that overthrew her father Boaz and opened the gates of Strong—Strong-in-the-Lord, it had been called then—to the Band. And in scuffles since, everyone did, but strategy was not her specialty.

"About taking the *Tallinnaskya* in," he amplified. "Which means we're not condemning them to death. Look, what are the Saurons going to do if the Tallinn valley *is* depopulated?" *One way or another,* he added to himself. Ruth was known as the Kapetein's Conscience, as Ilona was called the Band's Knife. There were times a man had to listen to his conscience—and times to ignore it.

"Ah," Ilona said. "Still . . . they could bring in farmers from elsewhere."

"Not all that many around," Ruth said, blinking in thought. "Rungpe, but they're mostly herders—Rungpe is only a half-thousand meters lower than the steppe. Santa Carmina, but they've only got a few hundred people left after the blights last year and the big Uighur raid."

Ilona laughed outright; Ruth winced slightly. They could all follow the logic. The best way to hurt the Saurons would be to make Tallinn a wasteland; rebuilding an agricultural base would be a labor of decades—and sustaining a force there over the seven hundred kilometer distance to the next Sauron base a nightmare. Yet a logistic strategy was likely to be bloody, and the helpless Tallinn dwellers would lose most of all.

"I see possibilities," Ilona said. "Devious, Piet my love, devious."

"*Die Boer mek sy plan,*" Piet replied with a trace of smugness. Addiction to frontal assaults had never been among his people's faults, not among those who served the old Empire as special-forces troops as he had, not back home on Frystaat or even in their ancestral lands on Terra.

"Trouble is," she went on, "those Sauron meshuggahs can be pretty *scheisse*-eating devious too."

That dampened Piet's smile slightly. Ilona finished her brandy.

"Meanwhile," she said, "since I've been wrangling sheep, punching muskeylope and sleeping alone for the past couple of T-months—" while the Band's herds were brought down to the stubble-fields "—I believe I have dibs on our delectable husband?"

"Why, of course, Ilona dear," Ruth said, flushing slightly. The Church of Eden was rather strict about some things, and even after all these years it still made her slightly uncomfortable to discuss them. "It is your, ah, turn."

"Unless," Ilona went on with a slow grin, "you'd like to join us?"

"*Ilona!*" The blush turned crimson.

Squad Assault Leader Mumak had a wooden arrow through the fleshy part of his shoulder. He did not let that slow him, as he and the four-Soldier section pursued the raiders. That or the killing wind, or the fine dust that cut visibility even for Soldier senses. The enemy were a kilometer away and mounted, but hampered by the herd of muskeylopes they were trying to run off. The Turks whose job it was to drive in the half-wild beasts had scattered to the four winds under cover of the storm. . . .

Deal with them later. It was dark, only a sliver of Cat's Eye up, and the skirmishing had gone on for nearly a day. Gone on while the winter duststorm built and built;

the wind was doing better than seventy KPH now, incon-
venient even for Soldiers, needling the sword-edged grit
of the plains into faces and under eyelids. With the wind-
chill the temperature was lower than minus-forty Celsius,
and it would be worse when Cat's Eye set. Seven Bandari
killed, for one Soldier; the troopers from Angband base
had been overconfident, to lose so heavily against cattle.
Tough cattle, he thought, as the flaying wind keened in
his ears.

They were well out on the steppe, two hundred klicks
northeast of Angband. The land rolled away from them,
never quite flat. There was not much snow, the steppe
had too little moisture for that. A dusting, in the lee of
hillocks or the twisted black-reddish native scrub that
grew in declivities. Half a T-day's journey to the north
was a black line, volcanic caprock eroded into badlands
long ago, when the climate was wetter and summers
warmer. Further eroded in duststorms since, a maze of
blind canyons and cul-de-sacs. The haBandari must have
hidden there, intending to take the Soldier's tribute-col-
lecting party by surprise and drive twice-stolen stock back
into the maze.

Mumak snarled silently and increased the pace. *In
range*, he decided, and fired from the hip, the barking
of the rifle lost in the banshee shrieking of the storm.
His troopers opened up as well, and even at extreme
range horses went down. Men too, some staying that
way, others rolling erect. Riders turned back briefly to
swing some up behind them, then galloped back north.
Mumak did not bother firing at the ones left behind; in
this muck a human-norm would be blind anyway. Perhaps they could take a prisoner.

That thought made him happy, and not only for the
approval it would bring from his superiors.

The Soldiers ran nearer, faster than horses, lighter on
their feet than leopards, even in this howling darkness.
Two Bandari stood at bay . . . or rather, one stood and
another lay tumbled beside a dead horse, and another

horse ran three-legged and shrilled its agony. The standing figure was muffled from head to toe in layer upon
layer of wool and fleece and quilting; sensible enough,
this weather was enough to kill a human norm in minutes
without such protection. It flourished a saber, defiance
at the darkness, and shouted an unfamiliar warcry:

"*Am Bandari Hai!*" in a voice only enhanced ears
could have heard.

Mumak closed in, slightly cautious. Some of the enemy
had Frystaat blood, the briefings said, which could make
them dangerous, even hand-to-hand . . . although a Frystaater would freeze solid like an icicle in this weather.

The saber came down at him; he slapped it out of the
other's hand with contemptuous ease. The pistol in the
other hand was hidden by the sleeve of the coat, and
only reflex saved him when he heard the *scritch* of flint
striking steel. His counter to *that* was a fist into the short
ribs, and the figure dropped like a loose sack of wet
sand. Dead, he knew; he had been careless. The other
Bandari was dying too. His leg had been broken by the
fall, but the death-wound was self-inflicted. Breath
remained for a mumble:

". . . rael; the Lord our God, the Lord—"

Then a rattle and twitch, and stillness; Mumak could
see the bodyheat fade quickly into the leaching wind,
ghost-fingers of red fading out into the black chill. As if
the soul left to ride the storm . . .

Superstition, he thought. His fingers snapped off the
arrowhead and pulled the shaft back through his arms.

"Get their equipment," he said. HaBandari gear was
low-tech but generally well made, and on Haven you
wasted nothing. "Count the herds."

"*No* losses?" Mumak said.

"Not that can't be accounted for, Assault Leader," the
Soldier said. "Some of the animals broke their necks or
froze to death while we were fighting and driving them
back and forth, but we've accounted for nearly all of

them. If anything," he went on jocularly, "there's more stock than we started out with!"

Then this enemy raid was a complete failure, Mumak thought with satisfaction. Or as much satisfaction as you could feel when the weather seemed to be settling down to a twenty-cycle midwinter snow-and-dust storm; it was blacker than a Cyborg's soul now that Cat's Eye was down, and the temperature was falling rapidly.

"We'll stop them over the ridge," Mumak decided.

There were old stone pens there; no telling who built them, this had been ranchland since Haven was first settled by the CoDominium, back in the twenty-first century. Nearly six hundred years ago. Huddled close together with walls to break the wind, the tribute stock should come through the storm well enough. Herding was not Soldier's work, but the Race was nothing if not adaptable.

The stock did survive, and the Soldiers huddled among them; they returned in triumph to Angband base with extra animals that would be food for the winter and extra breeding stock for the distant spring. The levied herds were driven into the valley's communal pens, where there was no shortage of hay, at least. Then Soldier and subject alike battened down for the long scores of cycles of storm and utter cold that could be expected, while Cat's Eye and Haven made their long slow circuit around Byers' Sun.

The footrot and paranthrax went unnoticed until far too late. By midwinter three-quarters of the new stock and half the old were dead, and most of the meat inedible.

The ice burned Hans Gimbutas' mouth; he spat it out and used a precious swig of hot milk and brandy from the ancient vacuum flask to warm his tongue.

"CO_2!" he whispered. "Pass it on!"

His lips had gone a little numb in the moment taken to speak; he rubbed them frantically with one mittened hand, as soon as the thick facemask was back in place.

At that, he was lucky they were at a broad point on the ledge, where he could use his hands without fearing the wind would pluck him off into the thousand-meter drop below.

Acknowledgments came slowly down the rope-line of climbers; now everyone knew that the crusted ice around them was carbon dioxide. He had suspected it, this well up into the Hollow Hills mountains, overlooking Tallinn Valley. Two thousand meters up, in air gray as despair, and thin, thin ... He shook his head, slapped himself; high-altitude anoxia took your attention-span first. Then gravity would kill you, in these mountains. Swinging the ice-axe back up into his right hand, he edged another step forward, stomach pressed to the rock. That left the pack on his back well out over the abyss; ten kilos of fulgurite, much of the Pale's remaining stock of high-intensity explosive. To his left the iron crampons of Spargo's boots grated on rock and ice as the engineer followed him, likewise burdened.

The cave was just where the map said it would be. *Praise Yeweh, from whom all goodness flows,* Hans thought. *And the luck of Piet.* Whatever the rabbi said, there were forces of the spirit in the world; maybe Haven was too far away for the High God to notice much. Piet and Tantie Ruth were much closer, and they couldn't be just ordinary folk, not with what they'd done and made.

Brigid was wheezing almost as loud as the pump before the little oil stove lit. Not much risk here behind a half-wall of rock, but you never knew with Saurons and their accursed IR vision. Hot eggbush tea thick with beet-sugar revived them all as they sat shoulder to shoulder about the low flame and ate, sweets and fat-rich dried stew, bodies aching for the calories lost keeping life going.

"Spargo?" Hans said at last.

"We're here," his younger brother rasped, unfolding the map; they were all hoarse, their throats air-burned despite every precaution. He leaned over, troll-bulky in his furs. The flickering light threw rough shadows dancing on the wall, against ancient volcanic redder than blood, over slick black patches of ice that had never melted, not since the cooling planet froze it half a billion years ago.

This must be what it's like to be old, Hans thought, as his joints groaned and crackled with protest at his motion. He leaned over the paper . . . no, *plastic*. More work of the Old Ones.

His father had trained him well on contour-maps; mapmaking was a Gimbutas skill.

"Another half-day to the springs?" he said.

"More like a day, way we're moving," Spargo croaked. "Yeweh and Perkunaz, I hope this works. Hate to come all this way for nothing."

The others were slumping; he kicked feet and shook shoulders. Iron clinked on stone, the steel drills and sledgehammers ringing like a percusor of the work to come.

"Rig the windscreen," he barked.

"It'll work," Spargo said, as they all huddled in the chilly darkness beneath the cloth. This was the only half-way-safe way to sleep, in a place like this. Madness to come here in summer, triple madness this time of year, except that the People's life demanded it. Air pressure dropped in winter, as gasses went solid.

"It'll work. The rock sea's unstable, where the hot springs come out. We'll bring twenty thousand tonnes down on it."

Hans grinned in the darkness, tasting salt warmth as his lips split.

"I accept full responsibility," Base First Rank Shagrut said, bracing to attention.

The commander's office was sealed from the outside, now; only a little warmer than it had been before the windows and shutters went in, though. The outside temperature had dropped that low, and fuel was very short.

It was dim as well, one shielded bulb, just enough for Soldier night-vision.

"Acknowledged," Cyborg Marln said. "In any case, the damage is repairable."

At a cost, they both knew. Thousands of tonnes of rock would have to be moved, or the Tallinn Valley's supply of summer irrigation water would be fatally reduced, diverted underwater by the explosion and rockslide. Left unrepaired for more than a Haven year—1.63 T-years— and the new flow would undermine the impermeable layer of basalt and wear a pathway through the soluble limestone beneath. Then without power-driven pumps it would be inaccessible forever. Most of the work would have to be done at high altitude—have to be done by Soldiers, who would then be unable to fulfill their military duties until the project was completed. There would be casualties, as well, from rockslides and accidents.

Shagrut fought an impulse to bare his teeth. He had three hundred—no, two hundred eighty-nine, now—Soldiers. More than enough to hold the entrance to Tallinn Valley, with the fort nearly done. Enough to prevent the Valley's cattle from rising against the Race. *Not* enough to guard the whole perimeter of the valley and the steppe grazing lands dependent on it, not without the cooperation of the *Tallinnayska.*

"Two hundred more of the cattle have left the valley," Shagrut pointed out. With the haBandari offering well-fed asylum, that was no surprise. Left unspoken was the truth that there was little point in stopping them; there was simply not enough left to feed them through the winter. Particularly when the Soldiers must patrol actively in cold weather, increasing still more their calorie intake. When summer came, their labor would be badly missed. Farming was labor-intensive work.

"Correct," the Cyborg said; almost absently.

"Fucking loonies," the rider beside Andries van Reenan said.

"Shut up," he hissed back at his sister.

It *was* eerie. The Edenite farmers who formed the square around them were singing as they made ready to fight, a deep rolling male chorus—

"—in the blood the Lamb has shed for us
We'll take our sacred bath:
'Till those unrighteous sinners feel
His scalding, cleansing wrath—"

Beyond was the aching dark-blue cleanliness of a winter's day. Only Byers' Sun was up, and two of the companion moons, so stars were visible at the edge of sight around the horizon where the high steppe met the sky. Frozen dirt and snow creaked beneath feet, hooves, wheels. Breath fogged upwards, in a huge silence where man's works vanished as small as toys.

The nomad winter-station was about a kilometer distant; Andries pushed back his bone snow goggles and brought up the binoculars. Just lenses and wood and metal, none of the half-living Imperial technology, but they served. Low domed shapes leaped out at him, patchwork of plastic and wood and bone covered with thick felt and thicker layers of earth. Trenches where slaughter-stock were buried in permafrost in the autumn, for dwellers who kept to the high plains year-round could keep only their breeding-stock over winter. There would be grain traded or extorted from farmers, and skin sacks of frozen yoghurt, dried milk, cheese, the yield of rich summer pasture. Everything the herdsmen needed to see them through the long cycles of cold, until the chill summer awoke the screwgrass and mutated alfa of the pastures.

Andries shivered a little, at more than the fingers of cold stealing beneath his jacket and boiled-leather breastplate. His father had seen that he read among the few books the Band had been able to preserve—more had been kept on computers, but those were scrap now—

and he knew as few others did that the camp might have been one on Terra itself, three thousand years ago, or ten thousand. Piet had often said how amazed he was at how much the plains-dwellers had reinvented in a single generation, often guided by no more than bits of folklore. The small minority that survived the Wasting, of course.

The survivors were tough. They showed that now, boiling out of their buildings and saddling ponies from the mud-walled pens, riding howling out to meet the invaders. The horses stretched like a dun clot across the brown-white winter steppe, the others who had been shadowing the fighters from the Pale looping in to join them. There would have been more, except that nobody had believed a raid was possible in deep winter, certainly not one by farmers. They milled for a few minutes, then shook themselves out into a loose crescent behind the banners of their leaders and trotted forward. There were nearly a thousand of them, and the earth shook a little beneath the unshod hooves. He turned the focusing screw of his binoculars and scanned. Faces leapt out at him, broad and dark, some longer and hook-nosed. Crude helmets hammered from kitchenware on some, or armor of bits and pieces of metal and synthetic laced onto muskeylope hide. Their arms were bows, spears, knives, the odd saber. Most of them were descended from Central Asian nationalist deportees or even purists, who had chosen to come here to preserve the ways of their ancestors. Many of those ways, such as mounted archery, had been kept alive as sports.

"No firearms," he said to his sister.

"Nice of the Saurons," she replied with a feral grin. The *soldati* cared little if cattle fought among themselves—they even encouraged it, to improve the genetic fitness of the tribute maidens they levied for breeding purposes—but they confiscated all modern weapons in every area they controlled, and these tribes were subject to Angband Base for several years.

"I estimate about eleven hundred riders."

Better odds than it sounded, although the fighters of
the Pale were only five hundred in all. The horses of the
Bandari riders in the center of the formation snorted out
puffs of breath-fog and stamped at the scents of the
nomad mounts, too well-trained to do more than shift
uneasily. There were a hundred cavalry around the half-
dozen wagons drawn by muskeylopes; equipped alike
with steel bucket-helmets with a cutout for the face,
body-armor of laminated leather, sabers, lances and
bows. Four hundred men on foot surrounded them. Tall
men of Americ blood, mostly, farmers. The first two
ranks of them carried long fifteen-foot pikes; behind
them were another two lines with crossbows. Their commander looked to Andries; the van Reenan nodded and
swung his arm up. Vehicles and riders halted; so did the
footmen. The steel cross on a long pole that was the
infantry's standard dipped.

"Pikepoints—*down*," the Edenite officer called.

As if they were puppets with cut strings, the first rank
of pikemen squatted, grounding the butts of their weapons and slanting them out, oval shields resting on their
shoulders and the ground. The next rank knelt behind
them, weapons making a bristling hedge of foot-long
steel points all around the formation; it was as if a giant
animal had curled in on itself, in defensive reflex. The
nomads were much closer now, the sound of their yelp-
ing cries almost as loud as the hooves. They checked
slightly as the spears leveled, then spurred their horses
the harder, howling and bending their stiff horn-backed
bows. The first shower of arrows rattled off the overlapping shields, and here and there a man reeled back
clutching at the iron that pierced his flesh, screaming or
slumping. Blood was very bright against the dun colors
of winter soil. Muskeylopes fretted in harness at the
scent, and their drivers walked along the lines, patting
and soothing.

The nomad wings were encircling the Pale formation,
and the Edenite looked back at Andries, eyes worried

beneath his iron-strapped leather helmet. The younger
man forced himself to impassiveness as he raised one
arm. He had fought before, often enough—everyone in
the Pale had, save for children and some Edenite women,
it was necessary—but this was his first time in independent command of so large a force.

"Now!" His arm chopped down, and beside him Miriam sounded a blatting cry on the ram's horn.

The first rank of crossbowmen fired, a deep thrum-
ming sound from their powerful steel-bowed weapons.
Horses and men screamed amid the onrushing nomads,
as the short heavy quarrels with their four-edged points
slammed home through leather and wood and metal.

The first rank stepped back, dropping the front ends
of their crossbows to the ground and pinning them with
one foot while they cranked at the windlasses that
rewound them. The second rank stepped into their
places, aimed. The ram's horn sounded again, and the
bolts snapped out almost too fast to see as they sleeted
into the horsemen. Behind Andries, the Band horse-
archers were loosing as well from the saddle, arching
shots over the infantry and into the rear ranks of the
herdsmen. The haBandari pulley-bow had almost as
much power as a steel crossbow, and more range.

Pa trained us well, Andries thought, looking at the
mounds of dead and wounded around three sides of the
square. Then the horsemen were at the line of pikes.
Weapons stabbed out, jabbing into bellies and chests;
horses reared, screaming like women in childbirth. Men
from the reserve darted forward, Edenites with long axes,
chopping blades on one side and hooks on the other;
others swung sledgehammers. He saw nomads pulled
from the saddle and beaten down under the iron. Then
there was a multiple ratcheting click as the crossbowmen
finished reloading and levelled their weapons. The
nomads were scattering away before the second volley
came.

"Open!" Andries shouted. His glove was a legacy from

his father, with a never-failing clock woven into the surface. Only five minutes since the first crossbow bolt.

One wall of the pike formation swung back, smoothly, like a great barn door. Around him the riders shifted, and lancepoints came down with pale Byers' light breaking off the honed edges. He took his own spear in hand, gripped the handle of the small round buckler in his left.

"HABANDAR!" the riders shouted.

Their horses pounded forward, building to a gallop. Those nomads still alive took one horrified look at the wedge-shaped mass of leveled points and steel-helmed riders and scattered like mercury on dry ice. A few could not get out of the way in time and turned to fight; riders and horses alike went down under the onrushing mass, nothing more than ripples in its flow as Bandari horses pig-jumped or sidled to avoid the bodies. Behind them, the pike-phalanx formed up and advanced at the quickstep, crushing enemy wounded and dead alike beneath their hobnails. Ahead there was frantic activity, as the nomads' women and children fled on whatever they could bridle. Surviving warriors darted in to snatch up families, tools, whatever valued bits could be taken in a moment.

Burn or poison everything we can't carry off, Andries reminded himself. There was nothing ahead of him but the buildings, now; he raised the lance to the vertical and slowed to a canter, letting the butt rest on the toe of his right boot. The whole formation fell into a jingling trot; some of the haBandari were yipping in derision at their fleeing enemies.

"Stow that!" he snarled, half-turning in the saddle. Behind him the banner whipped in the air, six-pointed star over a leaping antelope, flanked by burning swords. Abashed, the others fell silent; the Edenites behind had taken up their hymn of war, to the rhythm of their boots.

Nothing abashed Miriam. "Think this'll do it?" There was red on the blade of her lance; beads fell rattling and frozen as she resheathed the lower meter in the tube at the rear of her saddle to free her hand.

"Ja," he replied. "Enough to scare the others into migrating in winter to get away from us. There's a hundred thousand square kilometers out here, the Saurons can't keep a garrison in every *hotnot* camp." Yet the nomad herds were their last possible source of additional food before the next harvest.

"They *can* catch those farmers," Miriam said, jerking the short horsehair crest on her helmet at the Edenites behind them.

"So we move fast. I doubt any of the *hotnots* will bother heading for Tallinn with the news."

On Haven winter gave up its grip on the steppes reluctantly, with the long slow rotation of Cat's Eye about Byers' Sun, two-thirds again longer than Earth's year. The last hundred cycles of the cold season were a quiet bitterness, the coma of almost-death. Then the first fingers of returning light touched the far north, where nothing lived and drifts of frozen carbon dioxide lay for most of the death-season. Ice turned to gas and stormed southward, bitter in its cold, picking up a little moisture from the oceans. Over the continents it met warmer air rising from lowlands and the equatorial seas—warmer by comparison; only sheltered areas on the equator escaped midsummer night frosts, on this world. Where the fronts met, giants dueled in the sky.

The Soldier embassy riding south to the Bandari Pale had come through sleetstorms, hurricanes, tornadoes, even rain. It happened to be a clear cold morning when they rode through the Bashan Pass and down into the Eden Valley, air still and free even of dust, motionless and translucent as fine crystal. Byers' Sun was a small yellow-white disk overhead, halfway through the forty-three hour trueday. Floating high in the west Cat's Eye covered an arm's-stretch sector of the sky, an impossible banded jewel of yellow and green and crimson, glowing with its internal heat. The elongated red slot of the Pupil stared down, as baleful as the Lidless Eye banner that proceeded the Soldiers of the Citadel beside the white flag of truce. Lower and fainter were three of the sister-moons of Haven, pale shadows impaled on the high jagged peaks of the Afritsberg. Those glinted white and cruel, sterile as salt.

Cyborg Rank Marln ignored the scenery; every augmented sense was fine-tuned to wring useful militechnic data out of this visit. The necessity to come here at all was disagreeable enough. He would make it as useful as he could. Little enough data had been available on the steppe, mostly sign from herds driven out of visible range of the emissaries. Those had been disconcertingly numerous, though. He was pleased to note that Base First Rank Shagrut was equally alert, frowning in puzzlement at the badly-sited blockhouse beside the trail, a small structure of cemented boulders.

Puzzling because the rest of the fortifications in the pass were laid out well, as if from an old Imperial Marine text with some imaginative alterations. Bunkers, of course; many of them, on either side of the switchbacks they had climbed up from the steppe; more now as they headed down. From the looks, he suspected many gave into natural cave systems. Up to the right . . . *Yes. Those basalt boulders are set to avalanche across the roadway.* The road itself was also of interest. Imperial work, possibly even CoDo originally, blasting and mechanical excavation over the worst stretches. The surface had been repaired recently, though, with crushed rock and gravel to fill potholes, and the top was competently graded. Ruts were from iron-shod wooden wheels; dung had been swept up with straw brooms and collected.

Down into the valley; his senses confirmed the briefing. Very rich air, about equivalent to the 3,500 meter level on Terra, almost as rich as some parts of the great Shangri-La lowland over the mountains to the east. Much smaller, of course—thousands of square kilometers as opposed to millions—but comparable otherwise. Steep-sided on the west, with rolling foothill country to the east, a speckle of almost-trees. Dun-red-green pastureland between, with the thin thread of a perennial river, precious and rare. Old fields on the higher benchlands of the valley bottom had been abandoned here as elsewhere on Haven, with tractors and power-driven irrigation pumps a thing of the past.

There were differences from any other farming settlement he had seen. An earth barrage was three-quarters completed, ponding back the waters of the Langstroom in a scum of grey slit-stained ice and stretches of meltwater. Three skeletal shapes of welded girder stood beside it, long cloth-covered arms revolving in the constant breeze. The sound of their groaning came clearly to his ears, although they were several kilometers distant; wind-driven pumps. Canals snaked downstream, glinting slightly where water travelled to the thirsty loess earth of the bottomlands. Ploughmen were at work, their tools drawn by oxen or muskeylope; other workers dug distribution ditches, leveled fields, broke up clods. Marln focused closest attention on them as the party came down into the flatlands and headed for the cattle town. Men and women were well-clothed in heavy wool and linen, a contrast to the wool-and-sheepskin herder garb of the escorts. They appeared well-fed, none of the tell-tale signs of malnutrition. Older children were numerous, working beside their parents; that meant that younger ones were elsewhere, probably in schools. Rammed-earth houses half-sunken in the ground dotted the fields beyond a few hours' walk from the settlement. Closer than that were only sheds and pens. He nodded slightly; the workers would spend their nights behind the defenses.

Strong itself was also interesting. Smaller than it had been before the *Dol Guldur* came, obviously. Less shrinkage than in most other towns, since elsewhere townsmen had died first in the famines. The abandoned buildings had been thoroughly torn down, a process still under way, with brick and tile and precious timber and metal sorted into neat heaps. Yurt-like circular tents occupied much of the vacant space where homes had once stood, arranged in neat rectangular lines with open squares here and there. The tents were being struck and packed onto wagons, and the wagons and large herds were heading west, toward the passes over the Shield-of-God, up onto the high steppe for summer grazing.

They passed still closer; the escort-guard of Bandari lancers drew closer about the Soldiers, as clots and groups of people began to line the road. A few shaken fists and curses from the Edenite farmers, glowering hostility from the Band members, well reined in. Unusual. Soldiers were used to hostility from cattle, but it was more common to see it restrained by fear than by self-control.

"*Discipline,*" Marln observed in Soldier battle-language. Shagrut nodded, and took a deep breath through his nose.

Marln copied him. Massed humanity. Coal-smoke—significant, it would economize on precious wood and dung. Haven had very little coal, a few small beds where fossil peat had been compressed by volcanic action. Not much smell of excrement, but a tang of methane; some sort of sewage-digestion system, producing sludge for fertilizer and burnable gas. Also sulphur, which meant both geothermal hot water and the scarcest ingredient for gunpowder.

"I think, Cyborg First Rank," Shagrut said, "we may have conquered the wrong valley."

"No," the Cyborg replied. "These Band cattle chose the *right* one." A valuable prize, tended with a good husbandman's care, and simply too far away from the heartland of Soldier power to be conquerable. As was being demonstrated in this careful guided tour, of course.

Unconquerable as yet.

The walls were thick and high, earthfill faced with

stone and brick. Within streets were narrow, to keep
wind from stealing too much heat; houses turned massively built whitewashed adobe fronts to the cobble pave-
ments, for the same reason. Despite the embassy, folk
were at work, narrow slit windows carrying the noise of
pedal-driven looms, the clang of a blacksmith's forge, an
ear-pricking whine of lathes. In the central square the
exhibition was less subtle; a hundred picked troops drawn
up with automatic rifles, their quiet order as much a
statement as their weapons. Sunlight glinted on blued
iron and mottled wool camouflage smocks, a motionless
waiting that was not stiff but a carnivore readiness to
spring. . . . *Elite troops.* A slightly different odor from the
anger and fear outside, more of the rich hormonal stink
of aggression. The ranks were to either side of a house
larger than most; there the Pale's leaders waited, under
their banners.

Marln and his party dismounted, bringing their own
banners. His eyes read the waiting Bandari, looking for
the subliminal clues. *Van Reenan.* Older than he had
expected, although years younger than the Cyborg. A
hint of pain in the easy straddle-legged stance, a slight
smell of illness. He filed the datum. Two women flanking
him; one smelled of pregnancy. Several others, some with
the telltale brick build and startling muscularity of Frystaat, full or half-bred.

"We are the emissaries of the Citadel and the Unified
State," Marln said, after silence that stretched.

Van Reenan grinned, white against the dark skin. "The
Sauron Unified State is radioactive ash," he replied. His
dialect was the Anglic of Sparta, pure and crisp; the
Cyborg's analysis showed a trace of a guttural, clipped
accent, an overlay of the slurred archaic Americ of
Haven. "And we have received emissaries from the Citadel before."

The other three Soldiers had stirred imperceptibly at
the Bandari's taunting reference to Homeworld's fate.

Marln directed the hormones and blood-distribution of his brain away from anger.

"Your hostages stand guarantee for your good conduct," Marln noted. Soldiers had visited here twenty years ago, and they had not returned. That had been part of the original survey of the continent.

"They came demanding water and earth," van Reenan replied. His voice held subtones of amusement, and something else, a hieratic, ritual element.

Shagrut nodded stiffly. Earth and water were tokens of tributary status, in the folk-mythology of most of Haven's peoples. The Citadel made use of the symbology.

"We threw them down a well, where they could find plenty of both," van Reenan continued casually. "I hope you'll be more polite. In any case, we will talk."

He stood aside and gestured. Wordless, Marln led his party through the door.

Death's-head indeed, Piet thought, looking down the long table. There seemed to be little flesh on the bony face, or life in its muscles. The eyes, though, the eyes were full of life. *The problem is, it isn't human.* The negotiations were showing that, plainly enough. Just getting a word out of the Cyborg was a victory. . . .

"The mere fact that you're here demonstrates the success of our plan," he said. The Sauron 2–I–C stiffened very slightly. *Aha. Not quite the iron man, that one.* The Cyborg might have been a breathing statue.

"How so?" he said, in his nasal accent. "We maintain combat superiority."

"Relevant, if I were implementing a combat strategy; you will have noticed, we're not. Ours is a persisting logistics strategy."

"Archer Jones," Marln said.

". . . *Art of War in the Western World*," Piet finished, slightly surprised. *Not completely unknown for the* soldati *to be historians too*, he thought.

"In essence," Marln said, flatly, "you have found an

opportunity to use your superior numbers by avoiding combat and striking at our subsistence base. We are enough to fight, but not enough to guard. You have avoided turning our cattle against you—which would negate your numerical advantage—by offering them alternative means of subsistence yourselves. Yes. Quite a clever scheme. However, with spring, we can move significant forces into *your* outlying territories. You must then either abandon productive occupation and retreat to this valley, or meet us in open-field combat and be destroyed."

"If we *do* retreat," Piet said, keeping the enjoyment off his face with scrupulous care, "the likelihood of a successful siege is low."

"Debatable."

"Probable."

The other Bandari at the table were watching with awe, as their leader dropped into the same monotone that the demonic Sauron used.

"Therefore, a temporary accommodation is mutually beneficial," Piet said.

It always helps to be able to talk to a man in his own metaphors, he thought with grim amusement. Saurons thought in games theory: Cyborgs even more so, it was obvious if you looked at the grammar of their so-called battle language, or even the dialect of Anglic they spoke among themselves. Keep your logic clean and you could lead them by the nose, if you were careful. It was a major reason why they'd lost the war.

Of course, they had taken the Empire of Man down with them. The life of the Pale and its people depended on Piet van Reenan doing better than that.

"We have reached an impasse," Marln said.

"I thought we were making progress?" Shagrut said, slightly surprised.

The two Soldiers were alone in the common room of the quarters the Bandari had given them; adobe walls

with plain wool hangings, brick floors with sheepskins, a
brick stove and a bucket of coal. Elsewhere were a plain
kitchen, and four sleeping chambers. Bare enough,
although more comfortable than anything in Angband
Base. The three Soldiers of their escort were elsewhere;
despite the hostility of the populace, the attendants
assigned them were always female volunteers in the fertile phase of their cycles. Absently, Marln admired the
cunning of it. Spreading the genes of the Race was standard policy; the long-term goal of making Haven another
Homeworld was directly aided by it. The Bandari doubt-
less, and correctly, thought of it as a raid on the most
precious armory the Soldiers possessed.

"Less and less progress," Marln continued, staring
through the narrow iron slits of the stove into the low
red glow of the fire, admiring colors no human could see.
That was the only light inside, and more than enough for
them. "Our positions have reached a plateau. Each has
offered terms which represent their current minimal
positions for a truce. These remain irreconcilable,
although much closer than before. In fact, at worse we
could accept what they offer—until we are in a position
to renew hostilities, of course—and I suspect they could
do likewise with my latest proposal."

He allowed himself a slight frown and began to
methodically stoke himself with bread and cheese from
the table beside his chair, eating with the graceless economy of a wolf. Outside, beyond the double-doored vesti-
bule and thick walls, the haBandari guards were being
changed; the visible guards, that was. Multiple riflemen
in concealed positions guarded every entrance and exit
of the building; he could hear one of them cough and
shift position a hundred or so meters away, and the faint
click of a steel barrel against a windowsill. Upstairs mattress ropes creaked to the rhythm of faint panting grunts.
Absently, Marln correlated the pair's heartbeats, compar-
ing them with his own, Shagrut's, and those of the sleeping Soldiers' and their bedmates.

"Yet . . . perhaps this impasse is deliberate," Marln said.

Shagrut gave a faint twitch of surprise. "The Bandari chief seems to be exceptionally reasonable, for a cattle commander. Less given to counterproductive emotional bias."

"Exactly. His reason has been as a mirror held up to mine. Every move solidly grounded in logic and supported by concrete data. This is a facade. He is moving according to a metalogic which eludes me, but one which is carefully planned."

"Evidence?" Shagrut said.

"None. Intuitive leap."

The other soldier nodded. Not even a Cyborg's mental processes were all conscious; that was not the way of maximum efficiency. Gaining new insight often did not proceed in linear fashion; instead, the mind leapt to the conclusion and traced the lines of proof afterwards.

"We could abandon the negotiations," Shagrut said.

Marln could read a slight eagerness there, knew he himself shared it. Move forward, smash your enemies, impose your will—those were their people's cultural imperatives. Political imperatives as well; fear and invincible reputation were solid operational assets when dealing with human norm populations.

No. Cost-benefit. That was also a Soldier imperative, force as a rational tool in the service of Racial growth.

Uneasily, he remembered the Second Battle of Tanith. The Second Fleet had calculated well and wisely there; calculated that the Imperials would break off when losses exceeded damage inflicted, with allowance for needs elsewhere. First Citizen Diettinger had commanded a flotilla at that battle, or the first part of it. Instead the Empire of Man had stripped every outpost, abandoned every position. By the end of the battle ships were ramming each other as the Soldiers fought to disengage, and the Imperials blasted occupied cities on the surface of

Tanith to glassy craters, sacrificing millions to eliminate a few regiments of their enemies.

Homeworld had been next. A Cyborg's memory allowed no softening forgetfulness; he remembered green-blue skies turned red and black as the enemy fleets pushed inward against the last defenses. The mad scramble to launch, with the precious stores of ova, rendezvous with the *Fomoria*—*Dol Guldur*, as it became later. And one last glimpse of Sauron as the ship accelerated at eleven gravities for the Alderson point where they could go FTL, with the Imperial fighters in pursuit. Black cloud from pole to pole, with a long glowing slit where magma showed at the edge of a continental plate broken open to the core. *Like the Lidless Eye we adopted as our banner here*, he thought, with a complex of emotions. They were there, but his brain refused to analyze them. Odd.

"No," he said aloud. "We will continue for the present."

Neither spoke further as they sought the stairs and the waiting women.

"These proposals," Piet van Reenan said slowly, tapping the two sheets of paper, "are not actually that different. Both involve a temporary truce; amnesty for those *Tallinnaskaya* who wish to return to their homes; our sale of foodstuffs for the next two years—" Haven years, better than three T-years "—and then the resumption of normal relations."

Normal meaning hostile, of course. From the glares some of the other Bandari gave him, and even their own leader, Marln knew they would prefer to resume the war right now. *He sees more deeply than they*, the Cyborg thought. The pendulum of success was about to swing back to the Soldiers. Perhaps the prestige effects would be worth . . . no, Angband Base was the maximum priority now. Tallinn was as far as the resources and numbers of the Citadel would reach. Even if the garrison could destroy the Bandari, they could not occupy Eden and would probably be too weak to hold Tallinn itself. The frontier line would fall back as far as Firebase Ten, nearly a thousand kilometers northeast, allowing Fate-knew-what to brew down here. A strengthened Angband Base could deal with these troublesome cattle sooner or later. If nothing else, they would lose purpose and unity eventually, while the Soldiers would not—such was the nature of their respective breeds.

He waited patiently; then more alertly still, as the Bandari founder spoke. That overtone was in his voice again, as it had been on the first day. A bard's tone, or a priest's; the tone of someone speaking of a mystery.

"Let Fate decide the terms," Piet said quietly.

"You propose to flip a coin?" Marln said.

"No. Let it be a matter of blood and honor. Single combat to the death, without weapons, between our champion and yours. If we prevail, our draft becomes the binding treaty. If yours, then yours. And if ours wins the first fight, you shall choose one more champion, and if he falls—then you withdraw form Angband Base to your Firebase and trouble us no more."

Is he insane? was the Cyborg's first thought. No ordinary human norm could stand against a Soldier in unarmed combat. Then he checked, pulse, pupil dilation, hormonal scents. Nothing but the hint of ill-health he had detected before. *Exalted, yes, but not insane.* A crawling feeling started in the pit of his stomach, until he banished it. The jaws of a metalogical trap seemed poised about him, but—

Ah. Prestige factors indeed; he could *not* refuse such an offer. Psychological domination was the Soldier's true weapon, more potent than fusion bombs.

"Who will be your champion?" he said.

Piet van Reenan stood, a slight smile touching the heavy square face. His hands went wide, came together to touch his own chest.

"I will stand for my people," he said quietly.

Silence echoed, harsh with the sound of breathing. Marln stood.

"Agreed," he answered dryly. "Twenty Haven days from now, at the border marker agreed."

He turned on his heel and left, the other Soldiers tramping solidly in his wake. The Bandari waited until they collected their scant baggage and rode out the gate before the uproar started. Marln could still hear it as his horse paused, panting, at the summit of Bashan Pass.

"You're being a bloody fool, Piet van Reenan," Ruth said to her husband, voice steady despite the tears streaming down her face. "A *bloody* fool!"

Piet sighed with a weariness that seemed to reach bone, turning and looking at his wives. The warmth of the fire at his back seemed to reach no further than his skin, leaving the cold in his marrow. The bedroom was bright with dyed wool, slightly shabby with the comfortable ease of long occupancy . . . and as unreachable as Frystaat. *This was home*, he thought, looking at the angry faces of the women who loved him. *And I will never be home again*.

"I haven't six months more, my dears," he said to them both. "Allon's certain."

"Then you should spend those six months *here*," Ruth said. "And if you . . . if you must die, die here in your own bed, with us and our children around you!"

"Ruth, Ilona—it wouldn't be clean. Strokes, before the end, massive blood clotting. I'd rather not die a vegetable, or leave that as the family's last memory of me."

"So it's pride, is it?" Ilona said, throwing into the chair and speaking to a corner. "Your damned pride. The founder of a nation can't die like an ordinary man, no—he has to go out in a blaze of glory." She turned back and spat on the rug, almost crackling with her anger. *"Glory."*

"Partly," Piet said softly. "I won't lie to you two, never have, won't start now. But it's more than that. It's for the People, for our children."

"For the history books, you mean," Ruth said.

"No." They looked up at the emphatic tone of his voice. "Not that . . . we'll never be in history again."

"What do you mean?" Ruth asked, after a moment when only the flames spoke.

He held out his arms and they came to him, embracing all three together.

"I need your strength," he said at last. "It's a very lonely thing that I must do. Because—"

Kidmi Kasteel—Front Fort, in the slang of the Band's younger generation—hardly deserved the name. There was a well, and a few crude stone huts, set amid tumbled rocks that rose from the northern grazing lands of the Pale. Now it was crowded, with folk from the ranches and the Eden Valley, with half the Saurons of Angband and folk from further still, a babble of tongues and a milling beyond the broad oval where the combat was to take place. Byers' Sun was behind Cat's Eye, drowning the reddish light in a white glare that made the gas giant a blazing corona-clad presence hanging across a quarter of the sky. The light painted faces the color of blood, as the milling and the voices subsided. Only the wind remained, hooting thin and barely chill across the great emptiness that rippled around the settlement, wind on the sea of grass.

Piet van Reenan threw back his head and tasted the moving air, as his party rode toward the edge of the field of death. *How far I've come*, he thought, looking at the brightness above for an instant. He could remember Frystaat's sun, a blue-white point that would kill your eyes in a moment, and the shadows it cast, edged with black diamond they were so sharp. The metal taste of his home planet's winds, and the blue sands' eternal hissing. Sparta's sun, so gentle on the green world that was almost another Earth. Fire-shot air of landing fields in his soldier years, crouching sweating in a bunk as they dropped out of Alderson Drive into a new system; a swamp on Tanith and knowing that the Saurons were in the jungle too, the heavy clammy feel of an Imperial chameleon suit and the bonephone meshing its machine knowledge with his mind.

Haven. Hate and love and wandering, a home at last from the work of hands and mind, the slow grind of age that you did not notice and then it was accomplished . . . *And for all that travelling, I've made only the same journey that every man makes,* he thought with a sudden lightness of heart. *Every world where our children is born is Earth. It's time for me to rest with you, mother.*

He swung down from the saddle and ran a hand along the horse's neck; a simple action, done ten thousand times. Yet for everything, there had to be a last time. Old Allon was beside him for a moment; they shook hands.

"Don't take it too hard, Doctor," Piet said. "We all have the same long-term prognosis, hey?"

Something small and square passed from the *mediko's* hand to Piet's. *Another thing I'm getting the last of,* he thought. The last dose enclosed in its soluble plastic casing, preserved decades from an Army field-kit.

The family were silent; this was the *Kapetein's* goodbye, their father had taken his leave of them in private. Piet paused once by Andries, drawing the sheathed saber from his belt and handing it to the younger man.

"Just so everyone knows, son," he said quietly. "Use it well and only as needed."

Andries nodded. Beside him Miriam was fighting to keep her face still, and her cheeks jerked a little.

"Go out there and win, Pa," she said. "And . . . and if you don't, I'll avenge you. *Am Bandari Hai!*"

"The People live," he agreed, smiling and touching her cheek. "*Nie, nie . . . myn mooie meisie,* give me grandchildren instead. And don't mourn overmuch if I fall. Only a parent grieving for a child should do that."

He turned to Ilona and Ruth. "Take care of each other, my loves . . . and thank you. Thank you very much."

Aloud, to the gathering of his followers, he spoke with words that were heritage to Edenite and Ivrit alike:

"To every thing there is a season;
And a time for every purpose under heaven.
A time to be born, and a time to die—

One by one, they joined him.

When the *Kapetein* strode out onto the boulder-studded sand of the fighting ground, he was naked save for a rag loincloth twisted around his waist. That showed his body as few there had seen it, almost squat despite his height, legs like pillars on broad flat feet, body the same width from hips to meter-wide shoulders, arms seeming longer than was natural. Oil glistened on the huge knotted muscles of his limbs and torso, veins writhed over their surface, and the white hair was like a silver cap on his head. A dozen yards into the staked-out circle he stopped and raised his fists to Cat's Eye. He planted his feet wide, filled his barrel chest and shouted, an inhuman sound like the bellow of an aurochs that went on and on. It was almost shocking when it turned to words.

"*Saurons!*" he shouted. Twice a thousand listeners were crowded around. Every one could hear him, and every one could see; the ground was on a rise above the spectators. *"Thieves, murderers, invaders!*

"Saurons! Hear me! The land of the People sickens with your tread. Its hungry winter ghosts cry out for vengeance—send me your champion, that I may appease their anger with his blood!"

The crowd had murmured at the first sight of Piet. Now they fell silent with a hush that built like a wave, breaking in a sigh as the Sauron fighter walked in.

Piet was the old bull, swinging his frayed horns and flaring nostrils for the scent of challenge. The Sauron was a young leopard; taller, slimmer, cropped blond hair above an eagle's face, like a statue of ancient Greece

come to life. He moved like a dancer, like a ghost himself, and not a single watcher was deluded in to hope-
fulness by his slighter build. Those long-fingered hands
could rend metal, and to the mind that directed them
mercy was hardly even a name. In the manner of his
people the gene-engineered warrior wasted no time in
words or challenge. One instant he was poised and still;
the next he was charging in a blur of movement so pure
that its speed seemed leisurely.

Five meters from Piet he left the ground in a leap
that stretched him parallel to earth, right arm out and
fingers curved back almost against the wrist to present
the striking surface of the palm-heel. It was the ancient
flying crane of dead earth's martial schools, executed
with a speed and power beyond human rivalry. An oak-
staved cask would have shattered under that blow, much
less bone and flesh.

Only a handful of those watching understood what
happened next; Marln was one, and those among the
audience with the experience to see the individual strokes
of a ribbon-saber duel. There was only one counter to
the Flying Crane attack, and few men—few Soldiers,
even—were fast enough to use it. Piet van Reenan was
not one; but he began his move *before* the young Soldier
leapt, just after the moment of full commitment. Even
then the inhuman reflexes of the attacker nearly saved
him; he was jackknifing in midair and raking a bladed
palm down towards his opponent when it happened.

For Piet had gone over, over until all his weight was
on one foot and palm, pivoting diagonally from the Soldier's path. The other foot was driving up with every
ounce of force concentrated behind the heel. That drove
into the young warrior's pubic bone with a shattering
crack that made every man in hearing wince in reflexive
sympathy, with all the joint momentum and the power
of the tree-thick leg behind it.

Piet swung upright with the same motion and charged

at a pounding run, the side of his head streaming blood
where one ear had been ripped loose. Ten meters away
the young man writhed on the ground; still like a great
jungle cat, silent and striving to swing himself around to
face his enemy. The *Kapetein* seized him by shoulder
and thigh, swung the twisting body above his head. They
froze so for an instant, and then Piet threw him down
on a jagged basalt rock, hard enough that the corpse
bounced and rolled before it came to rest. Piet knelt by
its side to close the staring blue eyes, still set in astonishment and anger. Then he climbed erect and turned to
face the orderly grey ranks of the Soldiers.

"*Saurons,*" he shouted again, and the bull below was
louder still, hoarse and demanding. "*Send me no more
boys to do a man's work! Send me your champion! Your
Cyborg!*" Perhaps only Marln saw him move a hand
quickly across his lips, and his throat move in a swallow.

A murmur swelled to a stunned ecstatic shouting from
the crowd. Then it fell into a rhythmic stamping chorus:

"Piet!"

"Piet!"

"Piet!"

"Piet—"

Shagrut was startled into protest when he saw Marln
begin to unbuckle his gunbelt.

"Sir!"

"I am going to end this . . . this *mummery*, and that
immediately," Marln snapped. "That Frystaater has been
playing us like a violin, whatever his purpose is, and this
is *entirely* enough. Silence in the ranks!"

He was coldly angry as he strode forward, but the
anger was with himself. A Cyborg could not forget—but
he could neglect to connect ideas, to realize which datum
was relevant for recall and further analysis. Piet van
Reenan had been an officer in Jarnsveldt's Jaegers, the
Imperial special-forces unit. Who else would know Soldier battle-psychology well enough to risk his life on a
guess at an opponent's opening move? And the Soldier

had been selected for youth and reflex and strength, for
his personnel file's records of skill at unarmed combat.
Not for two lifetimes' experience of deadly struggle in
all its forms.

*I thought it would vitiate our propaganda victory if a
Cyborg was selected as our champion,* he thought bitterly. Cyborgs were demons to the ruck of cattle on
Haven; it would be like sending in a tank or an automech
battlesuit. Better for a rank-and-file Soldier to triumph,
to show that the most ordinary of the Race was the master of the pick of the cattle. *If van Reenan had not
insisted on second round, he would have walked away
from here with a considerable psych-war victory.* More
grimly still: *But his arrogance is my opportunity, as ours
was his.*

The chant ended as Marln took the ring. If the first
Soldier had been a young leopard against Piet's bull, now
Death faced the Minotaur. The Cyborg was thinner than
wire, flat straps of muscle like an anatomical diagram
stretched across a skeleton with a shrunk-on covering of
skin, below a grinning skull. Piet faced him, pivoting
slightly as they circled.

"Aha, angry now, aren't you, my walking battle-com-
puter," he said lightly. "You still don't understand, do
you, Sauron?"

Marln's unwavering gaze never left him. "I understand
that you will not leave this field alive," he answered.
His nostrils flared, seeking an elusive difference in his
opponent's scent. Under the iron-clad tang of blood, the
muskiness of blood heavy with adrenaline and
testosterone.

"I knew that. And I knew my purpose was accomplished, even if that youngster broke my spine—and he
was good, very good. My apotheosis, Sauron."

Marln checked for some fraction of a second. "You
are irrational after all," he said with a hint of . . . was it
disappointment? "Another of the myth-besotted cattle."

Astonishingly, Piet laughed; it was genuine amusement, soft and incongruously charming in the blood-streaked oiled skin of his face.

"Poor Saurons. Poor ultimate rationalists; you designed for utter utility. All you managed was to make was a caricature of your ancestors' ideal. Which is why you're strong only to destroy. Out in space you destroyed the Empire and your own world, and here on Haven you destroyed civilization—and ended history. So dooming yourselves, for what are Saurons if not the end-product of civilized history?"

Kill him now, instinct urged Marln. Pride was stronger, and curiosity.

"We are strong to master the chaos—"

Piet interrupted him, quoting softly:

"The ultimate chaos of man's existence
Is the human endeavor called War
By mastering War, we master the Universe.

"—yes, of course I know your Homeworld's songs, and your poetry. But you, poor self-blinded ones, you don't know their own power—or the power of another's songs."

"Songs?" Marln had to admit he *was* puzzled now. "You are engaged in music?"

"What comes after history, Sauron? Or before it? Why, the time of heroes; and before that, the time of legends. You destroyed civilization here—and now this is the time of legends once again. I made a treaty with you, but there's no glory in a treaty—no tragedy, no power. *That's* what I'm giving my people here. A legend, a myth, a dream to dream their dreams by, and to make them strong."

He laughed, louder and louder, limbs jerking suddenly.

"You don't understand what I am, and what you are now!"

Suddenly Marln recognized the clues; accelerated heartbeat racing far beyond design limits, until the great ribs jerked to it, the flaring of pupils, the flush across the other's skin as blood-vessels expanded. *Amok pill.* Chemical *berserkergang*, deadly dangerous to a fit young man of standard Terran stock. Death to a Frystaater, certain death to one of Piet's age. But in the seconds before that—

A wild laugh. "WE ARE THE ONES WHOSE SAC-RIFICE RENEWS THE LAND!"

They flowed together. What happened was too swift for conscious thought, even for Marln. All he knew was a rushing, and then he was sliding on his back across the rocky ground; little point in attempting to stand, with both his thigh-bones smashed. He could command blood to clot and pain to vanish, force shock back from his nervous system, even heal if given time, but he could not stand with the anchors of the muscle-levers snapped across.

Piet van Reenan stood with Cat's Eye at his back. One kneecap dangled; broken shards of white stuck through the running sheet of blood along his flank; a huge flap of scalp swung free. Yet still he had the strength to heave up a boulder and advance, one ground-shuddering step at a time. Then Marln heard the great heart stop and tear.

Piet's voice overrode it:

"WE ARE THE KINGS WHO DIE—

The rock dropped harmless from his hands, and blood poured from eyes and nose and mouth.

"—THE KINGS WHO DIE FOR THE PEOPLE."

The sound of his falling was endless, like the toppling of a tree. Marln felt himself falling also, into darkness softer than the mother's breast he had never known. He had time to feel the hands of his folk lifting him, and sense the moment's waiting stillness as eye met eye before the two chieftains were borne away.

PRAISE FOR
LOIS MCMASTER BUJOLD

What the critics say:

The Warrior's Apprentice: "Now here's a fun romp through the spaceways—not so much a space opera as space ballet.... it has all the 'right stuff.' A lot of thought and thoughtfulness stand behind the all-too-human characters. Enjoy this one, and look forward to the next." —Dean Lambe, *SF Reviews*

"The pace is breathless, the characterization thoughtful and emotionally powerful, and the author's narrative technique and command of language compelling. Highly recommended." —*Booklist*

Brothers in Arms: "... she gives it a geniune depth of character, while reveling in the wild turnings of her tale. ... Bujold is as audacious as her favorite hero, and as brilliantly (if sneakily) successful." —*Locus*

"Miles Vorkosigan is such a great character that I'll read anything Lois wants to write about him. ... a book to re-read on cold rainy days." —Robert Coulson, *Comics Buyer's Guide*

Borders of Infinity: "Bujold's series hero Miles Vorkosigan may be a lord by birth and an admiral by rank, but a bone disease that has left him hobbled and in frequent pain has sensitized him to the suffering of outcasts in his very hierarchical era.... Playing off Miles's reserve and cleverness, Bujold draws outrageous and outlandish foils to color her high-minded adventures." —*Publishers Weekly*

Falling Free: "In *Falling Free* Lois McMaster Bujold has written her fourth straight superb novel. ... How to break down a talent like Bujold's into analyzable components? Best not to try. Best to say 'Read, or you will be missing something extraordinary.'" —Roland Green, *Chicago Sun-Times*

The Vor Game: "The chronicles of Miles Vorkosigan are far too witty to be literary junk food, but they rouse the kind of craving that makes popcorn magically vanish during a double feature." —Faren Miller, *Locus*

MORE PRAISE FOR
LOIS MCMASTER BUJOLD

What the readers say:

"My copy of *Shards of Honor* is falling apart I've reread it so often.... I'll read whatever you write. You've certainly proved yourself a grand storyteller."
—Liesl Kolbe, Colorado Springs, CO

"I experience the stories of Miles Vorkosigan as almost viscerally uplifting.... But certainly, even the weightiest theme would have less impact than a cinder on snow were it not for a rousing good story, and good storytelling with it. This is the second thing I want to thank you for.... I suppose if you boiled down all I've said to its simplest expression, it would be that I immensely enjoy and admire your work. I submit that, as literature, your work raises the overall level of the science fiction genre, and spiritually, your work cannot avoid positively influencing all who read it."
—Glen Stonebraker, Gaithersburg, MD

" 'The Mountains of Mourning' [in *Borders of Infinity*] was one of the best-crafted, and simply best, works I'd ever read. When I finished it, I immediately turned back to the beginning and read it again, and I can't remember the last time I did that."   —Betsy Bizot, Lisle, IL

"I can only hope that you will continue to write, so that I can continue to read (and of course buy) your books, for they make me laugh and cry and think ... rare indeed."   —Steven Knott, Major, USAF

What do you say?

Send me these books!

Shards of Honor 72087-2 $4.99 _____
The Warrior's Apprentice 72066-X $4.50 _____
Ethan of Athos 65604-X $5.99 _____
Falling Free 65398-9 $4.99 _____
Brothers in Arms 69799-4 $5.99 _____
Borders of Infinity 69841-9 $4.99 _____
The Vor Game 72014-7 $4.99 _____
Barrayar 72083-X $4.99 _____
The Spirit Ring (hardcover) 72142-9 $17.00 _____
The Spirit Ring (paperback) 72188-7 $5.99 _____
Mirror Dance (hardcover) 72210-7 $21.00 _____

Lois McMaster Bujold:
Only from Baen Books

If these books are not available at your local bookstore, just check your choices above, fill out this coupon and send a check or money order for the cover price to Baen Books, Dept. BA, P.O. Box 1403, Riverdale, NY 10471.

NAME: _____

ADDRESS: _____

I have enclosed a check or money order in the amount of $ _____.

THE BEST OF THE BEST

For *anyone* who reads science fiction, this is an absolutely indispensable book. Since 1953, the annual Hugo Awards presented at the World Science Fiction Convention have been as coveted by SF writers as is the Oscar in the motion picture field—and SF fans recognize it as a certain indicator of quality in science fiction. Now the members of the World Science Fiction Convention— the people who *award* the Hugos—select the best of the best: *The Super Hugos*! Included in this volume are stories by such SF legends as Arthur C. Clarke, Isaac Asimov, Larry Niven, Clifford D. Simak, Harlan Ellison, Daniel Keyes, Anne McCaffrey and more. Presented and with an introduction by Charles Sheffield. This essential volume also includes a complete listing of all the Hugo winners to date in all categories and breakdowns and analyses of the voting in all categories, including the novel category.

And don't miss *The New Hugo Winners Volume I* (all the Hugo winning stories for the years 1983–1985) and *The New Hugo Winners Volume II* (all the Hugo winning stories for the years 1986–1988), both presented by Isaac Asimov.

"World Science Fiction Convention" and "Hugo Award" are service marks of the World Science Fiction Society, an unicorporated literary society.

The Super Hugos • 72135-6 • 432 pp. • $4.99 ☐
The New Hugo Winners Volume I • 72081-3 • 320 pp. • $4.50 ☐
The New Hugo Winners Volume II • 72103-8 • 384 pp. • $4.99 ☐

Available at your local bookstore. If not, fill out this coupon and send a check or money order for the cover price to Baen Books, Dept. BA, P.O. Box 1403, Riverdale, NY 10471.

NAME: _____

ADDRESS: _____

_____

I have enclosed a check or money order in the amount of $_____

EXPERIENCE THE BEST-SELLING WORLDS OF
JERRY POURNELLE

Chronicles of the CoDominium

Falkenberg's Legion	72018-X • 384 pp. • $4.99 ☐
(Combines *The Mercenary* and *West of Honor*)	
High Justice	69877-X • 288 pp. • $4.99 ☐
King David's Spaceship	72068-6 • 384 pp. • $4.95 ☐
Prince of Mercenaries	69811-7 • 352 pp. • $4.95 ☐
Go Tell the Spartans	72061-9 • 432 pp. • $5.99 ☐
(with S.M. Stirling)	
Prince of Sparta	72158-5 • 400 pp. • $4.99 ☐

Other Works

Exiles to Glory	72199-2 • 224 pp. • $4.99 ☐
Birth of Fire	65649-X • 256 pp. • $4.99 ☐
The Children's Hour	72089-9 • 368 pp. • $4.99 ☐
(with S.M. Stirling) A Novel of the Man-Kzin Wars	

Created by Jerry Pournelle

The Burning Eye: War World I	65420-9 • 384 pp. • $4.99 ☐
Death's Head Rebellion: War World II	
	72027-9 • 416 pp. • $4.99 ☐
Sauron Dominion: War World III	72072-4 • 416 pp. • $4.95 ☐
Codominium: Revolt on War World	
	72126-7 • 480 pp. • $5.99 ☐
Bloodfeuds	72150-X • 560 pp. • $5.99 ☐
Blood Vengeance	72201-8 • 400 pp. • $5.99 ☐

Available at your local bookstore. Or fill out this coupon and send a check or money order for the cover price(s) to Baen Books, Dept. BA, P.O. Box 1403, Riverdale, NY 10471.

NAME:_____

ADDRESS:_____

_____

I have enclosed a check or money order in the amount of $_____.

THE SHIP WHO SANG IS NOT ALONE!

Anne McCaffrey, with Margaret Ball, Mercedes Lackey, and S.M. Stirling, explores the universe she created with her ground-breaking novel, *The Ship Who Sang*.

☐ **PARTNERSHIP by Anne McCaffrey & Margaret Ball**
"[*PartnerShip*] captures the spirit of *The Ship Who Sang* to a surprising degree . . . a single, solid plot full of creative nastiness and the sort of egocentric villains you love to hate."—Carolyn Cushman, *Locus*
0-671-72109-7 • *336 pages* • *$5.99*

☐ **THE SHIP WHO SEARCHED by Anne McCaffrey & Mercedes Lackey**
Tia, a bright and spunky seven-year-old accompanying her exo-archaeologist parents on a dig is afflicted by a paralyzing alien virus. Tia won't be satisfied to glide through life like a ghost in a machine. Like her predecessor Helva, *The Ship Who Sang*, she would rather strap on a *spaceship*.
0-671-72129-1 • *320 pages* • *$5.99*

☐ **THE CITY WHO FOUGHT by Anne McCaffrey & S.M. Stirling**
Simeon was the "brain" running a peaceful space station—but when the invaders arrived, his only hope of protecting his crew and himself was to become *The City Who Fought*!
0-671-72166-6 • *432 pages* • *Hardcover* • *$19.00*

And don't miss The Planet Pirates series:
☐ **SASSINAK by Anne McCaffrey & Elizabeth Moon**
0-671-69863-X • *$5.99*
☐ **THE DEATH OF SLEEP by Anne McCaffrey & Jody Lynn Nye**
0-671-69884-2 • *$5.99*
☐ **GENERATION WARRIORS by Anne McCaffrey & Elizabeth Moon**
0-671-72041-4 • *$4.95*

Above three titles are available together as one huge trade paperback. Such a deal!
☐ **THE PLANET PIRATES** • *72187-9* • *$12.00* • *864 pages*

If not available at your local bookstore, fill out this coupon and send a check or money order for the cover price to Baen Books, Dept. BA, P.O. Box 1403, Riverdale, NY 10471.

Name: _____

Address: _____

_____

I have enclosed a check or money order in the amount of $ _____

BUG YOUR BOOKSTORE

We've said that a sure-fire way to improve the selection of SF at your local store was to communicate with that store. To let the manager and salespeople know when they weren't stocking a book or author that you wanted. To special order that book through the bookstore, rather than order it directly from the publisher. In order to encourage you to think about these things (and to satisfy our own curiosity), we asked you to send us a list of your five best and five worst reads of the past year. And hundreds of you responded.

So we got to thinking, too. Below you will find what we think are our top fifteen reads on our current list (in alphabetical order by author). If your bookstore doesn't stock them, it should. So bug your bookstore. You'll get a better selection of SF to choose from, and your store will have improved sales. To sweeten the deal, if you send us a copy of your special order form and the book or books ordered circled on the coupon below, we'll send you a free poster!

THE WARRIOR'S APPRENTICE, Lois McMaster Bujold, 0-671-72066-X, $4.50
BARRAYAR, Lois McMaster Bujold, 0-671-72083-X, $4.99
THE PALADIN, C.J. Cherryh, 0-671-65417-9, $4.99
HAMMER'S SLAMMERS, David Drake, 0-671-69867-2, $4.95
STARLINER, David Drake, 0-671-72121-6, $5.99
METHUSELAH'S CHILDREN, Robert A. Heinlein, 0-671-65597-3, $3.50
REVOLT IN 2100, Robert A. Heinlein, 0-671-65589-2, $4.99
BARDIC VOICES: THE LARK AND THE WREN, Mercedes Lackey, 0-671-72099-6, $5.99
THE SHIP WHO SEARCHED, Anne McCaffrey & Mercedes Lackey, 0-671-72129-1, $5.99
SASSINAK, Anne McCaffrey & Elizabeth Moon, 0-671-69863-X, $5.99
THE DEED OF PAKSENARRION, Elizabeth Moon, 0-671-72104-6, $15.00
THE MAN-KZIN WARS, created by Larry Niven, 0-671-72076-7, $5.99
MAN-KZIN WARS II, created by Larry Niven, 0-671-72036-8, $4.99
MAN-KZIN WARS III, created by Larry Niven, 0-671-72008-2, $4.99
PRINCE OF MERCENARIES, Jerry Pournelle, 0-671-69811-7, $4.95

For your FREE POSTER, fill out this coupon, attach special order form and send to Baen Books, Dept. BA, P.O. Box 1403, Riverdale, NY 10471.

NAME: _____

ADDRESS: _____